IMMORTALS

JOSHUA SMITH

IMMORTALS

©2019 JOSHUA SMITH

Print and eBook formatting, and cover design by Steve Beaulieu. Artwork provided by Tom Edwards.

Published by Aethon Books LLC. 2019

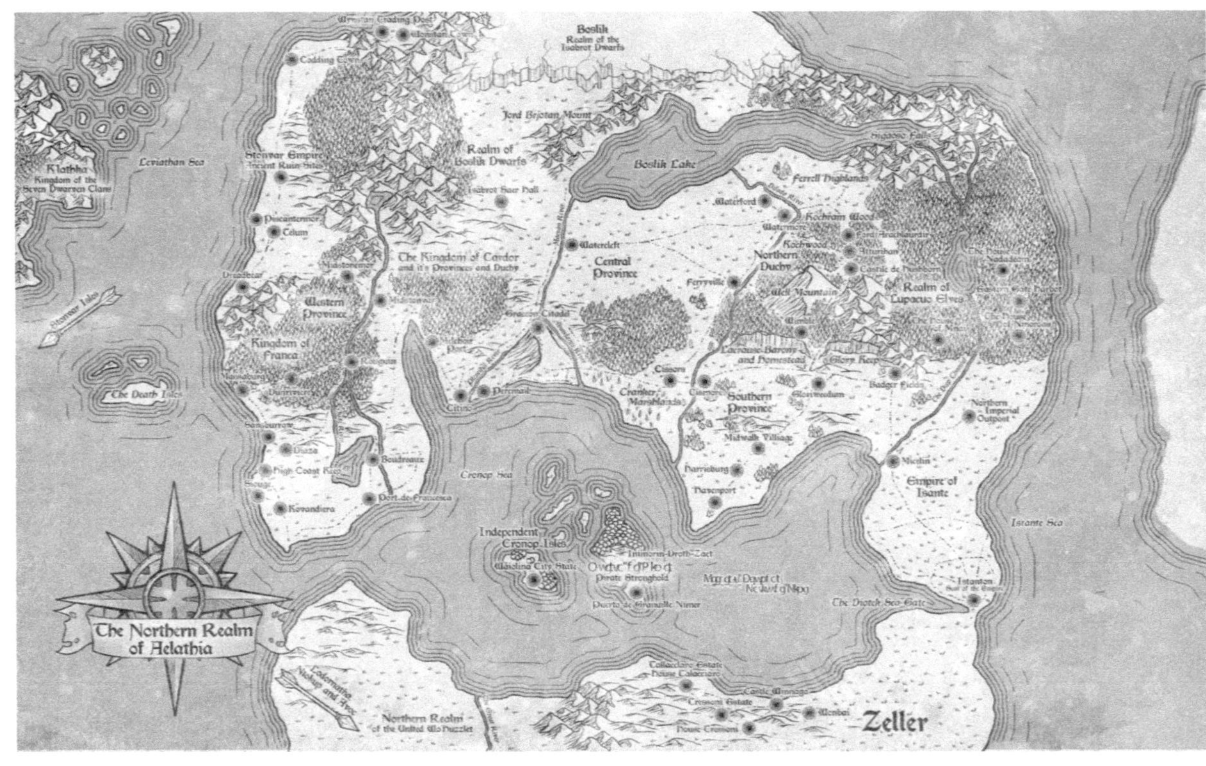

The Northern Realm of Helathia
Zeller
Leviathan Sea
Klathha — Kingdom of the Seven Dwarven Clans
The Death Isles
Stonvar Isles
Gronstan Trading Post
Cadding Town
Stonvar Empire — Ancient Ruin Sites
Realm of Boslik Dwarfs
Boslik — Realm of the Isobrot Dwarfs
Jord Brjotan Mount
Isobrot Saer Hall
Boslik Lake
Ferrell Highlands
Waterford
Kochrain Wood
Watermere
Pardt Arachlaurdir
Rochwood
Atturihan
Northern Duchy
Castle de Fusiborn
Realm of Lupacuc Elves
Central Province
Watercleft
Ferryville
Welt Mountain
Puscantervnor
Celum
The Kingdom of Cardor and it's Provinces and Duchy
Midotervnor
Drazelear
Western Province
Kingdom of Franca
Rougein
Arbor Port
Greater Citadel
Perrmail
Citine
Dunrvvere
Hanaburg
Sansburrow
Diaza
High Coast Keep
Scouge
Kovandiera
Port de Francesca
Cronop Sea
Independent Cronop Isles
Waisling City State
Irumorin-Droth-Zaet
Pirate Stronghold
Puerto de Gramalle Nener
Northern Realm of the United Glo Puzzlet
Lacrouse Barony and Homestead
Glory Keep
Badger Fields
Gloriwedum
Cissora
Crantar Marshlands
Ciarngro
Southern Province
Midwalh Village
Harrieburg
Davenport
Northern Imperial Outpost
Micthin
Empire of Isante
Isante Sea
Istanton — Seat of the Empire
The Dhotch Sea Gate
Callaeclave Estate — House Calaeciaro
Castle Winnago
Cressoni Estate
House Cressoni
Menbei

PROLOGUE

WELL MOUNTAIN ROSE ABOVE THE CRAGS AND RAVINES, A LONE
sentry. A range of ragged mountains carried on to the east and
north, covered in the everlasting green of pines, but Well Mountain dwarfed them all. It was singular. Powerful. Isolated. Agent
Bedel Riess identified with all of these things. He was one of the
world's most accomplished essencers. Some cultures revered
essencers, magic users, almost like gods. But they were just men.
Bedel knew more than most that there were some things simply
beyond the control of magic. The tides of fate and the events of
the world could conspire to separate him from his small team, his
few trusted confidants, and then once more would he be alone. In
the shadow of the great mountain, even Bedel felt small. Was that
why his father, the head of the kingdom's Magical Affairs
Commission, had summoned them here? To remind them of how
small they were? Or that no power of magic could save them if
their kingdom descended from peace into civil war?

The mountain marked the border between the southern province and the northern duchy. Far to the east, the wide Delado
River acted as a popular waterway from mighty Boslik lake in the
north to the Cronop Sea in the south. Well Mountain stood as a

bastion in the kingdom of Cardor's heartland. Duchess Sapphira controlled the northern area which bordered Lupacuo, home of Bedel's "grandfather" and his sentinels of history. Unlike other duchies, Sapphira's was its own nation as well as a province within Cardor. Bedel didn't know all the details, but long ago she was exiled there for betrayal against the Crown and Throne. She was confined, for now. Still, there were rumors her armies were expanding. Her ambition would not long be held in check by this border.

Not that the Southern Province lacked villainy. It was the kingdom's breadbasket, but it also held significant strongholds of the Slaver Coalition. The Slaver Coalition was a multinational industrial behemoth that didn't bat an eye at throwing people in chains, selling them, or even outright genocide. They openly defied the King in the west. His royal decree ending the slave trade hadn't slowed their predations. The Delado River was as much a trafficking pipeline as an essential waterway for the kingdom.

In the center of it all Wimble and Well Mountain created a neutral zone and likely last defense for the kingdom should there be civil war.

Being here was risky. Locals were distrustful of essencers. The mountain and its city were mysterious. So why had the team been ordered to meet here? Bedel looked up again, to where clouds obscured the mountain's height. Not just here, but up there?

They had opted to hike around Wimble and climb the steep north face. Three hours later, Bedel heaved himself up onto the ledge beneath a rock outcropping eight feet above him. The ledge was about three feet deep and tiered. Like stairs.

Bedel's muscles burned. He pressed his back against the granite, avoiding a trickle of water from above. There wasn't supposed to be any sort of structure up here. None of his team were amateurs. They would have seen something—anything—from below.

Rocks clattered. A hand appeared, covered in chalk. Bedel reached out and took Shai's hand. Chalk puffed out in a small cloud. She grunted her thanks as she joined him on the ledge.

Shai pushed loose strands of curly black hair behind her pointed, Elven ears, exposing her beautiful brown skin, clever eyes, and signature smirk.

"What the Kerdum is so important that they sent us to climb to the top?" she muttered, accepting a flask of water.

Bedel chuckled, forcing his tired fingers to loosen the top of his canteen. He took a swig, letting the water cool his dry throat.

"Something funny?" Shai asked, lacing the question with the sultry sarcastic tone she employed whenever they were on the verge of unlocking some mystery.

Bedel gestured with the flask at the tiered stone slabs. They wound up around the mountainside as the incline grew.

"Yeht," Shai murmured, sitting next to him. "These aren't supposed to exist. Is this why they sent us this way?"

Bedel shrugged. They both knew that myth didn't rule out reality. That knowledge was also their curse, but that unifying truth made for one hell of a team. "At least we get to walk for a while."

She shifted her chalk pouch to open her pack and pulled out a piece of venison jerky to munch on. "Can't wait to see Raynt's expression. Wonder if he'll be as awed as us."

Bedel gave her a chastising look.

She shrugged, taking another drink as a modest wind blew along the mountain, and began to retie her braid.

"We've been keeping him in the dark too long," Bedel said.

"What he doesn't know may not kill him," Shai said. "Sooner or later, it will us. You really think your father summoned us here for a meeting? We could have done that anywhere. Not a mythical ancient mountain tower, I guess. Can't see it, yet."

"Aye," Bedel said, leaning close to her. Their bodies were covered in sweat, dirt, and muck, but that had never stopped their closeness; at least not in sixty years. Both looked no older than thirty, but Bedel had recently celebrated his two hundredth birthing day. "Why did we never explore here?"

It was Shai's turn to give him that *unbelievable* gaze. "I guess we've just tried to avoid places that they may want to sacrifice you at. We should go back down."

"We can't," Bedel said, dark thoughts filling his mind. He looked away, at the beautiful scenery below. "Father had a reason. Besides, there's no blue stars. Nothing out of the ordinary. No breaking of the world. Just saber rattling."

"Is that what you call politics?" Shai shook her head. "Read between the lines, Bedel. Ancient structure that isn't supposed to exist. Mystery summons in the form of mission orders. We need to abort and get you to safety."

"Safety, huh?"

At the sound of Raynt's voice, Bedel and Shai crawled to the edge and helped their final companion over the edge.

"Thanks," he said, shaking his arms as he took a seat next to them. Raynt's mouth dropped as he stared at the ancient stairs, exposing his long canines. He shook his head, blinking with his four eyelids—two vertical, two horizontal—as his lips curved into a sly smile, exposing one elongated canine. "I can't believe it. The mountain tower it's real?"

When Raynt wanted to, his half-Glymph appearance could be vicious and terrifying, especially with the burn scars on his ears and the top of his head, which had left him mostly bald. But years of service together as agents of the Commission had given Bedel enough insight to know Raynt Lacrause as a loyal friend.

"When were you going to mention those?" Raynt said, his smile growing.

"Just about now," Shai said, offering him some jerky.

Raynt took the jerky in one large green-skinned hand and tore a piece off easily. "Any idea what we've gotten ourselves into?"

"Nothing good, I'm sure," Shai murmured, passing their half-Glymph friend the flask again. "So, who wants to say hello first?"

"After you," Raynt said, mouth full.

Shai shrugged and patted the stone. "Well," Shai said. "Hello, darling. I'm Shai, this is Bedel and Raynt. Do you have a name?"

The mountain was quiet, though another brief gust of wind brushed past them.

"She's shy," Shai said, palm still pressed against the stone. "But we can all feel her?"

The two men nodded.

"Lovely," Shai said. "We can sense you. Please, we'd like to be on friendly terms."

As essencers, each of them should have been able to use the mountain's essence, which to their eyes only appeared as colorful strings tied into threads and knots, woven together as the magic that composed reality called the world fabric. Essences were alive, sentient, and unvaryingly fickle. Bedel preferred to interpret any response as friendly—but such interpretations could end up being terribly false. Ploys and betrayals were normal here in Cardor, his homeland.

Finally, the thread underneath Shai's hand oscillated, as if plucked by a musician.

During the whole climb, they had tried to utilize the essences in an attempt to make life a little easier. They had sought to enhance their strength or create better handholds with *Soliditus*, or redirect the wind with *Gaseous*. The essences had ignored them. They obviously preferred another essencer's aether, like a child its favorite sweet candy. Yet another reason why this mountain made Bedel feel ineffectual and insignificant.

Whomever the essences belonged to, they could feel a presence watching them.

"We've got more than enough reasons to abort the mission," Shai whispered, though this wouldn't have prevented the mystery essencer from eavesdropping. "Come on, men, this is why I just don't think we should keep going."

Bedel shook his head. "I can't live in fear for another hundred years, Shai."

Raynt slowly turned his head, appraising him. If Shai had mastered the art of cynicism, Raynt could intimidate anyone with that critical focus, even with that good heart of his inside. It had been difficult hiding some truth from him all these years.

"What makes this mountain worse than any other mission we've accomplished?" Raynt asked, rolling his shoulders, keeping his muscles loose. "Our silent observer hasn't made any hostile moves. Discovery and intrigue is what we do. So, what are we really doing here?"

"That's the problem, Raynt," Bedel said, meeting his friend's hard gaze. "Xathon wasn't specific about the why. Just that we have to climb to the summit using this path."

"Using stairs he knew existed, but we didn't?"

Shai patted his arm.

In unison, they murmured every agent's frustration: "That's the Old Man."

Thanks, Father, Bedel thought.

"So, Raynt, you grew up near here." Shai stretched as she asked. "Any folktales about this place or maybe Wimble City?"

"I grew up in Gloriweedum, Shai, south of the Rock Wall and the woods."

"Your family has a barony, right?" Shai asked, handing him the flask back.

He took a long, slow drink. "My adopted parents are barons, yes. Their village is east of Gloriweedum, closer to Cismore. My adopted brother and I would climb the rock wall, but we never came this far north. It's beautiful."

"It is," Bedel said, taking in the view. From this elevation, the green pines looked like bushes among rolling hills. White clusters moved along actual pasture land; no doubt sheep flocks. The air up here seemed pure, with none of the smog of coal or wood-burning stoves of larger cities.

For a moment, Bedel allowed his aether to emanate outwards, gently pressing against the dozens, hundreds, thousands of essence strands or whole threads. Some trembled, as if the essences had taken a deep breath after a long dive. Bedel felt a hawk far away, felt the sun's heat off stone, he was with the baying sheep, grazing on a hill. For a moment, he was the stone of Wimble's walls, but then a force pushed him out. His aether descended into the mountain depths, but the rock rejected him. Bedel gasped as all the strands, like ethereal tentacles, retreated back into himself. He sighed as the thrill and glory of the world fabric reminded him, once again, how truly small he was.

"It is gorgeous," he whispered.

"Aye," Shai said, her regard softening. "It is."

"Aye," Raynt agreed. The three sat silently for a few minutes, resting, enjoying the solitude.

"What about you?" Raynt asked Shai.

"Hmm?" She asked.

"Have you ever climbed?"

"Branairds don't climb," Shai murmured. "Mountains aren't for us. We stuck to the low lands in the caravan, easier to get the animals and wagons across. As for Elves," she clucked and shook her head, then wiped sweat off her brow. "There's a reason they built airships. And I'm sorely ready to give whoever had us climb up here a piece of my mind."

Bedel and Raynt chuckled. Bedel pivoted slightly, metal harness buckles and rope anchors on his belt clattering against stone.

This mountainous stairway, which looked ancient, did indeed seem to go up a huge portion of the mountain. What waited above? No one had explained their mission, not even his father. All the Intel they had could be boiled down to 'reach the top' and 'use the ancient northern staircase.'

"What do we know about the stairway?" Bedel asked. "I only heard rumors, but even at" he chose his words carefully. He trusted Raynt but confiding in him too much would put him in as much danger as he and Shai had lived the last few decades. There were secrets some individuals would kill to keep from recorded history. "… in all my research, I've found nothing."

Shai pushed a bite to the side of her mouth. "Keepers."

Raynt blinked. "You're not serious."

Shai gestured upward. "Think about it. If Immortals exist, they're said to dwell in towers, set apart from civilization. If no one comes up the mountain, and someone has bribed the essences here to the point that they are controlled; who has that type of power?"

"You," Bedel said, kissing her on the cheek.

"Besides me," Shai said, turning to intercept the kiss with her lips. She locked eyes with him again. "If my father sent me for Elven Intelligence and your father sent the two of you from the Magical Affairs Commission, what are we missing? Why us three? A hostile Immortal? Or something else?"

Keepers and Immortals were one and the same: legends, nothing more. Pale, silver-haired folktale figures that lived longer than Elves and passed on their immortality—whatever that truly meant—through blood rituals. They were nothing more than scary stories told around a fire or to children to explain blights, bumper crops, and missing children, rather than address the real monsters like slavers. Keepers and Immortals belonged in the same tales as banshees, The Taurs, and Blood-Sages.

Likely, all of those legends were based on the Sorceress in Avoc. Bedel's contacts in Lodornatha verified some of the similarities, but she hadn't been seen in centuries. If powerful essencers, like the one who controlled the mountain, wanted the title Keeper or Immortal, so be it. Bedel had spent his life preparing for the worst of them; the one who had corrupted his brother. His family had never spoken of it, and Bedel had long played the innocent fool. Yet, even though Bedel had been an infant, his very first memory was of his brother's love for him while the taint consumed him, the battle that followed when he released the leader of a magical cult that later became an influential and powerful religion among other races. According to scholars, that Elf, the Dark Judicator, instigated an entire world cycle without the Sorceress.

And my brother set him free, Bedel thought. *But saved me at the same time? How can I hate him the way Father does?*

"It's plausible," Bedel said. "However, if there's a hostile Keeper living in Cardor, wouldn't we know?"

Raynt shrugged. "There's supposedly the Sorceress on the southern continent. She's a Keeper and conquered Avoc."

"Nothing supposed about her," Shai said. "My people used to tell stories they heard from the tribes and Lodornatha. She's very real, but her realm has been isolated."

"If there's a Keeper up there or speaking through the mountain, we would know," Bedel concluded.

Raynt shook his head. "While we're speculating, consider this. If a Keeper is up there and is hostile, why wouldn't he or she have attacked us by now? Then there's Wimble, the city on the doorstep of the mountain. Several hundred Boslik Dwarves immigrated there a few years ago and haven't been seen since. Wimble is large enough to be recognized by Count O'Crast and King

Relchar, but I can tell you that no more than three merchant caravans leave the city during the year. Their economy is self-contained, but the city and the outer villages are growing. I think we may be reading this situation wrong."

"Imagine that?" Shai muttered. "A single piece of info beyond 'find the stairs' could clarify everything. Who or what we are going to find up this mountain would have told us everything we needed to know. Grandfather was never keen on sharing facts."

Bedel nodded, finished off a piece of jerky, and then stood. His legs still burned, but the stairs should make the coming climb easier. "Only way we know is by heading up."

"Someday we're going to retire, Bedel."

He grinned wryly. They had rehashed their retirement plans so often, he could visualize the layout of the cabin they wanted to build. He'd even found a few potential locations.

Bedel helped Shai up, not that she needed it. She seemed comfortable. Already she'd cooled and appeared limber. Her steps were quiet and gentle, even on loose rock.

Raynt took point on the ascent. Bedel followed, and Shai took up the rear.

There was nothing remarkable about the stone slab stairs, at least, if he disregarded the fact that someone had managed to carve them out all the way up here. Bedel tried to keep up the pace, but Raynt's broad stride pushed him farther ahead.

A nagging feeling had Bedel reach for his belt, and the rope except there was no tether. How had they missed that? The entire vertical climb, they'd been connected. Bedel glanced behind him. Shai noticed.

"What?"

"Where's our tether?"

"Bloody fields," she muttered. "How is that possible?"

"Raynt!" Bedel shouted as he saw Shai turn back to the ledge. The rope was there, lying haphazardly on the ground.

How the Kerdum did that happen?

Raynt turned around. He shouted something, but a gust of wind rushed by them, carrying off his words.

Bedel stepped closer so he could hear Raynt.

The ground shifted, groaned, and cracked. A large fracture spread across the width of the stair. Bedel's legs wobbled as if he were aboard a ship on a turbulent sea. Loose rocks cascaded into the vertical drop. Bedel shifted his feet, about to jump, but another crack threw off his balance. Then the step slid off the edge of the cliff, taking him with it. Rocks cascaded against his shoes, while the ground jerking out from beneath him sent Bedel tumbling. He fell backward, suddenly gaping at the blue, partly cloudy sky above. Without hesitation, he reached out with his hands, thrusting himself into the rock, face first. Sharp edges cut through his tunic and sliced his hands. Stone and loose rocks clamored, tossed upwards into his face, cutting his chin.

He felt the open air beneath his legs and part of his torso. Bedel saw a loose, horizontal stone jutting from the rocky cliff. He lashed out, grabbing it as his body spun into midair. The horizontal stone was his anchor and his body the fulcrum. Rocks tumbled around him like rain as he slammed into the vertical drop. The cacophony of stone chaos muted Shai screaming his name.

Heart thudding, Bedel rested for a mere second, clutching his anchor.

I'm over the cliff, he thought, then said it aloud. "Bloody fields, I'm over the cliff." Somehow, talking to himself made the near-death experience a little better. All he wanted to do was scream with terror, but he forced his breathing to calm.

"Okay, Bedel, climb."

He dug his feet into minuscule ledges and lifted himself upward, nearly over the ledge.

With an ear-shattering snap, the horizontal stone broke off the wall.

Scree clattered down the cliff face as he slid farther, sharp jagged rock cutting and bruising his hands as he scrambled for any hold.

It was enough to keep him close to the wall, rather than spinning out to oblivion and a messy death. But he continued to slide.

Desperate, he tried the impossible. Bedel focused his mind, letting his ethereal aura flare out. Everyone had an aura, a murky, silver nimbus of aether that surrounded them. The auras of non-essencers were like a thin second skin, while someone like Bedel had an enveloping cloud. Theoretically, the aether inside an aura could be bartered to essences for their service. In this case, theory was a waste of time.

Essences were fickle, and the mountain already had a patron. Today, the world fabric seemed quite content to kill him.

Helpless, Bedel continued his never-ending slide. Flesh and clothes tore, Shai's screams became faint. His hands groped desperately for a handhold and came away bloody. Terror erupted in his belly. If he allowed it power, terror would kill him, clenching off breath by tightening his diaphragm. Bedel cleared his mind in that instant, concentrating on one thing: a flickering golden-white flame he sometimes saw in his sleep.

Bedel's fingertips found a narrow crack. He pressed in, with nothing but four fingers carrying his weight. He yanked to a halt, again hanging off the rock face. His muscles burned, but he channeled his thoughts into his hold on the mountain and the flame in his mind.

His legs hung below an outcrop of rock. It gave him a moment to concentrate. Bedel slowed his breathing even more, focused his mind. He could hear Shai and Raynt shouting above him, but he couldn't focus on them. Doing so was death.

He risked reaching behind to cover a hand in chalk from his

harness pouch. The dry, coarse texture burned against the cuts. He ignored the pain, silently hoping he could make it up before it distracted him. Bedel shifted his legs, using the spiked grips on his boots to push up. He lifted one leg, found a wider outcropping. He carefully edged his fingers up the crevice and held himself in place to catch his breath.

Hand over hand, he worked his way back up. He blocked thoughts of how far he'd fallen and kept moving, slowly and methodically. Wind picked up, blowing hard against him. He leaned into the mountain, securing himself with his fingers and partial footholds. His boots weren't helping, despite the spiked soles. The crevice narrowed. He found a new hold. Bedel inhaled deeply as he used his other hand to secure his position, then tried to dig his feet into a better foothold.

In a relatively steady position, Bedel reached out to the essences again. Misty-silver aether quested outwards from his aura. The essences ignored him. It was a bidding competition for their services; one that Bedel had lost.

"It's your mountain," Bedel muttered to the stone as he held on and prepared to move. "Killing us to prevent us from climbing won't change that. We're going up."

His breath was even again as he studied the mountain with the vision and scrutiny of an essencer. In his sight, the stone was like a massive knot; threads of gray and brown tied together over and over again.

"It's your mountain," Bedel repeated. "I need to get up."

Up is death, a woman's voice floated on the wind, a soft echo. *Go down. This is only the beginning. Up is death.*

Bedel felt the strain on his biceps and forearms. The mountain shook, pebbles and dust rained down. The crevice was *closing.* He had to climb faster, but if he moved too quickly, he could easily dislodge himself without the essencer's help.

Up is death.

"My mission is on top of this mountain," he maundered. "You know that."

Bedel secured a new handhold. The crevice he had just used sealed, as if it had never existed. Carefully, Bedel reached for a loose rock, the only other hold near him. From there, he could see a crevice he could use.

I know more than I wish, the voice on the wind said again. *They are all watching. The stars are changing. The cycle is coming. Up is death. I will save you.*

Keeping his breath steady, Bedel moved his hand from the rock to a new crevice. He blinked when his fingers entered a small stream of water. Panic clenched his throat. Bedel forced himself to relax, to shut it out, even as chalk washed from his hands. His fingers slipped. Immediately, he rested his weight on his boots and the fragile, thin ledge; or rather, on his toes. He scanned, looking for a better way. The water was a death sentence in itself. If it got on his boots, his ability to keep himself upright would disappear.

Bedel felt something hard press against his fingers, stone pushing him out, as if it grew beneath him. His stomach heaved once, but he forced himself to remain calm.

"Throwing me off a cliff won't save me! I can't fly. You own the mountain and the air here. I know."

Starblessed, flee from here.

Bedel tensed more, falling silent. No one knew that, except for Shai, his father, and his estranged brother. No one *should* know that.

"That's not me," he said, trying to keep her distracted, even his heart pounded in his chest. He could see the long fall to the rocks and sloped pasture land below, with trees so far away they looked like bushes. He'd never survive the fall, not even if he managed to find essences to help.

"Bedel!" he heard Shai's voice. "We're coming to get you!

Hold on!"

He didn't dare respond. Not yet.

I can stop the cycle, right now, the essencer's voice said, becoming clearer. She had a deep voice, whomever this essencer was. *Precisely 3.1415,* she said. *Do you know? 3.1415 and it continues. You cannot be. You change it. She changes it. He changes it. She changes it. 3.1415 does not equate to cycle parameters. Rules have been broken. One exists, therefore the other exists, therefore the stone knows. The stone speaks to me. Millions will die. You shouldn't even exist. I can reset the rules.*

Games with legends and myths. Unless she was a Keeper, Bedel thought. *Bloody fields, now wasn't the time to believe folktales!* Bedel suppressed an emotionally charged barb and tried to calculate his chances at jumping up, even as he pressed his boot on the quickly disappearing ledge.

There are two sides to every cycle, she continued. *If I don't kill you, Up will. Let me help you, and you help me save everyone. Your 3.1415 presence permits a breaking. It always does. Millions of lives in exchange for 3.1415 erased from play, Starblessed. Without a Reason, there is no pi, and no pi means a breaking is not guaranteed. We can stop it now.*

"No."

They taught you nothing.

Bedel worked his way up the crevice, even as the rock continued to seal itself. Hand over hand, Bedel paused. The memory of breaking into Menai Library with Shai and reading the forbidden books and scrolls flashed across his mind. That act carried a death sentence. Instead, he and Shai had received probation in exchange for elite service.

"I taught me," he whispered, anger seeping into his tone.

Forgive me, Reason.

Bedel had already tuned her out. He was closer to the top, and he saw a flurry of activity above him. He glimpsed Shai glancing over the edge, her dark curls falling over a shoulder. He kept climbing; each upward movement a fight for life. Stone pushed against his feet and fingers. He groaned with the weight of his body against his bloody fingertips.

Stone thrust out of the crevice, pushing his fingers out just as he used his arms and whole body to thrust upward.

"Shai!" he screamed.

He saw her beautiful face and long dark, curly hair appear over the ledge. Her arms reached out. The rock grew farther out, scraping and cutting his tunic, throwing off his leap.

"Now!" Shai shouted. She was almost completely over the ledge, hands open.

One of his hands found her forearm and closed around it. He swung, clinging to her.

"I've got you," Shai said. Then she shouted: "I've got him! Pull us up!"

Bedel strained and latched onto her other arm. He gazed into her deep, brown eyes, taking in her beauty.

She smiled. "I've got you, Bedel."

"Yes, you do," he murmured as Raynt strained up on the ledge.

Raynt pulled them up, one hand over the other. First Shai, then him.

Bedel gasped as he rolled onto the rocky, ancient stone stairs. He slowed his breathing, letting muscles relax. His legs felt oddly weak. Climbing wasn't in his usual magical espionage repertoire.

Shai laid her head next to his, her hair fell over his face as she moved. "Next time, leave the acrobatics to me."

Then she rolled on her side, kissing him upside down.

"I love you, Bedel."

"I love you," he said, reaching up and stroking her cheek.

"How bad is it?" Raynt asked.

Bedel groaned and sat up, back against the rock cliff. He half expected the mountain essencer to try and kill him again. That paranoia had kept him alive for two centuries.

"Scrapes and bruises, my friend," Bedel said, wincing as he looked at the long tears in his white tunic.

"Right," Shai said sarcastically, pouring water over his hands. They stung.

"Here." Raynt moved carefully between Shai and Bedel and dug around in Bedel's pack. He pulled out a small jar of ointment. "Salve."

"Perfect," Shai said. She applied it to Bedel's hands. His skin tingled across his spine as Shai's aether touched his own.

"Shai," Bedel whispered.

"Shush," she said. Her magic was different than others. She liked to say she could make something from nothing. The salve on his hands seeped into his fingers. Heat passed through his arms. A golden light burned through his blood. Shai met Bedel's stare and casually moved her hands over his, blocking the increasingly blinding golden light as Raynt tended the scrapes on Bedel's chin. Those wounds weren't deep enough to expose Bedel as truly *starblessed*.

"Stay still," Raynt muttered. "I'm not a healer."

"Aye, Bedel, stay still," Shai echoed him. She moved her hands underneath his. Dead, flayed skin tumbled away, as pinkish new strands of flesh wove together. The light beneath them was no longer visible.

Starblessed, the mountain had called him. Bedel had spent a lifetime preparing to fight powerful and terrifying essencers like the Dark Judicator, but an untainted essencer with a mountain had nearly killed him. *If I couldn't handle her,* he thought, *how would I fare against someone stronger? If the Dark Judicator discovered who I am, he'd return.*

"You're okay," Shai whispered. "You handled that well."

They both relaxed. Beads of sweat dripped down her face. She blinked sweat out of her eyes and continued to focus until his hands were whole.

"The mountain just tried to kill you," Raynt said, wiping his hands with a towel from the pack.

"You heard that, huh?" he glanced at his hands. The pain had faded, as had the warm, tingling sensation. Few people could heal, but creating new flesh rather than triggering the body's natural growth? Only Shai could do that.

Shai tossed hair out of her face and tied it behind her with a ribbon. "Heard it? Bedel, we saw it. Whoever has control of this rock doesn't like you much."

She squeezed his hands, gaze locked on his. She was trying to spin the words, hiding the rest of the truth from any unwelcome ears, even Raynt. It would keep Raynt alive when the time came.

"You heard her," Bedel said.

"I don't give a damn what that essencer thinks you are," Raynt muttered, securing his pack. He stared up at the stairwell path, evidently checking for further dangers. "You're Bedel. That's it. You're not some mystical tool."

He didn't see the light from my hands! Bedel sighed, relieved.

"Tell that to, oh, I don't know, every powerful being in the world," Shai said, moving closer to help Bedel spread the ointment. Bedel grimaced. He reached up, gently stroking the shape of her ears. "My grandfather, your father, and this mountain's essencer believe it. That's enough to be dangerous."

Raynt nodded. "Ideas can kill."

"But they won't touch us," Bedel said, his hand resting on her chin. "We made sure of that. As long as we know what they know."

Shai's regard darkened. "It's House Menai, Bedel. The Elves do what they want. Maybe we should turn back. If a cycle is coming, we need to hide you."

"I won't let them kill me."

"Tell that to the mountain," she retorted.

He smiled. "I did."

"Bedel, maybe she's right. Think about what Cardorians and Elves are capable of, just because of what we look like."

"Not you too, Raynt."

Raynt blinked and kept his mouth slightly open, so they could see his teeth. Shai ran a hand over her ears and subconsciously shielded her belly. Bedel looked away, wishing he could deny the argument's merit. He looked Istantese, but 'half-breeds' seldom lived this long or this free in the north.

Growling softly, Raynt continued. "Kerdum, Bedel. If powerful people believe you are part of some cosmic cycle, maybe we should hide you. We know enough about the myths. We know what they're capable of."

"I'm not running, Raynt."

Raynt shrugged and stood tall. He was at least a head higher than the others, another aspect of his particular heritage. He stared out over the northern edge of the cliff. East of the sloped hills around the mountain was a series of ravines and sharp peaks that formed a natural road between the Southern Province and the Northern Duchy. They were caught between two corrupt rulers. One controlled the slave trade, another amassed an army.

Bedel noticed Raynt was staring. "You two are always talking about that cabin. Now might be the right time to retire. Before the World Summit begins, or civil war breaks out. Even if there is no cycle."

Nations on the southern continent were coming to the king of Cardor's palace in just under three weeks, most likely to beg or barter for relief from a famine and drought, as well as the relentless slavery raids. Northern kingdoms, like Cardor, were flourishing while the other nations suffered.

"Think of it," Raynt said, as if reading the colors of Bedel's emotions on his aura. "Ever been in a stable or pen with a yeht in heat? One look in those beady red eyes, and it'll charge. Nothing survives those horns."

He seldom talked about his family's homestead. His adopted parents were barons, and Bedel knew something had happened with a potential marital match to sour a taste for home. When they had first met, Raynt would brag about his experiences. Abruptly, after a visit home, he never spoke of them again.

"Says the farmer," Shai said. Raynt shrugged. Shai smiled playfully and continued, "I've dodged a yeht or two in my time."

"No doubt, Lady Shai of Bombard," Raynt said, bowing, only half-jokingly.

She gracefully twirled her hand and bowed. Shai had been raised with a traveling menagerie. It helped her cover as a spy to be the famous acrobat and dancer. Both had first-hand experience of the brainless, brawny *ceratops* creatures which were often at the receiving end of jokes, curses, and common swear phrases.

Cardor and the Elven Houses of Lupacuo needed to be prepared, and intelligence gathering fell on individuals like Bedel, Raynt, and Shai. No matter what people thought of motley essencers like them.

"If the Summit fails, or the duchess launches a coup, we won't need a cycle." Raynt gestured at the land. "We'll be in a pen with a yeht."

Shai nodded fervently.

Can I honestly leave them now? Bedel thought.

A sudden, long squawk that ended in a roar sounded from above. Two more bestial voices answered it. *Gryphons.* Even though Bedel had expected something like that it certainly complicated matters.

Raynt gestured toward the sounds. "Decide before we finish going *up*." There was compassion in their colleague's look. "I love having you around, Bedel—you two at least see me as a person and not a freak—but I'd rather you vanish, so someone doesn't murder you for some mythical, insane, misguided sacrifice. You've both served for half a century. Maybe it's time to retire. You don't even have to tell me where. Plausible deniability. I'll know nothing."

He's right. We'd have to keep it from him. No one truly retires from the commission, or in Shai's case, from Elven Intelligence.

Shai tried to smile, but Bedel could feel her desperation. "Bedel, even Raynt is warning us. Imagine. Cabin by a lake. Just us and life. No intrigue. No lies. No espionage."

His heart ached. He laid one hand over hers as she touched his cheek.

"Please," she whispered. "We've done our share."

"If the cycles are real, Shai," Bedel said. He hesitated as the words caught in his throat.

"If the cycles are real, the world is going to need everyone. Including our mountain friend." He patted the stone next to him, emphasizing the point. Pebbles shook underneath his hand. *Was the essencer letting them go?*

"They're finally going to try, Bedel," Shai said, shaking her head in protest. "An Elf or even your father. Someone."

"But not you," he said, confidently. He directed the next comment to Raynt. "Nor you."

"If I had a mug, I'd say cheers on that, my friend, but she's right. Come on, I can go on without you two. Stall them. Both of you should just disappear."

Bedel sighed, then leaned his head against the mountain. "What about you, Raynt? After this mission, they'll send you back to take out the Slaver Coalition with the King's Men. Who will have your back?"

"Don't worry about me," Raynt said. "I'm used to being alone."

"That's the problem," Bedel said. His legs and arms no longer burned or trembled. He was ready to resume the climb. "We all are used to doing this on our own. If a cycle is coming, and if the myths are true, there won't be a place for us to hide."

Shai lowered her voice as she ran a hand over her ear timidly. "Bedel, we could make it work."

"For a while, but our mountain friend is right. There are two sides to a cycle. If chaos wins, it'll only be a matter of time before there's a breaking, and that will find us. If we stand together, no matter how they'll try to divide us, we help each other."

"Ancestors damn it, Bedel." Shai pulled away. "We can escape if we go now. We go up, we're committed to yet another mission. Why do you think we were summoned to meet here? On top of a mountain that is controlled by an over-zealous essencer."

Rock ground against rock. Pebbles and dust fell along the wall above them.

Shai shrugged. "No disrespect intended."

The mountain settled again.

Shai exhaled. "Please don't make me face them again."

"I will never make you do anything," Bedel said.

"You're sweet, but that's not a promise you can keep, my love."

"Shai," he protested, but she stood and eyed the long, winding stairs.

"We should watch our footing. Don't want the mountain to murder us before our own families try."

Bedel raised his hands in frustration.

Raynt helped him up, blinked once with all four eyelids, and then frowned. "Bedel, last chance."

"I think we have to, don't you?"

Raynt shook his head. "Most people view Shai and me as half-breeds, Bedel. Haven't we all done enough? You escape, I complete the mission, and then maybe I can retire with you all."

"I'd like that," Shai said, "although we're going to need to find you a woman."

"You can matchmake all you want when we've retired, Shai."

"Ooh! I have permission. Excellent. See how easy that was, Bedel?"

Bedel brushed off his short leather jacket. It was torn in places. He was still able to close it over the shredded tunic. "Shai. Raynt. We're needed."

Shai put her hands on her hips, turned away, and let out a string of curses.

Raynt shook his head, then gestured to the path.

Before long, they resumed the ascent. They kept less distance between each other and checked the ropes frequently. Wind blew hard against their backs, but the essencer didn't speak. She didn't have to. Bedel felt the mountain's essencer studying their every step.

The stone stairwell narrowed and curved sharply as the mountain grew steeper. Wind now cut in their faces, slowing progress. Above them, the sun peaked and lowered in the west, casting shadows along their steps.

At last, after they passed through layers of misty clouds, Bedel saw their destination. It wasn't the peak of the mountain itself. A stone double door, decorated in ancient Belasna runes, stood open, exposing the inside of Well Mountain. The cavern was dimly lit by oil lanterns, flames flickering inside crystal and stone cages. That light wasn't enough to push back the full darkness of the cave, or the odor and breathing of creatures within.

Raynt signaled with his hand, and they all slowed, moving as far to the right of the entrance as possible. Bedel could see a circular stairwell leading up, and thin slits in the mountain above, like windows. This was a tower carved inside the top of the mountain, but unlike dwarven architecture which tended to chisel the mountain down into exquisite and eye-captivating structures, the mountain still looked raw. Hidden.

Bedel heard the *whoosh* of breath, deep and low, as if a group of smithies methodically primed bellows to stoke one of the grand forges.

Bedel lowered his hand to a knife strapped to his thigh. They'd hidden most of their possessions before the climb, keeping only knives. Those small weapons wouldn't do much good against a gryphon.

Raynt withdrew two curved daggers, each engraved with Belasna runes, enhancing the steel. Without a word, Raynt's daggers ignited with a white-blue flame, one that would not harm him but would be painfully lethal to an opponent. Shai unsheathed her knife, with an outward-angled long blade.

Raynt used quick hand motions to direct them. Shai stealthily crept across the entrance and slipped behind the opposite stone door. Raynt and Bedel hugged the mountain wall.

A long, harsh scrape signaled talons or claws against the floor inside. Feathers rustled. A gryphon moved. If they were trained beasts—not tame, but trained—their riders were inside. If they were friendly, then this might resolve without someone being bitten in half. Might.

Scratch. Whoosh. Scrape.

Talons sounded on stone, and the breathing became shallower.

Raynt began counting down. It was better to fight a gryphon inside a closed space rather than the open air, where it could effortlessly swoop in and maul someone to death.

Raynt counted down. Three. Two. One. Swift gesture forward.

Raynt and Bedel ducked inside the right door, keeping to the edge, creeping into shadow.

A high-pitched caw cut the silence, followed by a roar that ignited every primal fear within Bedel.

The gryphon bolted from the darkness. Its brown furry mane, which overlaid its feathers, rustled as it darted forward. An open, sickle-shaped yellow beak, lined with small, slanted teeth, thrust at them. Bedel backpedaled, yanking Raynt by his shirt. The gryphon's beak snapped shut where Raynt had just been.

The creature moved forward, its massive body filling the doorway. Its furry mane transitioned into a forequarter of feathers. A long, fur tail whipped the air behind it, its tip flaring out into a beautiful fan of uneven feathers, white, brown, and black. The tail was raised in a threat position behind the gryphon's head, instantly making the creature look *larger*. The feathers shook as a tremor ran through the gryphon, much like a rattlesnake might give a vicious warning. Wide hind paws pounded the floor; retractable claws popping out, carving into the stone. The gryphon attacked. Swiping at them with its front talons, it tried to cut them down before finishing them off with its thick, muscular, fur-covered feline hind legs.

Raynt and Bedel separated, dodging the swift and relentless attacks from the beast. Bedel glimpsed two others behind, that dreadful combined gaze of lion and hawk seeking prey. The two others screeched and roared, anxious to get into the fight.

Shai began to move inside the door, but Bedel waved her off, thick talons swooshing inches from his head. Sharp and curved, they were long as a hand-and-a-half sword. One clean strike would certainly impale them.

Raynt rolled inside the front legs, which caused the bird to shift to one hind and one foreleg. A massive paw swiped at him, slamming into the stone. Raynt rolled, just as nimble as Bedel had seen Shai work. Crouching, using that split-second the creature was off-balance, Raynt pulled his arms back to deliver deep, cutting blows with his knives.

"Fireor! *Niecendent!*" A man barked. Bedel saw a hand gesture at the other gryphons. "*Niecendent!*"

One gryphon listened, but the other tried to push forward until a second voice echoed the first.

Raynt pulled back, hesitating to strike on the lead beast. The gryphon growled at him as it stepped back, resting on its hind legs.

Bedel exhaled sharply as a Hawk Knight, a member of Cardor's Gryphon Order, slipped around the bird. Wide shoulders and bulging muscles filled out the man's leather jerkin, the emblem of a gryphon in flight on his chest plate marking his status. The knight scowled, his stare sharp as the gryphons'. A saber, repeating crossbow, and full quiver hung from his belt. Blond hair marked him as a man from the far west, whether Dreadbear or farther, Bedel couldn't say.

Bedel and Raynt exchanged a look, then slowly backed away. Shai was silent as she rounded the door, back against the stone.

The knight patted the gryphon, speaking to it directly. Two more individuals moved behind him, but they weren't clearly seen past the gryphon's bulk.

"I was unaware the Gryphon Order had an outpost on this mountain," Bedel called to the man.

"We don't go around sharing all our secrets." The knight said. His presence and touch seemed to soothe the gryphon. He had a thick accent. It wasn't just of the folk of Dreadbear, but a mixture of Francan and Stonvar. "I was unaware an Istantese man, a half-Elf, and a half-Glymph went around casually climbing mountains that are alive."

The knight barely turned as he said the last, eying them suspiciously.

Bedel clenched his fist. Of course, the Cardorian threw out the same labels that long had made him and his companions consider finding a secret, new life. Bedel had never been to Istante, but he was judged because of his facial features, just as they labeled Shai and Raynt on their appearance.

Raynt snarled, his lip pulling back over his canines, almost shaking as the low sound came out. The flame on his daggers had extinguished, but he still gripped them.

"I was unaware the Gryphon Order raised Stonvar to knighthood," Raynt growled.

"I haven't been a Stonvar since I was a child, abandoned by raiders and raised by the Marquis of Souige in Franca," the knight said. His hand dropped to his saber. "Shall Fireor and I show you what his blessing led to?"

"Well, crow shit. This is going to be interesting," Shai murmured. She twirled her knife.

Raynt braced himself, raising his daggers. Bedel settled into a ground stance, easy enough to move from knife combat to hand-to-hand.

"That's enough, Sir Varn," another man snapped from the staircase.

Varn glared at the three of them, then removed his hand from his saber hilt. He clucked, and the gryphon Fireor followed him back to the stables.

On the staircase stood a man, his red robes a sharp contrast to the grim stonework. A gold medallion hung from his neck, engraved with symbols of the various essencer disciplines. His groomed white beard, thick mustache, and eyebrows appeared bushy. His look in their direction, an invasive scrutiny.

Xathon Morbrook's redwood staff *click-clacked* against the floor, but Bedel knew his father hardly required it to walk.

The staff itself, of raw wood, appeared like a twisted tree. Once, long ago, the staff had been carved like a dome set upon slender pillars. Bedel didn't know how it had come to be broken, in fact, he could only remember it this way. The staff pulsed with a quiet, hidden power, as some enchanted objects were known to do. Once Bedel had approached it as a child, taken it, and felt his mind transported elsewhere. A square room, dark, damp, with steel-reinforced doors and drawers one might find in a secure treasury vault. Bedel's mind explored the room, walking toward a young man with a brown beard, braided with colorful beads, who waited like an attendant. Bedel had felt the staff snatched from his hands, awakening to find his father glowering over him. He received a swift and severe lecture followed by a corporally punitive swat-by-wind-essence that he had never forgotten.

Shai and Raynt sheathed their weapons faster than Bedel. Raynt even saluted, hand over his heart. Bedel, however, stared at his father, wondering what it took to bring the Grand Essencer of the Magical Affairs Commission to the top of *this* mountain. Couldn't he just have delivered the orders over family dinner?

Xathon stood on a step, high enough he could stare down at them all.

"Well, hello, uncle," Shai said, wiggling her fingers in a wave.

Xathon acknowledged her with the barest of smiles.

"Sir Varn," Xathon said. "This is my son, Agent Bedel, and his colleagues Agent Raynt and Agent Shai of Elven Intelligence, as I'm sure you're aware."

The knight tended to his gryphon, tossing out salted meat in front of it to eat. "Agent Raynt stabbed Fireor, Grand Essencer."

"Fireor was going to rip me apart," Raynt muttered, shaking his head.

The gryphon flapped its wings as it sat on its haunches, its long fanned tail coiling behind it. One talon tapped the ground. It looked at them hungrily.

Varn shrugged. "I was going to stop him, but I had my mouth full. Ever try shouting commands without your tongue? I could have accidentally told him to maul you."

"Listen, Sir Varn," Shai said. "You're really not helping."

He shrugged and went back to work.

Xathon huffed, then said, "You three should come upstairs and rest and eat while we talk. I'm sure you had a perilous journey."

"Aye," Bedel said. "Father, our hostess in the mountain threw me off a cliff!"

"Be grateful Raynt and I were there," Shai snapped, hand on

hip. "She targeted Bedel alone. What are we to think, Grand Essencer?"

Xathon's lips pressed together tightly. Not quite a frown, nor chastised by their blunt accusations. Bedel couldn't tell what he thought, and that infuriated him.

"Did you know that was going to happen when you sent the three of us scaling the north side, Father? Why not send Hawk Knights for us? Or how many of them do you actually trust?"

"Hawk Knight?" Xathon said. "Varn."

Varn bowed, then pulled out a small, gold medallion, the same that Bedel and Raynt kept stowed in their bags for this journey. Bedel glanced, examining the man's aura.

"He's not an essencer."

"And I don't trust the Gryphon Order," Xathon said, partially turning to ascend the stairwell. "The Magical Affairs Commission doesn't always employ essencers as agents, Bedel Morbrook. Or had you forgotten that? Up we go."

Raynt shook his head, glanced at the two of them, and followed quickly. Shai and Bedel hung back. Few men really got under his skin as much as his own father.

"We're okay," Shai said, slipping her hand in his.

"*We're* okay," Bedel said, squeezing her hand. "This… something else is amiss."

Shai braced herself, then gave him a forced, playful smile. "Let's go solve the mystery."

They stepped inside the stone doors, feeling the temperature drop as they entered. Shai hesitated, pointing at one of the gryphons. Its saddle and harness were different than the others. Even its feathers had brighter colors. On the saddle was an engraved set of scales, one arm weighing a teardrop-shaped jewel, the other holding five stars. The crest of House Menai of Lupacuo.

Shai's eyes widened, and she glanced at the stairs.

Maybe the mountain had been right. Maybe they should have gone down.

"Together," Bedel whispered.

All traces of fear vanished from her face, but it was another moment before she released Bedel's arm.

They climbed the winding stairs. At the next landing was an arched door, leading to a circular room with stone chairs and a round table. Another table was at the far end of the room, where a cloaked man sat in near darkness, head bowed.

Xathon waved them into the room, but the three agents paused just inside the doorway. Xathon went to the seated man, whispering in his ear.

Bedel took in the two others in the room. One was a Magical Affairs Commission agent wearing the medallion. His skin looked pale, his neatly groomed hair and beard blond. He peered at them over wire-rimmed glasses.

Raynt leaned in to whisper in Bedel's ear. "Why is my tutor here? That's Stamford Farr, from Gloriweedum."

Next to him, a thin, muscular Elf with blond braided hair sat tall and straight. His stare was cold, judgmental, and contemplative.

"Well, Father," Shai said, controlling her voice from trembling. There was little love lost between Shai and the Elf who had impregnated her mother. "Fancy meeting you here."

"Shai," Lord Commander Nadael of House Menai said. Bedel noticed the long, curved dueling sword at his belt. He still wore armor, as if anticipating a fight. Though Shai would find some poetic justice in Nadael's paranoia on a murderous mountain, that couldn't be the reason. Bedel had seen Nadael in combat during the Trader Wars. He was swift and agile, his aim lethal, and he was a keen tactician. Worse still, his sister was Bedel's mother, Xathon's wife. Bedel greeted him with a nod.

Nadael recognized a threat. If not the mountain, nor the

people he sat with, could he be assessing Bedel's own team as an enemy? Why? Or perhaps the question with House Menai was—why not? Bedel opted to keep a close eye on Nadael.

"Grand Essencer, what's going on?" Raynt said, opening and closing his fists at his side.

"Why are we gathered?" Bedel said.

The praying man whispered to Xathon, but it was Xathon who turned to face them.

"War is coming," Xathon said. "An old enemy has returned."

Bedel felt a chill down his spine. Did he mean the Dark Judicator of Bedel's memories? Or someone else? Despite his shock, Bedel kept his face passive. These men needed to believe he didn't remember who had turned his own brother against them.

Xathon continued, "We have reason to believe that even now, before the World Summit, war councils are assembling." He paused to let the news sink in. "You will be divided into two teams. Raynt, you will continue your mission with the King's Men. If there are traitors in our realm, the King wants them found. It is time to shut the Slaver Coalition down.

Bedel and Shai, your secondary mission is to travel to Wonbai in Zeller. Obtain any and all intelligence to confirm our suspicions of war by any means necessary."

"Our secondary mission?" Bedel said when Xathon paused.

"I have suitable cover in Wonbai," Shai said. "But it is going to take time to get in and out, Grand Essencer. What are we supposed to do first?"

Xathon huffed, puffing out his white mustache. He sighed again, gritted his teeth, and said, "First, you will jointly travel to Lodornatha. Rangers will escort the three of you to the remnants of the Wo'Huzziet tribe."

"Count O'Crast's retainers wiped that tribe out in battle," Raynt said. "You're saying some survived?"

Lord Commander Nadael said, "If there are enough

Wo'Huzziet to reignite their jewel mines in the east, that flow will benefit both Cardor and Lupacuo's treasuries in the years to come."

"More exploitation," Shai muttered.

"Careful, agent," Nadael said sharply.

She nodded. "Lord Commander."

"No one will exploit anyone while I am here."

The seated man raised his head, but the shadows and his cloak still concealed him from view. Xathon stepped away from him as the man stood. He peeled back his hood, exposing a silver-white face, silver hair, and strangely kind, pale eyes.

An Immortal.

"Holy yeht—" Shai cut off the curse.

The pale stranger smiled at them. "My name is Alain son of Hokano, Keeper of the North. I am the emissary of Speakers and Keepers. I have come before myth and legends resume; before a cycle and a breaking. The stars that mark the cycle will appear within weeks, marking a few chosen individuals in celestial aura. One of those, we believe, is the daughter of the new Speaker of Men. He, though, requires convincing to leave the lands of the usurper, the Sorceress. I believe he will heed my advice."

Fear rose up within Bedel, clawing at his throat, churning his stomach. The mountain had known. Up was death.

Emissary Alain smiled. "The three of us, along with our Elven allies, are going into the Sorceress's domain. I need your help, Bedel *Ries* and Shai, to bring them out."

CHAPTER 1

A'BANNA MEZTLONI XITIA LET HERSELF SINK INTO THE WARM, blue water of the river. The lapping waves once a gentle reminder that there was good in the world. Usually, this was a favorite, peaceful place.

Each swell washed the northern man's blood off her. *Alain.*

Her bare toes sank into the riverbed, disturbing sand. Blood, sand, and water; a murky combination. No sane Avocan would bathe while covered in blood. Water drakes hunted here. The blood would only bait them.

But most Avocans were not destined to become the Sorceress's next high priestess as A'banna was. Nor did they have the experience of slitting a person's throat open over a stone bowl. A'banna had witnessed many such sacrifices, most often of trespassers into Avoc, but never before had she held the knife. Never before had a sacrificial victim shared the ageless silver skin and eyes of the very Sorceress who commanded her. Never before had a sacrifice died in prophesy, smiling.

The northern man's name had been Alain. He had trekked untold leagues to deliver his message, but A'banna had the temple guards strap him to the stone offering table. The Sorceress had looked on gleefully as A'banna whet the knife with which she'd slit his throat. Alain had broken the silence of the sacrifice with: "Tonight come the stars. Embrace them."

His prophecy had come true. The reflection of twenty-four distinct stars now glimmered in the water, their light undiminished by the sun, the tree canopy, or the blood staining the water around her.

A'banna no longer wanted her future as high priestess. But since she had slaughtered the messenger of the stars, what foreign gods would have her now? Perhaps death the way her ancestors perished, an offering to nature, was best. She had hunted in the jungle her entire life; had spent years exploring its wonders and communing with nature. Dying a hunter's death seemed more honorable than killing innocent wanderers. Or prophets.

Small fish swam by her body, feasting on tadpoles and other tinier prey thrown up in the murky cloud. A'banna closed her eyes and sank back into the water's embrace once more, allowing her inner senses to blossom. She felt the pulse of the ethereal world fabric which flowed through everything. It united her with the rhythm of beasts in the jungle, and the wind essences through the trees. Another wave serendipitously lifted her, and opening her eyes, she saw the water drake floating just inside the bay. She locked her gaze on the drake, letting it know she was aware of its presence. To emphasize her point, A'banna mentally stretched out aether from her aura, allowing it to pull free from the spirit of her body. It contained a part of her, a willingness, a submission to fight, if not perish. The shimmering ethereal strand streamed over the water like an arrow and merged with the water drake's own thin aura, one predator to another.

The drake shifted its position in water, signaling its intent. A'banna unsheathed the knife holstered at the small of her back.

The alarm cry of monkeys rose in the air as the water drake closed in to strike. Water trickled down along dark green scales and flowed around the stumps where wings could form should the beast gain its own territory. Its body was twice the length of a man, but the drake's tail stretched out far behind it, latent with power. From a long, triangular head orange reptilian eyes stared defiantly.

A jaguar growled somewhere in the trees. The animals of the forest knew the water drake for what it was.

A'banna's aether sensed all the animals, connected with them, was one with them beneath the trees. She could have used the essences to command it, *lead* its instincts to attack, but she only stared at those orange eyes and their black pupils.

The drake swished its tail, menacingly lifting its head a little higher. Water drakes were renowned for their capacity to travel at speeds in water a man or even a jaguar could not match on land. And this particular beast was on the cusp of adulthood, driven by the voracious need to feed and fuel its metamorphosis into a sea dragon. This close, with the traveler's blood in the water, she was the drake's prey.

And it was hers.

Up on the ridgeline above the water, trees and bushes shook, their leaves and branches rattling and rustling. A young ram burst from the underbrush, hawing in fright. A'banna risked a sideways glance as the ram beat the ground with its hooves in a futile attempt to slow before toppling into the water.

Screeches erupted from nearby. She momentarily dared to take her focus from the drake, spotting three *cuelatchanli*—raptors—pursuing the ram through the underbrush. A'banna studied the swift blurs behind vegetation. Their hips were at least as tall as a person. From tail to snout the smallest appeared to be around five yards. These were adults. A primed hunting pack, skilled at survival. These bird-like predators shared some reptilian similarities to the drake, despite being covered in feathers. They were wingless, but their arms and legs were powerful, with claws about ten inches long. Their feathers helped propel them across vast distances, one of the reasons her ancestors had built the city wall so tall. A'banna smiled, she recognized a soft yellow pattern on a male's feathered tail. They had rescued these hatchlings, raised them. From their birth to her death. Seemed fitting, even if she hadn't known they had returned to this territory. For every raptor that was seen, at least one hunted out of sight. There could be as many as nine more *cuelatchanli* in the forest that she couldn't see.

The ram teetered into open air and plunged toward the water. With lightning speed, the drake abandoned its lock on A'banna and lashed out, twisting its long neck. Huge jaws that could have ripped her in half plucked the ram from the air as the drake crashed down in a colossal splash. Desperate bleating silenced as the drake slipped below the surface. Water churned with the massive cranking of its tail. Blood foamed.

"One life for another," A'banna murmured a hunter's prayer. Emotion clenched her words, tears wet her cheeks. She ducked her head underneath the water, a ritual cleansing of self-pity. In death, one closes their eyes. The water seemed so blue, despite the blood and mud in it. The water was illuminated by the stars. She shut them tight, resisting the urge to open them even as the water urged her to breathe.

Alain, I am so sorry.

The memory was raw, like her hands had been when, as a child, A'banna first carelessly ran through the underbrush into thorns. A'banna remembered trembling as she stood over Alain, ceremonial knife in hand. He'd already smiled once. Steeling herself for the act, she pressed the knife to his throat, and he spoke. "A'banna." Her hand had felt frozen with fear, but she had lifted the blade barely a centimeter away. He was new to their lands! How did he know her name? He continued smiling. "Tonight come the stars. Embrace them, A'banna."

The Sorceress had glided toward them. A'banna never dared to look up at her. Not then, in hesitation. The Sorceress's pale fingers stroked through Alain's silver hair.

"Father says hello, Aunt Jocina."

"Last chance, Alain. Where are my children Hokano stole from me?"

"Once, my cousins told me you loved them. You can never win them back in evil." His pale eyes shifted to A'banna. "A'banna you—"

"Do it," the Sorceress snapped. "Longevity has dulled his mind."

A'banna obeyed. Cleaning wild game was routine, so she allowed her body to go through the same motions. But he was not an animal whose sacrifice blessed hunters. Alain's eyes widened with how sudden and swift it was. Then his gaze softened. Sorceress Jocina whispered in Alain's ear as he bled out.

"Rest with The Taurs," A'banna said remotely. "Find yourself in their embrace." Alain's smile barely wavered. He died with it on his face, having ignored the Sorceress completely. A'banna gasped when, with great effort, his arm broke his rope bonds, his hand grabbing A'banna's wrist. His body writhed in death, and his hand fell limp over the edge of the table. The Sorceress laughed.

"Well done, my child," the Sorceress had purred, salivating. She smelled him, as if savoring the aroma of a meal. Her lips peeled back over elongated canines. "Oh, dear, I'm getting ahead of myself. Bring me my cup, so I may drink him hot and fresh."

A'banna's had felt like it was laden with stone. She turned for the goblet but still heard the Sorceress whisper, "So we begin again, Hokano. Blood for blood. Poor little nephew." The Sorceress ran her hand through Alain's hair one last time.

A'banna shivered in the water, the memory over in a moment.

Alain's blood clouded the water around her, yet she could see clearer now than ever before.

"One predator against another," she said, pushing herself out of the water as if reborn. She was not absolved of the right to die —but she no longer felt so helpless.

At the edge of the forest, the giant raptors slowed, screeching angrily at the drake. The *cuelatchanli* did not advance beyond the shade of the trees. A'banna could make out beautiful blue and green plumage even in the dappling light of the waning sun. She heard one of their number click their claws on rocks, a taunting distraction before a charge. A'banna heard another raptor snarl. The tapping ceased abruptly on the alpha's reprimand. The *cuelatchanli* were excellent deceivers. They knew A'banna was there. The vibrant blue, green, and red males were the distraction. Bushes rustled gently as the encircling females positioned themselves for the kill.

A'banna climbed back up the river bank to face the pack, gripping her knife tightly. Water cascaded from her naked form, but she was unashamed as she turned to the three raptors. All three remained on the verge above the feeding drake, still protesting their claim on the prey. A fourth head rose from behind the males, with brown and red plumes. This one was larger than the others and must be the alpha; a female. A'banna lifted her arms from her sides and elevated her chin. She kept her eyes on the big female in the center.

"*Nie momatequia,*" A'banna said aloud in the ancient dialect of Belasna, growling like a jaguar. Her bearing was defiant, but internally, she was actually pleading. "*Ni mictici.*" *I wash my hands. Try to kill me.*

The raptors, suddenly attentive, all looked her way. One opened its great maw, rows of teeth inside. She deserved nothing less. Their black pupils were full of intelligence, weighing the risk of this new prey. A blur of brown, green, and red in the bushes to

A'banna's right signaled another female raptor was near, but then the leaves stopped swaying.

Leather groaned as A'banna's hand tightened around the knife. This was right. This was the time.

"*Cahuila!*" A voice snapped from behind. Arrow-like strands of aether whooshed past her, one for each threatening animal. She knew the structure of the one who had woven the essences—of obedience, fear, respect, of a more powerful predator—in that ethereal package. Her teacher *Beast Lead*, more powerfully perhaps than anyone in Avoc.

Just as with the drake, the raptors' auras absorbed the message. It boosted the command they had learned in their youth. The four giant birds screeched angrily but fled back into the shadows of the forest. Bushes not ten feet away rustled. A demur-colored *cuelatchanli* female revealed her chosen kill place. Instead, her eyes turned their focus away from A'banna. Her tail swiped the vegetation, then she retreated silently. In the river, twin trails of water streamed away as the drake submerged to finish its prey.

"Father," A'banna said. She sheathed her knife. Gaze lowered but chin still raised, she turned to face the voice.

Huahanna, High Priest for Jocina Queen of Avoc and Sorceress of the south, Voice of the Guides, stood in the sand, feet apart, seemingly in rest. One foot was slightly behind the other, knees bent. His muscles were like coiled springs, ready to propel him into action. His shield and spear looked ornamental but were practiced and deadly. Around his neck was a leather necklace with tusks, recent trophies of the hunt. The tusks laid over another necklace of multiple raptor's sickle claws which dangled above his embroidered tunic, marking him the premier *Beast Leader* of Avoc. He was the voice of all living, including every entity within the world fabric. And, as she had learned long ago, her father was difficult to deceive.

"A'banna, this was foolish. To bathe at dusk." He *Led* his aether to gently touch her own, creating an ethereal extension of his voice: *Why, my daughter? What prompted this? Whose blood is that?*

Clenching her jaw, she met his reprimanding regard, her heart troubled by his emotional questioning. She gestured to the sky. "New stars, Father. Just as the sacrifice predicted. Blue stars."

The new stars were so bright that in another hour they would outshine the moon.

A'banna knelt next to her clothing and slipped her white dress over her, then fastened her leather chest plate. She bound her black hair with a beaded rope of ram fur, tucking in the plumage of a male and female raptor. Her father gave her the consideration of looking away—though his senses were still alert to any signs of the *cuelatchanli* in the surrounds.

When she was ready, A'banna slipped on the orange and blue bracelet her mother had made for her womanhood day. She glanced at the sky, at the blue lights glowing brighter and brighter where they should not be. Then she faced him. "I killed a prophet. Is that what you do? Kill prophets?"

She thought back to Alain's last words. Why was he defiant of the Sorceress who allowed his death, but welcoming of the woman who wielded the knife? What had he said about her children? She'd never considered there were more than just Quin, but for an Immortal, perhaps it made sense. Were these children as evil as she? Not if they hid themselves from her. What kind of being *hid* themselves from Sorceress Jocina? Huahanna sighed, finally looking at his daughter. "We kill because The Taurs demand it, A'banna, not because I seek plea-sure in draining the life of another. We kill because she demands it."

A'banna remembered the northern man's eyes, fixed on her in both horror and sorrow—and pity.

"I do not want to be the Sorceress's priestess, my father. I cannot take another innocent life."

Huahanna's long, frayed black hair shook, and sadness filled his eyes. "So you would have the beasts of the forest and the water slay you instead?"

"I would have them try."

"My daughter," he whispered. His grip on the spear loosened then tightened as he turned it in his hand. "So this is what has been in your heart for so long? Who am I without my daughter?"

A'banna embraced her father. Her body rocked with emotion, a deep, guttural pain that she wanted to howl at the stars. Her head buried into his chest as her body heaved, but she bit down, refusing to allow a scream past her lips. The intensity ached her legs; such grief.

"Who will I be without you, Father?" she cried, unable to meet his eyes until the tears no longer felt quite so wet on her cheeks. "She'll kill you for me to take your place. It has happened before."

"Yes," he whispered into her ear, one strong arm wrapped around her. "But you are my daughter, last of my family. I need you. Do not throw your life away. I know your fear. Your anger. I see the stars."

At last, sniffling, A'banna broke away. She understood the danger in what she was about to say aloud.

"She makes a mockery of men and women in her witchcraft."

Huahanna's brown eyes darted toward her again. Their moment of father-daughter intimacy was over. Now came the consideration of hunters. His voice lowered. "She does as she and The Taurs see fit. It is the right of a Keeper."

Keeper, the Sorceress's other title. Absolute authority. It was the Sorceress who had ordered A'banna to kill the prophet Alain, not even waiting for Huahanna to return from a hunt to perform his ritualistic duties. What was she trying to hide? Vulnerability?

What had she questioned Alain about? Children? Not A'banna's betrothed, Huquin, obviously. Quin was at the palace. It had been a month since Quin's last journey abroad, though A'banna never pressed *where* he went. Nor had A'banna considered, in all the Sorceress's thousands of years, that she may have had other offspring. Where were they? What manner of person was Hokano, that he could *hide* them from Sorceress Jocina? A'banna shook her head. "I do not want this. I do not want Quin. I do not want the headdress."

"If you break the betrothal, she will never stop pursuing you. Her will dominates this land and all the living within it."

"Father, do you love me?"

His jaw stiffened. They both knew he need not answer.

"Then spare me this fate. Let my spirit return to the dust of the land and nourish the beasts of water or forest as I should. I am unfit for this world. I have slaughtered a prophet like a willing sacrifice. But he was not willing, Father. Today, I saw a man defiant with death at his throat, the Sorceress's voice in his ear! He told me to embrace the stars. His name was Alain."

She could not bear his look: grief in his eyes but resolute in his bearing. He did not try to dampen the colors as his aura flared with emotion. She watched the misty gray of sorrow flowing around him. Turning away, she re-focused her eyes on the still waters of the river.

"When they come to the altar, they know why. Every name you will have to bear. Every story, every prayer, every sacrifice for a greater good." Huahanna paused. "The Keeper explained about Alain. She wanted you to do it because I was with the hunting party. It is her way. She breaks you in, slowly. One draining at a time."

She couldn't bear the slaughter. How had he, all these years? Especially afterward, when the blood filled the Bowls of Life. She could still recall the look of lust on the Sorceress's face as she dipped her goblet into the still-hot liquid, oblivious to the death throes of the northerner.

Alain.

A'banna's voice cracked. "And you have seen her drink in pleasure?"

"These are perilous words, my daughter."

"The Sorceress and Huiquin will be dangerous for me, for I cannot follow both while these stars remain. I am to embrace one or the other, but my spirit says it cannot be both."

Her father continued to scan the forest, but of the *cuelatchanli,* there was no sign. "No, you cannot. Come with me."

A'banna exhaled nasally. "And to where does one who rejects the Avoc way go?"

The Avoc way was the Sorceress's way; and her way was that of The Taurs, their gods. They both knew the full consequences of everything she spoke.

Huahanna stepped closer, leaning the spear into the crook of his arm. "A'banna, to one who would break the Avoc way, I would say: Go and take gifts to the Lodornathan Dragon Hunters and Rangers north of the forest."

She had only heard of the Elves and Dwarves of Lodornatha. For many centuries, Lodornatha warred with Avoc over territory in the mountains and access to the dragon hives there. Lodornatha kept the dragons contained, and the tribes north of the forest, those of the Wo'Huzziet nation, benefited. The Sorceress wanted the dragons to become her pets of war, no doubt. Not long ago, rumors came that the tribes' villages north of the forest had been ransacked. The Wo'Huzziet city of Ntokup had fallen to foreign invaders. Lodornatha had retreated into itself and its mountain kingdom. Avoc raiding parties had been sent into the Elven and Dwarven realm. Those raiders never returned. What prevented the Sorceress from wiping out her enemies with her armies of experiments? The Marcher army of minotaurs? Snakes? The Velheron? There were stories of other creatures just as terrifying. When Avocans failed in war, would she send her creatures?

"What do I have that the Elves of Lodornatha would want from me?"

"Come, I will show you."

Her father turned and entered the narrow trail in the under-brush. She followed, her eyes surveying the surrounding forest. Any minor negligence, a single mistake, and the jungle could kill swiftly and silently. But like the drake and the *cuelatchanli*, the jungle was alive with other colors to A'banna. She saw what her father saw, but few others did.

Huahanna and A'banna increased their pace, moving rapidly along the thin path. She brushed through low ferns, her step light on the leaves and twigs of the ground. Not one broke. She, like the raptors, could conceal herself if necessary. All around them, the forest spoke. Monkeys swung overhead on vines, curving their tales and chattering loudly at them. Birds song rang out; a glorious and melodious orchestra. Insects swarmed and buzzed. Even in the shade, the heat had already summoned sweat, but the scent of vegetation, of life, refreshed her.

It wasn't long until new sounds could be heard. A baby, crying to be fed. A man and woman hollering at each other. A merchant hawking wares. The creak of wooden carts. And the loud stomping of the Sorceress's minotaurs patrolling the edge of the forest. This Marcher army had recently grown in number, humans morphed into the image of a High Taur. Very little of what made them Avocan remained; minotaurs were now the Sorceress's tools and a terrifying physical manifestation of The Taurs, always near, but often out of sight.

The stone walls emerged suddenly from the green jungle, civi-lization dwelling in the wild. Avoc-Nezlticoulti. Home.

Huahanna and A'banna stepped from the trail and skirted

along the city wall. They came to a gate-house, where huge iron-reinforced doors with a portcullis remained opened. It was tradition to keep the doors open wide for hunters and travelers caught in the jungle at dusk. Soon they would be shut and barred, the portcullis lowered. Fires had been lit in the braziers inside the gate, a warning to the animals of the forest. Guards patrolled the battlements. Most animals hunted at night.

The gate guards were alert this evening, watching the sprawling stone road that stretched deep into the wilderness for any late travelers.

When they saw the pair nearing, they sprang up and then bowed low.

"*Culhuavoc*," they said in the traditional greeting, nearly prostrating themselves before A'banna and Huahanna.

Nausea swept over A'banna, but she contained it, replying with a hollow blessing.

Those strange blue stars spoke of another god, one she had not known—or perhaps always had but chose to ignore in the endless devotion to The Taurs. She steadied herself and her thoughts. The Taurs saw much and were invisible to even her. Like most Avocans, she could only feel their unnaturally cold presence. Their representations, however, were everywhere in the city; life-like stone statues of the mystical Taur Guides were placed above doorways and at fountains. Their stone eyes glared out of ancient statues. Some boasted terrifying furry faces, cat-like ears, and snake bodies, often with furled or unfurled wings. Others were carved as giant bulls standing like men. These were constant reminders of the presence of fickle, wrathful gods, the true inspiration for the monsters the Sorceress created. So even if A'banna couldn't see a real Taur, she knew the shape the sources of fear took. The Guides were ever watching.

A scent of fresh bread exchanged the fear in her stomach for hunger and eased tension in her shoulders. It brought her back from her reverie to what she loved about the city; the people. A'banna clucked her tongue and slowed at a food vendor in front of the guard barracks, a towering ziggurat of dark stone. Her father turned, gave an ironic long-suffering sigh, and paid as A'banna thanked the woman. She shared a flatbread with her father as a man shouted for travelers to clear the road.

Scaly, three-horned yehts lumbered through the foot traffic; many pulled carts, their riders balanced behind the yeht's large frills. A'banna steered clear of the merchant caravan, wondering what drove them out so late.

On the opposite side of the road, two behemoth tamers thrust long electric eel-covered prods into a behemoth's shoulders. The long-necked creature bellowed as it lifted a roped platform. Workers removed tools and bricks from the platform, continuing construction on the new ziggurat's chimney. This structure was to be a great chamber for weapon smiths and an armory, dedicated to The Taurs. Quin had assured them it would equip Avocan warriors, but a passing glance at the armaments already cooling on racks showed weapons that required the strength of minotaurs: large scimitars, axes, hammers, and iron-covered clubs—all too heavy for a human to use. Ziggurats were only constructed for great buildings or the most elite of society. What was the real purpose here?

Two men on each side of the platform sat with large palm branches, feeding the behemoths and keeping them steady as a reward for their work. Scaled like most of the great beasts of the forest, the behemoths had two blue dotted lines running from their snout to the tip of the long, muscular tail. They were beautiful creatures, but dangerous if left unattended. A'banna stepped back, keeping away from the thick feet, remembering her father's saying, *the fool seeks shade next to a behemoth's foot or a breeze by its tail.*

They continued down the main road toward the large central

ziggurat of the palace and the round, black tower rising from its peak. Those were the Sorceress's private chambers, her laboratory and sanctuary. Clergy sometimes whispered that she governed the entire south, both land and sea, weather and creature, from those rooms. A balcony wrapped around the top of the tower, but the stone itself had been worn smooth. The tower rose above every structure in the city, including the grand Temple of Offering behind it, to the northeast.

Priests had forced Alain up the stairs. A'banna remembered when she first saw him ascending. He tripped over the hem of his sacrificial gown, so the priests plunged their eel prods into him. The eels, confined to their fate, bit and electrocuted. As Alain's body still trembled, they had whipped him until he stood again and climbed. Again and again, until Alain topped the stairs, flanked on either side by carved snakes that served as a railing. A'banna remembered a certain awe as he passed so bravely, unflinchingly, between the statues of the High Taurs—a minotaur more human than any other image, and a dragon, wings curled around itself, its head had lowered on its serpentine neck. The statues' eyes observed the coming of the dead, whose blood drained into the large Bowls of Life, one at the minotaur's feet, the other curled in the dragon's tail. A'banna distracted herself, whetting the knife. Alain smiled at A'banna. Sorceress Jocina barked that she must hurry. The Taurs and Jocina wanted blood.

Nausea tightened her abdomen as she endured the memory.

A'banna, the stars have come. She could almost hear Alain's voice. Tender, caring, and forgiving.

Approaching the palace from this angle, the statues of the High Taurs seemed to flank the palace tower—a visual illusion of the two ziggurats, built so close. A'banna felt a cold chill. Surely the statues couldn't be smiling? Impossible. The Bowls still glistened with red in the sunset, an offering A'banna knew wouldn't be there in the morning.

A'banna took another bite of bread, quelling her emotions.

Her thoughts turned to the city that had been her home. There was fear here, yes, but beauty and life, also. Streets were sensibly laid out with mathematical precision from the main thoroughfare to the palace and the temple. In a sense, she'd always viewed the rectangular, flat residential buildings as a reminder of the adoration they should have for the transcendent gods who dwelled above them, but often walked among them. More and more The Taurs had ceased to be her gods, despite how real they were, but as tens of thousands of people dwelled in the shadows of the ziggurats, so the blue stars now shined above. What kind of gods would the stars be? What kind of god could shape goodliness in a person like Alain?

Men, women, and even children stopped and bowed as A'banna and Huahanna passed them on the main road. A'banna could never understand what made her special in their eyes. Her position was a glorified executioner—and more often than not one of these precious people would be a willing sacrifice. Could she sacrifice the baker woman? The weaver? The hunters that went with her father? What about the builders? No. If she hated herself after Alain, there would be nothing left of her when one of these beautiful people came to offer themselves willingly.

As they passed, the people were free to rise. As usual, the questions and petitions came, but most would go unanswered until they visited the temple. They plead for favor for their womb, for their children, for their spouses, parents, other family. For those that had gone missing according to the Sorceress's rule. For the harvest and the planting season or the hunt. Those were normal requests.

Today was not a normal day.

A'banna's step faltered when she heard the first question about the stars from a little girl, who ran up beneath two adults offering their own petitions.

"My teacher said the stars mean the Sorceress's power will cause her enemies to kneel, Priestess! Will it be on one knee or two like we do at the temple?"

A'banna stared at the wide-eyed, innocent girl. She wanted to shout, plead with her, to see the lies as A'banna had discovered them. To gather her family and run away.

She crouched down and took the girl's hand, forcing yet one more fake smile. "It is what our legends, say, yes. And we shall ask her Silver Majesty when we arrive at the palace. You shall know soon."

"Bless the Sorceress and The Taurs!" an old woman shouted. In response, others broke into worshipful chants.

A'banna squeezed the child's hands, then rose. Her jaw dropped. Down the closest street headed west, someone had defaced a residential building's walls. Two silver eyes representing the Sorceresses were painted on the gray stone, with a red line, dripping like blood. There were always dissidents, and their short-lived rebellious acts never ended well. This was different. Someone had painted blue stars over the eyes and the line.

A'banna shivered, eyes fixated on the brash vandalism. It stirred something within her. Courage?

A man's voice shouted over the people dancing and singing in the street. "Silence! The stars mean our end."

That was the end of the peace. Someone shoved another person; someone else retaliated. The crowd became a mob as violence erupted.

"We do not know that!" Huahanna shouted, but the people did not settle.

Someone threw a cabbage at A'banna's feet. She spun, scanning the crowd as she would the bushes for prey or predator.

The same voice chastised the protestor. "The Sorceress will come for us in greater number than before, for she requires an army. Look at what she builds. If we fight ourselves, who will defy her?"

Some of the crowd remained bowed—A'banna and Huahanna had stopped, they could not stand, whether to join in the fight or be overcome by it. A'banna could see the city guards on the next street, standing in front of the defaced building, questioning tenants. Two broke off to see to the crowd. This would become brutal, quickly. At the worst, if the vandal was not found, the Sorceress would kill or take everyone in the building, one way or another.

Huahanna shouted again and slammed his spear into his shield. His aura spread out rapidly, hundreds of translucent white-silver tentacles roaming across the street, visible only to an essencer's eyes. Each briefly touched the auras of people in the panicked crowd. Through that *Leading* connection, he eased their fears, turned back any hint of violence. Folk calmed, though their angst was not completely satiated.

"We will pray and beseech The Taurs' guidance!" Huahanna called to the crowd. "I urge everyone not to overreact." He gestured at the defaced residential building. "Patience, calm. Already, the Sorceress has sacrificed in foresight of what was to come. Trust in the Truth. It will guide you."

It only took a few folks to nod, before others began to shuffle off. Some shook hands apologetically. Others lingered.

The crowd gradually parted, going their separate ways, but a hunter remained standing in the center. "You believe that?" he said. It was the voice of the dissident—but unlikely the vandal. The hunter was not ten yards away, as close as the drake had been in the water. His adornments, necklaces brandishing a variety of teeth, claws, talons, bones, feathers, and fur marked him as a veteran, a leader of hunts. She recognized him: Torresin. A good man, bereft father, and widower who defied the Sorceress's demands to worship The Taurs. He'd spoken to her before in the market but never visited the temple.

Torresin's hard eyes fixated on A'banna. "We aren't safe, are we?"

An unnatural cold swept across her skin. He shivered, too. Huahanna turned, eyes wide, imploring to them both. The Taurs were near. Their presence brought cold into heat, even if they were unseen.

"Torresin," Huahanna said, his voice with warning.

"Father, my friend." The hunter's eyes glanced at him, then looked again at A'banna. "They know. This is the first night of blue stars. If the Sorceress requires us, we won't last the duration. Are we in danger?"

"If you feel so," A'banna said, measuring her words. "Do as is our custom in the jungle, keep your weapon in your hand and one eye open." The man nodded. Had he seen her at the river? Had she missed him? "But, Torresin, as for me, I trust in the power of The Taurs to protect us and for the legends to come true."

"All the legends?"

"As many as the Sorceress requires," A'banna said. Her gut twisted with the words. She wanted to shout to the hunter, *danger!* She wanted to praise the artist who dared inspire resistance. She wanted to flee. Instead, she smiled. The hunter, jaw tight, glanced once more at Huahanna, and then fell in with the crowd.

"Well done," Huahanna said. "He is a clever man and good companion in the jungle."

"Yes, my father. You did well, also."

A'banna glanced up to the top of the Temple of Offering and the statues of the High Taurs; the dragon and the minotaur. No, the statues were *not* smiling. It had been her imagination, after all. Below them, carved ornamental snakes lined the grand stairs. Her eyes darted to the Sorceress's tower, rising from the palace ziggurat. Its wall slithered. The setting sun reflected off her enthralled snakes' orange and yellow scales in a beautiful, disconcerting mirage. Not a day passed that a chosen pet, despite regular feedings, didn't disappear for a time to snatch a poor citizen from their bed before rejoining the sinuous, rotating mass. If The Taurs knew her heart, they'd forever disown her. Stalk her. Kill her. Was this the life she wanted? To embrace stars as her new gods?

As darkness began to settle on the city, a swarm of bats flew above, feasting on insects and moving off into the night. The blue stars cast shadows upon the ground; a moving, flickering show of light and darkness.

They continued along the main street, even as some people called out, asking their high priest and future high priestess about the new stars.

"My *Culhali*! Is this a sign of The Taur's pleasure?" a woman called from a window, cradling her newborn as it nursed. "Are we blessed at last?"

"Hush, my child," Huahanna called back to her. "We shall seek their wisdom. I am certain the truth will be revealed."

He turned to A'banna. "We must make an offering and seek answers, else we are plain to see."

A'banna smiled at the woman in the window, a basket weaver who oversaw a store in the marketplace. The smile felt hollow as she thought about all the lies it projected. Always a sacrifice, and yet death was what lived in Avoc. The woman's other son had been taken to the breeding pits just last year. Too young to sire, not too young for the experiments. A'banna had watched the priests carry him off amid her wailing protests. The woman had tried to be dutiful, but even with A'banna's lingering gaze, she clutched her child a little tighter and closed the window a little faster than perhaps otherwise. Here someone needed their help, their truth, and they smiled as they lied to her.

A'banna had grown to hate this life.

If the only way to help her people was for her to leave, then leave she must.

They trekked to the palace and climbed its great stone stairs, ascending to the heavens. The higher they rose, the more visible the surrounding, dense forest was. In the stars' light, the tangle of trees and vines glimmered blue.

A palace guard, clothed in scaled drake armor, opened a door to their private chambers.

Once inside, hidden from human eyes and ears—who could account for The Taurs?—Huahanna quickly closed off a curtain. Hastily, he unstacked colorful pillows to reveal a chest. Taking one of the raptor claws from his necklace, Huahanna snapped off the back—a small key dropped out. He held it up, almost triumphantly, before unlocking the chest.

Huahanna handed A'banna a triangular device with round gold cylinders, engraved with runes, connected to each of the corners. The corners themselves were also engraved with runes, and each had a small blue jewel shaped like a teardrop set into it. Inspecting it closer, A'banna noticed deceptively fine, flat edges, carved symmetrically on each side of the jewel, giving it that water drop appearance. The device had been recently polished, though some parts of the artifact remained tarnished, probably through great age. The center was hollow, large enough for her to place both hands through.

After the triangular device came a book. Huahanna trembled as he lifted it. He glanced warily at A'banna.

She raised the triangular device.

"My father? What is this?"

His voice was barely a whisper. "The past. The present. The future. You hold in your hands an imager. It belonged to the ancient world. I learned that Elves called Larks teach of a goddess, Akasha, who stored her memories within her tears—like the shape of the quintessence at the center of our aura and these jewels in this artifact. These jewels store the essences of captured images, which can be transplanted upon a canvas, a wall, a medium. It is how they distributed art, literature, and pictures of their lives in action. You should have seen the stilled pictures before they were burned; people of many types, all together. The clothes they wore, different from what we know. The Sorceress wore a white coat, not a silver dress. She must be the last of her kind, for she was in a picture with others, standing together like equals. It was faded, but they all wore badges with the same symbol: a black arch over a cross with a serpent."

What an odd world he described. It sounded so different than what she knew.

A'banna shook as she gripped the strange item. The imager was half a rod across on each triangular side, and the jewels stretched outward from each corner. Metallic, cold but beautiful. The jewels themselves shimmered in the candlelight, making it seem like a thousand flames. "My father, this is priceless."

"It is an artifact passed down from one generation to the next, my daughter. It is how I made this."

He handed her the old leather-bound tome, its parchment pages yellowed, crinkled with humidity.

Gently cradling the imager, she ran her hand over the book before taking it. Its cover was coarse and thick. Hide of a behemoth, no doubt. So rare.

"Open it," Huahanna said.

A'banna lifted the cover. It creaked, and she inhaled the sweet aroma of its paper. Even A'banna, as heir to the high priest one of the few deemed worthy of education, had seldom been given access to books. These were priceless gifts, like the bracelet her mother had made for her.

"My father, this is not your handwriting. This is not our language. Belasna?"

"Yes," he said. "It is the original Belasna language, spoken and read by the ancient Elves and the people who came before, Immortals, of whom only the Sorceress survived."

"What does it say?"

"It describes how the Sorceress—from a group of Immortals called 'Doctors'—destroyed and remade the world. And how she plans to do it again with an Elf named Hurmlen."

"Huiquin's father? Hurmlen the Judicator of Truth?"

Huahanna nodded and pointed at the book and imager.

"Yes. They are the destroyers of worlds."

CHAPTER 2

A'banna stared at her father. "How do you know these
things if you cannot read it?"

On his knees, Huahanna crawled closer, so their faces nearly
touched over the tome. "Long ago, when I was young, and rela-
tions with the Lodornathan Dragon Hunters were less strained,
Elven and Dwarven scholars taught me the ancient written form.
Years later, after practicing for myself and honing my *Beast
Speak*, the Sorceress called me into her chambers. She was
writing in a similar tome, and I could see what she wrote." He
turned pages to near the back of the book. "This formula."

"Mathematics," A'banna whispered.

"The ancients called this chemistry," Huahanna clarified. "It is
the basis for every abomination she creates. For the snakes' evolu-
tion, for the Marchers, for the Velheron and for whatever comes
next."

A'banna hesitated. Even she didn't believe those Velheron
rumors. "The six-winged heron, my father, was seen but once."

"It is now a god in the far north. It brought a rose she created,
one that turns the skin of Elves blue, while the skin of other races
hardens like her snakes, but in the image of The Taurs. Goblins

may kill freely in bloodlust and dine on their enemies, but in their own way, even they respect the dead with ceremony once their lust is quenched. Not these new beasts. Not the Vel. Last week there was an accident at the breeding pens. The Vel escaped and first found a full company of soldiers. They slaughtered them, ate them, but were drawn by the screams to a dormitory. Prisoners waiting for their turn. The Vel killed them all and left the flesh for the crows, but it was not crows who came, nor snakes, nor minotaurs. A flock of Velheron descended on the bodies. What remained was left as carrion, not even burned."

A'banna gasped in horror. "You saw this."

"As high priestess, you will see many, many horrible things. If you stay."

"If I stay? But I am determined to leave."

"Then the monsters may pursue you. The Marchers were only the beginning. The Vel worshipped the Velheron as they feasted. For now, their numbers are small, but in the harbors of southern Avoc, whale ships are packed with crates of red eater-ants and snakes. The forges of the Marchers in the mountains of the west glow at all hours and whole villages have disappeared."

"But more Marchers are seen," she finished for him, staring dreadfully at the text below her. She couldn't read a word. But why would her father lie? Why tell these things unless the Sorceress had chosen a path for Avoc she had not told anyone? And then there were the new stars, prophesied by the traveler A'banna had sacrificed. Yet, here in this city, a new forge was under construction, facing the newly anointed barracks waiting to be filled with troops. "How can she end the world?"

Huahanna nodded, turning more pages. "Once I learned of this, I began using our family's imager to slowly take pictures of every page, risking my life more than once." He paused and took a deep breath. "I used guards and Marchers to feed the snakes so as to be undisturbed. It was the only way."

He found the page and pointed. Another formula she didn't understand, more scrawled text belonging to the Sorceress herself. "They have already begun," he said. "They began so long ago. The end begins in the past, with lies and deception to create a new world from the old. She failed once, perhaps twice, but with Dark Judicator Hurmlen, their son Huiquin and these monsters it has been said, in hushed whispers among the wise of our people, that the stars we see tonight mark the beginning of her plans. She will try again. Soon."

After closing the book, Huahanna placed a second, much smaller one on top of it. He slid both toward her.

"This is why you must warn Lodornatha and the other nations that once stood against her. Zeller once proudly protected the north, but their newer god—a dragon they call him—has sided with Hurmlen and Jocina, and Greneld in the east is governed by the new Judicator, no doubt the pupil or puppet of Hurmlen. With the Wo'Huzziet splintered, Lodornatha stands alone."

"What of my sister? Surely, she stands." A'banna watched her father for a response, but they revealed nothing.

A'banna thought of the young girl that was raised with her by her father and mother. They weren't birth-parent sisters, but they had loved the half-Glymph as if they were blood. Not even the raptors or water drakes had bested the woman now in exile.

"Against her own father? Her step-mother and brother?" Huahanna lowered his head in sorrow. "I fear we failed her, also."

"But she is strong. She will resist."

"She will survive and keep the forest safe. That is all we may ask from her." He sighed. "Lodornatha is alone. If Lodornatha falls, the fire dragons will spread." Huahanna paused.

A'banna knew that look. Huahanna carried the weight of the world upon his shoulders, and his gifts in magic did not help lighten his load.

"What have you learned?"

Huahanna took her hand. "Farther north lies an ancient kingdom, younger than the new world, older than Avoc. It is called Cardor, and in my dreams, I see you there in war against the Glymphs, fighting alongside a man of Istante and a half-Glymph, like your sister, but with blue flames in his hands. There is a man with golden hair, bearing one of the ancient swords from the Realm War, dressed as a dragon, and a regal woman with you—a warrior like yourself in the colors we see, and the fifth and final man I cannot see, for he rides on the wind on a beast, half eagle and lion.

"And the *cuelatchanli* bow before you."

A'banna shivered. Raptors bowing before her? If not for her father's prophetic dreams in the past, she would have silenced him, but his eyes watered with pride. His dreams always came to pass. Though she did not feel comfortable calling them dreams, what other word had she to use? He could see between realms and walk in the spirit; it was no mere dream.

"You have dreamed again? My father, why did you not tell me? Your old dreams made you scream and shudder in your sleep."

Huahanna smiled and placed a calloused palm on her cheek. "Because I see you alive and well. And I see the world will gain some hope."

Myriad emotions coursed through A'banna, and she leaned into his touch. "My father, you should come with me."

"Both of us gone? For so long? They will know. If I stay, you have a chance. The beasts still speak with me. I love you, my daughter, but now that you have decided in your heart and now that you *know*, you must go."

A hard *rap-tap-tap* sounded on the inner door. Someone inside the palace wanted to see them.

Before she could react, Huahanna snatched the items from her hands and stuffed them back into the chest, locking it swiftly. He pulled back the curtain, covering the chest in pillows, and smiled at her.

"Priestess," he said.

Hardening herself for the playacting, A'banna nodded.

"What is it?" Huahanna growled, crossing his large chambers. "Who interrupts our prayers?"

Her father opened the wooden plank door—there stood a beautifully handsome man. Silver hair cascaded around slightly pointed ears, framing his exquisite pale-skinned face. Elongated canines were visible with his half-smile. Huiquin, son of the Sorceress and Hurmlen.

A'banna's skin felt like it could crawl away, but she was well-practiced in hiding even her emotional colors inside her aura's quintessence. The quintessence was that shape, much like a teardrop jewel, near the center of a being's *aura* that contained their core personality. Weakness brought out certain hungers within Huiquin while they were alone. She wanted to flee. To run. But Huiquin liked such games. They always ended in her pain.

Huahanna swiftly bowed. "Your Highness, I was unaware."

"My priest father," the man said. His cold silver eyes swept over the room. When he blinked, each eye displayed two sets of eyelids—one set horizontal, one vertical—and his red lips curled as he caught sight of A'banna, who also bowed upon his entrance.

"My future husband," she said, spreading her arms wide, trying not to panic. Had he heard anything? *Breathe as though in battle,* she thought. Could he hear her heartbeat as she could? Deafening. *Breathe.*

The Sorceress's son bowed at the waist, according to Avoc tradition. "My future wife. *Culhali.*" Huahanna nodded at the priestly greeting as Quin continued. "How went the hunt?"

"We brought back a sabre-boar for feasting," Huahanna replied. "The kitchen should be preparing it tonight in honor of

The Taurs," he gestured to a small cabinet. "May I offer you a respite?"

"No, but you have my thanks. I come to call upon A'banna."

Huahanna nodded, smiling as if pleased. "Ah. My daughter."

Her heart skipped a beat. *No, no. Stay calm.* Instead, she smiled and moved toward Quin. She took his arm—thick and strong—and met his gaze. So much like his mother. Those finely pointed ears were attractive beneath his unique silver hair. She'd lie if Quin wasn't one to admire outwardly, but everything else about him repelled her.

Quin led her into the hall, and she walked near him, as they were prone to do. A'banna had rehearsed remaining calm, being ready for anything, even leaving. Why the thought of that latter act simultaneously scared and empowered her the most, she didn't understand.

Both were quiet as Huiquin led A'banna to the balcony jutting between one of the layers of the ziggurat. Far above them, A'banna could hear the slithering on the Sorceress's tower.

"My mother told me of the sacrifice today," he said. "It is not easy to first take a human life."

A lump formed in her throat. "No. No, it isn't. But I will learn what The Taurs have called me to do."

He smiled at her, his red lips curving slightly above those thick canines. "I am confident of that."

Without warning, Quin grabbed her by the back of her head and pulled her deep into a kiss, his teeth slightly cutting her lips in the usual places. She kissed back, resisting the pain. She let her hands wander, simultaneously grateful for the intimacy and repulsed by his aggression. He had been a part of her destiny, her future; betrothed from the moment A'banna could speak to the animals.

And he was a murderer, a sadist who drank of the same sacrificed blood as his mother.

When they stopped, she let her hands brush him, saying in that touch what she would never speak: goodbye. Her hands only lacked a dagger.

Breathing heavily, A'banna wiped her chin clean of the small trickle of blood from where Quin's teeth had left their marks. She leaned against the rail, watching the city below and remaining silent. When she turned, he was licking her blood from his teeth, crimson against his pale skin.

He was a monster, but she still needed to pretend.

"What do you make of these new stars?" She gestured toward the blanket of sky.

"Ill news. This is not from the Guides," he said. By Guides, he meant The Taurs. The Taurs only chose to reveal themselves to the best of students. The greatest of The Taurs personally guided the Sorceress.

"I feared as much. Father and I were just about to seek their guidance."

He smiled, and she wanted to run and hide.

"You are ever faithful and persistent," he whispered. "A'banna, my mother says we should wed soon."

"Soon? She is ready for the priestly exchange?" Her heart rammed against her chest. She swallowed bile. If the Sorceress wanted this, she would be near. Waiting.

"The Taurs are," he said. Excitement entered his voice, glimmered from his eyes. "You should be pleased. I am glad they have chosen you. I have."

She touched her gloved hand to his cheek. "Oh, Quin, I am, too. I need some time to say farewell to my father."

He nodded, putting one hand over hers. "Of course. You shall bear us most excellent children, A'banna Beast-Speaker."

She smiled. "I shall go and prepare."

Quin nodded. "I will stay here and study these stars from the Oppressor."

Of course! That prophet Alain must have come from the Great Enemy of The Taurs, the Light Giver, also called the Oppressor. She'd been too foolish to see. Alain *worried* Quin. What if the Sorceress hadn't been the last of her kind? Alain had been pale, also. Did the Immortals her father spoke of still exist somewhere? Did they threaten the Sorceress's rule and thereby Quin's authority? He always walked her back to their chambers. Always. Perhaps she was right to follow the stars.

She kissed his cheek—as was expected—but his smile was preoccupied. He looked to the stars as she left.

A'banna entered the palace. She sighed once on the other side of the doors. *We should leave. Together. Her father would see reason. Tonight.*

"A'banna, my dearest."

A'banna froze. A door near the balcony was open that hadn't been before. It was a lounge often used by only the highest of Avoc nobility. Looking in, she could see the large lounge chair with its red cushioned back facing a blazing fire. This fire was coated in an oily black flame, casting shadows that moved independent of the flames, like men and animals and other creatures dancing upon the walls. Surely, they were only shadows. Seated in the chair, the Sorceress' pale white arm clutched a goblet, encrusted with black jewels.

The room was frigid and thick with tension. The Taurs were always around this woman. A'banna could feel them.

Her eyes flickered back to the shadows.

"Come sit with me, my dear," the Sorceress called. "Just for a few moments."

"Your Silver Majesty," A'banna said, bowing deeply at the door, heart pounding in her chest. She kept her thoughts and emotions guarded, wiping them clean as if once again on the hunt.

A'banna had been correct. Quin had known the Sorceress was waiting.

"Oh, A'banna darling, you flatter me. Quickly now, it is much too cold in this room."

Every few steps, A'banna bowed again, lower and lower, prostrating herself by the woman's feet. Sudden movement at the Sorceress's strapped sandals drew A'banna's gaze. Her eyes met the golden beads of a small writhing viper. The snake slithered up and down the woman's calf, waiting on its mistress' command.

"Rise, child," the Sorceress said.

A'banna pushed herself up, and the viper reared. She inhaled, watching its movements carefully.

"Isn't it adorable?" the Sorceress said, slowly leaning down to pet the snake with one pale finger. At the touch, the viper let out a sigh and leaned into her finger. "Only a few days old. This hatchling ate most of its brothers and sisters. I couldn't be more proud."

A'banna nodded, keeping her eyes lowered in respect. The silver-strapped sandals disappeared below the hem of a glittering silver dress.

The Sorceress sighed and rose, crossing the room gracefully, almost as if she floated. She appeared ageless and majestic and utterly powerful. Her silver hair draped well below the small of her back like a cloak. The viper tightened around her calf as she moved, but kept its golden stare on A'banna.

"I know this transfer of authority is not easy, my daughter," the Sorceress said as she neared a credenza, pouring a pitcher of wine. There were no servants here, only above in the Keeper's Tower. The rest were sent home or to their own quarters after a sacrifice. The wine's aroma was sweet, sourced from the southwestern fields of Avoc, where the grapes had conquered the ice and rock of the bottom of the world. A'banna had never traveled to those cities or villages, but she knew the span of the Sorceress's realm—from the great forest and the Dragon Wall in the north to the icy end of the world, from coast to coast. Even the southern seas were under her power.

Focus, A'banna thought. *Keep your colors clear.*

The Sorceress continued. "Nor is the first bloodletting easy, as Quin and I and your father well know. I know Quin has told you of the transfer, it is difficult. We will miss Huahanna's presence, certainly."

A'banna inhaled sharply.

With her back still turned, the Sorceress froze, hand raised with the newly refilled goblet. "There is something different about you tonight. It is the stars." She drank until the goblet was empty. "After today's sacrifice. I should have told you about them, and why it is imperative we stay our course and trust The Taurs." The Sorceress refilled her goblet slowly. "I've seen them before, long ago, a sign that the other gods, particularly the Oppressor, are setting a plan into motion to destroy us." As she lifted the goblet to her lips, her voice took on a ringing quality. "We simply cannot allow that. Which is why we strike first, like the smartest viper."

A'banna realized she'd been holding her breath. She released it slowly.

"But shrewd stable masters never kill their prize stallion unless necessary. A'banna, The Taurs and I are willing to let Huahanna live and sire more children, all like you when united with other strong bloodlines, if it will help facilitate your transition."

A'banna had seen the breeding pits and houses. It was the life of slavery and experimentation.

"It is a kind and gracious gesture by our gods, your Silver Majesty."

"Rare, A'banna." The Sorceress twirled, and A'banna barely had time to lower her gaze before seeing those pale lips curve into a terrible, toothy smile. "I would take such an opportunity while it exists, yes?"

"I will notify my father."

"Then you will wed Quin tomorrow night and ascend to high priestess."

"As you and The Taurs wish."

The Sorceress lifted a hand, and the goblet floated empty in front of her. A'banna knew the woman stared through her and saw everything. "I give you freedom child. The Oppressor is much more of a masterful strategist, using his servants as pawns. Easily discarded. I give my servants power, authority, choices, greatness beyond their genetic worth. Remember that. Then one day, A'banna, the Oppressor's most valued, will face me." She frowned, her voice took on one of faux sorrow. "They will face me in battle. To great loss."

The Sorceress swept from the room with the goblet gliding in front of her. The fire in the hearth snuffed out, the shadows and cold following her like the train of her dress.

Alone, A'banna shivered. She took one last look at the room that had been a private sanctuary and hurried back to Huahanna's quarters.

She didn't knock nor did she speak until safely inside, curtains pulled. "We both need to leave."

Huahanna smiled, gave her the key to the chest, and unlatched one of his spears from the wall. "Only one of us will get far."

"You don't know that, my father."

"Gather your things quickly. Pack food and drink. We have but minutes before they arrive. She knows."

A'banna didn't debate him. She quickly unlocked the chest, gathered the book and the imager and settled them inside her satchel. Flatbread and dried meats she wrapped in a towel, with some root vegetables and fruit. "This is not enough for two to make a journey through the forest to the north."

When she turned, Huahanna was already fully dressed in a leather breastplate and greaves, his traditional shield with raptor feathers in one arm, scimitar hanging from the leather strap belt around his waist. More feathers adorned his hair, while his face was striped with blue and green paint.

"No, my daughter, it is only enough for one. Quickly!"

She grabbed a scimitar from the wall, strapped it on, and dipped her hand in brown paint, marking her face. Tying her skirt, she slipped on boots, and double checked the knife at the small of her back. Her satchel hung off one side, to the other a quiver of darts and a blow stick. Beside them, she carefully tightened the vial of snake venom mixed with the decoction of toxic fish.

Father and daughter slipped out through the entryway, silently and swiftly slitting the throats of two guards who attempted to draw swords on sight of the high priest and priestess. Behind them, came the sounds of other guards already pounding on their front door.

It was a night for death, A'banna thought.

They dragged the guards' corpse into a small alcove. A'banna and Huahanna crept in the shadows of the ziggurat stairs, alert to the slightest thing that moved. Stealthily, they reached the bottom just as a loud cry rang out in the great heights above.

A deafening shriek shook the whole palace to its core.

"Run," Huahanna said.

Above, in the blue starlight, the circular movement of the thousands of snakes under the Sorceress's command all froze as one. They turned and slithered downward, serpentine rain cascading off the black stone. Their hisses and shrieks were loud and clear; a horrific music of death, a lament for her mistress, and a battle song to those who had betrayed her. The overwhelming sound and fury of the snakes pursued them, pressing in on A'banna's mind. Imaginary vipers rose up behind her so close they could strike. There was nothing left now, but to run.

CHAPTER 3

A THIN LAYER OF FOG SHROUDED THE ISLAND'S HARBOR AND clung to the cobblestone streets. Street lamps shone like hallowed yellow stars, too far apart to fully light the city that Raynt Lacrause knew covered those rolling hills, fighting for space against the island's tropical forest. In those spaces without light—not even illuminated by those startling blue stars above—there were dangers. Puerto de Granuille Nimer was larger than could be seen from the hill-encircled bay. The Cronop Isles were renowned for being a sanctuary for all people, no matter their race or background. That included the more colorful vagrants—pirates, slavers, thieves, prostitutes, and criminals looking for a new lease or a new mark. Nestled in the hills of the southern tip of the big island of Cronop, Puerto de Granuille had become a safe haven for every race that both saw the sky and those that dwelled away from it.

Just the sort of place that the captain who had transported Raynt's friends almost three weeks ago would have hidden, given the amount of gold the Magical Affairs Commission had provided for their discreet transport and escort of the Immortal. But that was four and a half weeks ago. The captain had been hired to stay anchored in the Great River to wait for Bedel and Shai's return. Instead, Raynt gazed across the bay at the very ship, anchored south of them, sails stowed and most of the crew apparently below deck or visiting some tavern or brothel in the city. An obvious breach of contract.

Despite the innumerable faint lights the ships or the beam of the one tall lighthouse that stood on the crest of one of the hills the locals called a 'mountain,' the fog had a bluish tint to it. Raynt looked away from the ship across the bay and studied the twenty-four bright new stars shining above the land, forming constellations that should never have existed. Most of the sailors on this ship, *The Red Hand*, had immediately headed indoors, wary of the sea's wrath or some other unspoken omen or curse these stars heralded.

Raynt knew better. It made everything they had learned at the clandestine meeting at the top of Well Mountain that much more frightening, more surreal. Bedel and Shai had expressed their fear to him, but he hadn't fully understood it. Now they were gone. Three weeks had passed since their last scheduled mission update across the magical communication network. Three weeks without a word of what had happened to the Immortal, or to them, which nagged at Raynt's concern. In all their years of service to the Magical Affairs Commission, they had never missed a deadline or disappeared without completing a mission—not without some sort of knowledge or warning ahead of time. They wouldn't have chosen this time to follow through on their plans to disappear to that safe haven they dreamed about. So, what had happened?

"What did you witness?" Raynt muttered to the strange new stars above. He felt foolish, but his worry ate at him. Bedel had almost been taken out by an essencer who controlled a mountain. Raynt had faced his own foes before, those who could match him blow for blow. There was nothing quite like the dreadful call of mortality to put everything into perspective.

Footsteps, steel-toed boots on wood, clacked across the deck as a figure approached. The pirate captain, Dans Forbens, came to stand beside him. Forbens gestured at the stars. "I don't have a single godsdamn map with those on it."

"No, I doubt you would have."

"What do you know?" Forbens said, leaning casually on the rail. There was nothing casual in the directness of his question. Years ago, Forbens had been an elite member of Franca's navy, but on one mission, he had been entrusted with ferrying the queen of Franca to Cardor and back. They were ambushed by Stonvar raiders, and Queen de Gerac had fallen in the battle. He was exiled from Franca but had become a very valuable associate of the Magical Affairs Commission. Still, Raynt didn't trust him. Raynt was a trained assassin. Both men were essencers, but *The Red Hand* was Forbens' ship, which put Raynt at the disadvantage. All that said, Forbens had kept his word so far. "My men are chattering on about omens and curses and the peoples of the sea rising up to kill us all. You and I know that's yeht shit. But you're Commission. Does the Old Man know what these constellations mean?"

"He does," Raynt confessed. "And it could be everything they said, or it could be the salvation of the world. Kerdum if I know."

"What you meant was, they are omens."

"I didn't say that," Raynt rushed to correct him. Perhaps too fast.

Forbens shrugged and shook his head, his beaded dreadlocks clattering softly. "I have a friend, a Goblin shaman, in a village up the river to the north. We could be there by daybreak. If anyone would have answers, I'd bet on him. They don't call him Speaker because he likes to keep his mouth shut."

Speaker? Speaker! The Speaker of Gaul—otherwise known as Goblins—was dead. The dominant clans in Luchik had made that known by hanging his distinctively tattooed head and those of his disciples—Goblins, Elves, and humans—outside their main gates.

"You're joking."

"About him never shutting up? No, afraid not."

"You know what I mean."

Forbens pulled a pipe from his belt and lit a match, covering the flame with his hand as he carefully puffed. "Kerdum take it all, yes, I do."

"When? When did it happen?"

"A couple months ago. You could ask him more if we sailed there."

That was a tantalizing option. If what Bedel, Shai, and Raynt knew about the stars and a "cycle" they were supposed to herald, one of the prophetic signs was the restoration of Speakers for Theantros to each of the races. Xathon had sent Bedel and Shai with Immortal Alain after the new human Speaker and his daughter, but they didn't know a new Goblin Speaker hid in the wilds of Cronop. It would be an incredible discovery, if true, one that could even threaten the balance of power the professed Speaker in Cardor's religion held over politics and the economy.

No, he thought. Focus on finding a lead on Bedel and Shai's situation.

Raynt used an eyeglass to peer across the bay. It was hard to see, but the *Batoidea* mercenary ship was anchored there, plain as day. Their large ray figurehead seemed to float above the fog, its long wings curled back, tail and barb wrapped around the bowsprit. If he had only known the *Batoidea* had been hired by the Slaver Coalition to participate in the Battle of Ntokup, which led to the genocide of the Wo'Huzziet weeks earlier, he'd never have allowed Bedel and Shai to board it. Only if they had known!

"Ah," Forbens said. "Those lively bastards." Raynt turned slightly, enough to see that Forbens had woven air and water essences together to form his own eyeglass. "Their captain is a greedy prick by the name of Braissen McCormack. He's an essencer, like us."

"You casually manipulate essences in front of your crew?" Raynt observed.

"Most of them can't see it, but they are glad the winds and sea favor us." Forbens grinned, showing off a few gold-capped teeth. "They think we're blessed."

Raynt continued studying *Batoidea*. Twelve ports per side for ballistae and a catapult on deck. At the moment, the few crew that were on deck were drinking and laughing. Why in Kerdum had Bedel and Shai chosen this ship and not one of Cardor's naval frigates?

"Could you take on that ship, if you had to?"

The pirate's grin faded. "I would need a trunkload of gold and a damn good reason."

"They killed my people, Captain," a man said behind them.

Raynt and Forbens turned as Nchoji, the ship's bosun, walked through the mist. His skin was dark, and the night hid him as well as the mist flowing around him. "The Last Battle of Ntokup. We Wo'Huzziet stood with our Lodornatha neighbors and fought to the last spear, but I was not among them."

"Crows know it, Nchoji," Forbens said. "I can't stand looking at the bastards, either."

Nchoji cocked his head and gestured at the ship. "But when you do so, you know that someday, if pardoned, you can go home. Your home, your city, still stands, yes? They razed mine to the ground. Fourteen thousand people defeated by a witch and her brothers, dead or enslaved. I was here, serving *The Red Hand*. My dead deserve justice. Together, we can give that to them."

"Avenging your people is good enough for me," Raynt said. "However, someone on that ship knows where some of my colleagues disappeared to. They were friends."

Nchoji scoffed. "Cardorian justice. You first. Us Wo'Huzziet later. We've waited decades, and finally, they destroyed us. When will your people finish waiting and strike?"

Raynt stepped into the light so they could see him clearly, just in case they had forgotten. He removed the hat with upturned brims he'd been wearing, feeling the texture across his nearly bald head and the burn scars. He blinked twice, two sets of eyelids—one horizontal, the other vertical—opening and closing simultaneously.

"I'm half-Glymph, Master Nchoji. I don't have a people. But you are right. I'm told Naminia used to say the same things."

Nchoji quieted and leaned against the rail. He stared hard ahead, through the fog, though Raynt wondered just how good the man's eyesight was.

Forbens sighed. "That ship hires out to slavers, Raynt. For you Commission types, that's not the company you care to keep. Why did they hire *Batoidea*?"

"I don't know. I'm surprised they did. Unless someone misled them, then I want to know who."

"Betrayed from within, eh? As much as that's the Old Man's style, I don't think he'd do that to his own."

"No, he wouldn't." Raynt raised the eyeglass. "Nchoji, what can you tell me about your chief's daughter, Naminia?"

Nchoji lowered his chin to his chest and breathed deep. "She was taken during the first raid on Ntokup, over ten years ago. Aboard a ship, but we were told the only survivor died from her wounds before she finished reporting. There isn't much of my people left, but every Wo'Huzziet would respect the rightful chieftess. She has the mark. Like stars."

An interesting comparison, Raynt thought.

"I have reason to believe she's alive," Raynt said, not willing to divulge much more about his primary mission. "Naminia tried to testify in Cardorian court against the Slaver Coalition five years ago. Before the trial could begin, assassins killed most of the witnesses and lawprotectors. Naminia was abducted again and sent back into slavery."

Nchoji hissed.

Raynt nodded his agreement, then continued. "We lost her trail for many years, but she may have been found last week. We complete this mission, and I return to help them break her free, to return to you the star of the Wo'Huzziet, your chief's daughter."

"Our chieftess," Nchoji said.

"Yes, your chieftess. During the course of my second mission, after my friends left, we obtained records showing who some of the hired thugs were from."

Forbens grimaced and stared ahead. "*Batoidea*."

"*Batoidea*," Raynt agreed.

"Ancients take them all!" Nchoji hissed.

Raynt nodded. "If we work together, that could still happen. This Captain McCormack has been dogging our peoples for too long, eating away."

"Captain?" Nchoji's dark pupils seemed to burn the unspoken request. "We can settle the score with *Batoidea*."

"I agree, Master Nchoji," Forbens said. "Agent Raynt?"

"I need McCormack, then I'll go with you."

"You lose him, and he'll get on board, take her, and run," Forbens warned.

"And if we sink her first, I may get nothing about what happened to my friends. So where would they possibly go to hide, if I manage to get McCormack to talk."

"I have an idea." Forbens pulled out a small map of the island. He snapped his fingers, and a small flame ignited in the air. Ice formed around it, like glass. The effect was beautiful, a multicolored shimmering, more illuminating than any normal lamp hanging above them. Forbens pointed at the map. "Here's where we are, Puerto de Granuille Nimer. This is Inimorin-Droth-Zaet, where my friend the Goblin shaman and some possible reinforcements are." He pointed to a small bay in between each. "This is Muerta de Nimer. If a pirate vessel that's part of a certain accord, the likes we don't partake in, needs safe harbor, they go here. Any ship of that accord that opens fire in the bay risks every ship's wrath that's anchored there. You want to start a blood feud between my ship and a whole fleet of ships and captains just as cruel as them there, this is where it'll go down."

"And if we leave, *Batoidea* may sail away."

"Seems like you have yourself a little dilemma, agent. What are you willing to risk for your friends' welfare?"

Raynt stared ahead at the *Batoidea*, bobbing gently in the water, men drinking on deck, celebrating. It was sickening. Forbens was right, though. They'd need help to take the ship and the captain.

Except Raynt was drawn to the burning passion of revenge he could feel from Nchoji. Not just feel, though. Raynt watched the man's aura. Essences the color of red, yellow, and green swirled around him. Those flashes of emotion spoke to the depth of his need. Nchoji needed justice for the Wo'Huzziet.

Back on mainland Cardor, Raynt's partners, the King's Men knights, were busy infiltrating Slaver Coalition strongholds in the city of Havenport, setting up Raynt's mission. If they were correct, the chieftess was somewhere in that city. Restoring her to the remnants of her people would be a powerful statement for the kingdom to make. Besides, Raynt's involvement in Naminia's absence was personal. He had chosen to rescue lawprotector Yeltson Greggor, now a King's Men captain coordinating the mission preparations, rather than stop the slavers who took Naminia.

What did that mean for Nchoji and every Wo'Huzziet in freedom or suffering in slavery?

Raynt's decided. "I have an alternative plan. Lend me Nchoji. He can act as my guide and backup, while *The Red Hand* sails to

Inimorin. Bring reinforcements back by evening tomorrow, and we make these bastards pay."

"A fine plan if ever I heard one," Nchoji said.

"Don't risk this man's life, agent, understand me?"

"And how exactly will I manage that?" Raynt murmured.

"Tomorrow evening, then. Stay alive."

Forbens offered his hand, and Raynt shook it.

"Let's get ashore," Nchoji said. Raynt turned to find two bags, packed and resting on a crate on deck.

"You knew," Raynt said.

"Aye, sir. It was obvious."

"How?"

Nchoji double-checked his own bag, which had a green hood in it.

"You were a ranger from Lodornatha," Raynt whispered. "I wasn't aware they took non-Lodoronathans into their ranks."

Nchoji hesitated, his hand gripping the hood as if it were a lifeline. "It is not mine."

Raynt was speechless as the muscular man put their bags into the dingy. Once aboard, sailors lowered the boat into the gentle waves. He was surprised that it was just the two of them. Nchoji rowed, occasionally glancing at the stars, then across the water, then back at the ship they moved away from. Closer to the harbor, Raynt heard the chimes of bells of ships, mostly fishing vessels. Larger ships, frigates, galleons, and others, had to anchor inside the bay. For a brief moment, they were far enough away from any ship that the enveloping fog concealed them almost completely. Only a small lantern hung at the bow of the ship signaled to others they were on the water.

In that moment of silence, Nchoji said: "It belonged to my Warrior-Bound."

Warrior-bound. Raynt had heard the term before. Marriage among the Wo'Huzziet differed from the northerners. It was more fluid, easily annulled, or could even happen between more than one individual, no matter the gender.

"I'm sorry. What happened?"

"She was taken in the final battle. She led the Lodornathan forces. I wasn't aware of her intent to fight. I was on *The Red Hand*."

"Crows, Nchoji, I'm so sorry."

"I will always remember her smile," he said. "The way her hair tucked behind her ears. I had agreed to marry her, but as one of the Rda, the elite guard, I was ordered to guard the last shipment of jewels *The Red Hand* carried. Captain Forbens took me on."

"Where did the funds go?"

"To one of the last strongholds of the Wo'Huzziet and our allies."

"And your Warrior-Bound?"

Nchoji shook his head. "Do you know where Edelissi Onoarel disappeared to?"

"Onoarel?" Raynt was stunned. Lodoronatha so seldom reached out to those in the northeast because of the distrust between Elves but if an Onoarel had also been abducted. "One of the great houses of Lodornatha?"

Nchoji held his silence. The only sound was the gentle slap of the oars on the water.

"I'm sorry. I don't."

He cleared his throat. "Then there are two women held by the slavers we must find."

"We'll do our best, Nchoji, but I can't raise your hopes. It's taken us five years to even get a hint of where Naminia might be. We're still not completely convinced she's there, but I have people working on confirmation. I've just never heard of slavers abducting Elves."

"And Dwarves. The industry expands even as you close around it. So I have come with you, to end them."

"We'll do our best," Raynt said, afraid to offer the man any more. At least the man was from Rda, meaning he was an elite fighter. That would prove to be an asset.

"Aye, we will."

The boat slid quietly through the harbor. It bumped quietly against the wood dock. Wordlessly, Nchoji tossed Raynt the rope to secure to the dock cleat. Nchoji gestured quickly to get Raynt's attention. The harbormaster marched toward them, round stomach and bare chest puffed out with a bamboo-covered ledger with a quill and ink jar attached at the top.

Raynt tipped his hat forward a little, providing a bit of shadow over his face and concealing his features better. Even in the fog and with the tricorn hat, there was no telling if the harbormaster could identify Raynt very well. There wasn't a known place in the world where halflings of any race were accepted, especially Glymphs.

"What you here for?" he muttered, long pipe bobbing up and down as he peered at the boat.

Nchoji smiled. "I'm acting as a guide and escort for our friend here."

"Heh, heh. That's you, huh, Nchoji?" Belamy said. "Captain Forbens has you running around for 'em again? Babysitting the upper crust, eh?"

"No more than usual, or I'd buy you a drink at Under the Goblin," Nchoji said back, taking a jar of chew out of his pouch. He popped some weed into his mouth then offered the harbormaster some. "Old times' sake?"

"Old times' sake," the man said, nodding. He turned to Raynt. "Here for pleasure or business?"

"Does it matter what I say?"

"Godsdammit, no, it doesn't." Master Belamy stood to the side as he scribbled onto the ledger. "Name?"

"Shaun Tennant," Raynt answered, careful to not smile too wide so to hide those long canines or to blink and expose his two pairs of eyelids, one vertical and one horizontal.

"That your real name, Master Tennant?"

"Is your name really Master Belamy?" Raynt said, playing into the role, adding a south-central Cardorian accent to his voice. South-central cities of Cardor bordered the capital and were wealthy. He moved his duster coat aside, so the man could see one of two curved daggers on his belt. "Here I thought Puerto de Granuille Nimer was a place of privacy!"

The large harbormaster let out a huff, then stood aside. "So it is. So it is. Just doing my duty, Master Tennant."

Raynt paid Nchoji, giving him a grateful nod. Nchoji nodded back. "Think of us again, Master Tennant."

Nchoji joined Raynt on the dock with their bags, acting the part of a porter. Raynt held out a few gold Kings, which Master Belamy immediately grabbed.

"For your discretion, good sir, you have my thanks."

"Indeed, Master Tennant," Belamy said, studying the coins. "Think nothing of it."

Raynt offered another coin. "Which way to Under the Goblin?"

The harbormaster bowed as he snatched the coin out of the air. "Take Balkins Street, over there."

"My thanks." Raynt turned on his heels, cloak and mist rolling around him like wisps of snow in a flurry. Their footfalls were quiet as they disappeared into the mist. Neither spoke. Raynt kept his head on a moderate swivel, taking in the scenes, studying every doorway, every dock, every boat with a cover, the shadows behind a crate. He listened to the rhythm of the water.

They fell into lockstep, with Nchoji a pace behind, as they

traversed the cobblestone streets, maintaining the ruse of master and servant. A ship's bell chimed somewhere off to the northeast, while a few night birds and bats swirled above or dove to catch fish drawn in by whatever weary dockworkers tossed into the water. Bats swarmed around lampposts. Yellow light flickered and danced inside tavern windows, as raucous sounds mixed with the eclectic music common in the isles. The night would otherwise have veiled the cove outside the city, but tonight that wasn't quite the case. No, the stars prophesied by Alain the Immortal now outshone even the half-moon.

"Balkins Street, sir," Nchoji said.

They turned down it, away from the harbor. The street was on a slight incline. Raynt halted briefly, taking in the architecture. At best, it was haphazard, representative of a half-dozen different cultures. He could spot the wood and plaster paneling resembling homes of the Southern Province of Cardor. Some buildings had roofs which curved to a point, stone gardens, and cherry trees planted outside, which made Raynt think of Istantese homes. Partial stone buildings reflected Francan and western Cardor's Stonvar roots. Flat-roofed adobe homes resembled those from Zeller and Greneld; some even had walled courtyards with fountains. Raynt had never seen before the assortment of styles. It made him pause, wishing he could have lingered in the city for a holiday, a short leave even,-rather than just be here for a mission. He hesitated again outside an adobe house. Windows were open, and he could hear a family inside, laughing. The aroma of meat roasting, the scent of spices, and bread baking wafted out. Raynt had a passing thought of home, of his mother's fine cooking on the barony homestead. Like many of the buildings, this one had a small lawn or garden with a palm tree at the edge of the street. He was so rarely around a palm tree, Raynt pulled off his glove and touched the trunk, tracing the rough contours of the bark. He smiled and pulled on the glove again.

Raynt was pleased the world was kind to some individuals. He only wished them peace and happiness in the future, knowing that no matter the nation he was in, his service ensured their tranquility, even in a dangerous city like this Puerto de Granuille Nimer. Maybe that's what partially had gotten under Bedel and Shai's usual demeanor. They had served for decades, even if they looked no older than him. Desire for a family and time away from espionage could be a terrible burden that often competed with the need to be in the heart of the action.

Both Nchoji and he exchanged a knowing glance, nodded, and moved forward.

Their route went further up the inclined street. It was surprisingly quiet the farther away from the dock they walked. Lights streamed from street lamps, but the fog made their benefit minimal. Its antithesis was the stars shining above, creating an unusual azure haze clinging to the city. On the side of the street were iron crates, emanating the odor of sewage. They had seen people near the taverns and inns or even some of the warehouses, but few seemed to be abroad in the streets. Raynt wondered if nightfall meant crime. That would be enough to drive any sensible person indoors.

He felt watched. Just a sense. Not even magical. They were being watched. Raynt continued walking but never ceased being aware of what could hide in the darkness or the fog, even as it gradually cleared the farther they moved from the docks.

In an alleyway between buildings, a face peered out of the shadows. Across the intersection, there were others. Now that intuition made sense. Whatever force drove most of the people indoors wasn't in the consideration of street urchins and other homeless. The most desperate thieves, no doubt, weighed their chances of assaulting the two men. Raynt discounted any innate desire to give a few coins out to them. That cold scrutiny and the glint of light on a dagger blade made clear that doing so would only escalate danger. As it was, Raynt noticed both he and Nchoji walked with shoulders and back straight, heads alert, weapons hanging from belts, and with the calm stature of men familiar with fighting. Neither swaggered. Soldiers had an air about them that made others consider the risk of tussle.

Raynt and Nchoji slowed when they heard voices ahead. A hulking figure lumbered out of a rowdy tavern across the road. The large, four-armed man slapped the sign with one hand as he held a laughing woman close with another two. A Glymph and a human! They disappeared inside an adobe home down the road. Raynt grinned. If he ever found Bedel and Shai, he might add this to their list of possible retirement options. A place where everyone could live together even if there were pirates and slavers anchored in the bay, thieves in the shadows, homeless lurking in the alleyways, and no sensible form of government!

Raynt studied the swinging sign: Under the Goblin Tavern.

Nchoji shook his head. "Dockworkers and average sailors go there. You won't find someone like a pirate captain there. Not one as prestigious as him."

They kept going.

A two-story inn hugged the side of the road, built with wood plank and plaster, as well as a stone foundation. Light streamed out of the large windows. Music and the clamor of voices drifted out of the open front doors. The sign boasted, The Bronze Pug, with a drooling dog in the center. Nchoji only nodded, so they entered.

The grand room was surrounded by arches, which housed individual booths for those wishing for a bit of privacy. At one end of the room was a stage, where a trio of musicians played drums, bamboo flute, and a long-stemmed, thin lute. They played a lively tune that combined Branaird beat with Zelvatore harmony. In front of the musicians, a group of men danced in a circle, arms around each other, while a smaller group of women danced in the center, each person in step with the others. Black boots and shoes kicked in and out, tossing skirts or billowy trousers. Women, with arms raised, tapped small hand cymbals as they moved lively as one. The men, however, had arms draped around each other and only used their feet and waists to dance, twisting and kicking with the music. At a certain point in the song, every dancer ululated at once, then broke into laughter as they continued. The dancers were of varied ages, but none younger than adolescents, and all shared varied shades of olive-brown skin tones and dark brown, black, or graying hair. At first, Raynt felt a twinge of shame at thinking how dangerous the Zelvatore group was. Surely even Zelvatore people could settle here? It was his own prejudice, his own fear, his own shock. One dancer twisted with the rest, facing the door, even as the two circles moved counter to one another.

Raynt stared at one of the King's Men's most decorated spies from their Intelligence Order, and a man Raynt had been serving with for years.

Sir Rurik's eyes widened when he saw Raynt on the second twist. Raynt averted his gaze, careful not to give Sir Rurik away. A glance back showed Rurik had stayed composed, was even laughing quite naturally, dancing with his own people; the people he had run from years ago.

The tavern was full of off-duty, casual Swords of Baktur—religious zealots who believed that the only way to balance the world fabric was to assassinate essencers. Wispy shadows swirled with them, though none of the Baktur wore the traditional wraps that signified they were on the hunt. A gathering of Baktur this size would keep a knowledgeable citizen indoors—and wisely so. They were celebrating and laughing now, which was an odd sight. Every essencer avoided Baktur if they knew how to value their life. Baktur may not have been able to manipulate the essences—except for the ability to blend into or wrap shadows around themselves to the point of invisibility—but they could sense when someone used aether or manipulated the world fabric. Their very goal was to bring balance to the world, allowing nature to take its course without the influence of essencers like Raynt. They were, quite simply, lethally proficient in their work.

Raynt gestured to Nchoji and put up a false front as they moved between tables next to a potted fern. Nchoji watched the group curiously.

"Never seen a proper Zelvatore dance before," Nchoji said. "It looks fun."

"You dance?" Raynt said, amused that this warrior-turned-pirate would enjoy simple pleasures.

"Don't be an ass," Nchoji chuckled, shaking his head. "Of course, I dance! How do you think we learned the spear? By drills alone?"

Amused, Raynt leaned back against the wall, trying to act casual, all the while surveying the room. There was an exit by the bar. Not far away, a woman in a green gown and apron glared at them as she pointed to the shelves behind her, bearing numerous weapons. Raynt pretended not to notice.

Crow shit, Raynt thought. I can't fight two dozen Baktur. And what the Kerdum was Sir Rurik doing here? He'd trained Raynt and his fellow King's Men to fight Baktur, but Rurik had warned them not to be fooled. When they hunted, little stood between them and their quarry. That said, Rurik was no longer a Baktur, even if one never lost the innate ability gained through the meditation of nature and ancestors. If the King's Men spy was here, blending in, there was a damn good reason, and Raynt needed not to blow Rurik's cover.

"I can't stay here," Raynt whispered to Nchoji.

"Afraid of dancing, are you?" Nchoji's brow furrowed. "He'll be here."

Raynt fought a grin. Damn, he liked banter. "You afraid I

might show you some of my moves? Or are spears the only weapon dances can be attuned for?"

Nchoji let out a deep, single laugh. But he locked gaze with Raynt for a moment, enough to question the motivation to leave. "This is the inn he'll be at."

Raynt choked down an exasperated sigh. He couldn't just discuss this here! Renowned pirate captains, like Forbens, tended to have some essencer abilities, whether confined strictly to elemental or trickier disciplines. Captain McCormack of the *Batoidea* would never let himself be in such a compromising position, with a threat of an en masse Baktur assault.

"He's probably—" Raynt started, then stopped.

Past the bar and the exit were private meeting rooms. Light filtered through the bottom of a door. A servant woman with a full tray of goblets of wine and a platter of meat, cheese, and exotic fruits opened that door, wide enough for Raynt to see inside.

On one side of a wooden table sat a Baktur, wearing a traditional elder's black robe, beside his wife. She wore a traditional gold wrap dress embroidered with horses. When she lifted a wine glass, a blue silk shawl slid down her arm to the crook of her elbow. Her black hair was done up in a tasteful braided bun, while her husband wore his hair pulled back into a triple warrior-bun, a style further-advertising his status.

They were the lord and lady of House Talacciaro, who controlled a third of Zeller's fleet, contributed thousands to the Baktur army, and even raised Zelvatora horses, rumored to be the fastest breed. They were also Rurik's parents, whom he had run from years ago.

Across the table from them sat a man with a white-peppered beard and braided hair. Several scars traced his cheek. He wore a dark leather coat and jewelry. A finely embroidered tricorn hat hung on a hook next to the window.

"Bloody fields, Nchoji," Raynt whispered. "You're right."

"Who is he with?"

"Best for you not to know."

"That bad?"

"Worse…" Raynt's voice trailed off.

Behind Captain McCormack, a heavily scarred man lounged casually in a chaise. His cloak was tossed neatly over the chaise back. Raynt could see his aura, its nimbus thick and billowy, pressed tightly against McCormack's. This second man was Raynt's age and smartly wore a vest over a white, loose-fitting pleated shirt. Pouches and a long knife hung from his belt.

This man and Raynt had history. Five years ago, the Slaver Coalition's main fixer had led the *Batoidea* force in slaughtering witnesses and a lawprotector. They nearly killed Raynt's friend and colleague—and Rurik's commanding officer—Yeltson. That intervention had cost them the Wo'Huzziet heiress. Few things troubled Raynt, but this man, known only as Contact, was the stuff of his nightmares. Besides Bedel, he was the only essencer Raynt knew of that could match him in both magic and melee combat. Contact might just be unbeatable and now sat in a meeting with the infamous pirate captain and one of the leading houses of Zeller and the Swords of Baktur.

Raynt's stare hardened on Contact, who furrowed his brow and glanced up. Raynt turned away, just in time. The serving woman came and went, the door closed behind her.

"Crows! Did he see me?" Raynt asked, looking out the window.

"Who? The other man?"

"Yes," Raynt breathed on an exhale.

"I don't know," Nchoji said as dancers circled, ululating along with the music, laughing, and only moving faster as the music reached a crescendo.

"We need to leave," Raynt said again. He didn't wait for

Nchoji to agree. Raynt headed to the back door, hailing the bartender. "Are the stables through that door?"

"Why?" the woman said. "You paying for a horse or did you bring your own?"

Raynt reached into his money pouch and pulled out five gold-silver Kings. The coin was gold, with a silver imprint of one of Cardor's former queens beside the King's image. These were worth four times as much as a single gold King. She knew it, too. "My lords, I got two fine steeds, bought them this morning off a high lord and lady from Zeller. Tell Alonko you bought them from me."

"Thank you kindly," Raynt said.

They quickly entered a short stone hallway as the music ended and the crowd cheered. Raynt shut the door behind them. Light poured out of an archway to their left, along with the sounds of a kitchen. There was another door beyond that, which appeared to be a storeroom. Raynt and Nchoji pressed themselves against the wall, looking inside the room. A single cook moved back and forth, checking between a boiling pot and bread in the oven. Cheeses and salted meat sat on a carving table. The large man kept his back to them, humming a Zelvatore tune to himself. A soft crash sounded, and the cook glanced inside an additional door to the storeroom, cursing and uttering the name, "Alonko!" An apologetic voice came from within as the cook hurried to help the stablehand, who was apparently doubling as the sous chef.

It was the best opening they were likely to get. "Door," Raynt whispered as the two men argued inside the storeroom. Nchoji reached for the lock, but the door opened. Raynt instinctively reached for his daggers.

Rurik locked eyes with Raynt, said nothing and shut the door.

Nchoji's brow raised with understanding. Each man quickly passed the kitchen and went through the stable door. Raynt's senses were hit by the smells of animals, hay, manure, and the surprisingly dim light. The stables were inside a cave carved into the hill, with a gated entrance at its opening. Two dozen horses grazed in a pen freely, while several others had their own stalls. A few chickens clucked at them from inside a pen, and a dog sat up, watching them carefully.

"Crows, Raynt, what are you doing here?" Rurik adjusted his tunic, showing off a belt of small throwing knives. He hadn't sweated from the dance, and the cave was cool enough to chill Raynt from the sweat gained by the humidity outside.

"I could ask you the same, Rurik," Raynt said, still scanning the surrounds. He didn't see anyone, not even in the shadows. "Do you know who is in that meeting room?"

"He knows," a female voice said from the doorway. They all spun around. Lady Eleyana Talacciaro stood there, one jeweled hand on the door. Her eyes darted between the three men, then the shadows, then back into the hallway, as if she was considering going back.

"Mother," Rurik whispered.

Raynt glanced at Nchoji, who didn't speak.

"Eight years, Rurik," she whispered, then nodded at the men. "Who are they?"

"Friends," Rurik said, hands out in front of him.

Lady Talacciaro pursed her lips, then closed the door behind her. Revealed by lantern light as she gracefully moved, the hilt of her traditional dagger glittered from its hiding places in the folds of her sleeve. Every Zelvatore woman carried one, he'd heard. There was some religious belief behind it, as well as making them secretly deadly.

Rurik, you better know what you're doing, Raynt thought.

"I have only a minute," Lady Talacciaro said.

"Take a walk," Rurik said. "Please."

Raynt and Nchoji nodded. Raynt bowed at his waist. "Your ladyship."

Talacciaro raised her other hand, bracelets and rings jingling. "Wait. If you are my son's friend, and if you are what I think you are. I think you should run from here."

"Respectfully, your ladyship, you've seen us. I need to know you'll let us leave peacefully. Your son, too."

She threw her hands up in the air. Her accent was thick as she spoke in the common tongue. Raynt actually enjoyed listening to the Zelvatorian roll of her r's, all the while dreading what she might say. "I can't work with people like him, Rurik."

"Mother, please."

"Eight years."

"Father killed Rhonna Tessoni before I could marry her, and he was going to kill me, all because we opposed the Veccil'ni, who is still in power. What did you expect me to do?"

Raynt gave her a hard stare over Rurik's shoulder before he and Nchoji crossed to the cave entrance. The street outside was quiet, though they could still hear laughter from the tavern great room. They weren't far enough away from Rurik and his mother to avoid the uncomfortable discussion.

Talacciaro's expression had softened. She shrugged, then pulled her blue shawl across her shoulders. "Write home every other year, perhaps!" She shook her head, then reached out for him. He came close and embraced her. She kissed his cheeks. "Ancestors damn it, my beautiful son, what have we done to you?"

"There is no way I can share years in a few minutes."

She smiled, then stroked his shortly cropped hair as if it was a mystery. "No, no. I don't think we could. I do not know if you believe it, but I love you. Your father still does, even if he and your brothers are bound by their oaths to kill you on sight."

"Which is why I'm leaving, and why I never allowed him to see me."

"Though he does not comprehend it, you are our son, indeed." She closed her eyes. "Oh ancients, what do you need?"

"Your help. If a war is coming, I have friends attempting to prevent a war, but something has happened, and they're running behind. They need details to confirm."

"Rurik! I can't defy your father or the Veccil'ni like that! I am proud of what our house has accomplished! Do you want us watched like the Tressoni family? Day and night dogged by the Veccil'ni's spies? Or the Dark Judicator? Do you know what you're asking of me?"

"I'm sorry. Yes, I do know. So, war is coming?"

"Make amends," she pleaded. "Pledge allegiance to the Red Dragon. Let us spare you."

"He is not what our ancestors believed."

She broke into a sad smile. "Oh, my son! No, he is not. I have always cherished your bravery, no matter what I have had to say or do to stay alive." She put her palm on his chest. "You have held to the old ways and made the old code of Baktur proud. I am proud of you. Tell me exactly what you need."

Rurik bit his lower lip. "Troop numbers and movements. What is the reasoning behind the war? How can we change it? We need to prevent this conflict."

She shook her head sadly. "You have one chance, only one chance. The King of Cardor must officially end the slave trade and provide Zeller and Greneld food and water. The drought has lasted long, and though we survive in the north with plenty, I fear for the rest of our people. Convince your leaders to commit to a treaty, and then you might undermine the gods that plunge us into more horrors. You are young, you don't remember the Trader Wars." Talacciaro held each of the three men's gaze. "You are all too young, but I survived it. Your father survived it. The Baktur tried to remain neutral, but we had no Veccil'ni then. No god of war dictating to us, but we should have defended our people! When Cardor took Castle Winnago from us for a few days, when our people fought back, the death toll and fighting was horrific. Your father led the charge that took the wall, side by side with Goblin mercenaries! When soldiers invaded our home, I cut them back."

Raynt's eyes widened as he listened to Talacciaro. He'd never actually listened to the enemy after the war. How they saw his people.

"I cut them back," she repeated. "With nothing but my dagger, I defended you and your brothers as you slept in your beds."

"I remember," Rurik whispered.

"You remember?"

"I woke up. You told me to go back into the bedroom, but I saw the soldiers' bodies, the blood, I saw our servants who had fought with you."

Lady Talacciaro closed her eyes and bowed her head. "Ah, so that had been you. I should have asked you children if you knew what we fought for, what we lost, what we'll fight for again. Harder now than before. I remember feeding you olives, because the fig trees stopped producing when the northern essencers whisked our water away."

"I hate olives, now," Rurik whispered, smiling.

She chuckled, but her gaze slid to Raynt, almost threateningly so.

"Your ladyship, on what our people did before us, I wish I could make it right. I'm sorry for the essencer's involvement."

"But you don't starve in the north, do you?" She pressed, turning from Rurik. "No, Raynt Lacrause, hand of the Grand Essencer. Yes, I know you. Your people do not starve like ours do. Who needs irrigation when you have essencers to make it rain, eh? Who cares where the water comes from to make your crops grow when your people drained our lakes and left our riverbeds dry. You are on the wrong side of this, Lord Raynt."

Rurik's jaw had dropped slightly. "Help us get all of us on the right side, Mother. If we do as you say, appeal to the rulers rather than the gods, we have a chance, don't we?"

"And essencers?"

"What if you ask for some of ours who specialize in agriculture? Let me get home, and I'll put in a word with Xathon. We help correct the wrongs of the past."

She bristled, straightened her back. "And we allow essencers to work our lands, help us, against everything we've believed since the world revived from the long winter? Since Baktur laid down our code!" her hand cut through the air in a sharp slash. "You'd have us abandon our beliefs?"

"For the sake of peace and the survival of your people," Raynt said, opening his arms. "Anything is possible."

Talacciaro turned back to Rurik. "Your friend speaks truth, my son. He is a rare breed. You have my word I'll do just as you ask, but if your father finds out."

"We can't let him then," Rurik said. "Your contact will meet you in Wonbai in exactly a week's time at a party. You'll know her. She's one of a kind. In the meantime, you have to be."

"Baktur," Talacciaro said, pride filling her. The shadows suddenly came to her, curling around her blue shawl first, then blossoming from the horses like twisted flowers. "That means you must run, my son."

She leaned forward, kissed him on both cheeks.

Raynt barely had time to shout a warning.

Talacciaro unsheathed her jeweled dagger and plunged it into Rurik's abdomen. Rurik gasped and doubled over, his gaze pleading with his mother.

"I love you, and I am so sorry," she said. "But this is how I get your people what you asked for."

"Damn you!" Raynt said, running to him.

Talacciaro was more agile on her feet than she first appeared.

She shed the shawl like a net, thrusting it over Nchoji's head and pulling him off his feet. He rolled, knives slicing through it. In the same movement, Talacciaro ripped the knife out of her son, blood flicking from the blade, and slashed at Raynt, but Raynt had already pulled out his own dagger. The blades clanged, and with his palm, he slapped Talacciaro's hand. She cried out as her dagger flew. Straw puffed up into the air as she adjusted her feet, driving her extended hand into Raynt's throat. He gasped, doubled back.

She pressed in, hit after hit to his chest. He felt a rib pop.

"Hit me!" she hissed. "If you want to live, hit me!"

"Damn it!" Raynt grunted, and he punched her in the jaw.

Talacciaro doubled back, gasping, blood trickling from her nose. Nchoji tried to attack from behind, but the sheepdog leapt up. He dodged its snapping jaws and wrapped his arm around its throat, falling to the ground with his legs wrapped around its torso. "Sleep, valiant dog. Sleep."

The dog snapped and kicked furiously.

"I wish it had been another way," Raynt told Talacciaro as she steadied herself on her feet.

Spitting, she scooped up her dagger, straw sticking out of her fingers. "Oh, essencer, are you so blind you can't see what I'm doing?"

She slashed at him, but Raynt stepped back, hitting the stone wall. He considered her attacks, then realized that she hadn't thrust at all. Raynt raised his knife, the blade cutting across her arm and slicing through her dress. She gasped. "Kick me."

Raynt howled as he did what she asked. She fell back into the hay, near Rurik.

"Help him," she said in a raspy, pained tone. "Run so I can scream."

The dog had succumbed to Nchoji's choke, and he slid out from underneath it's now sleeping form, placing it gently on the hay. Together, he and Raynt lifted Rurik, whose head dangled limply from his shoulders. He was breathing, though. Raynt tore off a sleeve and pressed it into his side. He knew that area there were no organs. It wasn't lethal. Talacciaro had struck with surgical proficiency.

"By the ancients, run!" she hissed, hair unkempt. She spat blood and screamed in Zelvatore. "Essencers! Help me!"

"Crows!"

Nchoji kicked open the stable doorway, and they dragged Rurik into the street, just as the door inside the cave opened. Angry and shocked voices exchanged something with Lady Talacciaro. Then came a frightening ululating war cry.

She had just told the entire assembly of Baktur they had assaulted her. Good for her task of espionage; crow-shit odds for their lives.

"Come on, brother, wake the yeht up!" Raynt growled into Rurik's ear, even as his blood soaked the cloth in Raynt's hand.

"Raynt, we gotta hide!" Nchoji said, pulling out a long knife from its leg sheathe. "Where we going?"

All around them, lights flickered on in house windows—or were instantly extinguished.

"Raynt?" Nchoji cursed.

Rurik may keep his organs, but this was too much blood.

And then the essences trembled. Strings of wind plucked, then continued to wobble as someone manipulated them into a *Windstream*. *Windstreams* were used by those who could fly or even add strength to a ship's sails and were frustratingly hard to command without training, which meant only the best could use them. Raynt could fly, but he couldn't carry two others with him.

One of the essencers was coming for them.

Raynt heard a clatter on a rooftop. Shadows circled a plain-clothed Baktur, jumping from house to house, following them.

Behind them, a strange blob of darkness seemed to slink along the street.

Nchoji cursed. "Raynt! We need a plan!"

Raynt tossed aside the soaked cloth and slowed to rip his other sleeve off. Rurik gasped when he pressed it to the wound. His eyes opened wide as pain flooded his body.

Raynt slapped his cheek. "Hey, hey! I need a plan!"

Rurik blinked. "That alley," he muttered. "Take it."

Raynt saw the faces of urchins and possible thieves dart back into the darkness. "Well, crow shit."

They fled into the alley, consumed by darkness.

CHAPTER 4

A'BANNA SPRINTED AND TURNED DOWN AN ALLEY, BETWEEN TWO pyramidal homes. She could hear children calling for parents inside, their voices shrill with terror. A wooden window slammed shut above her. A'banna jumped at the sound.

Again, she was being hunted, but had she brought terror upon the people of the city too?

A'banna searched the darkness for her father, but Huahanna had vanished.

"My father!" she whispered, trailing back to the main city thoroughfare.

A sudden wave of emotion washed over her. Pain, anger, fear, jealousy, betrayal all erupted within her. She wanted to fight, to hurt, to defend those she loved—against the Sorceress and those who bore her silver mark. A'banna steadied herself, stunned by the visceral reactions.

This was magic.

This is Leading.

Person Leading. But it was more. Pride in the herd, danger to the nest, the stalking of predators.

Someone wove *Person Leading* and *Beast Speech* simultaneously. Unlike anything she'd ever experienced. The wave continued, passing through her and every living thing, through wood and stone and cloth. It was wide. She could see, within it, wispy silver ethereal strings—like a worm in water—each surging for a host. Each string bearing individual packages of emotions in smaller strings, color-coded and organized, so that whether they struck beast or person, the result would be the same.

Knowing what was happening, A'banna stilled herself, calming the violent agitations. In that moment, she caught a breath and exhaled, "My father."

What had he done? For her? For a prophetic dream? Fighting to save the world felt instantly foolish. Would she even survive the Sorceress's hunters? Was any of this worth what was about to happen to her people?

Visceral howls and bellows sounded throughout the city. Growls and screeches. All at once, every beast in the city had been affected. She heard shouting and confusion. Men and women in their homes, calling for their neighbors. *Rebellion,* was the word. *Overthrow the Sorceress before she kills us!* A'banna risked glancing back into the main street. Exposed by the starlight and the many large braziers along the street, she witnessed something she could scarcely imagine.

A great long-necked behemoth tore away from its keepers by the forge, stomped one of them, and then charged the palace as a legion of guards emerged. It spun, massive tail flicking outward, colliding with the guards on the lower stairs, sending them flying into the night sky like dolls tossed by an angry child. Yehts' joined in; a thudding charge, horns tearing and ripping into the Sorceress's guards, decimating the ranks.

A new roar joined the cacophony. Hundreds of voices. The marchers had come; men mutated and morphed into boar-like half-men, with tusks and fur and beady eyes, giant clawed hands and cloven feet. The Sorceress called them her minotaurs, as if they were blessed for being in the image of the Guides. The boar-men charged, war axes and scimitars hacking at the attacking animals and guards alike. Blood, darkened in the night, splattered and sprayed as the marchers brayed their great joy.

The behemoth struck again with its tail, a great trumpeting bellow emitting from its chest. The tail whipped into the minotaurs, breaking their charge. Yehts turned upon them, horns glistening. Bodies flew. Then came cats, monkeys, and jaguars, still trailing the rattling chains of their masters behind them. They leapt into the fray. Claws, teeth, and hands cast shadows as the pets of the wealthy, or the honored teemed as one, assaulting the marchers and remaining guards wherever a yeht or the behemoth had not.

Another pulse of *Person Leading* surged over A'banna. She heard angry shouts, no doubt the first of many. Those who had been on the streets gathered into a mob or fled for their lives. Pitchforks and shovels, axes and hammers, short swords and daggers, spears and bows all rose in the hands of furious citizens. They started at a slow march and began a full charge toward the palace; toward her.

A'banna ran, dodging angry people as they joined the action. Torches, lanterns, and braziers around the city flared, illuminating people glancing outside their windows in great panic or growing fury. The front line of the mob neared. She wouldn't break through. A'banna darted between two buildings. She pressed herself against the stone wall, took a breath, and watched the mob —nearly a hundred people already—charge past. When the last stragglers were gone, A'banna glanced back.

Another swing of the behemoth's tail battered an entire section of stone housing. Debris rained into the street, crushing marchers and guardsmen alike. A mournful wail came from the behemoth as it moved its bloodied tail, bent awkwardly as if broken. In the gaping spaces of the homes, families clung to each other, watching the battle from far too close.

A'banna darted back into the street, determined to help the behemoth and the people. At the least, she could evacuate the families and convince the behemoth to move away from battle. Sounds that she dreaded cascaded from the palace: scratching, slithering dissonance.

"No!" she whispered, skidding to a halt.

Thousands of monstrous snakes, released by the Sorceress, poured from the ziggurat and down its stairs. Her venomous servants spared no one. The largest—avocondas as long as three yehts horn to tail—wrapped themselves around people and animals alike. Citizens caught in the battle ran and sought cover, but the snakes were hungry and attacked without prejudice.

Marchers dashed toward the behemoth with spears. The behemoth let out a bellow as thundering stomps crushed a few marchers beneath its wide feet. A'banna gasped, clutching her stomach. *This is just the start of the brutality. People and animals. My city!*

A'banna let fury engulf her. She clenched a fist and ducked as a marcher broke ranks and swung a club at her. She tried to draw her weapon, but the earth shook beneath her. A gray pillar-like leg stomped on the marcher, while a second dragged against the street, throwing up stone with its thick toes. The creature's bulk pushed her to the ground, away from the battle, as the second behemoth lumbered between her and the marcher wave.

Yehts charged, the earth shaking beneath them, trampling a wave of marchers. Their frills formed a sort of shield wall, blocking several spears thrown in A'banna's direction. The ceratops surrounded the behemoth, skewering attacking marchers with their long horns.

A'banna pushed herself to her feet, stunned by the animals who had suddenly formed her honor guard. The behemoth's long neck lowered, its head no larger than her torso. Tears streamed from its hazel, reptilian pupils. It gently brushed her back.

"Let me help!" A'banna told it, knowing that her father felt the animal's aura. She could sense him through the behemoth. Its gaze was his gaze. Its concern was his concern.

It brushed her again, more urgently this time, then it raised its neck, returning to war. Its massive bulk swiveled, its long tail swatting marchers away like flies.

The minotaurs kept up the assault, no matter their losses. They shoved people, and even other marchers, onto yehts' horns, using the distraction to scale the frills and hop onto the yehts' backs, attacking ferociously with scimitars and axes. The tails of the behemoths slammed against them, again and again, but still they continued to hack back. The first beast, swaying as if off-balance, reared up to use its massive feet instead.

A'banna scrambled back. Her father was using the animals to shove her out of the battle! But she wouldn't be outdone. As she had done in the jungle, she extended her aether, filled it with a mixture of essences to strengthen a person's resolve. Dozens of these arrow-like ethereal strings sprang out from her aura. In that moment, she could sense how every snake and every marcher was connected via a long, tentacle-like connection, one that enabled a lasting *Lead*, far more powerful than the one A'banna had just created. If she attempted to affect them, the Sorceress would find her. Quickly. And A'banna would fail. The Sorceress controlled those essences, she was more powerful. A'banna could feel her, even now. Searching. A'banna groaned, cutting off her essence manipulations. She gripped her stomach as nausea hit again. A'banna ducked back between buildings, unable to see the effect of her effort on the battle itself.

People rushed to the gates. A group thronged between the buildings she hid behind, a wave pushing her back out into the street. Some went to the gate, but a great many joined the battle.

She saw citizens in their doorways, some with families, some carrying makeshift weapons. One woman even had a pot and butcher knife. Laborers used scaffolding to throw bricks and small stones. With a loud angry cry, the mob joined as one and leapt to defend neighbors, livestock, or pets. Pitchforks and old scimitars, spears and shields, all clashed as this makeshift army crashed against the minotaurs and the vanguard of snakes. All of their fear, the anger, their resentment poured out on the boar-men, who met them with furious berserker abandon. People ran between the legs of the second behemoth as it stomped on the attackers, even smashing multiple snakes into the stone ground. But the first behemoth's weakening cries signaled the end was near.

A'banna sent out a string of aether, trying to ease the behemoth's pain. A group of marchers used the behemoth's lumbering gait to flank the animals and people. Instead of attacking the rear guard, they stormed houses right behind her. A'banna heard a woman and her baby scream.

She eyed a passing jaguar prowling along a roof and a hawk overhead. *Help them*, she said through a tiny ethereal arrow, filled with protective and offensive instincts. The two animals hesitated. The jaguar pawed the ground; the hawk stretched out its wings, and soared in a circle. At last, they turned. The jaguar leapt through an open door while the hawk flew through a window. A tumult came from inside. The cat growl, the flapping of wings, the hoarse grunts and squeals of a boar-man. The sound of ripping flesh and a fierce struggle, as furniture crashed. Moments later, the woman, clutching her baby, ran out of the building. It was the basket weaver they had met earlier! She joined a small group gathering at the edge of the street. A'banna sent streams of *Person Leading* toward the entire group, urging them to flee.

Not far from them, in front of the forges, stood Torresin, the hunter from earlier; the dissident. Torresin nimbly dodged the assault of a lone marcher, driving his spear into its porcine neck. A'banna sent streams of protection, leadership, and wisdom toward him. His thin aura rippled as the *Lead* was absorbed. Torresin hesitated as the marcher fell. The hunter shook his head for clarity. Then he saw the crowd at the edge of the street; freeing his spear from the monster's throat, he ran to join them.

Sighing with relief, A'banna watched Torresin and the group have a brief exchange. Her heart lodged in her throat. *Go,* she thought. *Flee.* There was only one way this could end. After what felt like dozens of life cycles, the group followed the hunter to the gate. A'banna edged forward, risking a clearer line of sight. The doors were wide open, the portcullis raised, and the armaments abandoned. The flock of people joined several others headed toward the open road.

A'banna's lips quivered as she watched those she had known and cared for fleeing the horrors to come. *Wherever they planned to go, may they survive.* It was the least payment she could offer.

Her gaze returned to the battle in front of the palace.

The full onslaught of snakes had arrived, slithering with such great power and force that they blanketed the ground, the animals, everything except the marchers who ceased their bloodletting and stood silently as the Sorceress's pets extacted vengeance. In the fire and starlight, the snakes were a cacophony of orange, blue, red, yellow, and black. Much like the dark fire the Sorceress embraced, her pets were a writhing and brutal sea.

Many people attempted to run but were swiftly overtaken. A few defiant, rebellious men and women fought to stay aloft against the sheer force and number of the snakes, only to be drowned by them. Monkeys tossed stones and leapt for higher ground, shoving potted plants, vases, and rain barrels onto the snakes. A lucky jaguar severed a large viper, but three more struck it and the mighty cat was felled. Hunters, farmers, and laborers slashed with their makeshift weapons, long knives, or other armaments taken off of the fallen. Yet they too were soon surrounded in the nightmare. Reptilian eyes glowed yellow. Light glinted off the swift reveal of fangs or teeth. Scales shimmered in the starlight. They bit and struck at whatever was near, beasts gone mad.

In all of it, A'banna could see auras flashing or swirling with shades of red, yellow, purple, black, white, brown, and orange; hues in which she could only begin to comprehend the complexity of aggression, rage, defiance, stubbornness, revolt, suppression, terror, courage, and more. This was battle. They were all on the cusp of life and death. Here, man, beast, and monster shared a shifting rainbow storm of unbridled emotion and instinct, stoked by mastery A'banna could only dream of. On such a scale; hundreds of people and animals clawing at each other like a field of elite warriors; this was a masterful manipulation beyond her ability.

The sight disgusted her.

A'banna turned back towards the gate, lurching as if lost in a stupor. She followed strings of darkness and wispy silver aether weaving between each other, touching one person and then another individual to fight them moments later. The marchers and the snakes seemed covered by this darkness, threaded by faint red.

Flames erupted within a nearby building, spilling out onto the combatants. Screams, clashing of weapons, the cries of agony or despair or anger filled the night, while she coughed against the smell of smoke. She stepped in a warm puddle and lifted her foot from the sticky liquid. Blood flowed between cobblestones.

Stunned, A'banna scanned the battle, the burning city, the temple, and the palace. A pale woman in a silver gown stood in a balcony of the black tower, watching it all.

"What have you done, Father?" A'banna whispered. How were they any different than the tyrant on the tower balcony?

A hand groped in the darkness and grabbed her arm. Instinctively, she unsheathed her dagger and pressed it into the neck of her ambusher. But Huahanna only advanced himself into a sliver of light, showing his face. "We will grieve for man and beast later," he said, voice quiet. "Come."

Amazed by her father's power, she followed, pressed against the wall. They ran quickly, stopping only at a section of the wall she'd never seen before. "My father?"

"I have long prepared for the inevitable," he said and then rammed his shoulder against the mossy stone. Astonished, she watched part of it cave in, bricks clattering together as they tumbled from the wall. "Get through," he said. "Remember, Marchers roam outside the walls as well. If we are separated, follow the great river north. Be mindful of the raptors and drakes and other beasts. Use them if you must but do not trust what will kill you if it can."

"My father," she gripped his forearm. "How did you manage all of the animals in the city?"

"Listen to the oppressed and ease their suffering, my child, and they may help you one day."

A'banna felt horrified. "You used them."

"I gave them a chance to be free, as I did for us." He pointed at the hole in the wall.

A'banna planted her feet and shook her head. "That is what you call freedom? Any survivors will be butchered or experimented on!"

Huahanna growled with frustration. "She plans on doing that anyway. Don't you see? If you do not escape, the world will become like this city! We will return for them when we can, when you are stronger and united with the others."

A'banna ground her teeth and turned away. She pushed herself through the tunnel, feeling the skin of her shoulders scraping on ancient mortar and brick. She dropped to the ground on the other side.

With war and rebellion still raging in the city, the night sounds of the jungle greeted her; the buzzing and intoning of insects, the chirping of birds in the trees, even as those trees shook in the night. A'banna glanced up at the shadows of prowlers, big cats, and monkeys—an army of animals passed overhead, rattling tree branches and shaking leaves. Boughs and branches groaned under the weight as claws dug in and creatures shimmied upward. Dark shapes fell upon the guards on the wall, whose torchlight and gaze were transfixed inward. More and more animals from the outside were being drawn to the violence within Avoc-Nezlticoulti.

Words choked in her throat. Her chest tightened. She wanted to rush back into the city and die fighting with them, but her father's words resonated in her head.

"No," she whispered.

What was the world to her people? This forest?

Huahanna crawled through the tunnel and dropped down next to her. They hugged the wall as his gaze roamed. "Hundreds will find safety in the forest and work their way to the tribes and Lodornatha," Huahanna whispered. "It is the only hope they have."

"Really?" she whispered, disdain dripping from her words. "If they can't survive the battle in there, how can they survive the wild?"

Huahanna took her arm. "Listen, my child. We only escaped because Jocina was completely distracted. I wanted her to feel the loss of it all. Her mind is bent on finding us. She will ignore any who fled while she tracks us. If we travel fast enough, I have friends beyond the jungle in the old Wo'Huzziet lands. They can help us, like they helped Alain."

A'banna gasped.

"It only took a single nudge," he continued. "You know our people were on edge, A'banna. They have been. The increased feedings and abductions! Beloved children, spouses, brothers, and sisters turned into monsters with only the hunger to shed blood and serve the Sorceress. You heard their fears. Alain tipped the scales when he prophesied before the Sorceress had him slaughtered."

"Had me slaughter him, you mean? If it hadn't been me—"

"A'banna, one way or another, she would have made certain you held the knife. He knew that."

A'banna felt her legs weaken.

"How did he know that?" she murmured. "How would *you* know?"

Huahanna swallowed, composed himself, and then continued. "The faster we go, the safer the others will be. She cannot let us escape. What I did to make those emotions turn violent; the instincts of fear and aggression and self-preservation to rise; I did so we would not have to stand here arguing. We could have covered twice the distance by now!"

A'banna growled at his deflection, all the while blinking back tears. "All those lives! Our people! And the beasts of the forests, too?"

Who was this man that she had loved? What manner of man was her father?

He looked at her squarely, certain. "Yes, A'banna. All those lives. Some escaped, and with the forest turning on the Sorceress, they have a chance. But we've slowed her advance by stripping her of her capital city. I had to. The animals understood. Marchers roam their lands and disrupt nature! They heard the call. Perhaps it will be enough to destroy her army. Now, release the colors of passivity so we may pass unharmed."

A'banna shuddered at the horror befalling her people. She could leave her father and track through the forest alone. Yet, her father had a point. The marchers were out in the jungle. She owed it to her people to live, at least for now. A'banna growled but acquiesced—for now. She projected blues to lower the perception of her temperature, bright colors of green and yellow and orange so others might see her as a predator or poisonous enough to avoid. At last, gray, to pass unseen to the animals without color sight.

"We hunt for our passage north and stay off the road," he said.

A'banna nodded. She took one last look at the great city, listening to the horrors within. Every action she had taken as priestess, as a servant to the Sorceress, and now this; the abandonment of her people? Likely ten or twenty thousand remained in the city. And the animals of the forest? Her hands felt more than drenched in blood. Had she made the right choice? Should she have let the drake or raptors kill her? If she had, perhaps these people would be alive or have hope of it upon tomorrow.

A'banna stared back at the walls, listening to the sounds. She palmed tears away. *This is my fault.*

Alain hadn't just been any traveler or any other prophet; he had been the first person of any race to share the pale skin and silver hair and eyes of the Sorceress and Quin. This traveler, if her father's tales were true, may have been like the Sorceress; an Immortal from the elder age. But he knew the Sorceress, and she knew him. She was *afraid* of Alain. And then the prophet had known A'banna, without her name ever being spoken, and foretold the stars. He even pitied her. He had tried reasoning with the Sorceress, but the Sorceress had refused, calling him by name: Alain. And then A'banna had drained him upon the altar to The Taurs, whom he denounced to the crowd gathered below.

The Keeper of the South had set the kindling, the prophet had struck the match, and her father ignited the fire. Thousands more of their people would be killed or tortured.

Huahanna moved by her. Dark stains grew under his arms, at his wrists, his chest. Not sweat, but blood. Every person was surrounded by an aura connected to their body at key points. For one who could touch and use the world fabric, giving of that ethereal nimbus was required. When someone had no more aether, the cost came in blood.

"Your aura," she said.

"We can tend to it later."

Huahanna disappeared into the darkness of the forest, the rhythmic bobbing and soft shuffling of leaves signaled his passing. In the canopy above, all manner of beasts crawled and jumped between trees toward the city wall. Thousands of wings beat the air as bats, hawks, and other flying creatures went to the massacre. Would the animals reach the Sorceress? Could they defeat her?

A'banna stepped into the jungle without an answer.

CHAPTER 5

THE ALLEY STUNK OF HUMAN FECES AND ROTTING TRASH. RAYNT took point since Rurik was now awake. The bleeding from the knife wound had slowed, but that hadn't made the situation any less dangerous. The spy kept his breathing even, even though his own mother had stabbed him just minutes before and then blamed them for assaulting her. Sure, she all but guaranteed her new cover as their informant intact, but Raynt had to worry about whether or not his colleague would survive if they had to fight. Rurik preferred the bow, but he was just as equally capable in hand-to-hand. None of that mattered if he lost too much blood. Meanwhile, Nchoji brought up the rear, supporting Rurik with his arm around his shoulder.

"We have to get out of sight," Nchoji whispered.

"No," Rurik objected, trying not to cough. "Baktur can sense if Raynt uses magic, and we have two essencers tracking us who can easily spot Raynt's aura. If they follow my blood trail, hiding isn't possible.

Raynt's boot splashed in a puddle that suddenly smelled like urine and blood. Unconsciously, he bit back the stench and told

"

himself it was no different than spending time in a barrack's privy. They came to an intersection, and Raynt carefully glanced around the side of a building. That's when a figure dropped from the roof above. Stealthily, he rolled. Raynt saw a street lamp's light flash across a thin metal blade. Raynt hopped back as the Baktur's baklana made a horizontal slash that nearly disemboweled him. Rurik grunted; a bow twanged. Small feathers brushed against Raynt's ear, before embedding into the Baktur's nostril. The zealot came forward, stumbled and fell face-first into the cobblestone alley.

"Crows, that hurt."

"Where were you hiding that?" Nchoji muttered as Raynt turned to see Rurik lowering a small crossbow.

"The ancients never tell their secrets," Rurik murmured. "I need the bolt."

Raynt shrugged, leaned down, and yanked the bolt out of their attacker's face. He wiped it off on the man's clothes than handed it to Rurik. "Any secrets you want to share?"

"Yeah." Groaning, he pulled back on the string and locked it into place before replacing the bloodied bolt. "Keep moving."

Nchoji pried the baklana from the attacker's stiffening fingers, examined the fine, thin blade, and grunted. He unbuckled the sheath from the corpse and clipped it to his belt, stowing the sword.

"Salvage," Nchoji muttered.

"They'll be looking for that," Rurik warned. "Swords are personal heirlooms."

"Let them come, then." Nchoji pulled his belt tight, then reached out to support Rurik.

They hastened their pace crossing the street and into the next alley. Most houses by now had begun to dim their lights or pull shades or close window panels. Raynt heard the slam of bolt-locks as they passed one house, though he couldn't see the people moving inside. Were they all this scared of Baktur and the essencers?

"Anyone seen any of the alley folk from earlier?" Raynt murmured as he guided them through.

"No," Raynt said. "It's like they all disappeared."

People like that just don't disappear. Hide well, yes, but disappear? No, they usually saw everything. What had they seen that he hadn't? That thought nagged at Raynt.

A woman's shrill scream split the night, just a few streets over. Ahead of them, not behind.

"What in Kerdum?" Rurik murmured. "The Baktur are behind us."

Raynt checked inside a slightly open iron rod gate. "Gentlemen, if you've got ideas on what I'm missing, tell me now."

"Taurs if I know," Nchoji muttered.

"Yeah, I would like to avoid that."

Nchoji grunted his agreement.

A door opened. It was barely audible, its path arrested just before the hinges creaked. Raynt turned to the sound and looked down. In the shadows, a young, dirty face stared at him, one hand pressed against a cellar door. A child.

"Coin," she whispered.

Raynt was relieved to find his coin pouch was still tied to his belt. He reached in, not caring what he dropped into the girl's extended hand.

Beaming, she hissed low. "Goblins in the streets!"

"Goblins? In Cronop?" Raynt asked.

As if to answer that question, someone else screamed.

"And Swords of Baktur, sir. I ain't lying. Run or hide; they find you in the open."

"Get safe," Raynt whispered. "And thank you."

The girl held up the coin. "Didn't do it for you, but sure, you're welcome."

Without another word, the girl shut and locked the cellar hatch.

"Nchoji?" Raynt asked. "Are these the captain's friends?"

"You've got Goblins for friends?" Rurik asked incredulously.

Nchoji shrugged. "Doesn't everybody?" His tone turned serious. "I don't know."

"Keep moving," Raynt ordered.

Doors slammed a few streets over, but they didn't hear any sounds of violence, which didn't rule out Goblins.

"Raynt," Rurik hissed.

Behind them, a glob of darkness tightened to fill the alleyway. In the dense space, they could hear footsteps gently and quickly advancing. The three men broke into a run, darting into the next street. Raynt gasped and backpedaled, barely missing a horse and a wagon. The horse reared and snorted, and the owner cursed, then whipped the horse forward. There was no hesitation. Nchoji helped Rurik up as Raynt bolted into the bed. As the horse began to gallop, Raynt reached out, grasped Nchoji's forearms, and pulled him aboard.

"Get the waving winds off my bloody wagon!" the driver cursed at them.

"Just keep driving and we will," Raynt growled.

"It's Goblins, damn it!" the driver shouted back at them, whipping his horse to move faster.

The wagon rocked and jostled on the street.

Raynt turned and pulled up Rurik's drenched shirt. He startled at the belt of knives strapped to the spy's side. "You're full of surprises."

"Don't tell anyone. You'll ruin my allure."

Raynt chuckled as he unsheathed a dagger. Its blade suddenly lit with a searing blue flame. "This will hurt."

Rurik nodded.

His initial thought was correct, the wound had been a surgical strike. Lady Talacciaro was anything if nothing highly skilled at defense. She could have killed or maimed them all with that surprise attack, but she hadn't. "You know, your mom is one damn good fighter."

Rurik grimaced. "You interrupted my operation—"

In the middle of the sentence, Raynt pressed his dagger's blade into the wound, searing it closed. Rurik cried out in surprise, then clenched his jaw, muffling his response. Burning flesh drifted up.

The flame on Raynt's dagger extinguished. "You'll live, my friend."

"Crows. Thanks."

Raynt smiled, relieved that he finally got Rurik of all people to crack a little. Raynt had been serving with King's Men for the better part of six years and known Rurik for over half that time. It was now a matter of personal pride that he had *surprised* him. "Anytime, brother."

The driver shouted back at them. "You all get into trouble? Because this ain't the wagon for you!"

"Just take us to the edge of town," Nchoji called.

"I can't leave," Rurik said. "I have a cover."

"It's blown here," Raynt said. "My apologies for that."

"No, you don't understand." Rurik grimaced as he pulled Raynt closed. "Revive, we found her."

Raynt sat back on his heels and held onto the side of the wagon for balance.

"Who's that?" Nchoji asked.

Target Revive was the name of the operation Raynt had been planning with the King's Men to rescue Naminia, heir as chieftess of the Wo'Huzziet. "The woman we discussed earlier."

Nchoji gasped. "Where? Where is she?"

"Hey, I can't tell you." Nchoji grabbed Rurik by the shirt, the whites in his eyes wide as he held Rurik to his nose. "I said I can't tell you," Rurik repeated. "Calm down, man. There's a plan in place. You were right, Raynt. That group is moving."

Raynt hissed, shaking his head. How could he search for Bedel and Shai when he should be back north stopping the Slaver Coalition from raising its defenses and consolidating its slaves to an undisclosed location?

"I've got a cover in place," Rurik whispered, his voice barely audible in the clop-clop-clop of the horse's hooves and the rattle of the wagon. "I have to get back north as soon as possible. Do you trust me?"

"Yes."

"Good. We haven't heard from our colleagues, but the plan stands the same. She should be in Wonbai in a week. If not, the Old Man has a contingency in place. Now, we have a reliable secondary source. That's why I'm here."

"Not to back me up?"

"I work better alone."

Raynt smiled. "Maybe."

Rurik chuckled. He reached under the wagon's blanket. There was a travel bag with fresh clothes. "You gotta drop me off. I can't be seen anymore."

Raynt shook his head. "You're wounded."

"Ever stopped you?"

"Your mother stabbed you."

Rurik nodded and looked away. "Aye, that was pretty much the tip of it all."

"That was a shitty joke," Raynt said, chuckling. He checked Rurik's wound again, then helped him with the bag while the driver's back was turned. Rurik stripped of his shirt, revealing the shoulder harness with throwing knives and a second collapsible small crossbow. He grunted and pulled on the shirt, which was slightly large on him. Here in the islands, that would hardly be noticed during the day.

"Until we meet again," Nchoji whispered. They gripped each other's elbows.

"Ancients preserve you."

"And guide your hands."

Rurik smiled at the traditional farewell of two warriors. Long ago, the Rda and Baktur were aligned, even sharing some beliefs. Obviously, commonalities still remained.

"Be safe," Raynt whispered. "Tell the Old Man and Yeltson I'm on my way."

"See you soon," Rurik whispered. He smiled. "Glad I ran into you."

With that, Rurik rolled off the wagon and onto the street. In moments he was on his feet and sprinting between houses. Shadows wrapped around him and he vanished.

"What about us?" Nchoji said, searching the street for hostiles.

"We—" The essences trembled, like plucked strings on an instrument. Goose flesh sent shivers up his arms. "No!"

Out of everything Raynt could have said, that was it?

The street heaved as if it took a deep, rolling breath. The horse stumbled. The wagon lurched, sending the driver flopping on his side, struggling to stay on the bench. Nchoji and Raynt tumbled into each other, ramming against the side. The ground had risen up, covering the wheels. The horse rose, pulled hard. Tack broke, and the horse ran into the night. The ground heaved again as Raynt felt *someone* fly above them. Raynt turned to try and pull the driver to safety, but this time the rumble was accompanied by a rush of heat, as though a furnace had been opened below them.

"Jump!" he shouted.

The driver struggled, pinned in his seat by wood planks. Nchoji had already jumped off the wagon, and Raynt barely had time to reach out for the driver before brick and flame erupted like a geyser, incinerating the man and wagon. Raynt rolled back as the flames consumed the carriage, as bricks cascaded like hail.

Raynt rolled to a crouch and reached out, his silver ethereal aura acted like hands catching bricks from the air. He whirled on his heels, one hand around the makeshift net of aether and air, and released it at the figure who landed in the middle of the street.

Contact, the essencer mercenary, jumped out of the way as the molten bricks passed him.

"Miss me, Agent Raynt?"

"You know these sons of the damned?" shouted Captain McCormack, lowering through the air.

"Only the one," Contact said, gesturing from beneath his hood. "It has been a long time, hasn't it agent?"

"Traitor," Raynt growled, glancing between the two. Contact had been serving the Slaver Coalition for years, and their last serious fight had ended in a draw. Captain McCormack of the *Batoidea* had ruled the seas as one of the most violent and competitive pirates around. That he now was linked to the fall of the Wo'Huzziet had only made this more of a fight. Raynt didn't know the man's fighting style, but he doubted it was anything but dirty. McCormack rounded the hole in the street, which still bubbled with tar and fire. Flames licked the side of the wagon; smoke billowing into the air. McCormack drew a cutlass with a gold and silver encrusted hilt. Six hexagonal jewels were set inside the hilt's guard. Various colors swirled within each jewel, representative of essences stored therein.

Tactically, it was a sound move to have additional essences on hand for combat, especially if he preferred close quarters quick hand-to-hand melee. He'd draw previously-stored essences from them, using those to close the distance of the attack. Raynt knew

Contact would most likely stay back and observe the conflict; he always did, unless absolutely necessary. He'd also attempt to eliminate weaker opponents first, like Nchoji, rather than give Raynt the upper hand. But maybe Contact was simply narcissistic and wanted a victory over him? They'd beaten each other senseless before but never defeated the other. What would Contact choose tonight? They were both masterful at hand-to-hand combat. What would it be? Contact drew no weapon now. Did he have an ulterior motive? Yes, clearly, Raynt could see it in the man's eyes. As soon as Raynt engaged McCormack, Contact would run—but would Contact fight Nchoji? Or just flee like after their first encounter? If Raynt was wrong, how would he keep Nchoji safe?

As soon as those questions passed through his tactical checklist, he realized it was impossible.

You can't keep a man safe who doesn't want it.

Nchoji dashed forward with not even a roar. He moved faster than Raynt anticipated, his long knife in hand.

"Either a fool or man with a vendetta!" McCormack declared, standing ready for the assault.

He'd slaughter Nchoji.

Raynt glanced back at Contact who smiled cheerily, bowed slightly, and said, "One of my clients doesn't want you harmed today, old friend." Contact pulled up his hood.

"Huh?" Raynt muttered, raising his knives expectantly. "Just like that? A client?"

"Contracts are sacred things," Contact said with a shrug. "Conflicts of interests can be tricky. Until next time?"

That was as much pomp as Contact needed. He backed into the furthest alley.

Pursue the mercenary or save a man's life?

"Until next time," Raynt growled.

Raynt summoned air. It lifted him up above the street. As he reached down to unsheathe his knives, Raynt's thoughts communed with the wind. Hand open, Raynt watched strings of essences gather in his palm, like a small funnel. He pushed outwards, releasing the gust of wind.

McCormack grinned, tracking Nchoji, waiting to cut him down.

The wind funnel appeared as a spinning thread of rope, tightening around itself until it curved, almost deformed with the energy packed into it. Raynt used his aether to push that tightening, rushing wind forward, lifting up what remained of the wagon and the loose bricks, still glowing red from the heat. Flame curled up inside the funnel, churning out smoke. Raynt used his free hand to control the essences; his way of making the assault more personal. Slowly, his hand clenched into a fist, then he opened it. The thread of wind snapped, loose strings of essence splaying at all the tightened knots it had formed. Instead of a single funnel filled with debris and fire, it multiplied into ten. With a roar, the swirling funnels surrounded the pirate captain, calling to themselves the other air essences McCormack had summoned to try and undo Raynt's weave. The wind surrounded him, blasting him with bricks and fire and splintered wood, as wheel spokes flew through the air like oversized throwing knives.

Just when Raynt thought the man would be utterly pummeled or burned to death, the ground shook. The cobblestone street heaved, slithered. Stone and brick ground together as it rose, surrounding McCormack in a flowing cloak of stone and brick and dirt. The two weaves met. Flame sizzled and quenched. The winds shoved a part of McCormack's shield away, but it wasn't enough, though a single wheel spoke slid through a gap. Raynt felt the impact; the sound of the wind too loud in his own ears for much else, save for McCormack's shouting. He staggered, uttering curses as he dodged flaming bricks, trying to keep himself upright. His armor had fallen away, some of it swept up in Raynt's wind funnels.

Raynt forced the wind essences to turn as though he were flying. Six funnels remained, rotating. One impacted the outer wall of a homestead, stripping the gate, wall, and some of the plants from inside the courtyard up. Raynt grimaced when he saw it. Collateral damage, the Magical Affairs Commission called it, but he knew there was no collateral that family had to repair their broken wall. At least he hadn't destroyed the home. This momentary reflection didn't ease his conscience any as the funnels spun back toward McCormack.

Except that was the only distraction McCormack needed. A hammer formed out of bricks, circling McCormack's arm like a sinister gauntlet. He swung, battering aside flying debris. Raynt had lowered himself back to the ground all too soon. McCormack pressed through. Raynt thought he saw the man's face through the conjured armor; McCormack's beard had singed. The brick and stone shell and the hammer made him resemble a crab, but he moved lithely in the duel.

The pirate reared back with the hammer. Raynt dodged as the hammer split the air where he had just been, revealing that the bricks had formed a sort of blade.

Raynt rolled as McCormack made a horizontal swipe. Brick cut across Raynt's bicep. It burned. He felt blood on his arm, but he couldn't stop. The funnels hit McCormack from behind. It threw him off balance, enough that he let go of the shell, for a second, giving Raynt a fraction of a second to strike. He lunged forward, beneath a blanket of brick. McCormack, on his hands and knees, saw him coming—and grinned. His teeth were black in spots, and others had been replaced with gold. His brown eyes glistened with pride.

"You are one damned fool," McCormack said. Raynt prepared to stab the pirate with his dagger, but McCormack spun, a long, jagged knife slipping from a concealed sheathe in his sleeve. He rose up, the brick armor spreading around them like a small tower.

Raynt gasped as the thin blade slid between ribs. The pain was excruciating. There was something else—a burning sensation, more than just the pain of being stabbed. The limbs on that side went numb.

McCormack snickered. "You thought you could take me, did you now?"

He shoved the blade deeper, then ripped it out. Raynt gasped and collapsed to his knees. The blade was a long, thin knife that looked more like polished bone with indigo-colored sacks—perfect to poison a weapon.

"A ray in the ocean is a pretty thing," McCormack droned. "Until you get close to its godsdamn tail. Then it cuts you."

Raynt struggled to breathe. It came out with a liquid rasp. *No, no, not like this!* Raynt struggled to pull on McCormack's arm, but he could barely stand. He heard stone bricks falling around him as his own wind whistled past, harmless. The essences returned to their neutral, passive state; their essencer dance was over—because Raynt had gotten careless.

McCormack grinned as he carefully wiped the barb clean, then carefully sheathed it on his wrist, before pulling his coat over it.

Raynt felt warmth spread across the outside of his chest. He breathed, and a bubble popped from his lips.

McCormack stared down at him. "I suppose it's pointless now, boy, but why in the sea's depths did you try to knife me? Me!"

"Bedel," Raynt gasped, his vision clouding. His limbs felt heavy. "Shai."

"Oh. That?" McCormack scoffed. "I got them where they were going, but there's one lady on land I don't try to screw around with, and her little bird said leave. You all have no idea what it's like when you bring two Immortals within—"

A long, thin sword shoved through McCormack's chest. "Ancients reject your spirit to the realm of the wandering lost," Nchoji whispered in his ear as blood blossomed on McCormack's white shirt. McCormack tried to turn, to rip the blade from Nchoji's grasp, but the Rda warrior used the old pirate's movement against him. As the barb popped out, Nchoji grabbed McCormack's elbow and stabbed the barb into McCormack's throat. Blood gurgled out, staining his beard. The pirate's face twitched, a last dying fury of an old man. Then he tumbled over.

Raynt's breaths were becoming more and more ragged, harder to pull.

Nchoji knelt next to him. "You've been poisoned, it's natural. Hold on."

The Rda heaved Raynt over his shoulders and turned to follow Rurik except shadows now filled the entire street. The Baktur strode, forming a line, eyes wide and horrified at the catastrophe before them.

Raynt's chest muscles pulled, his throat tightened, he couldn't speak.

Swords flashed in the lamplight. The Baktur moved forward, weapons poised for the kill. They charged.

Out of the alleyways flowed a wave of green and brown. The Baktur barely had time to turn to this new threat before nearly three dozen blurred forms wove around them. Raynt struggled to keep his eyes open to see what was happening. Baktur slashed down at the whirling figures which barely rose above their waists. Howls rose up, claws and blades flashed. Raynt thought he saw reptilian, bulbous yellow eyes blink before disappearing into another frenzy of activity. Then, out of the struggle, an olive-green figure in rolled-up trousers and a brown tunic leapt up on the back of a Baktur. Its bald head reached around as webbed fingers clutched the man's shirt. He tried to pull it off, but the Goblin opened its wide mouth, sinking sharp, nearly shark-like teeth into the man's throat. It pulled back, tearing flesh and cloth away in a bloody spray. As the Baktur fell, the Goblin leapt to another's back. The man fell, collapsing into a veil of mounting bodies. It was chaos. Whenever a Baktur managed to skewer a Goblin, often with the help of another Baktur, the greenskins swarmed them, slashing at their legs and bringing them down, or leaping on their backs, carving up spines and necks.

By the end of the carnage, bodies filled the street: Baktur, Goblins, and McCormack.

Nchoji stood still, Raynt on his shoulders. But feeling had begun to drain from Raynt altogether. None of this mattered. He was desperately tired.

The Goblins slowed from their frenzy. A few younger ones gorged a bit more on enemy corpses, indulging in an act so heinous Raynt couldn't comprehend it, not in his poisoned state. An elder passed through the group, slapping the heads of those feeding on the dead or nodding to the older Goblins who gathered the bodies of their fallen, lips smacking at the temptation so near. The elder spoke something in a chattering language, full of clicks and clucks. All eyes focused on him, snapping out of the blood-craze. The elder turned to face them.

Raynt tried to gasp, to tell Nchoji to run, but he couldn't find the words. Red and black swam at the edge of his vision, blinding him to anything but pain and the nearly three dozen sets of eyes now focused upon them.

Goblins sneered and growled, blood leaking from around their extended nostrils and lips. Tongues slithered around their faces, reflexively cleaning themselves as they drew close, weapons still drawn. Not that Goblins needed them. Goblins *were* weapons.

Raynt felt Nchoji tense, even though he said: "Trust me."

If there was anything Raynt had learned from the tales of

heroes of the Trader Wars, it was this: don't trust a Goblin. The bloody mess of what once were Baktur was exactly what you gained. Raynt struggled to try to warn Nchoji. He could hardly think, let alone speak. In fact, he could barely keep his eyes open.

The lead Goblin bowed.

Raynt's eyes closed, as exhaustion and pain overcame him.

CHAPTER 6

THEY TRAVELED THROUGH THE NIGHT AND INTO THE NEXT DAY, stopping to eat only when necessary. On one of those breaks, A'banna tore cloth from her skirt and dressed her father's wounds. Mindful of threats smaller than the eye usually saw, they kept a closer watch on where Huahanna's aura had pulled itself away from his body. In time, it would regenerate, but now it left a potentially dangerous trail.

That night they lit no fire, but climbed high into a massive tree. Mosquitoes and flies beset them, making the most of their rest. A'banna resisted the urge to use ethereal to influence the insects, not that it was easy with mosquitoes. Those were the worst to work with. A sloth slunk by for a visit. A'banna greeted the sloth with a wide smile.

A'banna and Huahanna sat quietly as the sloth moved on. They ate flatbread and drank water from their hide skins. They slept in shifts. A'banna's dreams were violent horrors of a sea of snakes that devoured and obliterated the people, land, and animals she had loved. Her wandering spirit whisked up the tower, floating in front of the Sorceress on the balcony. She'd scream in frustration and order more death. Then there was her father, who casually ignited the genocide in the city. And through it, all silver eyes searched for her, dark voices called, and shadows of another realm slid around her dreams.

When she awoke, A'banna heard howling and wailing from the animals, as if grief had stricken them. Huahanna shuddered in the branch beside her, cradling his knees to his chest. He was glowing a quiet blue in the starlight, and already she could see his aura regenerating. Darker shades of yellow and brown swam like fish in a stream within his ethereal nimbus, hidden behind the blue glow. They were signs of the emotional weight her father carried. Guilt, sorrow, and hope. Nevertheless, he disgusted her.

A'banna said nothing, not even a comforting word. They both knew what the Sorceress would be doing to any survivors who did not fight for her. For every good intention Huahanna had, the Sorceress's army would grow quickly now, and her pets would be well fed. A'banna clutched the satchel with the imager and book inside. She was complicit. For that, she deserved death. So why did she want to live? Who would she be exposing if she followed through on this plan? The Sorceress? What about her father? She couldn't discard her father's dreams, either. Maybe she could fight alongside these mysterious others? Her dark thoughts returned to the city. At least she had urged some to flee, even if she had manipulated them. With a hunter, their group might survive in the forest if they got far enough away.

When the sun rose in the east, they climbed down and began their trek. It wasn't long before they discovered the bodies of marchers—their limbs were strewn across a clearing, torsos gutted and throats slashed. They had died quickly. Loose feathers and the severed limb of a raptor near a bloodied axe told them everything they needed to know: Even the great hunters had been outmatched.

A'banna and Huahanna circled around, staying clear of the

horror under the clearing. *Cuelatchanli* ruled here. She and her father were only guests, and this was not their kill.

As they trekked, they continued their wary vigil on the territory and its shadows.

A'banna's clothes clung to her with sweat, and they stopped only briefly to drink. Later in the day, thunder rumbled far in the distance as the sweet aroma of coming rain swept through the trees on a cool breeze. They paused long enough for Huahanna to take out leather hoods to cover their heads.

The storm neared. Lightning streaked the skies. Thunder slammed A'banna's hearing as wind whipped the trees, shaking leaves and branches in a dance of madness. The animals of the forest took shelter, but she and her father kept pressing forward. Mosquitos and flies joined them, making an uncomfortable journey worse. Several times, to their east, she could see the great river, water gradually overfilling its banks. In the murky water, long, scaly drakes lurked, observing the bank for any who came too close to the water's edge. The skies opened. Rain washed the canopy above and soaked A'banna's leather hood. It was a wet, cold downpour, which turned the forest floor into a slurping, black mud.

"We should stop," Huahanna said after leading them up a slope into the forest and well away from the drakes.

Shivering, A'banna nodded. When he stopped at the bottom of a tree and didn't try to climb, she considered objecting. They were surrounded by foliage and other thick trees, providing cover for any potential ambush. The rain itself made visibility difficult and hearing limited. Yet, other than the colors of insects, bugs, and a squirrel shivering in the rain, there was a surprising lack of the ethereal signs of life. She was too tired to argue.

They immediately began pulling down tree limbs for a covering. Huahanna unfolded a treated leather tarp, which they stretched and tied to the trees. As he did, part of the tarp brushed his cheek, wiping away a smudge of flesh-colored paint.

A'banna froze, staring at her father and the newly visible tattoos. She let go of her end of the tarp and neared him. At first, he flinched and pulled back. Studying him, she wiped more of the paint away. It smeared on her fingertips. Makeup, like the women of the high houses used, mixed with war paint for its durability.

"Here," he whispered. He took a cloth from his bag and wiped more away. A'banna gasped and folded her arms as he slowly revealed intricate, detailed tattoos around his mouth and eyes. They were drawn as if his mouth were the sun with bright rays. Runes like that of the words of Belasna were around each. Four pointed stars arched around his eyes, and deep, curved lines stretched from those to the upward shined rays.

"What is this?"

"Come, let us finish the shelter and I will tell you all."

Reluctant and shivering, A'banna set to work again. They secured the tarp, gathered grass and moss, and cut down a bush bedding. Draping a leather coat colored like the texture of the tree over them, they huddled beneath their meager shelter. At least the trunk was wide enough they could both lean against it. She preferred having her flank protected while resting.

Her thoughts turned to her father. She wanted to reach up, touch his tattoos.

"Why hide these? They're beautiful," she whispered.

"For the Keeper of the South, the Sorceress, they are blasphemy and treachery," Huahanna said.

He smiled wearily as he touched the tattoos, as if rediscovering them. "There are"

He paused. "There are other gods of this world, A'banna. One she and The Taurs call the Oppressor. You can recognize his servants and prophets easily enough when his spirit selects them. These tattoos appeared the night I met Theantros, alone in these woods after your mother died." He touched his chest. She knew there were scars from a long battle with a *cuelatchanli* pack. It was how he obtained the claws dangling from his necklace. "As I was bleeding out, I was given a gift that night. Theantros came to me—he is Oppressor to The Taurs, though, in reality, he's more like a balance, a guardian to keep their actions in check with the rest of nature."

A'banna nodded, teeth chattering. Children often found guidelines and rules restricting. She did. "What does it mean?"

"They call me a Speaker. It is the sign of the gift of Speaker of Men. Right now, there are only four of us out of the various races, but it is my job to speak truth, justice, kindness, and the humility of Theantros."

A'banna shook her head. "And he lets you pray to the other gods?"

"Did I say that?"

"Father, who gave them to you?"

"Rouha, the spirit of Theantros. These are not the work of a mortal craftsman."

She sighed again. The chill seemed to grow colder; and her father's words were confusing, to say the least.

"I hid them, A'banna, because I wasn't ready. I didn't believe I could break the bonds of the Sorceress as high priest, not fully or publicly, until you showed me how."

"Me?" A'banna let out a despairing chuckle and gently patted the satchel hanging from her shoulders. "You copied and stole her work."

He shrugged. "I did much in the shadows."

Like destroy our people, she thought. "Did Theantros tell you to send our people into a war they couldn't win?"

"No," he said simply. "I did that. I ignored the plan. For that, Alain is dead."

"You knew him."

"We have spoken for many years, but I only met him last week. He was supposed to get you out."

"Me? What of you? Where did you meet Alain? How have you spoken to him for years? Why kill our people?"

He didn't answer. But she knew the answer. "You ignored your new god. You set me up to murder a man that came to help me."

"Yes," he said hoarsely. "I chose your life and mine over others. Even Alain. Over the world. Over our people. And now, unless you find a way to fulfill what I saw in my dreams—your purpose destined by the stars—my choices will come back as twenty thousand vengeful monsters to ruin the world I disregarded, because I ignored Theantros, the god who saved me."

A'banna scoffed, and for a moment they did not speak. But the forest did. The trees, the earth, the beasts scuffling out of one hiding spot and into another. They were afraid.

"My father" teeth chattering, A'banna scanned the forest. Small streams of water and mud cascaded down a gradual incline to the river below. "Something doesn't feel normal."

"I agree," Huahanna whispered. He pulled his daughter in closer, rubbed her chilly limbs. She was too numb and on edge to really welcome the touch. "It is too quiet."

She pointed to the streams.

"Yes, we should move soon."

Soon might not be quick enough, she thought. They both knew what this was. Glancing behind and above, she could see the steep hills covered in forest but heard nothing. The animals had fallen silent. Predators were near. She was grateful for her father's warmth, even if he refused to actually get up and move.

Huahanna continued. "In two days, we should be out of the forest and in the plains of the tribal peoples. Should we be separated, follow the river and search for the ruins of a tribe? Their huts are old, but their influence in the region was strong. We'll be met."

"By Elves?"

"Friends of ours from the northern nations and a remnant of the Wo'Huzziet. We are about to enter a much larger world, A'banna. I met with them just a few days ago, while I was out 'hunting.' Lodornatha Rangers had escorted the prophet Alain through the woods before he had them turn back. I should not have waited. Alain was going to get you out of the city, safely, if you were willing."

Stunned, she pulled away and stared at him, covered in those intricate tattoos, a man she barely knew. "My father! How? Why? So many people are dead now. Why? How could you let me?"

"Because I thought I knew my own way. I was wrong and selfish." He teared up. He looked away and smiled sadly. "Your mother asked me those same questions about letting you enter the priesthood after they took your house-sister. Your mother trusted Theantros after they met. Then Jocina sacrificed her—"

He used the Sorceress's name!

"It wasn't a question of if I would tell you, but when, and—"

Suddenly, a thick, yellow-nailed hand darted underneath the tarp, fingers curling around Huahanna's leather jerkin, and yanked upward, ripping away part of their meager covering.

Huahanna smacked into a tree branch. His spear fell into the mud; shield tipping over from where it had rested on the tree. The hand pulled him free and tossed him into the air. Huahanna skidded in the dark mud.

A'banna looked up to see a marcher.

The breath from its long snout turned to steam in the rain. Its bulky frame lumbered forward, hooves sinking in the mud. It unsheathed a long scimitar from its baldric and pounded toward Huahanna. Her father shook his head, mud and water cascading off him. He lunged for his spear, slipped in the mud, and barely grabbed hold of it. Its tip sank into the minotaur's shoulder, and Huahanna slid, maneuvering the blade deeper. The boar-man bellowed, and all around them, the same deep, guttural cry answered.

Foolish! They'd been surrounded as they rested. But A'banna didn't process that thought; she unsheathed her knife and scimitar, leapt, and stabbed at the marcher's neck with quick precision. Blood ran fast with rain as both A'banna and her father pulled their weapons free.

Another minotaur came barreling from the underbrush. Head low, it slammed into Huahanna, tusks goring his side. It flicked its massive, sinewy neck and Huahanna rolled into a tree. Before Huahanna hit the ground, the marcher twisted, jamming a horned mace into his side. Huahanna flew into the underbrush. The marcher chuckled as it stomped after him.

Bushes rattled to her right. A'banna snapped her head to look, expecting to see a marcher, but instead found the long reptilian snout of a raptor, a *cuelatchanli*. Its golden eyes with black vertical crescent pupils widened with surprise and reflected her image—wet, frightened, prey. It stared forward. She could see blue and green feathers, soaked down against its skin. It screeched and charged, long arms with three clawed fingers stretched out toward her.

Another minotaur rammed the *cuelatchanli*, sending it flying. The raptor's spine cracked against a tree as the minotaur turned toward A'banna—but a second raptor and then a third pounced from the underbrush. In a flurry of teeth and claws and slashing feet, the raptors ripped out the neck and severed two limbs from the beast before splattering the ground with its entrails.

Two more marchers entered the area, and the groups charged each other. The collision of the massive predators cracked in the storm. The minotaurs hacked at the raptors with their swords, while the raptors slashed with giant claws on their feet. Both cut through skin and flesh. One *cuelatchanli* bit down on a marcher's torso and kicked high, sweeping its claws across the minotaur's neck.

A'banna didn't stay to watch further. She dropped to her knees and leaned against her heels as a mace swung over her head, cracking into a fourth raptor that had leapt into the fray. A marcher growled at her and went to dispatch the raptor, which had skidded to a halt in the mud. As the marcher approached, the raptor lunged, maw and claws opened wide. A high-pitch shriek pierced her hearing, but A'banna couldn't stop and cover her ears. She made a mental calculation of her father's wounds and blood. He needed her.

Sounds of fighting, clanging of blade against blade, signaled a struggle behind a large bush and trees to the north. A'banna circled south of their broken tent, putting a few of the massive trees between her and the action. She glimpsed Huahanna using his sword to parry away a long, curved blade, thinner than most marchers used. She darted to a second tree with a massive trunk, barely escaping another minotaur's view as its huge frame lumbered by. Its heavy footsteps slowed. A'banna heard its deep breathing on the other side of the tree.

Just behind her.

A'banna's heart pounded as images of what the marcher was capable of flashed through her mind. It had a strong concentration of dark fire within its aura, a sordid blend of the person it once was and the mindless monster it was forced to become. She stilled her breathing, like the hunter she was. Two predators tracking one other.

To her left, mud slurped around cloven feet.

She moved right, keeping the tree trunk and a tall fern between them. Her hand tightened on the scimitar's hilt. She paused, listening. Mud squelched, heading away from her position. A'banna inhaled, prepared to flank the marcher, and spun between the fern and the tree. But a wide, gaping, toothy mouth was there instead. She gasped, slid in reverse as the raptor's jaws snapped shut. It focused on her. The bush rustled as it emerged. *Prey,* she read in the aura colors.

A giant, furry hand sank into the raptor's neck plumage and yanked it backward. The *cuelatchanli* howled, lashing out with its limbs at the minotaur. A'banna risked the danger of the raptor's claws, dodging the black, slashing talons. As she swiveled, she sank into mud and ducked under the feathered whipping tail. She drove her scimitar into the marcher's gray underarm and sliced free. Blood sprayed as the marcher lost its grip; the raptor turned free and lunged at the shocked minotaur's throat. As it pulled away flesh, it let out several low hoots, lowering its head at A'banna. She saw its aura colors change from the red of hunt and prey to shades of blue, yellow, green.

Trust.

Leaving the raptor to its work, A'banna ran toward the clanging sounds of battle, sheathing her knife. Her father couldn't last long against a marcher, not in his condition. She scooped up his spear from where it had fallen in the mud and readied it for a thrust.

She was too resolute and distracted to recognize the blur of movement in her peripheral vision. The blow came from behind bushes and between trees on a gradual incline. The momentum added to the force. A massive hand that felt as heavy as stone slammed against her head, sending her sprawling.

Focus, she thought, even as stars and darkness crowded her vision. Suddenly, she remembered how cold she was.

Her body slid into mud, grime and water caking her. Desperately, she kept hold of her sword and Huahanna's spear. Covered in the soil of the earth, she groaned, rolled up, and readied the spear as the minotaur charged her. A'banna screamed a war cry, throaty and high pitched—and the bushes behind her parted. A brown and red shape leapt up above her spear, full-on, into the minotaur. The alpha female of the raptor pack slit the marcher's gut open with both legs while its clawed fingers dug into the marcher's shoulders. The alpha raptor sank its teeth into the neck, ripping away furry flesh in a gush of red.

A'banna froze in awe. The alpha female had decided to attack the marcher—not her—and there was no visible *Beast Speech* happening. No one had influenced her. Yet, her colors were the same as the last raptor regarding A'banna: *trust, the pack.*

The *cuelatchanli* shrieked again as it dug in for more, but A'banna swiveled and darted through the foliage. She gasped, sliding to a halt. A massive, leather-armored marcher stood as sentry. It growled when it saw her. Behind its thick and muscular frame, she saw her father fighting, but couldn't see the minotaur battling him. She ducked the sentry's mace as it splintered the bark of a tree and thrust up with the spear, lodging it between the marcher's armor and its shoulder. It roared and reached for her with the damaged arm. With a twist, its brawny torso shattered the spear shaft as it backhanded her into the tree. A jolt rattled down her spine as she bounced off the stuck mace. More stars and darkness swam in her vision. Her skull ached as the sentry reached out and tossed her through bushes and mud. She slid, her head hitting tree roots and a rock.

"Oh gods," she whispered, pain stabbing throughout her body, the cold numbing it at the same time. Her clothes, armor, and skin were filthy with mud and blood. The ground shook as the minotaur made its way toward her. The pounding accentuated the throb in her head, and she saw its free burly fingers curl and uncurl.

Up, she ordered herself.

But her body shivered against the tree. One arm stung as with a thousand needles, but her fingers still searched the muddy soil for the scimitar. Groaning and screaming against the pain in her left arm, she pushed herself upwards as the marcher took hold of her. It was only then that she saw the blood dripping from its tusks. A jolt coursed through her body when it grabbed her, raising her off the ground. Those beady eyes held some strange reflection of humanity, but there was fury and murder there, not an actual identity. Snarling, a web of saliva spread across its long, pointed teeth. Hot, wet breath reeked when it snorted in her face. It held her. Her consciousness and its connected. A'banna thrust her sword into its neck. The minotaur grabbed her wrist and squeezed. Pain shot through A'banna's arm as she lost her grip on the scimitar. Her knife slipped from its sheath, and both weapons smacked into the mud.

Only then did she realize the clanging of weaponry had stopped.

"Don't kill her," came an all-too-familiar voice. The marcher grunted and turned A'banna so she could see. She gasped: her former betrothed, son of the Sorceress, pale and glorious in his silver scaled armor. Quin's long, curved sword touched the neck of her father. Huahanna had been forced to kneel in the mud, his body lacerated from multiple wounds, including his back thigh— hamstrung. Quin pressed a boot on his leg, taking pleasure in Huahanna flinching in pain, the barely audible groan, and the crimson red mixing with sludge. His face was half-caked with mud, but the tattoos were mostly visible, even as the rain washed the grime away. Streams of water now cascaded down the hill, carrying away mud and debris, causing everyone to shift their feet to stay upright. Quin even moved the sword briefly.

"A'banna," Quin said, his red lips spread into an ominous smile, displaying his long canines. "We don't have a lot of time. Once that raptor pack finishes with the others, I'm afraid we'll be next."

"Let us go," she said. Her head swam with pain and shock.

"Letting you go would be an offense to the thousands of people killed hours ago. To my mother. No, no, my beloved. I know what that traveler told you. What your father here has probably said, being a Speaker of Theantros and all." Huahanna jerked back, but Quin yanked his hair harder, the sword cut a little deeper, keeping him in place. Quin continued. "But this doesn't end in some heroic act of glory under the starlight of an oppressive god. That would be too poetic."

Quin slit open her father's neck.

A'banna screamed. Huahanna kept his gaze on her. He breathed deep, trying to remain calm. His tattoos seemed to blaze and shimmer with light. Fear seeped out of him, and only determination remained.

A single silver strand of aether left him. A'banna's own aura received it, embraced it.

I love you, my daughter. Your help comes from the hills.

Quin grinned mockingly and shook his head, patting Huahanna on his back as his head rolled lopsided, blood gushing from his neck. "Still sending messages in the dark, old man? And mother called you her 'prized stallion.' If it's a comfort, you hid well. Damn war paint." Grinning with sadistic pleasure, Quin leaned forward, eye-level with Huahanna. He shrugged, mocking him. "Just not well enough."

Huahanna opened his mouth to speak, but blood gushed and bubbled from his throat and mouth. His defiant eyes said enough.

Weeping, A'banna watched as her father's cycle ended. His body went limp and fell into the mud. The muscles within her tensed. She vomited over the marcher's hand. It growled.

Quin flicked blood from his blade. "I've always wanted to kill a Speaker. It's so nice to make that gift disappear again. You know he was trying to give it to you, A'banna? From one high priest to another priestess? Poor, poor Huahanna." Quin sneered. He stepped on her father's head, driving it deep into the mud.

Miles away, on the slopes of the western mountains, wood

cracked and groaned, and the sound of rushing water met their ears.

Quin reacted, spinning to look.

"That son of a bloody Keeper!" he shouted. The marcher looked at him oddly, confusion in its small, once-human hazel eyes.

In between the weeping and the tears, A'banna looked up to the hills. What she had feared—and why she had urged her father to flee—came true. Trees bent and were plucked from the ground as a massive wave of mud, rock, and water cascaded down the hills. The forest's trees and bushes became a rolling mass of tangled limbs in the landslide.

A'banna screamed, swung, climbed the minotaur's knee, and twisted. Cloth and leather ripped in its grasp, but she dropped to the ground, snatching her knife and sheathing it before darting away. Quin rushed at her, and the marcher followed, even as the landslide engulfed where they had just been.

Through the trees to her right, she saw the drake-haunted river. If she could run fast enough, she might be able to clear the area. Her limbs ached as she ran, slipping and trying to keep ahead against the oncoming wrath of the forest and the mountains beyond.

"Damn you, A'banna!" Quin shouted, even as the minotaur's hooves slipped and it slid down the hill.

Through the canopy, A'banna could see the blue stars. The blue stars that had changed her life.

The landslide became a deafening roar. She saw the massive trees on its outer edge and the bubbling froth of mud.

Then it engulfed her.

CHAPTER 7

SHE WAS THE EARTH, THE WATER, THE TREES. IN THEIR WRATH and violence, she spun head over heels. All sense of up, down, any direction at all became meaningless. A'banna had no air with which to scream, and rocks and trees pummeled and stabbed her. Her arm clutched the satchel her father had given her. She joined the tumult into the air above the river and plunged. Water, mud, and forest collided. An enraged drake roared from the spinning madness and snapped its jaws at her, but a tree crushed its head even as the force of the landslide drove her deeper into the river. The great river's current was unmerciful, embracing her and the avalanching debris in its grasp. The water cleared for a brief moment, and she saw blue light streaming downward. Gasping, she swam toward the light, but a tree trunk hit her, and she spun under the water with it. Then once more she was free, thrust into the water and the leaves and twigs and mud. She gasped as her head rose above the water. A'banna blinked away blood and water, pushing her hair aside to see.

A tree, now stripped of its branches, spun overhead like the downward arch of an axe. Blue starlight glimmered off the tree's bare trunk as it rose high in the air. A'banna sucked in air, kicked, and pulled herself through the debris. Her hands gripped trees and pushed aside what the forest had expelled.

Behind her, the tree slammed into the water, pushing down other trees and sending up a slight wave that carried her downstream. The river continued to rush forward. There was pain, cold, numbness, the fear of what jaws might lurk below, and the constant agony of nature's wrath. In a moment of clarity, she thought of her father and grabbed again at the satchel, but it was gone.

A'banna howled as the river and the debris forced her underneath the water's surface. She struggled to breathe. She pushed against the hard row of logs above her for an opening. At last, she found it. She struggled up onto the grouping of about five logs. Halfway out of the water, she turned and looked into the open glare of the sentry marcher. Its mouth was curled in fury and fear, tusks ready to devour, one hand curled at her, but when the current forced it afloat, she could see the tree that had impaled its gut. The minotaur was dead. The river carried the corpse away.

Up, get up, she thought, seemingly for the hundredth time. She heaved as logs bobbed along. Forcing one leg onto the wood, she gasped as pain wracked her body. The other leg refused to move, so she bent over, seeing the open, gaping wounds of her arms, then her legs. A sharp, broken tree root, as thick as a dagger hilt, was impaled in her thigh. If she passed out, she'd bleed out— or wake up in an animal's maw.

She tugged her broken leg onto the floating logs and reached for her skirt. It hung off her by threads. She tore pieces from it and urgently tried to dress what wounds she could. At last, her numb fingers curled around the tree root in her thigh. With her other hand, she put a stick in her mouth and bit down.

With both hands, she pulled.

A'banna screamed as the root ripped free. Red and stars flooded her vision as pain shot through her. Tremoring, she felt hot blood on her fingers. She forced her scream to end, though it was lost in another rumble and mudslide not far from where she'd been. More trees and earth were sent into the depths of the river, displacing a wake that pushed against her. In moments, she could either be crushed or drowned. She closed her eyes, clutching her leg, but the debris rammed her trees, pushing them ahead of the tumult. Gasping, she calmed herself and used the rags to bandage her leg with unsteady, numb fingers. She was prepared to do more, wanted to do more, but when she pulled tight, the pain coursed through her, draining her of what little strength she had left. A'banna fell back. Darkness crept at her vision. She felt lost to the world, to consciousness.

The current continued to pull her makeshift raft downriver. She sprawled out against the trees, kept together only by the force of nature itself.

A'banna was weak, tired, broken, and alone. Still breathing heavily, she gazed up at the blue stars and questioned why. Why had she even bothered to live?

Omens, she thought, as if she heard someone else's voice. Distant and far away.

Silence, the man with the golden hair and the sword of light replied. She sat on the edge of a small boat with him, looking at the troops, at the iron-hard gaze he cast at the shore. But she was only hallucinating.

Then she slept.

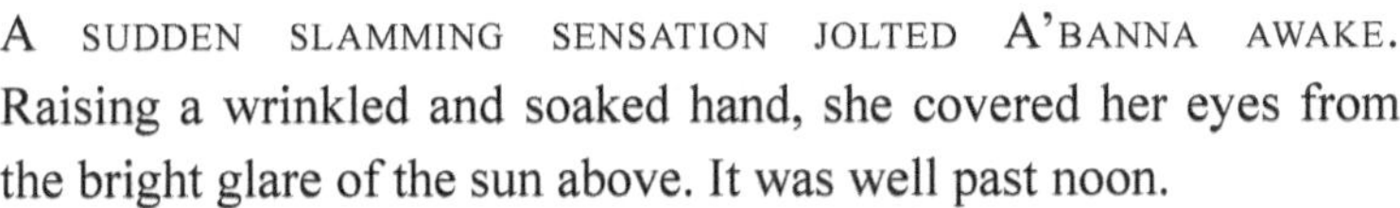

A SUDDEN SLAMMING SENSATION JOLTED A'BANNA AWAKE. Raising a wrinkled and soaked hand, she covered her eyes from the bright glare of the sun above. It was well past noon.

Gods.

A'banna gingerly touched the wood beneath her. It was

steady; she was afloat. She struggled to sit up. Her makeshift raft was no more than a streak of blind luck. Four trees that had retained some of their branches and roots had snagged together like interwoven vines. And they had just slammed into a rocky beach. Beyond that, the forest had begun to change. The trees were different, like the palms of the northern wall of the forest. A'banna stared, knowing she was less than a day away from reaching the tribal plains. But she had failed: The satchel and the book were gone. Her leg—she cried out as she tried to move it. It was bruised and bleeding from the many wounds. She was sure the other was broken. She almost laughed. She couldn't walk if she tried. She had indeed failed. Her father was dead, his dream was dead, and whatever gods—even the gods of the stars—had left her to die slowly, finally getting the end of her cycle as she deserved.

"Hello? Can you hear me?"

More hallucinations?

"Just kill me," she cried out to the god of the stars. "I wanted to die! Why did you take him and leave me?" She wailed. "My father, my father! Long had he served you."

"Avocan, I do not plan on killing anyone today. Wake up. Those river crankers will not wait forever."

"Then let it be," she said. "I trusted you."

She wept at the sun, used her one good arm to bat at its light.

"Forgive me," the voice said again. Strong arms—touch of human flesh—lifted her. She was too tired to fight. She tried to raise her head and only saw the man. He was young, with almond-shaped eyes, and his aura radiated with the light of the sun and the moon. Behind him, in the shadows of the forest, were men clothed in black. Spears and bows notched with dark fletching, they stalked through the trees. Tracking both, the shadows darted from tree to tree, as well as the drakes now converging on the raft.

"We've got you," the man who carried her said. "Just hold on. Camp is"

A'banna's strength flooded out from her, and she drifted to sleep, to go where *cuelatchanli* roam.

— · — ·•·—·•◉•·— ·•· — · —

At first, she ran with the *cuelatchanli*, keeping pace with the alpha female that had come to their aid during the battle. She nestled with their pack and mourned with them when they found their dead along the river bank. And she joined them when they took vengeance where the drakes had eaten of their corpses. She found comfort in their warmth and their strength, and their dogged determination to return all of their pack from the great wrath of the forest.

It wasn't until the light and heat of another person's aura, their presence, tore her away from her quest in the wilderness that her dreams became fitful. She dreamed of Quin killing her father, the massacre back at the city, the battle in the forest, the horror of the mudslide, the altar on which she sacrificed the pale prophet. At times, she felt the warmth of furs and blankets, the comfort of a bed. At others, she felt the searing pain of wounds being treated. She felt someone's aether gently touching her own; a healer's aura connecting to hers. The *cuelatchanli* declared his presence most unwelcome.

In her dreams, she would see the man from the river tending to her wounds—the liquid on the cloth he used burned.

When she opened her eyes again, she saw the man from the river now held her hand. She felt their auras joined, felt his strength and guidance enter her. It was beautiful, as beautiful as he was, but it was not requested. She pulled away with a brief burst of pain, but his grip was strong, solid, like her father's had been.

Rest, he said. He seemed clothed in golden and blue light. He touched her cheek. *I have to remove the infections before they take root in your wounds.*

I need to die, she said. *I deserve it.*

Your friends don't seem to feel that way. He gave her a sly smile, and she didn't snatch her hand away.

My friends?

The raptors. Your connection is remarkable. If they will you to live, isn't that enough?

No, no. It is. But it isn't. You don't know.

You're correct. I don't know. But to survive what you have, there is strength in you. Fight a little longer. And tell your friends we mean no harm.

He appeared troubled, but she rested in his ethereal embrace. A'banna wanted to protest, but sleep overcame her. She could feel him and knew he was near. So were the *cuelatchanli* pack, her new family.

CHAPTER 8

Bedel Riess Morbrook rose from the Avocan woman's bedside. He stretched, easing the tension in his muscles. Bedel was skilled at many magical disciplines, but healing took effort. He didn't want to exhaust the patient's body more than necessary, so he had used more of his own aether than was safe. He winced at the blood dripping from his wrist, where aether had pulled from his aura. But she lived. That mattered. Bedel applied salve on his wrist. His gaze hesitated on the open wound, just below some scars that remained from his encounter with the mountain essencer. That had been half a world away and more than a month ago.

Bedel glanced back to the woman on the bed. When they found her, she'd been caked with mud, blood, debris, splinters of wood and leaves. The river drakes had almost made a meal out of her. Given the debris the river had washed northwards, he guessed she'd been caught in a landslide. The Lodornathan rangers agreed. Without the Elves and the village's apothecaries, she would have died from infection on the first night. After two days, she seemed peaceful. Her black hair had sweeping over her dark face. She breathed normally.

She was beautiful.

Sighing, Bedel took up the washbowl off the bed stand and elbowed open the cloth door to the old Wo'Huzziet shack. One of the rangers, Pol, sat on a tree stump. He gave a curt nod at Bedel, then continued sharpening a curved blade. Pol paused, lifted the blade, and sliced hairs from his beard.

"Sharp enough?" Bedel said, smirking.

"Almost," Pol grumbled. He was shorter and stockier than most Elves. Facial hair betrayed Dwarven lineage, but that wasn't uncommon. Lodornatha was the only place in the world where Dwarves and Elves lived side by side in peace. There were at least three other Dwarves or part-Dwarves among the rangers.

They weren't in Lodornatha. The rangers had met Bedel's group weeks ago at the tip of the Great River, outside a small city-state that sometimes built its economy on fishing, and slavery in the offseason. Thankfully, the rangers arrived shortly before Captain McCormack had reneged on their contract and abandoned them. Some of the sailors said an albatross had told the captain to. The bird had been following the ship since the Cronop Isles. Bedel had only seen the huge broad-winged shape at night and in fog, but to him, it had felt more than a bird. Even Immortal Alain had seemed unsettled. He had pushed them to move faster on foot after that. From albatross to giant ground-raptors.

Fantastic, Bedel thought.

Bedel gave Pol a nod, then headed for the boma wall. He needed to dump the bloodied water.

"Agent Bedel," Pol called. "I wouldn't head too far out. Those raptors are still prowling around the village perimeter."

Bedel slowed, looked back at Pol. Before he had met the rangers or arrived at the Wo'Huzziet village, Bedel thought he and Shai had been paranoid. Still, no amount of awareness had convinced Emissary Alain from disappearing with little more than a note. Down here, in the wild, nature seemed content to kill whenever it could. Or maybe he was still thinking of the mountain…

Sighing with frustration, Bedel walked between wooden thatch huts. This was where the Wo'Huzziet had started over, but there were still signs of the last raid. The outer edge of the village had been burned down. Livestock that normally kept the grass low had been kept penned since the raptors' arrival.

The village wall was a ring of thorny bushes stacked on top of each other. Through the tiny gaps, he could see grass shift as a large blue and red shape darted through it.

Dirt crunched softly behind him. Bedel swiveled, hand on a dagger at his belt. His mind reached out, steadying the essences within the bowl. The Elven captain materialized from the husk of an old building. Veiled and clad in tight, green and brown leather armor, the ranger was well camouflaged in the shadows. Bedel sighed, then released his weapon to focus on the ground.

"She bonded the raptors, Bedel," the ranger said.

Bedel shrugged as he used some aether to coax *Soliditus* to move. A deep hole appeared in the ground near him. He could see the colors of brown and gray shifting in the world fabric.

"What gave it away, Idrin? The ambush after we pulled her from the river or the fact they tracked us outside their territory?" Bedel said.

The ranger captain, Idrin, said: "We have reason to believe we entered a different pack's territory. This one came from farther south. Following her."

"That is unsettling."

"Raptors are intelligent predators," Idrin said matter-of-factly. "It should be unsettling."

Bedel poured the bloodied water and tossed the rag into the hole, then requested essences cover it. "This should block the scent."

"Unlikely or unnecessary. They found a food source."

"Such positivity, Idrin, I'm encouraged about our chances of survival."

Idrin pulled the veil down below his chin, revealing tufts of blond hair hidden beneath his hood. He was lean, muscular, and gripped his bow with an arrow notched. A small, dog-sized, brown blur darted around Idrin's feet. Idrin's mountain ferret's tail wagged. The ferret's oval eyes flickered from Bedel to the land beyond the boma wall. Unlike ferrets from the kingdom of Cardor in the north, this Lodornathan mountain predator was twice as large and just as fast and as deadly as other predators its size. It was a worthy companion. A spear leaned against the wall behind the ranger and his ferret, and all of his sheathes had been unclipped, leaving his swords and daggers on a broken stool.

Idrin's gaze continued to pan over the area. It was an ominous effect underneath the leaf-like hood.

"I did not mean to put your defenses at ease."

Bedel rolled his eyes, playfully. Truth was, he kind of liked these hyper-vigilant rangers. Mostly.

"We have a saying in the mountains," Idrin continued, barely moving. "Love is the most pleasant distraction when the hunt is over, but when the dragon flies overhead, love itself is peril."

Bedel nodded. "I'll keep that in mind."

Idrin pointed at Bedel's bandaged wrist. "Will you?"

A swath of grass rustled and swayed. Without summoning *Invisitus* to enhance his sight, Bedel could see yellow reptilian eyes, watching him through the gaps in the boma wall. At Idrin's feet, the large Lodornathan ferret hopped and pawed the ground. The small companion circled and hissed a warning to the raptor on the other side.

"She's a patient and an asset, Idrin. Nothing more."

Idrin said nothing but slowly drifted back into the shadows. The ferret followed. Somewhere in the village–came a bird-like whistle. Three other shrill voices answered.

As he turned, Bedel nodded to the curious raptor, scanned the grass for any others, and headed back into the village center.

When the last great assault of the slavers happened a few months ago, the slavers hadn't left much standing of the great Wo'Huzziet tribes. Their city, Ntokup, had been home of hundreds of thousands of people and hundreds of united tribes. Over a few decades, the slavers had razed Ntokup multiple times, but that hadn't been the end of their depredations. To reinforce their dominance, raiders also attacked outlying villages like this one. They destroyed most of the outer wall, burned half of the homes to cinder and slaughtered any Lodornathans and tribal warriors who resisted. The Last Battle of Ntokup had seen hundreds of Men, Elves, and Dwarves prisoners of war taken to the ships on the river. Only after McCormack had abandoned them did Idrin recognize the *Batoidea* as one of the Slaver Coalition's flagships. Had they known! Bedel shook his head at his own naiveté. He'd ignored hiring his father's preferred captain out of familial spite and instead, contracted the largest, most powerful ship in the harbor. Foolish and arrogant! As far as the world believed, this land was desolate, raped by evil northern industry. Even McCormack believed there wasn't enough of a viable population to keep raiding this far south.

Unbelievably, and thankfully, they were wrong.

The stubborn and tenacious Wo'Huzziet had *survived*. Most of the tribes remained united even after the fall of Ntokup because of the survival of their high chief's steward. They spread out their villages and kept their locations to themselves. Not even the rangers knew all of them. Two tribes had gathered here, the Gahna and Bomingo, from which the royal family descended, or so they had told Bedel. The villagers stared at Bedel as he passed —not so much because he was an outsider, but he was an outsider who allowed the raptors to follow him.

Old women clutched their grandchildren in doorways, half-concealed by hanging blue and orange woven tapestries. Outside the huts, old men sharpened their forward-bent knives while sitting on their heels. One elder had the shaved head of the Rda, the nation's elite guard. There was a gaping hole where his right eye had been, and his other eye seemed to see everything at once. He rested on his heels beside a sharpened spear, and a belt of throwing knives and a short, inward curved sword hung from his waist. A trio of shaven-headed adolescents—two young men and one woman—formed a wall of spears that wouldn't hold against an entire raptor pack. But the Wo'Huzziet didn't know the difference between *wouldn't* and glorious death, and it was a testament to their resolve that the young people had taken up the Rda ways. Still, this raptor migration had everyone on edge. One horse and a yeht calf had already gone missing. In the village pen, goats and aurochs bleated. Yehts stomped the ground. Bedel saw another Rda, younger than Bominga the Rda elder, covered in scars from northern blades, dart in their direction, spear and hide-covered shield in hand.

Their chief, Martuza Cougareyes, seemed to emerge from the shadows. His hair was gray and beaded. Trophies hung from a necklace. His body was old and scarred. Once the steward to the high chief, he had united most of the survivors. Martuza's bearing was so hardened that sometimes, he would only stare and speak when needed. After scanning the village, he crouched, joints popping.

"Great Chief," Bedel greeted him. Martuza met his eyes, nodded, but maintained his silent vigil.

Bedel paused at the center of the village. Empty market stands were part of the perimeter. He could only imagine what these villages were like full and hopeful. Bedel leaned against a post. Beautiful and serene, Shai sat at a table studying the contents of the satchel they'd pulled from the river. Bedel watched his lover as she hunched over a book, writing furiously with a quill and ink on a piece of parchment. Shai stopped to massage her temples before glancing up at Bedel.

"How's it coming?" he asked.

Shai shook her head. Long dark locks fell around pointed ears. She held up the golden jeweled artifact. "I'm sure this is the imager Huahanna mentioned, but I can't figure out how to release the images—or take them. Look at this."

Bedel leaned over the tome. What they could read was written in an ancient form of Belasna, but much of it was damaged by water and muck. He glanced at the triangular artifact. "Well, it is an imager."

"How insightful," Shai mused.

"I've only seen one once," he said. "In the vaults below the Commission. Xathon won't even touch it."

Shai rubbed her temples again, cringing under the stress. Their conferences hadn't gone entirely to plan. Alain's meeting with Huahanna had caused both of them to go missing. "Not help-ing, Agent Bedel."

"Let me." He moved her hands aside and began massaging. She relaxed and leaned in, then shook her head.

"Not yet," she whispered. "I need to keep my mind clear."

Bedel stopped, then pulled over a stool and sat beside her.

"You sure the copies are still in there?"

Nodding, Shai pointed to the jewels. "Ever seen the Memory Larks? Those jewels are carved just like this. Maybe a cut or two in difference. Similar color, too. If they can retain thousands of years of history, imagine what these hold? If Speaker Huahanna duplicated Jocina's private text using this imager, we could recreate everything we lost."

"And there aren't many imagers left in the world, nor people who know how to use them."

"Aye." She slipped the artifact into a new leather satchel. The one they'd found snagged on a root off the river bed was ruined. "You know, my people in Lodornatha or Lupacuo could help with this, but our second mission time table is closing, Bedel. We need to get to Zeller."

Everything had happened too fast. Emissary Alain had invited the new Speaker of Men to this small Wo'Huzziet stronghold. They'd argued for more than a day and disappeared with almost no warning. It pricked Bedel and Shai's frustration. While they searched the jungle for those two men, only the mystery woman and this satchel appeared in the debris from a mudslide. Bedel couldn't argue with Shai wanting to leave. Their agencies needed invasion plans if they existed. Instead, playing intercessor to two defiant religious men was tedious—and that was before they took off on their own well over a week ago. The fact that Shai and Bedel were tasked with both guarding the mystical servants of the Well and also making it to Wonbai in time was a testament to how thinly stretched each agency was.

Bedel glanced back at the hut, where the woman lay healing. "She needs at least one more night's sleep. We just drained the infections this morning. Her body has finally taken over the healing itself. None of us here are healers. If we move her too soon"

Shai's thumb gestured at the camp perimeter. "And while she rests, our window of opportunity in Zeller closes, and those raptors get hungrier. Then there's Huahanna. Are we sure that's his daughter? Then where is he?"

Bedel crossed his arms. "I think we know where the Speaker is."

She glared up at him. What had she expected them to do? Tie them up? Huahanna had made his decision to leave in the night. He even disarmed and gagged a ranger in the process.

"Both Alain and Huahanna knew the risk when they chose to leave," Bedel said. *Even if they had done so independent of the other,* he thought. "Perhaps when she awakes, she can share the same information."

"You heard Alain. Huahanna had never really embraced his calling. Who knows what he actually shared? With anyone. This may be all we have from him." Shai paused.

After a moment, she slapped the table. "We've lost an Immortal and the Speaker of Men in one week. We have a Chosen. We're done here, Elizenzer. I need to get this to people who can help. If we don't make the mission north—"

"We will," he said.

"You Cardorians. So sure of yourselves." Shai crossed her arms and leaned back. "We were entrusted with two of the most important people in the world, and they're dead, Bedel. I need to have a valid reason why."

"They didn't want protection." He gestured to the sky, then intoned: "Theantros will help us." Shai cracked a smile at that. It was a decent Alain impersonation. "I can't protect someone who refuses it. None of us can."

Bedel sat across from her.

"If she is a Chosen, she was Alain's mission—our mission. She needs to recover before we attempt travel. If that is also Huahanna's daughter, A'banna—which I think she is based on the healing bond we've shared—then she'll know what happened to her father, the Speaker. Consider what else she could know. They were the highest nobility in Avoc, close to the Sorceress herself. And if they were close to her, we've never had an opportunity like this."

He hesitated. The memory, from when he was so young he had difficulty understanding it now, flooded his mind uninvited. Blood, death, salty water, the groan of a ship, harsh wind, and a man standing on a deck with a sword wreathed in dark flame. He had analyzed rumors and facts, and they led to Avoc; to a horrifying union between the terror who held a sword and a Sorceress who allegedly experimented on her own people.

Bedel leaned forward. "Just because the mission has changed doesn't mean we've failed. The world is teetering on the edge of Kerdum. One life saved is a victory. Her life, by the time this is over, may mean victory or defeat. This imager—even if we can't read it yet—is a victory."

Shai's response came in a hoarse whisper. "But we still have to leave here to make any of it worthwhile. You're bonding to her too quickly, Elizenzer. She's bonded to bloody raptors who put us all at risk. From this little village to Peremaih and probably Lupacuo. Our peoples are at risk. The whole damn world." She tossed down the quill and groaned in frustration, rubbing her eyelids. "As much as I want to know what the Keeper of the South is up to and where the new Speaker disappeared to—"

Bedel kept his voice as soft as possible. "If they were in the same landslide, then he's dead, Shai. Huahanna is dead."

"That's another problem," she said after a harsh moment of silence. If she was trying to goad him into Cardor's spiritual affairs, it wasn't going to happen. He knew they'd failed to bring back a contender for Speaker of Men. The imposter who opposed everything Bedel and his agency believed in continued to manipulate the faiths of his nation's people. No one had to tell him that. She continued. "Now, I'm more concerned about the warlords meeting in Wonbai next week. This World Summit is only a cover for the war. You know that. I've got to have time to build up my cover story to get actionable intelligence while we can. My team needs me."

"I know." He glanced across the village, scanning through the boma wall for the shadows darting in the tall grass at the edge of the prairie. "If she is bonded, we can make the pack let us pass."

"You don't spend enough time in this part of the world," she grumbled.

He grunted affirmatively.

"Raptors don't let you pass, Bedel. One night, they'll start pulling people from their beds. There's screaming and weeping until there isn't anyone left to weep. But if we take the road to Lodornatha or north, they'll hunt and ambush us from every direction—especially if we travel at night. And if we make it out, the rest of the Wo'Huzziet are as good as dead because those raptors will come back to where there is food. None of us can *Beast Lead* like she can. She better damn well wake up, or you're going to have to fly us out of here and explain to—*everyone*—why so many people died."

Bedel held firm. Both his king and Grand Essencer Xathon had wanted the Wo'Huzziet survivors to stay secret, so the slavers didn't return. But the Wo'Huzziet were as stubborn as Huahanna had been. They refused to leave. Now other predators surrounded them. "You're not wrong, Shai. However, if we act too quickly and awaken her before her body has had time to heal itself, we'll slow the process. Maybe halt it. Shai, she might not walk again."

Shai's mouth quivered, but the half-Elf had gained control of her emotions again. "That would be unfortunate."

"I thought you'd understand."

She swatted at a fly buzzing nearby. "Bedel, I can empathize. If I lost the use of my legs, my whole life would be over. But there's a world war coming—and something perhaps worse than that—and I can't solve anything here in the middle of a ruined civilization. Maybe if there had been anything left of the Ntokup Archives, but you saw the rubble. I need books. Advancers' help. You're going to have to wake her." She hesitated, not making eye contact with a group of women staring at them from a hut. "These people don't need us here, either. Our people have hurt them enough."

"One last night's rest for the patient," Bedel said. "We can get started in the early morning. As you eloquently phrased it, the last thing we want is to travel at night."

Shai shrugged. "I'll accept the consequences as long as we can get to Wonbai. From there, we start our next mission." Shai rested her hand on the imager. "Then I'll take this to my people; see what the Advancers or scholars can do. What the Memory Lark can tell me."

Bedel stood. "I'm going to get some sleep."

Shai chuckled.

"Did I miss something else, Lady Shai?"

She shook her head. "You and I. We sit here talking about the deaths of a Keeper and Speaker—our spiritual leaders—and we don't even shed a tear. Why?"

"Never met either of them before this week. Neither wanted to stay long, either."

"Or maybe we just don't care?"

"Maybe not. But neither of us believes that. So we keep her alive. I think we know they went back for her, despite what they didn't say. If she was worth their lives—"

"Don't finish that sentence."

"—then maybe Huahanna's daughter is our mission now, Shai."

"Crows, Bedel." She was actually even more attractive when she swore like a Cardorian.

"I'm not the mystic," he said.

"No," she said. "You're the damn jar baby."

Bedel felt his face harden. Moment ruined. He'd shared what little he remembered with so few people, to hear an insult from someone he trusted

"Get some sleep, Shai."

"I will shortly," she said, cracking a smile.

His silence spoke enough. Her expression changed to remorse, just slightly. Bedel sighed and shook his head. They were tired, scared, and hot as Kerdum itself. Bedel pried his sweaty shirt off his back to let air in. He let one hand brush Shai's hair. She smiled.

Bedel left her at the table and weaved his way through the poles and two other tables, where village women had brought laundry to hang around to dry. Huts lined the center of the village in a semi-circle, with the chief's longhouse at the opposite end. A large fire pit sat in the very middle. Granted, it was a cookfire—but this was a strange place. *Was it necessary?* Two rangers finished their meal, sitting and chatting with a pretty Wo'Huzziet woman who kept a traditional long, inward curved short-sword at her belt. They looked unconcerned with the heat—or with the stars above. He nodded to them and headed to the hut the tribe had provided. Night had come quickly, and with it, the blue stars fixed in their places. They formed constellations, or at least it was easier to consider them that way. One of the great long-necked beasts of the south, a bow, a gryphon or dragon—he couldn't decide which—and a serpentine shape. But the stars themselves were beautiful, strange, and still as bright as two days ago when they first appeared.

The Wo'Huzziet called them omens, but that didn't keep them inside or afraid. The rangers looked sorrowful, but wouldn't explain why. And he and Shai? Though lit in the blue light of stars, they were in the dark. Failing at even this.

Bedel entered his hut. A Wo'Huzziet had started a fire in the floor pit. Wasn't it hot enough? He took off his shoes, then climbed on the creaky cot, pushing aside the itchy yeht hair blanket and pulling up the net to keep bugs off.

The door opened.

"Really?" he said.

Shai unpinned her long, curly hair and let it fall around her shoulders. "I shouldn't have said that. I apologize."

"We don't even know if that's true," he said, watching her as she undressed.

"Don't we?" she asked. "Those imagers are from a different time. A different history. The only ones who know that history try to hide it. You're from that history, whether you want to believe it or not."

Either that, or I'm a bastard of the greatest essencer alive. It was a thought he didn't welcome.

With one bare foot, she tossed her clothes onto a stool. *Fields, she was beautiful.* Bedel let her climb in beside him. Noses touching, the powerful tenderness of her beside him rewarding. He was not alone.

"And this history," he whispered, hands wandering. "Ties all of this together."

"I'm afraid, Bedel Elizenzer Riess," she whispered as he wrapped the insect net around them, then pulled her closer with his arm. Elizenzer, Elvish for lover.

He smiled and stroked her hair behind her pointed ear. "I am, too, Shai."

Few people in all the world were entrusted with some of the most dangerous and foreboding secrets. Knowing that some truths were kept from the general populace, Bedel and Shai had long assumed Xathon and Mnai were grooming them for something more—like these two missions.

"I need to know the man everyone's afraid of isn't involved in the war to come," she said. "I don't know if we can stop him."

"My father did, once."

"Your father doesn't know you remember."

"I'd like to keep it that way."

She kissed him—and he returned it with the dread that

conversation carried. At once their auras joined, a beautiful flash of silver-white light that only they could see. They made love, shadows dancing on the hut wall. Passion and grief carried them into tears and joy, tender and desperate, and it seemed the terrors that haunted the world drained away.

CHAPTER 9

BEDEL WALKED IN BLUE STARLIGHT. A STONE WALL, TALL AND strong, was behind him. It hid the sounds of the battle, the abominations cutting down the citizens of the city, his charges.

My charges? he thought. *This is a dream.*

He turned. A woman stared at him. She wept.

"What did he do?" the woman asked through her tears.

"Where are we?" Bedel asked, realizing he was naked before her and she didn't care. This was their bond, forged in his efforts to heal her.

What had he done?

"My home," she replied.

Falling leaves and shaking branches drew his attention. He turned away from her and gaped as animals of every sort used the trees to reach the top of the walls, like some sort of siege. He looked back to the woman, but Huahanna stood there instead.

No, not exactly Huahanna. His form was translucent, silvery, ethereal. Without warning, Huahanna fell to the ground, a long blade at his throat. Whoever held the blade was shrouded in darkness; the blade itself seemed to float. Suddenly, Bedel understood.

Huahanna had tried to send a message, all this time, buried within the woman's quintessence.

Her name was A'banna.

"I couldn't give the Speaker gift to her. I didn't have time," Huahanna said, the tattoos around his eyes, mouth, and nose seeming to shine. "Everything I did was for her. Alain was correct. If I had listened to him, we'd be alive. They would be alive." He gazed back at the looming city wall, tears flowing down his cheeks. "She is conflicted about me now."

"Who she is? Who is A'banna?" Bedel demanded.

"My daughter," Huahanna said, pointing upward to the blue stars shining through the canopy. One of the new constellations was long, serpentine—like one of the great sea monsters.

"My daughter is the Leviathan. All the Speakers and the Keeper agreed," Huahanna continued. "Alain and I had to go back to get her out, but I couldn't tell you or her."

"Huahanna," Bedel said. He could feel A'banna somewhere, prowling. "What happened?"

"Horrible things." His eyes shifted, looking elsewhere. "I love you, my daughter. Your help comes from the hills."

Behind Huahanna, a massive cascade of mud, rock, and uprooted trees came rushing down the side of the mountain like the thundering host of ten thousand mounted knights, the hiss of a thousand serpents, the cacophony of screams, hoots, and calls of a thousand people and animals, and the roar of a red dragon. There were eyes above it all. Two pairs—one silver and cold, exuding patience and malevolence, the other black as night, with threads of a raging fire within.

Bedel ran. He glanced away for a moment to see her again. A'banna looked at him. She was horrified and surprised.

Then the mudslide engulfed them.

BEDEL AWOKE. HIS MIND RACED WITH WHAT HE HAD SEEN—AND how it could have happened. Shai was correct. In his efforts to heal A'banna, he had connected with her deeply. His mind wandered with the possibilities.

He relaxed against Shai, pressed together in the darkness. The fire was nothing more than red coals. They still had each other.

Just as he nearly settled to sleep, he heard wood groan, cloth rustle as it was pushed away.

Shai moved, ever so gently. She'd unsheathed a dagger under the pillow. He could feel her muscles tensed, coiled for action.

A hard, thick breathing filled the room. It was a raptor, silent and warm. Its dark shadow seemed to consume the entire space. The fire barely lit it. Feathers of blue, green, yellow, and a red underbelly speckled with brown. Black claws unfurled from two lanky hands. It sniffed at the roof, at their clothes, then its long snout shifted toward them. One eye, illuminated by the dying fire, was black as night. Its teeth were yellow-white. Its breath was hot and stank of death, even as it cascaded over their naked forms.

Bedel should have been terrified—but there was a single ethereal thread, clear as day, trailing from it through the wall and toward where A'banna slept. She was connected. How and why didn't matter.

Shai's warning from earlier crossed his mind. *First, they come in the night, dragging people from their beds.*

Not this time. Not her. Not him. Bedel held Shai close, as if he might lose her, then projected a long thin string of his silvery ethereal to the raptor. Instead of cutting off the thread, though, he joined with it. In that moment, he felt A'banna shudder, and suddenly saw through a dozen eyes. The raptor was decorated with more color than its bright plumage—and these colors radiated anger, curiosity, determination, and hunger.

The *cuelatchanli* reared back, yet a new color flashed along its thin, beastly aura: shock. He could read it now, feel it. Its intent was the hunt and to set its pack female free.

She will come with you, he said through the connection. The raptor shuffled backward, feet scattering the coals, fire singing and filling the area with the brief odor of burnt flesh. The raptor snarled, hooted.

Shai sat up, pushing the netting aside, and held the dagger ready. Bedel slowly rose behind Shai, both naked, exposed, vulnerable.

"Get dressed," he whispered. Slowly, he slid into his underwear, but the rest of his clothes were out of reach.

With the raptor inside, there was hardly room to move. Everywhere, they would be within striking distance of its jaws or the vicious dew claws arched casually in the air. Even with the thick feathers, the raptor was heavily muscular. A fight in here was questionable.

"Bedel, what in Kerdum are you doing?"

"You know what!"

The raptor moved forward. He pressed back.

Bedel threw a glance at Shai. "Get dressed!"

Dagger out, Shai crouched atop their bed and slowly moved along the perimeter of the hut. She fetched their clothes. Still, the *cuelatchanli* lowered its head, snarling at her.

"Hey!" Bedel barked and threw more of his ethereal into the thread. It took a step forward, dirt turned to a puff of air in the movement.

Say it! A'banna's voice in his mind advised. *You can hear the words. You can hear me, as I can feel you.*

"Cahuila!" Bedel said, the foreign tongue surprising both him and the *cuelatchanli*. The raptor's head swiveled back as the aura flared red. It snorted at him.

Bedel felt as though he could hear its vague thoughts. It did not know this—him—as anything but prey.

Bloody fields, Bedel thought.

Bedel's heart began to hammer his chest. Shai stood, clothed. Silent, she reached out, leaning as far to him as possible, his clothes in her hand. Her extended arm was so close, that when the raptor breathed, Shai shivered.

Trembled.

No.

The raptor lunged at her arm.

Cahuila! A'banna cried out in his mind.

Bedel sent a desperate cut of ethereal into the air, urging it to action. The essences answered, hardening into an invisible shield between Shai and the predator. The raptor's head slammed hardened air. The raptor staggered. Shai gasped. That shield wouldn't hold a second time. Bedel lurched forward and unsheathed a short-sword from its hiding place below the bed.

Bedel shouted and ran forward, driving the sword at the raptor's neck—but it moved at the last moment. The blade sank into the beast's torso, missing anything vital. A'banna screamed, and the raptor squealed. Blood spurted as it flapped its wing-like arms. Bedel hopped, barely dodging a big curved claw that lashed out at his neck and then torso. Shai screamed and leapt forward, knife out, shoving it into the raptor's eye.

"Down!" Bedel ordered it, hopping onto its back and still gripping the sword. The raptor was huge, a good twice his height. It rocked, trying to buck him off, but he pressed his thighs in. Claws reached back to rake against his shoulders, but his grip limited those. Shai's grip kept its head from turning and biting, but eventually, it ripped itself free, and she dodged, rolling out of the way and against the wall of the hut.

Down! Lay down! Bedel repeated, this time through the ethereal. Though he knew it was futile. He'd wounded the predator; it had no intention of doing anything but killing him.

The raptor hooted again—and something answered it.

In the dim light of the fading fire, Bedel saw Shai's face, terrified. Wood splintered as the entire hut buckled. A long, yellow snout slammed through the hut wall, snarling and snapping.

Shai scrambled back and snatched a hot rock. Skin sizzled. She screamed and slammed the rock on its snout.

Bedel placed a hand on the raptor's neck and poured ethereal and the essences of calm into it, though his own heart slammed in his chest. He tried to focus on a single essence to calm himself, but he was pouring too much in trying to forge a connection with this hunter. It knew only one thing. Bedel ripped out his sword, felt hot blood on his skin, and slammed the pommel down. The raptor rose on its hind legs, tail whipping behind it, knocking over a small table. It reared again. Bedel fell back, hitting the wall. A leg kicked toward him, long black claws shining. He lurched to the side, barely missing the deadly blow. Instead, the claws lodged into the wall.

Bedel rolled, reaching for his sword, even as the raptor twisted free. Wood splintered, dust and shards flew. It snapped at him, massive jaws, hideous and huge, its great teeth not even a handbreadth away.

He sensed another menacing presence in the doorway. Shai cursed, but he didn't have time to look over. He scrambled up, barely missing another bite. The raptor swung its head. Sharp extended teeth sliced Bedel's chest as he was thrown backward and hit the wall.

Air rushed out of his chest. He shook his head, fighting off blurry vision. Shai dodged a second raptor. She rolled, snatching her dagger, and sprang to her feet. Even as she did, her free hand circled the dagger, which glowed with all the colors imaginable.

This was her magic. Steel stretched, as if an unseen hand pulled it, yet it did not thin.

The first raptor turned on Bedel.

Don't make me do this, he thought. The raptor snarled, rearing back. Bedel shook his head and called out to the essences. The bed levitated as if floating on water. Bedel had air upend the bed, slamming it into the predator. Before it hit, straw and twigs rained down on his head. Bedel glanced up, expecting to see another raptor—but it was A'banna. His patient leaned forward into the hole she'd made, the dagger still extended.

"Cahuila!" The raptors stilled at her command, then slowly backed out of the hut. They hooted, before darting for the boma wall. The Wo'Huzziet couldn't let them pass. Any predator that had penetrated their defenses would do so again. He felt an odd pity for the beasts who had just tried to kill him.

Bedel called out to the essences, and the furniture tumbled to the floor.

He looked up again at the young woman with beautiful large brown eyes and hair darker than even Shai's. She stared back, her lips quivering. She tried to jump into their hut but instead fell. Bedel caught her, tried to steady her. He could see the thin, wispy, ethereal line stretched between them.

"No," he whispered. "No."

A'banna stared at him. "Riess," she said.

"Bedel Riess," he corrected.

The Avocan smiled wearily. Her eyes rolled back into her head, and she went limp in his arms. She still breathed, though shallowly. Exhaustion had overtaken her weary body.

"Shai?" he called.

His half-Elf lover stood in the doorway, looking oddly at them, elongated knife in her hand. Bedel swallowed. Here he was, naked and holding another woman in his arms. A woman he'd been bonded to. He knew Shai could see it. Heat rose in his neck.

"I'm fine," Shai said, a single eyebrow raised. "I think. Is she?"

"Alive." He shrugged at the discarded furniture. "Uh, I threw the bed."

"Right." Shai turned it over then helped him lay A'banna down.

Outside, the twang of bows, followed by two howls and large thuds. *A waste*, he and A'banna thought. *A horrible waste.*

He felt Shai's warm breath on his cheek, a hand on his shoulder. "As my lover, I can say you are very attractive without clothes, but not all of that blood is from a raptor."

Bedel let go of the woman's hand and turned to Shai. He reached out gently with his aura. She was terrified, grieving, but uninjured. Shai held his clothes.

"The villagers?" he asked, dressing quickly.

They both looked toward the door, but a ranger stood, discreet enough to keep his back to them and face hooded. The ranger's hood shifted slightly as he said, "All accounted for. The predators were put down. We've called everyone to the walls."

"Bedel, if she's fine, let me tend you."

He brushed a strand of hair from A'banna's face, recalling his dream of her and Huahanna, then went to the stool. The village apothecary didn't bother averting her eyes as Bedel finished dressing. She set down bandages and a bowl. "Another dose of our medication, to assist the healing and resist infection."

"Thank you," Bedel said. "There's a noticeable difference. I don't think she could have broken the fever without it."

"No, she could not have," the apothecary agreed, giving him a warm smile. She helped A'banna drink it, then tidied up.

"That'll be all," Shai said curtly. Both Bedel and the apothecary stiffened at the dismissal. The Wo'Huzziet woman, however, grunted, her glare turned dangerous.

"Thank you, is what Lady Shai meant," Bedel said.

"She shall remember your example next time, I am sure." With that, the apothecary left, shoulders back, chin high, bowl in both hands. She snorted as she passed Shai. She disappeared into the darkness outside the hut; displaying Wo'Huzziet prowess.

"A little respect? She's been helpful."

"I warned you," Shai said, washing away blood with a rag. "I told you what could happen if you pushed yourself too far. She's unconscious—and even if she was awake—she's too unstable and untrained." A rag pressed into the wound on his chest. Bedel winced.

On the bed, A'banna moaned. The silver thread connecting them was thicker, far more solid than before.

Shai held his gaze. "You can't undo this, Bedel. You forged a *Zitaya*."

Bedel shivered as she resumed dressing his injuries.

"No essencer in their right mind would form a *Zitaya* with anyone." Her hand hesitated. "Not anyone they didn't expect to spend the rest of their lives with, together."

"I don't know how it happened," he said, trying to assure her.

"Of course not." She huffed. Her shoulders shook. A tear rolled down her cheek.

"I love you," Bedel said. "We'll find a way."

Shai put her hand on an uninjured cheek. "Bedel Riess, for being one of the best agents the Magical Affairs Commission has to offer, you are truly a fool, aren't you?"

"Shai."

She shook her head and hurried with the poultice. "There is one way to break a *Zitaya*, or do they not teach that at your precious Academy?"

"They only give a warning. I know it, but there has to be a way."

Finished, Shai stood and went to the door. Her stare was professional, drained of the emotion that had filled her moments before. "Get dressed. There is only one way to break a *Zitaya*, Bedel. One of you has to die. In that moment, so does the other."

Bedel had barely finished dressing when Shai abruptly left. His stomach clenched. Surely they'd get through this. There had to be a way. She had to be worth the risk, right?

What risk? The woman's voice sounded alien in his head. Bedel could see her, running through a field, keeping pace with five raptors. But that couldn't be accurate. The Avocan woman was lying on his bed, still.

Why does the lord of the stars sound like my father?

Bedel nearly cursed. The Avocan woman stirred.

"I'm not lord of the stars," he said aloud.

The Avocan groaned, her head turning in his direction. He could see movement behind closed eyelids as if she were in deep sleep.

Bedel shifted his gaze to the door. Shai couldn't be far. Surely there was a way.

Long ago, he and Shai had discovered knowledge few living knew about the history of their world; how magic and cycles and history functioned, and about the meaning of the stars above. Forbidden knowledge that had cost people their lives. It was why they lived on a knife's edge when it came to the Elven side of Shai's family or, at times, even his own father. There was no doubt in either of their minds that they lived because of their abilities and use to those in power. Missions like this were evidence of that. Both had pushed the boundaries far, but they always had each other.

Bedel looked down at the Avocan, sleeping peacefully. Did she know?

History and prophecy were often intertwined. If the Avocan was the Leviathan of the stars well, Leviathans never survived the star cycle. If history stayed consistent, the Avocan would be killed, and he would die, and Shai would be alone.

Bedel gazed at the Avocan as she slept. How things changed. He picked at the bedpost, unwilling to admit they had lost all hope. The Avocan had become his mission and likely something more. There had to be a way to sever the *Zitaya*. Shai was wrong, on occasion. His hand gently touched the thick thread of ethereal stretching from him to the Avocan. He could hear her, a soft voice that seemed to come from within him.

My name is A'banna, star emissary.

I'm not I'm Bedel.

Her grief merged with his regret. In the whirlpool of emotion, their memories swirled, reflected as the sun shimmered in water. They experienced it as if through their own vision: Huahanna sat in a room by a chest, surrounded by pillows, smiling as he held a raptor claw; Alain laid on a stone table, strapped down, smiling up; Bedel's brother hiding him in a barrel from the evil Judicator; blue stars shining above them, illuminating the forests and domed buildings of Lupacuo as they pledged their love; Raynt as he urged him and Shai to disappear rather than climb that bloody mountain. The clamor of war and images of battle and death of man and beast from each of them swirled, melding. Grief, guilt, love, regret. Huahanna's message repeated over and over between memories. The speed and detail of it all was staggering. All at once, the whirlpool of emotion burst, like a vase shattering and spilling liters of water as rain. Each of them gasped for breath. Water dripped steadily. Those were the only sounds as A'banna, and he stood alone in a dark chamber, water just below their ankles. All around them were secured doors; the vault experience from when he had touched his father's staff. Yet his father Xathon was there, clad in red, critically evaluating. A raptor shrieked. Unseen forces wrapped around both he and A'banna, pulling them away from each other and out of the room.

Bedel shook as he kept his footing. He was in the hut, but he could still hear the genocide in Avoc-Nezlticoulti as if he had been there. He'd seen battle before. Like any soldier, he needed sleep, though it would be light. After retrieving the short-sword from where it lay, Bedel cleaned it with a rag and placed the blade across his lap. Arms crossed, he leaned against the wall of the hut and slept.

CHAPTER 10

IN THE TALL GRASS, A'BANNA WAS ONE WITH THE PACK AND THE pack one with her. Every few minutes, the man would come and join them, kneeling next to her. The pack sniffed him. The alpha female hooted at him, both in anger and frustrated acceptance.

A'banna, I'm sorry.

So am I, Bedel, son of the stars.

I'm not lord of the wait, son? How do you know that? He asked, shifting to look at her. He crouched with his elbows on his knees. His beautiful hazel eyes peered at her.

I don't, she said. It was confusing, eluding, but somehow she felt her father's knowledge inside of her. *But my father did. The others told him. I think he gave that to me when he died.*

I didn't see that in the—whatever that was. How did he die, A'banna?

Her dreams turned into a nightmare.

But Bedel was there. He watched as she wiped the war paint from her father's face, exposing the tattoos of another religious order she knew nothing of. He listened to Huahanna share his story with her. When the raptors and marchers came, Bedel embraced her tightly. He witnessed Quin murder Huahanna.

Bedel took her hand and walked her away from her father's draining body, from Quin and the marcher and the mudslide. On their walk atop the river surface, Bedel pointed out the rangers he had been with when they found her.

I'm not god, Bedel said as they watched the memory of him carrying her through the jungle. *Just a person. Like you.*

You're more than that.

A'banna showed him the memory of his brother hiding him, but Bedel waved his hand. The memory rippled away.

A'banna, did Quin survive?

I don't know, she said, feeling afraid.

Next time, we'll handle him together, he said.

I don't want there to be a next time.

I understand, he said.

And together they were on the ship. Fire spread. The deck was stained with blood and littered with corpses, and Hurmlen standing proud and defiant on the deck. *Quin has his stance, in the way he holds the sword,* A'banna observed. Black and red fire surrounded Hurmlen's jagged sword, and wind snapped his coat tale.

Now we both know, Bedel said at last. *They are all coming for us.*

A'banna squeezed his hand. *How is this possible?*

I'll explain when you wake, he said. All at once, they were inside the village again. When she opened her eyes, Bedel was gone, but she could feel him nearby. A'banna slept, feeling safe.

⸻ ⸻

"BOAR-MEN! HAVE YOU LOST YOUR MIND?"

A'banna stirred at the shouting. She knew that voice. The half-Elf.

"As you said, Shai, we're bonded. I see her dreams. Her memories."

"Great. I hope you damn well enjoy reliving our times together."

"If the Sorceress has your magic—"

"No one who has the Gift uses it to turn people into monsters."

"How can you be sure?"

"How are you? Hurmlen siring a little bastard with the bitch I understand. *Beast Leading* thousands of snakes, I understand. Making people into monsters? Unheard of yeht shit. Bedel, I expected better from you."

A'banna stirred, groaned. Her entire body ached. She felt the pain in her legs, her head. She dimly recalled carving a hole into the hut's roof to save them. But she still remembered the mudslide, the trauma vividly. A'banna coughed, rolled onto her side. She looked up, surprised at the sun shining through the doorway, of the figures outside like shadows in the light.

The half-Elf barged past Bedel, hands on her hips. "It's about damn time. I thought we might be in another planting season by the time you awoke."

Exhausted, A'banna gave her a hard stare. *Unreasonable.* She held the glare as she tried to sit up. "Sorry to keep you waiting, Shai."

Without warning and holding nothing back, Shai backhanded A'banna, throwing her back. A'banna felt the hut shudder as she hit the wall. Pain arched through her face, neck, and shoulders. She tasted copper.

"You had no right," Shai whispered. "To form the bond. No right."

A'banna tossed hair out of her face and wiped blood from her lips. She groaned as she tried to move again, sit up. It was slow, but that worked in her favor. As Shai started to turn away,

A'banna lashed out, fist curled, knuckles connecting with Shai. The impact on flesh and bone of Shai's chin threw her backward. A'banna's feet scattered the cold gray ash and coals of the fire pit.

"I did not try, essencer," A'banna snarled, then collapsed back onto the bed. "It just happened."

"For not trying, you stole him from me," Shai said, regaining her feet.

"Shai," Bedel said, stepping into the hut. "It was life or death."

Bedel moved further in, trying to put some space between them. "It started with the healing—and that raptor would have killed you—"

Both women raised a hand. "Stay out of it," they both snapped.

They glared at each other.

"Did you know that the man you slaughtered on that damned altar of yours was the son of the Keeper of the North?" Shai said, angrily. "Now, the Keeper is the only one holding the Sorceress in check."

A'banna's jaw dropped; she pressed a hand to her stomach, trying to quench the nausea. But battle didn't wait for vomit and grief.

"In check?" A'banna laughed bitterly. "You think he's worked a magical ward to keep her south? She will bide her time, but she is coming, Elf. And when she does and brings her *Marchers*, you will wish you had listened to me." A'banna hesitated, glancing at Bedel. "Listened to him, I mean."

"Because of you," Shai snapped, "there is no one to take the Keeper's place when the immortal finally becomes mortal. It will happen."

"It hasn't happened to the Sorceress," A'banna said. Her legs felt weak, but rage filled her.

"She killed to get where she is."

"Thousands of years ago."

"A different history."

The two women were nose to nose, each bleeding from their mouths where they'd hit each other, bruises swelling. Their hands were clenched into fists.

"I never wanted this," A'banna said.

"But both Keeper Alain and Speaker Huahanna believed you needed it," Shai said, shaking her head. "You were a waste of good lives."

A'banna swallowed. "Then train me, if you are so powerful. Both the Sorceress and her son liked me wild." A'banna bit at the air. "They refused to let anyone train me. Who is to say the death of the forest animals and the city is not my father's fault, but mine?"

She jabbed at Bedel, who stood with his arms crossed. "Because he dream-walks with me? I am the murderer you wish to kill, Shai." She lifted her chin, exposing her throat. A'banna's eyes stayed locked onto Shai's. "*Ni mictici.* Kill me."

Shai's hands rose, and then she looked away, hands falling to her side. "I can't."

"Why not?"

"If I kill you, your bond will instantly kill Bedel. It's called a *Zitaya* life bond. Once my people used it to deepen the love of marriage. Because both of you did not manage your own connection with the world fabric and all that moves within it, you created one, solidified it through that raptor. You can dream with him. Hear him when he is away. Feel his pain, though not like he feels it. You may speak across the greatest distance we can know. And for all of that, every moment I could share with my lover becomes one, I would have to be willing to let you share as well. Bedel has been the one person in this world who knows what I know, has seen what I have seen, and knows the end of our history is near.

Have you ever known relief? Passion? An escape from the burdens you have to carry?"

"No."

Shai's face twisted into remorse and grief. "Then enjoy what you stole from me. I won't forget."

Bedel shook his head and leaned against the wall, back to them.

"What's he thinking, feeling, right now, bitch?"

"My name is A'banna."

Shai raised an eyebrow.

"Shai, please," Bedel said.

A'banna tremored, frowning. She could sense his depths without needing to read his aura's colors. It was like swimming, becoming one in a dance with the water's rhythm leading. It was wonderful, rich and soothing, yet his emotions were as tumultuous as a storm.

"He grieves his mistake. He is grieving you. He is worried about your grief. It kills Elves. Is that true?"

Bedel's head fell, blocked from view by his thick arms. Shai backed away, trembling.

"No more than raptors in my bedroom," Shai whispered.

"They are masters in the forest," A'banna said. "I cannot control them on a leash."

Such an obvious point should not have needed speaking, but the half-Elf was in grief.

"You did a good job last night," Bedel said. "I did what you suggested. It didn't work."

"They don't know you."

"But they know you?"

"My father and I have hunted their pack since my youth. Some I cradled when they were young, and the nest was abandoned. Yes, they know me. They came to us in the wild. We had nowhere else to run. But knowing and not killing is not always the same thing."

"They will hunt again tonight," a stern voice in the doorway said.

A'banna sensed the animal accompanying him. The snake-eater. An Elf stood there, clothed in browns and greens, bow and quiver and spear sheathed on his baldric. A large ferret stared at her, like a dog at its master's feet.

Bedel gestured toward her. "Idrin, this is A'banna, daughter of Huahanna, Speaker of Men."

"Idrin," A'banna said. "Are you a ranger from Lodornatha?"

He saluted, fists over his heart. He bowed, eyes strained skyward. "I live for the hunt and the people of all lands," he said. "Huahanna was known to us, favored by the high kings and queens of our mountain realm."

A'banna nodded. "He said your scholars taught him, Idrin. My imager was found in the river, yes? Along with the book my father made from the Sorceress's diary?"

Shai glanced at Bedel. "That's right," she said sharply.

"It should go with Idrin for his high kings and queens."

"I should keep it," Shai insisted. "It should go to Lupacuo."

A'banna shook her head, dark locks flailing. "No. My father dreamed of a man who looked like Bedel and one with green skin. He saw that I would fight in the north, in a land called Cardor."

"Well, I'll be yeht—"

"Are you sure?" Bedel interrupted as Shai finished a string of swearing.

"Our dream walk was real last night, Bedel Riess, son of stars."

"Bedel!" Shai shrieked, horrified. "How could you?"

A'banna sensed his fear—real fear. This was not something she should know.

Stay out, she heard him say.

But Alain said I should embrace the stars. If you are their son—

"No," Bedel snapped. Everyone looked at him curiously.

You don't understand, he told her.

I wish to.

I know.

He sighed and tried again. "I didn't tell her. Huahanna shared that within the ethereal cylinder of memories. It took a bond to find them. Healing started it."

"The dream walk finished it," A'banna said. "My father lied to me and all our people for a very long time. Now we know the truth, but Quin, bastard son of the Sorceress—" she glared at Shai, whose eyebrows were raised, "—slaughtered him before the hills' wrath came."

"But she knows," Shai said, gesturing at A'banna then the ranger. "Now, Idrin. Can we trust you?"

Idrin stared at Bedel with a new fascination. "I will forget I know the Gatekeeper has appeared." He bowed slightly, in his odd manner.

"Thank you," Shai and Bedel said together.

"But are there Taurs here? Have they heard?" Shai ran a hand through her hair. "Ancestors and crow spawn, Bedel, I—I can't protect you anymore." She gestured to A'banna again. "You bonded to a suicidal, murderous, self-absorbed witch of a priestess. Good job, hope-of-the-whole-damned-world. If she kills herself, all of Aelathia is damned to a Taur-infested Kerdum. Thanks ever so much."

"You know of The Taurs?" asked A'banna.

Shai didn't answer.

"The Sorceress worships them," A'banna said. "She said they wanted Alain as an offering."

"I'm sure they did," Shai said, looking at Bedel with a desperate expression.

"Can the stars stop them?" A'banna glanced between the three. Surely, someone would have an answer!

For a moment, no one spoke.

Shai started, but Bedel held up his hand, interrupting her. "It's not about the power within the stars, Shai, but what and who they represent. It's a cycle, one with no discernible timeframe or predictable occurrence. All we know is what happens after they appear. Five people are anointed with power to face a threat that endangers the whole of the world. The gift of Speakers is returned to the races that have lost it. And a Gatekeeper is born, to keep The Taurs from infesting our world like they did, a long, long time ago."

"And you are the Gatekeeper?" A'banna asked.

No one answered.

Bedel shuffled in place. "Do you remember the dream walk by that city wall?"

"Yes," she whispered. "Right before I woke up and the raptors attacked you."

Shai gasped and turned away, pointed ears red. A'banna wondered what she felt. *Embarrassment? Anger?* Shai muted her colors, a deliberate effect, making it hard to ascertain. *Or control. She fears me.*

Do you blame her? Bedel said, letting his frustration at A'banna's lack of mental restraint come through their connection. *Her world changed, too.*

"Your father appeared," Bedel said aloud, as his thoughts finished in her mind. "He called you the Leviathan, which is why both he and Alain felt they needed to return."

"What do the great sea serpents have to do with me?" A'banna asked. "I have never seen one. They are of the north and colder waters."

"It is not an actual beast he's referring to, your Grace," Idrin said.

Shai started to protest the title but stopped.

"I don't understand," A'banna said.

"It's a correlation to the stars," Shai said, still turned away. "Leviathan is one of the four current constellations the new blue stars make. The others are the Letter, the Dragon, and the Behemoth. Eventually, they'll form the Rose."

Bedel completed the thought. "The newly returned gift of Speaker of Men was lost, along with the future Keeper, to save one of the five Chosen. You."

"Chosen for what?"

Shai turned and looked to Bedel, then to A'banna. "To save the whole world. I think you should tell us more about the boarmen. And then we really need to talk."

CHAPTER 11

No one deserved to have *CUELATCHANLI* threatening an already struggling civilization. They were A'banna's problem, and she intended to see it closed, one way or another. A'banna stood at the front of the boma wall gates with nothing but a Wo'Huzziet inward curved knife strapped to her back and wearing a bleached white hide dress. Two feathers from the fallen raptors had been braided into her hair. The heat beat down upon her. The scent of the tall grass filled her nose. Her body broke out with gooseflesh, sensing the predators concealed by the overgrown field around her, .

Where are you? She thought, scanning the grass for movement, for color, anything. Wind rustled the tips, causing her mind to race. Even if she returned to the dirt path that stretched to the southwest from the village, the raptors could ambush her there. She hastily made her own clearing, chopping at the brown grass with her long knife.

Creaking wood made her turn. The gates opened. Bedel stood in the forefront, wearing Wo'Huzziet leather and holding a sword and buckler. Behind him, the three Rda warriors and their young trainees stood in a line behind him, spears up. Their expressions were grim, ready for death. Each of them had a long, oblong shield strapped to their opposite arm. Chief Martuza stood behind them, with Shai next to him. Rangers flanked them on all sides. On top of a wooden platform on the other side of the gate, their ranger captain, Idrin, crouched with an arrow notched in his bow. Other archers—both Wo'Huzziet and ranger—stepped up on platforms around the boma wall, whistling to each other.

No contact, she sensed Bedel's thought. *They don't see the cuelatchanli. It'll be an ambush.*

Bedel stepped through the gate—and it shut behind him.

"No!" she shouted. "The cuelatchanli are my problem I brought on you all."

"That's the most pressing problem, but not our only one. Shai and I came here to rescue you."

"I don't need to be rescued," A'banna said, turning away from him. She needed to be sharp, undivided.

Bedel came near, touching her shoulder with his fingers, letting her know it was him at her back.

"You shouldn't have come," she said.

"Well, I thought if these cuelatchanli are going to kill you, I'd prefer a notice before I die, too." Bedel offered her a small smile.

"I can't save the whole world."

"Good news is you don't have to do it alone. And now that we're stuck together, we better get used to it."

A'banna rolled her shoulders, sighed, and stepped back into the tall grass, tracing her hands along the prickly tops. Whorls scratched gently against her skin. Each step parted the grass like water, and she waded in. But there was no escaping walking blindly into the mercy of the raptors. No way to return Bedel and Shai's freedom and hope. A'banna still wasn't sure how she formed the bond in the first place. It was new to her. To him. To them.

A streak of fear lashed through her like she hadn't experienced since she was a child. Terror distorted her world, transforming every leaf into the barrel or a mast of a great ship, engulfing her in the chill of driving rain and dreadful cold, when actually the morning sun had just begun its oppressive vigil. Death stalked here with a sword flaming black and red, sizzling but never extinguished. Black eyes—silver eyes—with streaks of crimson in them searched.

Hurmlen, Quin, Jocina. They were one and the same. They were death stalking them.

Control your fear, she thought. *They are drawn to it. Feed off of it.*

An image of a floating flame passed across her mind. The terror was gone. Packaged away.

We are one, aren't we?

In thought, emotions, and more, he thought. *Yes. Thank you for wanting to end the bond.*

But we can't, she thought, remembering his fear.

No. We need not to die. Let's talk. Aloud.

"Hurmlen hunts you as the Sorceress hunts me," she said, voice soft, searching the long grass for anything extraordinary. "And the raptors and The Taurs hunt us both."

"This marvelous life," he said.

Two watchers whistled staccato bird noises.

They saw one. Bedel's thoughts had grown firm, hard to understand. It didn't matter now, the watchers were correct.

To her left, grass swayed as something brushed against it.

Another whistle as a streak of blue and red darted behind a single crooked tree to their right, its large expanse offering the only shade she could see.

"They're trying to flank us," he whispered.

"You'll make a good hunter, yet."

Love's fine until a dragon flies overhead, he thought. *Or something like that. So helpful, Idrin.*

"Why would love change, then?" A'banna asked. "Love is needed even when there is danger. Why would he say differently?"

She felt Bedel's embarrassment, and flashes of attraction for her, and deep loss for Shai. Bedel grunted. "We'll need to find a way of gaining some privacy if this is going to continue."

She nodded.

Grass swayed off on her right. A straight line, headed for them. She could feel her raptors, but they were silent to her. Another blur darted directly ahead, across the path.

"When they come, use your hands, not your blades unless absolutely necessary."

"Aye," Bedel said. "If you would let the archers fire."

"No! No more death."

A'banna and Bedel both pivoted, tracking the same streak as whistles sound from the wall. A'banna kept her head on a swivel, searching, taking nothing for granted in the field.

"I see one behind us. It's running circles around us."

"A distraction. Watch your sides."

She could see three lanes of grass rustling. One adjusted, moving left as if it sensed her. She saw a blur of brown and red feathers. Silence. In the village, an auroch mooed, and a yeht stomped the ground. A dog barked. Then they too went silent. The only sound was the watchers' bird whistles.

A long whistle followed by a short sound.

Idrin has a shot.

No!

Bedel whistled back, three short sounds.

A'banna fought the urge to turn and glance at the red-blue beast that was running in shrinking circles around them. All of the grass suddenly settled, rustling only in the wind.

She tensed and relaxed her hands. Fear gnawed at the back of her mind, but she couldn't give in to it. Grabbing the knife was unacceptable now.

A black-gold reptilian eye watched her from the grass, about sixteen rods left of her center.

"Yeht, A'banna, I just saw a fifth one."

She swallowed and hooted, sounding very much like a raptor. She wanted them to know she approached peacefully. "Impossible. The Wo'Huzziet killed two last night."

"Did they? I only saw them roasting one."

A'banna hooted again. *Keep your eye on it,* she thought to Bedel.

Bedel whistled: *I count five. You?*

Idrin whistled five low staccato tones.

Confirmed, Bedel thought. *Five raptors.* He paused. *For being deadly predators, they're beautiful.*

A'banna abruptly smiled.

And something roared. Four hoots responded. The streaks resumed, circling outward. And then they were gone.

"That's no raptor," Bedel said.

One of the Wo'Huzziet archers stood on his platform, shouting in their language. A second archer stood, echoing the first. They sounded panicked.

"What in Kerdum was that?" Bedel whispered.

A'banna unsheathed her knife, bracing herself while keeping her vision as wide and focused as possible. On Bedel's wrist, a knife blade popped forth from a bracer. A second was in his hand, ready to throw. Where it had come from she hadn't seen.

Heavy footfalls heralded the unseen predator. But the grass swayed, and the blur was a golden yellow.

"Hold your fire!" Idrin shouted in common. "Hold your—" His voice drifted off. She could sense Bedel trying to make sense of why he had frozen in place, staring ahead. Bedel turned and stepped beside her.

A man stepped out from the grass. Steel and silver-plated armor covered him, but white-gold light shone between thin gaps on his armpits and knees. He was bearded. Despite this, he did not sweat, as if heat had no effect on him. A sword of glimmering jewels shimmered from his belt—no sheath to hide its beautiful blade. He held a simple rod staff, crooked at the end. But his skin had a fine crystalline texture, glistening, like a ruby or sapphire. His eyes blazed with the blue-white fire of stars.

"Bedel Riess, A'banna daughter of Huahanna, I greet you in the name of Theantros."

The armored man bowed.

"The Oppressor?" A'banna asked.

The man chuckled as he straightened. "They've always seen it that way, haven't they? I am Epus, Caur of Beasts."

"I don't care who you are," Bedel said, looking away. "There are five raptors out here."

"Indeed, and I bring a friend for someone I cannot meet in the north. Leviathan, Gatekeeper, when you meet the Dragon, send my regards and this companion."

Epus started to turn back into the long grass. A'banna felt Bedel's curiosity rise. The man was fearless.

"Wait," Bedel called. "Who are you, Epus Caur of Beasts?"

He slowly turned at the hip, just enough that they could see some regret on a suddenly shining face. It burst into blue flame, burning and withering the grass around him. The fire engulfed him, turning his staff into a pillar of shimmering blue-white light. The heat was almost unbearable, the brilliance near-blinding. They shielded their eyes.

"An old god," Epus said, his voice coming from the flame. A blue-white hand gestured behind him. "My gifts to the Chosen of Theantros. And for the sake of my kin who want this war, my apologies for what we ask of you."

"He is a star," A'banna whispered in terror. She prostrated

herself in the dirt before this god. The one she had searched for. "My lord, my lord!"

"Dear sweet child, you bear my magic. Only if the stars were as kind. You are still searching for answers, but I can only give you what I have. Fire and beasts. I do not know if we will meet again."

A'banna wept, she did not know why, but when she finally forced herself up, Bedel was on his knees, practically thrown backward. The noise of shouts and weeping rose up behind the boma wall.

What had been the figure of a man, Epus, now shone with the brightness of a blue star as it rose above the ground. The man was no more, only a ball of light. And then the light disappeared.

Flickers of color consumed A'banna's vision. Every muscle in her body trembled.

"God Epus, return, my lord!" she cried out. "Forgive me!"

The only sound was weeping. Her own, and the villagers. Bedel's thoughts raised with vague ideas, concepts, the words Caur and Taur interchanging with the image of a moving eye, gazing out of a mountain.

Where Epus had stood was now charred, blackened earth.

A breeze rustled the grass, tossed her hair, stroked her cheek. A woman whispered.

"Epus has always been fond of exits," the breeze said. The leaves of a nearby tree were carried upon it, and for a moment, A'banna was certain she saw a woman. Her skin appeared like translucent crystal but also clear water shimmering in the sun. The woman was adorned in a colorful dress of leaves with turbulent wind for hair, standing over the spot where Epus had just been.

"And a gift for both you and the Gatekeeper, my dear children." The female Caur touched the blackened ground. Soil rose, exposing rock and stone beneath. The mound split open, and fresh green grass sprouted like cascading water, dotted with flowers of shapes and types A'banna had never seen before, and mushrooms that glowed blue, making the colors stand out even more. They blossomed in blues, pinks, purples, yellows, reds, and inside them a ring of rare mushrooms and herbs, good for medicine and health. Most had stopped growing in Avoc years ago. Ferns grew quickly, stretching high above like a protective wall. In the center of the mound, rocks split, tiny stones fell away until they crumbled as small as sand. There, in what had been the rocky center, were three perfectly formed ingots, enshrined in the newly grown vegetation. The ingots were silver and gray, like steel, yet with runes carved throughout, lines and circles, shapes and designs she couldn't process. The runes flared with blue and gold light when the sun's rays fell on them. Beautiful metal wreathed in green life.

The female Caur smiled and gestured toward the garden. "My gift of earth and starlight steel. Seeds for your survival. The village apothecaries will understand. I will be watching."

Then she, too, burst into a blue light and shot into the sky. In that moment, the breeze disappeared.

Movement caught A'banna's eye. Not all the grass burned, nor did the fires spread. A wall of grass surrounded them, far from the garden mound.

From the wall, Idrin's hasty staccato whistle came—five notes punctuated by a shocking sixth.

Five raptors emerged from the grass wall, lined up like soldiers for an inspection. The males displayed their red underbellies and expanded their colorful tail plumage like peacocks on display. Without a sound, they opened their toothy jaws and clicked razor-sharp claws on their long fingers. The two females, with their feathers' demur colors and sleek brown snouts, topped with four teal spikes like a long mane, stood silent and matronly. The largest of them all was the alpha female who had helped A'banna in the woods.

They stepped around the clearing but not inside. Each foot had one sickle-shaped claw on the inside toe, pulled back from the dainty arch into the leathery pocket. This was death, standing at attention.

A'banna shook as she and Bedel stood. He had blanched. They stood side by side, their silver ethereal bond uniting them.

Each raptor shifted a foot forward, claws retracted even more; raising their tails, they bowed their heads. Close to the alpha female was the raptor who had attacked them last night, whose eye had been cut by Shai and shoulder injured by Bedel. No animosity, no gesture of a threat, no colors signified danger.

Out of the tall grass stepped a massive, muscular lion, mane thick and golden, head held high. It trod forward to stop in front of the raptors. The lion and the alpha raptor acknowledged each other, with a passing glance. Anything more meant they had the intention to kill the other.

The lion's eyes blazed with blue starlight.

Impossible, Bedel thought.

The lion also bowed to them.

A'banna felt her aura rattle as a voice rumbled over it. Bedel shared the shock across their bond, his thoughts drowned out by the sound of the voice. *I pledge myself to service to the Chosen, until we face the Red Dragon, The Taurs, and their Chosen. When they hear our roar, the dragons' power ends. Until then, I must remain silent. Courage, my friends.*

The blue starlight faded from the lion's eyes.

It's not a lion, A'banna thought to herself.

A'banna's heart thumped loudly in her chest. Her mind raced with thoughts she couldn't answer or give voice to. In the midst, she remembered her father describing his dream; how he saw the *cuelatchanli* would bow before her. She thought of the man with golden hair in the rowboat, how he had commanded the sailors and those behind him. And there was a lion among her raptors.

"The gift for the Dragon," Bedel whispered, as if he had realized something. "The controversy?"

"What does the Dragon want with a lion if it defeats itself?"

Bedel gained a measure of courage, and stood, feet spread apart, arms at his sides. He nodded to each beast, as if greeting new companions. A'banna smiled, meeting partial gaze with each of them—but not daring to make direct eye contact with an untamed predator, no matter how peaceful they appeared now. *Cuelatchanli* could attack at any time, if they chose, and it only took one to set them all off. She couldn't risk it.

Bedel went to The Caurs' garden, stooped over, and hefted the ingots. Finally, he stared at A'banna. He was shaking.

"I don't even know where to begin."

Bedel held up the ingots. The runes shone with white-gold light, just like Bedel's eyes.

The lion stepped toward him, nostrils flaring. It bowed lower, as if the Caur-lion was in the presence of a mightier god than itself.

A'banna gasped, touched his elbow, and then she too began to glow with the white-gold light, spread across their silver ethereal bond. They shone like the sun. Both of them felt like they were being watched. They turned together, both mutually realizing it was foolish to turn their back on these predators, but the power was it did something within them. Brought something alive.

It also brought reality.

Shai, Idrin, Martuza, nearly all the rangers and villagers had gathered on the platforms, or in the newly opened gate; those that could not fit were trying to see between the spaces of the boma wall.

"Hail the Chosen!" Chief Martuza shouted. The village broke out, ululating. The Rda warriors beat their spears against shields, swaying to the beat the villagers made. The Elven and Dwarven rangers cheered, following Captain Idrin in raising their weapons with every, "Hail!"

The people the Wo'Huzziet they're smiling, Bedel thought, astonished. *But Shai*

The animals half surrounded A'banna and Bedel, like honor guard. Soon even the raptors hooted in time, and the lion purred.

A'banna looked where she felt Bedel did. On the platform behind Idrin, Shai lowered her head so her long hair hid her face. Then she climbed down from the wall and disappeared into the village.

Up, Bedel thought. *I went up.*

CHAPTER 12

THE RAPTORS AND THE LION LAY DOWN OUTSIDE THE GATE together. Not a Wo'Huzziet in the village passed that gate without a spear or blade in hand, steeled for the hunt. Archers were paired with a warrior on the wood platforms, keeping an eye on the visitors. Vigilant rangers worked with a few craftsmen and the Rda to erect makeshift wood platforms. Bows nocked. The sun started its decline in the sky, and the blue stars shined on.

Whispers were everywhere. The beasts were divine gifts. The Caurs had come. Had Theantros remembered us? Bedel grimaced as he moved through the crowds gathering in the village center. Some reached out to touch him, as if the glow would return or maybe he could heal them. Their voices called out, desperate. He felt so inadequate; he was standing in the presence of survivors and still denied himself. He smiled, desperately wishing he could tell them they didn't need him to save them.

He tried to say something to A'banna but heard her say, "He's a lovely child. You are a survivor and should be proud you can tell those tales to the baby."

Bedel's mouth dropped as he swiveled on his heel, people misreading his intentions by crowding around him.

A'banna took the baby a woman held out. Laughing, she smiled and made cooing sounds as she cradled it. A tear streamed down her cheek.

Quin again. The pain throughout her body; his teeth on her lips. The force of him. The desire for marriage. For love. For children. How much Quin said he loved, but it was hate. I wish I knew he was dead. But how long had she wanted to hold a child?

Bedel blinked, trying to slow the rush of emotions he felt from her. Then he allowed himself to see the way she cared for the villagers. She was as close in skin color to them. She was no northern false savior. They knew it. They knew she was bonded to him. Bedel smiled and took an elderly woman's hands. In her Wo'Huzziet dialect, she began listing off names, weeping.

"Forgive us," he managed when the woman slowed. It was in that moment he noticed the scars where a blunt weapon had hit her head, took in the lines of middle-age on her face, the fury and fervor in which she tried to communicate her message. He was deaf to it.

A man cleared his voice. The crowd paused, turning to face the chief's longhouse. Built on a wooden platform a foot above ground on pylons, it was a natural place for a speaker. Beside Martuza stood the village apothecary and the elder Rda, the one missing an eye, effortlessly bounded up the wooden steps behind them.

"We cannot offer you that," Martuza said. "We Wo'Huzziet were attacked, we were brutalized. We offer you to find us justice by bringing those who led these acts of war to justice. That is the atonement the north can provide. But you, Bedel Riess Morbrook, have not caused us the harm you think you have." Martuza then cast his gaze wide on the gathered villagers. "My people, I need to speak to the Chosen. Let them be and take heart. We are not forgotten. We will continue to rise above the ashes the north tried to reduce us to. We are Wo'Huzziet."

A few people cheered, but they let A'banna and Bedel through. They followed Martuza inside the longhouse, flanked by Idrin, the Rda elder, and the apothecary.

Benches and tables lined the longhouse walls. Roots, vegetables, and herbs hung drying from the rafters and rounded struts, as smoke from a fire rose through an opening in the wood and grass roof, curved at a beautiful angle that belied the architectural capabilities of this civilization. At the far end was a loft, and a wall. Beyond that, before the war, would have been the chief's livestock. Now it served as a storeroom. In front of that wall, on a small dais, was the chief's chair. Bedel studied the design, metal and wood, carved and smelted together in angles and curves, with a hexagon shape carved above the chief's head. The hexagon was designed with runes and six enchanted essence jewels, one at each point. The center of the hexagon was indented with a smaller hexagonal shape, but this lay empty.

"It's beautiful. Those runes, those designs. They are like the tattoos on my father's face." Bedel felt a wave of emotion from A'banna. "He had the spirit of a Speaker, he said, of the god, Theantros. Which god is greater? The Caurs or Theantros? Or are they Theantros' servants? Like the center of the carving, I feel empty without knowledge."

Martuza, who had made his way to the front and had yet to sit in the chair, turned. His gaze softened, framed by his gray long hair and beard. He looked grandfatherly. "Dear Chosen, you have spoken true. True, indeed."

Without answering, Chief Martuza Cougareyes stepped onto the dais and took his seat. The seat was draped with hide and fur coverings and claws hanging from leather chains; the latter jingled like chimes when he stood or sat. "We will take counsel, now. Captain Idrin, serve us wine from your people, a generous gift from old friends and warrior brethren. Your people bled, died, and were taken with ours. They are family."

Out of the sheath of a fur, he withdrew a rusty blade, hilt inlaid with beads and jewels. Blade down, he struck it into an armrest. "We begin."

Idrin bowed his head then walked to a serving table where a barrel of Lodornathan wine had been tapped. They'd brought several with them as a gift. Idrin filled goblets and mugs as were available and passed one to each person present. After he served the apothecary, Idrin stood before the elder Rda, his one eye locked onto Idrin's, and he nodded his thanks without ever breaking his brooding glare. The rangers and the Rda, the great warriors of their time, and drinking allies. Their attendants, two young people, stood behind them. "Go on," the apothecary said.

The young man, holding the Rda's spear, looked to him. The elder nodded once. Idrin gave them each a partial mug of wine. Both bowed.

Bedel brought forth the three silver-gray starlight steel ingots and set them on the short table in front of the dais, practically at the chief's feet.

A'banna and Bedel gratefully accepted the wine. Idrin stood to the right of the chief and met Shai's gaze. "Your ladyship, if you wish to share, the tale is yours."

"I wish to be on the road. I don't know what magic she pulled out there—"

Idrin's face hardened, and Shai silenced.

"Enough!" Martuza snapped. "I have six of the deadliest predators napping at my people's gate! I called for counsel. I said we drink together as one. But if you Lodornathan and Lupacuo Elves desire to fight amongst one another, I will *not* have it here. Not anymore. I want answers. Quickly. No more Elven games."

Shai and Idrin both seemed to bristle with that, glaring across the table at each other.

Idrin bowed slightly. "It has never been a game to the people of Lodornatha, Great Chief."

The old warrior, once steward to the lost great house of Bloodskulls turned chief, growled.

Idrin gestured for the half-Lupacuo Elf to say something. All she added was: "I am also Branaird, and was raised as a gypsy. I am Lupacuo out of need, not out of desire. The dissent between the Elven peoples is true, but though I am their agent, I do not wish that upon anyone here. I do not seek conflict, great Chief." Her voice softened, avoiding Bedel's gaze. "I never wanted conflict."

The chief nodded approvingly. "We are, then, making progress. Lupacuo did not betray my people like Cardor." His harsh, judgmental gaze swung briefly over to Bedel. "But I know our allies there. I received word that an Agent Raynt went searching for you two, Bedel and Shai. He joined with one of our Rda, who killed one of the great northern heroes who made war against us."

"Raynt?" Bedel said, breaking into a smile. He and Shai exchanged knowingly, even happy glances. "How do you know this? Can we communicate with them?"

"I have few messenger birds, Bedel Riess Morbrook. The Magical Affairs Commission must be content to rely on its own network until they return."

A friend? A'banna asked, excitement in her voice. *Both of you seem relieved.*

Raynt is an ally if we ever needed one. The three of us have served often enough, together.

I look forward to meeting him.

"Great Chief," Bedel said. "You said Raynt and your Rda killed a hero from the Slaver Coalition. Do you know who?"

"Captain Braissen McCormack, captain of the Black Ship *Batoidea*, which led the fiery siege on Ntokup for a decade. Your transport, it seems."

"It was a mistake, and a relief to learn he has been killed. But he has lieutenants. Children in service to the Coalition."

Martuza and the other Wo'Huzziet present all spat. "Claudia and Kestov McCormack. We know. When all three are brought to the justice of our ancestors, then we shall seek peace with some in the north again, in earnest."

"It couldn't happen soon enough," Shai muttered. "But they're dangerous. Worse than their father."

Martuza stared at her, nodded. The claws on his chair chimed. "On that, we agree. They killed High Chief and Chieftess Bloodskull in battle, stole their daughter Naminia from us, and stole my children. I remember how they tore through our Ntokup, slaughtering like rabid animals wont to do. Help your friend bring them to Wo'Huzziet justice, and we welcome talks with the Magical Affairs Commission again. My wife was denied battle by Claudia herself. I shall have justice for us all."

Bedel and Shai both bowed. "It will be our pleasure and honor, Great Chief."

The Wo'Huzziet in the back of the room let out a short, elated ululation in support.

"Excellent," Martuza said. "Now, The Caurs visit us. You shine like the sun. An Immortal leaves our land and the woman who arrives, claiming to have been warned by him, is the daughter of the Speaker who left my hospitality without farewell. Now, these great predators act as housecats. Tell me what is upon us."

The ranger, Idrin, set down his iron forged cup and bowed. "Once, long ago, my people told the tale of the death of the world," Idrin began. "From its ashes came the Sorceress we've learned more of from Alain, Huahanna, and now A'banna. But in the death of the world were gods and there was a great sundering of them. Some embraced the darkness and fire that became the death and breaking of the world. We know them as The Taurs.

Others sought the light of the stars and became more beautiful than their brethren."

"Myths my ancestors do not tell, my lord Idrin," Chief Martuza said, brow furled. "Our archives in Ntokup spoke of the breaking and the Sorceress, but not as myths. But you say The Taurs and The Caurs were once one and the same?"

"Yes."

"Is this told in the north?"

"No, Great Chief Cougareyes. Most ancestors do not tell, do they Lady Shai? Agent Bedel?"

"My people," Shai said. "Of the Elves, at least, say this is nothing more than a myth. The Taurs have always been The Taurs, and only Theantros exists to keep them in balance."

"But keep them in balance with what?" Idrin said, eyebrows raised.

"The fire and the stars?" Shai murmured.

"Or is it a balance between types of fire?" A'banna said. "I have seen the Sorceress use a dark, oily fire that is cold and yet burns and destroys and gives life. The Taurs dwell with her. Today, we saw The Caurs. And I felt another fire."

"The Taurs and The Caurs," Idrin said when no one else answered. He frowned sadly. He put one hand on Bedel's shoulder. "Dark fire and the Well of Light."

"Don't," Shai said.

"Lady Shai, ignoring the truth does not make it less true, nor prevent what must come in the end."

Bedel grimaced and shook off Idrin's hand.

"It would be simpler if that were so, Captain Idrin," Shai said, her voice even, but her stare threw daggers. "But the fire we saw today isn't easily accessed but by a rare few. Dark fire is embraced by radicals and villains, but a hint of it remains throughout the world fabric. Ethereal is spawned from star fire, which the more religious of us would say comes from The Caurs.

The only balance here is ethereal and dark fire, not a battle between the Well and everything else."

Bedel stayed still, trying to ignore A'banna's thoughts questioning which of them were correct—or if they both were.

Idrin's voice hardened as he moved to the center of the room. The normally quiet man gestured to accentuate each point:

"The stars have come. They burn blue as a Caur. The Taurs have come, or you would not be afraid, Agent Shai. The Gatekeeper was reborn as prophecy predicts."

"Sorry to obliterate that reasoning, but I've been around for a while," Bedel said. "Whatever The Caurs or The Taurs want to call me is wrong. I'm not a Gatekeeper."

"The Gate, as it stands, is unreachable now," Martuza whispered.

Shai bristled. Bedel looked away. A'banna gawked. They all understood. The implications were horrifying, if true, but was there enough proof?

He knows where it is, just as we had feared. All that time Shai and I spent in her grandfather's library, we uncovered the truth. Which meant my father can't think that. I can't think he'd deliver me into the hands of Elves and an Immortal near the tear between realms itself. Not Xathon. Unless my adopted brother, Jacob, had been right about him. Was that why he betrayed us?

"Continue and ignore my pondering," Martuza said.

"As I was saying," Idrin continued. "The gift of Speaker was returned to Men and perhaps others. And five are Chosen, including the Leviathan."

A'banna shifted in her seat as Idrin pointed to her.

"The Caur mentioned the Dragon, and there's a dragon constellation in the northern sky," A'banna said.

"Correct, your Grace. Many of the scholars and astronomers of my people say it was improperly labeled. It should be a Lion. Perhaps the common misconception is why the Caur introduced the mysterious addition as such. Ignoring the truth does not make it any less true."

Bedel felt A'banna's tension. Her raised pulse, the thumping of her heart. Yet, despite her fear, she was overjoyed and also ready to weep. *This is why I didn't die,* she thought to herself. He was glad she found some meaning in this. Even though he knew the varied teachings and lore they discussed, it was frightening. The only meaning any of it gave to him was suffering and death —and whether she wanted that now, it would be hers, too.

I am a lamb to the slaughter.

A'banna turned, wide-eyed, searching his face. He shifted away.

"Damnation, Idrin," Shai said. "No wonder Lupacuo and Lodornatha don't get along." She gestured to the ingots. "Why don't you fill in the rest of the story? How about the Bloom? Or what starlight steel is supposed to let you accomplish? Theoretically. Considering all of the Dwarf smiths who knew how to work the metal died thousands of years ago. Unless the knowledge was saved from the archives?"

Martuza cast a critical gaze at Idrin. The answer was *no,* then.

"She speaks truth, Chief Cougareyes," Idrin said. "All of the great starlight smiths are dead, but some of their forged weapons exist to this day. The one Chosen as Dragon—or Lion—will bear one. They are mortal Man's defense against the dark fire of The Taurs and their servants." Idrin faced Shai. "I do not believe these ingots were given by the Lady Chinweda, Caur of Earth and Light, to A'banna and Bedel hoping they will throw them at the enemy like rocks." One of the Wo'Huzziet youngsters chuckled, but Martuza cast a displeased look in that direction. Idrin continued, "Nor do I believe she could have forged these alone. There were other Caur who did not present themselves, just as at times The Taurs hide themselves from those in our realm."

"I understand that," A'banna whispered. "The terrible cold, as if kissed by the point of a dagger or thorn, a soft hideous caress you wish to hide from."

"The Caurs were purified by the Well, A'banna," Idrin advised. "You have no need to fear them. Did you feel chilled?"

"No," she said, considering Idrin curiously.

"What of a large bird?" Martuza asked. "You served the Sorceress. Does she have large birds at her disposal?"

A'banna gasped. "The Velheron. She made them like the other monsters. How did you know?"

Martuza's expression was blank. "Six-winged birds were seen watching the last battle of Ntokup, until at last the smoke stilled and the morning came. And our Rda warrior aiding Agent Raynt reported one watching the Black Ship *Batoidea*. So she has an interest in the destruction of my people, then."

"I am afraid that can be the only explanation. She sends them as her eyes, her ears, and occasionally her agents."

Bedel noted the elder Rda and Martuza exchanged knowing glances. The Rda ducked out of the longhouse, then returned a minute later. "A watch has been set, Chief Cougareyes," the elder spoke.

"Well done, Bominga."

Idrin nodded approvingly. "It is logical if she learns of us or The Caurs assistance, she will send her minions."

"Yes," A'banna agreed. "She will."

Martuza growled. He sounded very much like a cougar. He gripped the rusty blade and dug it a little further into the chair, lips peeled over his white teeth. "I await their arrival."

"The forest still resists her," A'banna said. "Though I nearly died in its wrath, it will hold her back for as long as it can."

"If only we all had such faith that the essences cared that much for us," Shai said, shaking her head. "The essences are fickle and do as they like. Whether they aided you or not, you can't know or trust they'll do it again."

She's always been a bit of a cynic, Bedel said over their bond.

Why do you think she's the cynic? A'banna thought back, eyebrows raised. *I hear your thoughts, remember.*

Bedel felt heat in his cheeks. *A touché, indeed. It's a dueling term.*

I understand dueling, A'banna said, shaking her head and crossing her arms. *I'm no fool, even if I have much to learn. Stop treating me as such.*

Idrin spoke on about the ingots and said Shai's name, drawing Bedel out of his thoughts.

Shai had sat back. She shook her head and gestured at the metal bars. "Those are Belasna-blessed. Same runes as that Wo'Huzziet crown jewel—and Speaker tattoos. I cannot safely work with any material that has been inscribed with Belasna." All focused on her now. She crossed her arms again. "You can't ask me."

Disappointment and tension settled in the pit of Bedel's stomach like a heavy weight. "Shai."

She gave a pleading look to Bedel.

Not this time. "You wove a boy child in the womb of the Queen of Cardor at their request," Bedel said. "You can do this."

"That was different," she said.

Chief Martuza Cougareyes rose to his feet, and all the Wo'Huzziet reached for weapons. "What manner of magic is this, Shai? You crafted a child?"

Shai grimaced. "They needed an heir, Great Chief. Their rule was threatened, and the new Rultritans are the only ones trying to stop the slave trade that has ravaged your people and lands—and the roads traveled by my mmother and the Branairds who raised me. I did what I had to do—what they requested of me." She hesitated, looking at the ingots, then at Bedel. "My magic isn't like others. And I had a template, so to speak."

Bedel felt the tension between his shoulders release.

Martuza slowly sat, fingers on one hand clenched, the other edged closer to the ceremonial dagger. Bedel glanced to the back of the room, at the small court. The apothecaries seemed intrigued but silent.

What does this mean? Why do you think of yourself? A'banna asked through their connection.

Not now, he thought sternly.

The Sorceress has breeding pits. Does Shai?

Breeding what? No! Bedel thought, sternly. *I am not a fool, either.* Then added, *Please.*

It was a logical question, A'banna thought, exhaling audibly.

The leather of Idrin's armor crackled as he stepped forward. "Will you attempt to forge weapons for the Leviathan and Agent Bedel?"

"The three of us will discuss their preferred weapons." Shai raised a finger. There was a glint in her eye. She had thought of something. "But I cannot promise success."

Idrin gave her a half bow.

Shai met Bedel's gaze. She was terrified. For him.

"I know you're afraid, we all are."

"Are we, Bedel?" She half-rose from her seat. "Do you know what they're asking me to do? When you leave this village holding starlight steel weapons, at some point, very soon now that there is a cycle, someone is going to notice."

Her finger tapped out code for a name. *Raynt.* Could she be right? Were Raynt's knives starlight steel? It would explain the flames. Then where did he get them?

Shai continued. "The Taurs will hunt you down if they learn of it. If Idrin and Lodornatha—or my father and Lupacuo—have their way, you're going to die by the end of all of this. Along with probably half of the Chosen, if not more. I—"

"Everyone dies," Martuza said from his throne.

"Great Chief," was all she could manage.

"Even those we love. It is for those of us who live that victory or defeat is sweet or bitter."

Shai nodded, deflated. There was a dark quiet over the room, as if the dead and the absent were listening.

Idrin stepped to the serving table, grabbed a knife from a chunk of meat, and lodged it into the wall. "This represents Avoc in the far south. Jocina the Sorceress is here." He pointed at the wall. With another fast action, he grabbed a fork and stabbed higher. "This is the north. Cardor. Where the gap between realms is believed to be. The Seven Larks disagree on its exact location. It seems that their disagreement is valid, Great Chief."

Martuza did not move or speak.

If Idrin suspected what they did, what would that mean for Lodornatha Elves? Where did they stand on sacrificing him to close the tear? And how would it work exactly?

Idrin continued. "I believe Shai is most concerned about what happens when you head north again, across the Keeper Boundary."

"That boundary stops the Sorceress from coming north, but it won't keep out dark fire essencers," Bedel added, trying to move the conversation away from the gateway. An impossible task.

"Or The Taurs," Shai murmured. "And not all corrupt essencers use dark fire."

"Indeed," Idrin said, gesturing his thanks to both. "We expect you will find and unite with the other Chosen, preventing The Taurs from crossing into this realm by the thousands or millions."

"They save the world," Shai said in a hushed tone.

Idrin nodded. "Precisely. Meanwhile, in the South, Jocina makes her strategic move, whatever it is. Keeper Hokano's son is dead, and therefore, his lineage is gone. Unless he can sire a new heir, if Jocina can draw him from his circle of power, thereby shifting the boundary, the magic that traps her here—" He pointed to the bottom of his makeshift map. "Is gone."

Dear gods, A'banna thought. "That explains so much of what she's been doing. Why she hurriedly had him killed."

Idrin's face paled as A'banna spoke. "Many of us remember the last time she made such a gamble, yes?"

Martuza's chin raised. Bedel crossed his arms and leaned against a table. The Wo'Huzziet in the back stirred. Idrin himself had a forlorn look, as if he was deep in memory.

Grief, Bedel thought. A'banna met his gaze.

Idrin took a deep breath. "Idrin," Shai whispered.

"This is what you wanted, Lady Shai," Idrin said. "The whole truth. Dragons rained their fire upon my mountain city, burning everything."

"As Chief Cougareyes said—" Shai spoke quickly. It wasn't what she wanted, not truly. Bedel knew that much about her. But she had pressed him so far!

"Everyone dies," Idrin said, cutting her off. He looked to A'banna with a haunted expression. "Have you heard the story? Do they tell it in Avoc? When the Sorceress acquired a dragon? It happened while we celebrated a wedding during the Feast of Stars in Lodoronatha. The new Dwarven king married his beautiful bride. Hair so long and golden it was the train of her gown draped behind her. We were still adjusting to living among Dwarves; we did not fathom how their festivities and ours might diminish our attentiveness. During the drunken revelries, the rangers slacked their duties. Dragons and drakes emerged from their hives, drawn to the drums and flutes in the night." He paused, his eyes welled with emotion. "Hundreds of thousands of Elves and Dwarves died in the fires. My mother shielded my sister and I with her body. Thus, we survived.

"When the dragons were finished, and their drakes had their fill of ash and flesh, we climbed out from beneath what was left of her. And then Jocina learned to command a dragon. She flew it from the burning ruins of our upper city to Zeller. Chief Cougareyes, I know your ancestors tell that tale."

The Chief nodded. Only once in history had the dragons broken past the ranger's boundary. No one had forgotten.

"It's remarkable anything grew back in the ashen land," Bedel said, stopping Idrin from continuing. Idrin blinked, then sighed. *Step back, my friend,* Bedel thought to himself. "Rest," he whispered to Idrin. He offered a very fake smile to A'banna.

This is horrible, Bedel, A'banna thought to him. *You do not have to make it pleasant.*

I won't. All of us should remember. Idrin risked himself to tell the tale, A'banna. We all should remember what is at stake here, whether I agree with Shai's motives or not.

"Thank you, my friend," Idrin said, suddenly weary. "The worst is passed."

Bedel nodded and stepped aside.

Idrin paused, composing himself, then began again. "But the blue stars appeared. Many thanked The Caurs while wailing was heard from the heights of Lodornatha and all of the Wo'Huzziet tribes. The Speaker of Men, who was a woman then, anointed a blacksmith named Aruna as the Dragon and then the other Chosen. They set a trap and were able to kill the dragon before it crossed the Lakarth Mountains into Zeller, barely saving half a dozen civilizations. Jocina escaped. Children in Cardor and Franca tell it as a happy story. The triumph of love and faith. Aruna the Hammer, they call it, or Aruna and the Dragon."

"They don't even mention the Speaker," Shai said, not staring at the map. "Ironically enough, he would have failed without her or the others."

"Yes, Shai, Aruna would have failed without Speaker Aleesha-Saraine and the other four Chosen." Mouth open, she shifted his direction.

Point made, Bedel thought.

"It is a very different story we are told," A'banna said quietly. "She will try again. The signs are there, including our scouts reporting that Lodornatha rangers have pulled back from key outposts along the mountains that keep the dragons in."

We need each other, A'banna thought. *All of us. You wanted to remind her.*

Yes, A'banna. We need all of us. But no, I did not want to do this to Shai.

Bedel exhaled sharply, remembering the mountain, and that drew A'banna's gaze.

Bedel, what is 3.1415?

Forget it for now.

A'banna felt watched. She shifted slightly. Shai remained unblinking, evaluating A'banna.

Does she know?

A'banna, I said forget it for now. Please.

A'banna bristled at the second retort. He felt her resolve, and he hoped she could feel his regret at having to shut that down.

"It's all been real," Bedel said. "From the very first."

Idrin inhaled sharply. "What little intelligence the two of you have discovered, along with the testimonies of A'banna and Huahanna, it seems Sorceress Jocina has made elaborate plans to return. A single poison-laced, miraculously aimed ballista and a heavy hammer are not going to save the north. It's not going to save the south."

A'banna thought of the Sorceress with the viper wrapped around her leg while she drank wine, unafraid. And earlier, when A'banna had seen her gleefully drink the blood of the human sacrifice, licking it off her red-stained lips and her silver gown.

"No," A'banna said. "Jocina is no fool. She's creating an army with foul magic. Taking people and turning them into monsters."

"That's a lot of poisoned arrows," Shai said.

Clearly, Shai, Bedel thought.

A'banna stood. "At the rate the abductions were occurring when we left, the Sorceress will have the entire populace of Avoc mutated within two years. About one hundred thousand people. That's if she doesn't find a new method." She settled back onto the bench, glancing from Shai to Bedel.

Idrin stepped closer to the dais, directly beseeching the chief. "Great Chief Cougareyes. Bedel, Lady Shai, and my company are here because we were tasked to escort an Immortal and evacuate the new Speaker. Instead, the Speaker and the Keeper's Heir brought us a Chosen they valued greater than their own life. The Wo'Huzziet people have suffered. Lodornatha has suffered. Our forces are diminished, and yet it is at this time the stars appear and the Sorceress presses her advantage. She has allies of terrible power rooted in dark fire. We have reason to believe that the Glymphs of Greneld and the people of Zeller have allied against the north."

Bedel stood. "He's correct, Chief Cougareyes. We believe they're allied with the Slaver Coalition."

"My Rda warrior confirmed that," Martuza said.

"You knew?" Shai said. "We stayed here, tending to A'banna!"

A'banna glanced away. Bedel felt her guilt.

Martuza raised a hand. "Now, your friends will know when they receive my reply. The Rda, with Raynt and another one of your spies, revealed that. He said you have more to do and it is prepared for you."

"It's ready?" Shai blurted out, half standing in shock. "Bedel!" Then before she said more, she clamped her mouth shut and erased her expression quickly.

Bedel's heart beat quickly. *Raynt, my friend, there is a round on me when we meet again!*

"Thank you, Great Chief. It is a relief to us. We have no credible intelligence on what the Goblins, Istante, or Franca are going to do. If the Goblins or Istante join in, we'll have to fulfill the prophecy in the midst of world war," Bedel said. "Now we know all of this will likely occur while we find a way to stop Sorceress Jocina from attempting to destroy everyone." He had their attention. The question is, were they all friendly? There was only one way to find out. "We know the gateway's location is believed to be in the north by everyone but those in this room."

"No, on that point you are wrong," Martuza said. "If the Sorceress indeed has these birds, and they are her agents, she has doubts also."

Bedel and Shai exchanged blank glances. *We were right. Damn it! Father sent me here where they could have easily killed me. Which meant Alain knew. The mountain had known. Idrin might know. Father betrayed me—no not father, he's only the Old Man. Mission before family. That's what Jacob had meant when he hid me, so long ago. He was trying to save me from all of them, even Hurmlen.*

They would kill you like a lamb? A'banna thought, trying to get his attention.

It is how ancient civilizations used to worship gods, sacrifice.

Not ancients. Avoc, too. It's what she made me

Of course. I became inward-focused. My apologies.

A'banna ran a hand through her hair along her ear. She tried smiling, but they both knew there would be no easing the irony that she was groomed to sacrifice people, and he was destined to be a human sacrifice, and they were both now magically bound together—through necessity and by accident—until death.

Shai stood and seamlessly picked up where Bedel left off. "We know the north is about to be invaded." She gestured to the map on the wall while drawing Bedel out of his own thoughts. "We know Jocina is raising an army and has a history of obsession with the north. That's the bloody truth of it. Those stars are moving. The Bloom is near. Even if we all figure out the rest of the puzzle, the Chosen are not going to survive long enough to close the Gateway, especially if we can't find it."

Martuza cocked his head, chin out, as if amused by her direct confrontation.

A'banna's mouth hung open. She was stunned. Mortified. "No. No, we can't" She turned in her seat to Bedel. *How do we stop them? She can't let them do that to you! She wouldn't!*

No, Bedel thought. *She has no intention of letting it happen. She called out what they've been dancing around. She saw what they weren't saying and had to show all of us.*

Light flickered off a blade. Bedel only moved his eyes. The Rda elder had his spear. Somehow, his apprentice had a knife, hilt and blade partially concealed by his sleeve. The elder's one eye seemed to take in all of them but wasn't focused on a single individual.

Even if she needed to ignite a bonfire, Bedel finished. *Shai knows how to be a scalpel, hammer, salve, or a fire.*

And I can be a spear or a knife in the tall grass, A'banna said with a sneer as she cast a murderous gaze of her own at the Rda elder. She half rose out of her seat.

To his credit, Idrin stayed still, hands at his side, observing. It didn't ease a potential conflict of interest—meaning whether or not he'd let Bedel live—but the fact he stayed still enough to cast doubt on that question. Possibly. One of his feet moved behind him; the opening footwork for an Elven surprise hand-to-hand assault.

Helpful to know, Bedel thought to A'banna.

A'banna let out a soft growl, like a raptor and a lion, directed at Idrin and the Rda. Outside, Wo'Huzziet and Lodornathan voices and whistles sound loudly. A'banna's eyes flashed reptilian and back to her own. The wave of emotion from the animals staggered Bedel. He sensed they were ready to break the gate and storm the village to protect the pack.

In the back of the room, the apothecary and her attendant grew nervous, and even the young Rda attendant let his knife lower as they glanced at the door of the longhouse.

Shai raised an eyebrow at A'banna, pursed her lips, then cocked her head back at Martuza, eyebrow still raised defiantly. The chief's hand gripped the rusty knife's hilt tightly, grinding the blade into the wood. He had no illusions it would stay lodged in the chair for much longer.

Hastily, Bedel slid from the bench and stood beside Shai. His hand settled on her elbow. She started to pull back, but he stepped closer. Whispering so only Martuza and A'banna could hear, he spoke to what she didn't say, either.

"It's better to try to save a life, any and all lives possible, than to simply give up. Run away."

Martuza's brow furled as Shai's gaze left his. Her eyes centered on Bedel's. He had flashes of their decades together, their love, all bound in her watery gaze.

"I only ever wanted us to escape and forget the world. We should have never gone to that mountain, Bedel."

"I know," Bedel said, feeling the entire tension on the room—and probably the fate of the world—riding on this single exchange.

A tear escaped, running down Shai's cheek, but she didn't hide it or wipe it away. The more she spoke, the more deeply grieved and hoarse her voice became, until the final sentence came like a broken dam releasing all of its water. "We could have lived old together. Build that cabin on a lake, far away from all of this. You, me. Now, they're going to kill you. And her, too. We failed. I don't fail, Bedel. I love you."

Martuza cleared his throat. Bedel nearly jumped, expecting the chief to attack, but instead, he glared in Idrin's direction. Idrin had moved, a stride or two closer to the front. Martuza's bellow caused him to pause. The Elf kept his face expressionless.

"Continue, agents," Martuza said, loud enough for all to hear.

Still whispering, Bedel nearly choked on his words as he focused back on Shai. "Life doesn't give us what we want."

"Be honest," she said. "Your gods and our fathers don't give us what we want."

Wood and leather nearby gave a soft swish sound, as something hard released tension on it. Martuza's hand settled on the chair's armrest, leaving the ceremonial blade in the wood.

"I have no intent to allow human sacrifice on Wo'Huzziet lands," Martuza's voice rumbled. As if pronouncing a great, sorrowful sentence that grieved him also, he met Bedel and Shai's gaze, then A'banna's. When his scrutiny turned on Idrin, it morphed into a baleful, ire-filled scowl. "There is no great Gate here. Communicate this with my friends, your lords, to the northwest, and to those who govern in the northeast, should they desire peace."

Exhaling slowly, the tension in Idrin's body visibly released as he bowed.

"Remember The Caurs," Martuza finished. Idrin hesitated in rising from his bow for a split second longer.

Whispering so only the four of them could hear, with a face turned from the others in the back, Shai said, "My lord Cougareyes, thank you."

He gave her the simplest of nods, before turning back to A'banna. Bedel saw she was close to weeping. Her eyes changed again! They flashed to the reptilian pupils of raptors and back to hers. Moments later, whistles and cries of alarm and relief came as the guards signaled the predators had calmed.

"We have peace?" Martuza asked.

"We have peace, Great Chief," A'banna said, bowing.

"Very good," Martuza said. "Captain Idrin, do we have peace?"

"Yes, Great Chief."

"Very good. Now, why would the Grand Essencer of Cardor and the High Lord of the Elven Houses of Lupacuo conceal certain histories and information? If the Sorceress conquers and releases the dragons or some other horror, we will face disaster whether they wish it or not. The preoccupation on the Gateway does not stop that reality, nor will it. The Taurs are not needed for dragons to breed in their hives. And she has access to magic that is foreign to most of us."

Shai shifted but maintained a neutral expression.

Martuza continued. "Did you know that I have heard from Gaul—a group that parted from the Goblins—that their race returned to violent ways because of a man named Jacob Morbrook?"

"Impossible," Bedel whispered. "Jacob he's been missing for years. Even then, he defied Dark Judicator Hurmlen and spared my life when we were young."

"Not according to the trusted sources, including the Rda," Martuza said. "When family departs from us to evil, it is a vile and painful thing. But we must face it."

All of the time they'd been in this village, all of the consultations and meetings, and Martuza had failed to say this.

"Great Chief, you are saying my adopted brother, the biological son of the Grand Essencer, helped corrupt the Goblins to their blood-crazed ways?"

"It would make sense why Luchchik doesn't respond to messengers, and why they executed their Speaker," Idrin said. "And hung his head on a pike outside their main gates."

"Goblins are intelligent folk," Bedel said. "Some say they rival Elves and Dwarves in their science. Why would they reduce themselves to embracing dark fire?"

"Using dark fire is not unintelligent," Shai said. "And just because they are more violent and aggressive doesn't mean they are any less intelligent in the sciences. That's what makes them terrifying."

"I know this is horrifying news," A'banna said. "But your brother, Bedel? Why?"

Bedel still didn't believe it. Corrupting an entire race? "When Jacob turned, I was three years old and have memories too young for me," Bedel said. "I'm not supposed to remember, but I do. Hurmlen used my brother Jacob, but Jacob also stood against the Elves in my defense. And I remember him hiding me from Hurmlen."

Shai exhaled and gestured at the makeshift map. "Where do you think Hurmlen is? Not in Avoc." A'banna shook her head. "Greneld, then? Maybe. Where's Jacob? None of us know, but there is this one fact: we believe they've allied with the Sorceress. Bedel, you need to stay out of all of this. Stay safe, and I'll come back for you. For that cabin. Wherever you want it."

The idea was so appealing, so emotionally thrilling, Bedel had to caution himself. He could hear two heartbeats: his own, and A'banna's. And A'banna could feel his. She felt helpless, a sideshow in the middle of a village who had not chosen to be there. Or worse. She had invaded their lives. With her, came The Caurs, the revelation of power.

They were Chosen.

"I can't."

"If you go north, Xathon will want you. Mnai and Nadael already tried to play us, isn't that right, Idrin?" The Elf said nothing. Shai shook her head. "They're liars. Only Ismerdalia might keep you safe."

"She's my mother."

"Adopted."

"She birthed Jacob."

"Jacob is an evil tool. Some figs don't fall far from the tree." Shai glared at Idrin. "What about Lodornatha?"

"You already know our forces are just holding back the dragons and repelling the Sorceress' assaults from the south," Idrin said. "We are in the war. We always have been."

Shai growled. "Chief Cougareyes, with your leave, I will attempt to smith weapons from the ingots."

"And for my people?" the chief replied. "To defend ourselves?"

"I will do what I can," she said, voice hoarse.

A'banna stood as Shai approached the dais. Shai held out her hand, halting A'banna in her path.

"Great Chief," she whispered, her voice hollow. She took the three ingots and turned, holding each of the heavy and large metals in her hands. "I need a fire, a lot of workspace, no interruptions, and a good bed afterward."

"See to her needs," Martuza ordered. The Wo'Huzziet youth darted from the room.

Shai stopped, picked up Idrin's cup. "To death." She swallowed the harsh ranger beverage and slammed the cup on the table. "Burns. Good brew."

"Made with flowers grown near dragon hives."

"At least something grows from ashes."

"There is always life after death."

Shai shook her head, readjusted her grip on the ingots, and followed the old warrior out of the longhouse.

Idrin turned to Martuza, Bedel, and A'banna. "My knowledge is yours."

"Tell them about the Bloom," Bedel told Idrin and followed Shai.

"Where are you going?" A'banna called.

"To watch," he said.

Bedel followed Shai from the longhouse, but not before hearing A'banna say: "Tell me later."

The warm evening air seemed cooler outside. Bedel looked for Shai, who had headed to the massive fire pit.

"Shai?"

She set the ingots down on a log. "So, for you? An ancestral Istantese sword? I know you've always admired the design. Pity the Baktur had to go and make it their own."

"Shai."

"Bedel. What more do you want from me?"

He grimaced and looked skywards. Blue stars hovered in the bright, glittering night. "I don't know. Maybe a little more patience? Professionalism?"

She chuckled bitterly. "Oh, but we agreed that between you and I, we could leave all of that at the door."

"You ended you and I."

Shai rose from stoking the fire and pointed the red poker at him. "You and she ended you and I. Plus your devotion to these realm walkers."

Bedel knew A'banna was behind him. He could feel her, even though she stood outside the fire ring.

Shai continued as she worked, setting up her own little forge. "Don't be fooled, A'banna. The Caurs aren't gods any more than The Taurs are, or Theantros is. They're a bunch of supernal beings from another plane of existence that get to cross over into ours and masquerade as being omnipotent, so we'll bow down and do their will. They're realm walkers, pure and simple. And bastards for manipulating us into fighting their own little war."

The two youths brought back strips of leather, a table, tongs, a hammer, and an apron. "I'll need fire and lots of it," she told them. "Something hard" two of the old men lugged an anvil on wheels. "That'll work perfectly." The youths ran off for wood.

Shai shrugged. "And they've been hiding this where for four weeks?"

Bedel chuckled and shook his head. Shai deflected tension with humor. He enjoyed it. Usually.

"Why do you hate them?" A'banna said. "They've saved my life so many times."

"Did they? Or was that, hmm, maybe Alain, your father, and Bedel here. Not to mention the village herbalist and Idrin's people helped. Oh yes, so did I. Takes a village to bring back the almost dead."

A'banna shuddered. "I survived the mudslide by the grace of the stars."

Shai shook her head as she tied her hair back. "You survived because you're a damn good fighter and quick on your feet. When Bedel pulled you out of the river—just be grateful."

Bedel shook his head. "The two of you are making me crazy. I'm in love with you, Shai."

Shai scoffed. "Oh, move on, Bedel. She can hear everything you think. 'Banna, how about for you? More of those knives the Wo'Huzziet like so much?"

"And a shield," she said. "I had a shield."

Shai adjusted her tools. "See, she's practical. I like that, even if she is a thieving wench."

"Stop calling her those things. You're the one acting like a bitch."

Shai paused and stared at him, mouth agape. "Well, your balls are back."

"Crows, woman."

He turned and left the ring. Shai called after him, "And there's that Cardor slang I so missed!"

A'banna stepped closer as the youths prepared the wood stack in the fire, and another person carried over buckets of water.

"Why do you treat him that way?"

"I wasn't aware I needed a reason."

"You're disrespectful, arrogant, rude."

Shai sized A'banna up before setting back to work. "Oh, little precious Avocan princess, I don't know. Maybe it's because I'm an illegitimate child of the House of Menai. That's the ruling house of Lupacuo, if you didn't know." Shai stared at the fire, whispered to it, and it suddenly blazed hot and roared. A'banna stepped back from the sudden heat. "So technically, even though he's adopted, that means I'm sleeping with my second cousin. Or was."

Shai's hands hovered over an ingot, and it rose in the air, directed by her, until it settled into the blazing flame.

"Maybe it's because I was raised by my Branaird mother in a traveling caravan. Do you know what it's like to be the only Elven-looking child amongst a bunch of nomads? I was Branaird in every way except for these ears and lighter skin. You know what free Branairds are like? Beautiful. I remember the years right before the north figured they could start taking our people as slaves, and the Trader Wars began. We were free. We laughed, we traversed the road, selling wares and trading. We embraced the music of the world fabric. We were one with nature. Happy. Self-sufficient. You should have seen our wagons—they were canvasses for a tribe of artists, or the nights we camped and sang and danced. And then slavers came, and they've been coming ever since. My mother helped save us. She is the only healer known to not be a part of their Healing Order and that political Conclave in Cardor. That was how we survived. She leveraged herself politically. It didn't stop the anger, the resentment. And my people were right to be. We were peaceful nomads until the slavers came. And I looked partially northern."

She shrugged. "They needed a scapegoat. We were all angry, and it shouldn't have been at each other. But once again, Mother cared. Finally, a few years ago, she let me find my father, Lord Commander of the Elven High Guard and cousin to Bedel's mother—are you still following me? Anyway, they turned me into a spy. Much easier than having their bastard daughter at home, you know."

"Is that what the Menai lied about?" A'banna asked as she watched Shai's hands move, sweat speckling on her forehead. Inside the pit, wood crackled under the fire and metal sizzled. Something was growing, moving within.

"Only to themselves," Shai said, short of breath. "All of the history Idrin and I shared in there, no one knew. Or it was some fancy fairytale to tell children at bedtime. But the House of Menai knew. They locked it away in a hidden study of theirs."

"How did you find it?"

Shai cracked a mischievous smile. Her accent changed to something closer to Bedel's. "My father made me a spy, remember? I picked the damn lock when they weren't looking and read until dawn. Now, they can't kill me. I made a name for myself. No one can kill Shai the Acrobat or Shai the Artist without some backlash and the wrath of the Conclave. No one wants to make a healer mad. They stop healing. Something to be said for popularity among the masses. Everyone loves it when—as an essencer —you don't harm the world fabric, even the Swords of Baktur.

"My magic, see" she strained under some hidden pressure. "Is art. I make something from something else. Most people think I make something from nothing, but I have to have something to start with. I repurpose the essences, no real manipulation involved. I don't buy them with ethereal, I don't force them to listen. I don't even have to whisper any Belasna phrase. We just get along. Something beautiful comes from it."

Shai reached into the fire with tongs and pulled out a long, elongated piece of metal.

"What is that?" A'banna asked.

"Bedel's present." She started hammering. "Water. Bring me that bucket!"

A'banna hurried, snatched the bucket, and set it down beside

Shai. The searing hot blade barely missed A'banna's hair as Shai drove it into the water. Hot steam sizzled upward.

"Dear gods," A'banna said, getting her first glimpse at what already looked like an elegant blade.

Shai shot her a frustrated look. Sweat dripped from her nose. "Dear, that was just the first round." She quickly withdrew it from the water and plunged it back into the fire. "I'm forcing the essences to hurry, so the normal folding process is sped up."

"How long will it take?"

"For the kind of weapon he wants? Without me, you'd be here for a week." She quickly repeated the process. With each blow, she continued: "But. I simply. Don't. Have. That. Kind. Of time." Water boiled and sizzled. Repeat. "We need to leave at noon. I'll sleep in the wagon, if it's all the same to everyone."

"No sleep tonight?"

Shai gestured with the tongs and hammer. "Don't worry. Got used to it when we traveled. Among the caravans, you always slept with one eye open. Pretty half-Elf thing, source of their people's problems. I mean, it was people who looked like me that made the Wo'Huzziet non-existent and killed, raped, and pillaged the Branairds. This village is all that's left of the once greatest southern tribe because of slavery. And you, Avocan, with that skin and black hair, are going to be a hot commodity in Cardor, so watch your back, front, and sides. And have your raptors bite any man who looks at you sideways."

A'banna gaped.

"I don't have time for modesty. You have a lot to learn about the north before you get there. And I—" the smithing process had already begun again. "I have to keep you alive to keep him alive." Her brow furled as she looked at a scrap piece of metal. "I don't know if I like the idea of you staying at the cabin with us. Maybe another one farther down the road. I'm sure it'll make sex real interesting."

A'banna stood dumbfounded as Shai worked. After an hour or two, A'banna sat and helped stoke the fire. She fetched more water, switched out tongs, and got a new pair of gloves. They talked, the stars arching high over their heads. At some point, Bedel returned to the longhouse. She could hear the men discussing routes and maps and the ranger's involvement and a rendezvous with Shai's caravan. None of that was as important as what Shai showed and explained. And then Shai asked her about Avoc. So she answered.

Eventually, they laughed as they cleaned the first blade and the second. A'banna turned quickly with the smaller blade, and Shai let out a yelp, holding her wrist. "Careful!"

A'banna was on the other side of the fire. "I don't understand."

Shai's eyebrows raised. "You don't know what these can do?"

"Fight The Taurs?"

"And more. No sudden movements while we're still smithing, all right?"

A'banna nodded. From then on, she was careful, slowly maneuvering the blades. Then came a set of bracers, a round shield with spikes, A'banna's knives, and another small outward curved knife. Shai grinned and produced a silver arrow that was sleek, firm, and light. It was dawn when they finally sat back from their work, smiling at each other. They drank and ate heartily from a tray Bedel brought them. And they let him sit. Shai showed him the bracers then began fitting leather strips and small gear mechanisms that she'd made when A'banna hadn't watched. They talked. Joked. Eventually, he laughed, too. And everything felt right.

It was, A'banna realized, *fun*.

Even Shai smiled—and Bedel was right—she was quite pretty. Shai's eyes flickered between the two of them and then to the fire. She hid her face behind the large goblet, but A'banna could see she was still sad. The colors of her aura were muted, in check. Sadness was only a fraction of what she really felt, but she hid those emotions even from the trained eye. There were moments that Shai looked like a true hunter. Still, they all laughed together. And the stars passed overhead, and then the sun rose, a beautiful red-orange light behind them.

For the first time in her life, and against her training, A'banna chose not to see the world fabric, the colors surrounding each person, the animals. For a short time, all she wanted was to be present. It was foolish, but she wanted life to stay this way. With laughter, with hard work, with people who she found herself caring for. Even if she had to try ignoring Shai's aura, with all of its flares of grief, anger, and passion wreathed in pulsing dark fire.

CHAPTER 13

TIME WAS LOST TO THE POISON AND PAIN. TWO PAIRS OF EYELIDS opened and closed simultaneously—horizontal and vertical. He felt webbed hands place him on a tight cloth, he heard Nchoji speaking to them in a language he didn't know. He heard air whistling, then realized it was his own wheezing breath. He saw bulbous yellow eyes staring at him, felt someone's hands press into his side.

Raynt Lacrause screamed in pain. His body shoved him back into the depths of sleep again.

He awoke to the sounds of insects and leaves rustling. The stars were blotted out, then appeared. No, a tree canopy. Forest. The Cronop Jungle. He barely heard footsteps, soft and padded.

"Rest, my friend," Nchoji said, his accent heavy. "Trust me."

Raynt did. The Rda warrior had earned his trust. All Raynt wanted was sleep.

His dreams were erratic. Captain McCormack had found Bedel and Shai and killed them. His friends. He saw the King's Men company, waiting for him, bloodied; one of the men was dead. Where were you? Captain Yeltson Greggor asked. I trusted you.

"I'm coming," Raynt murmured. "I still have three days to search. Three more days. Wait for me. We'll find her."

"Raynt," he heard Nchoji say. "You're dreaming."

Raynt felt his body lurch.

"Careful!" another voice said.

At last, Raynt was set on something soft while a woman counted. He felt warmth spread through his body. "Bring it," she said. "His lung is punctured. Which weapon caused this?"

Raynt heard bone clink against metal.

"Pierced and poisoned, Lady Healer."

"Ancients," she whispered.

"Can you save him?"

Raynt gasped as he felt someone lift his head and pour a soft, sweet, and earthy liquid down his throat.

"Please be patient, Brother Nchoji. Speak to him, he can hear you."

Raynt felt the warmth inside him, in his chest, in the pain. He felt the healer.

"No, it can't be."

"What is his magic?" the woman asked.

"I saw nothing out of the ordinary," Nchoji answered.

"But can you see?" she said. "No, no. I can. Never mind."

Raynt felt something in his chest. His eyes opened and saw a blinding light above him.

A woman hunched over him—the healer. He could barely discern her features. "Peace, friend," she said. What Wo'Huzziet dialect was that?

Raynt's eyelids fluttered, closed.

In his sleep, Raynt heard voices chittering and clucking as they rose in emphasis and passion. That same passion sounded animalistic when in crescendo, like a bird and a reptile cawing and shrieking at once. Then a dozen voices joined it, followed by a woman ululating in a variance of a Wo'Huzziet dialect. He heard songs. He heard drums and a flute. He felt something prick his skin, over and over, but Raynt Lacrause couldn't open his eyes. His body simply didn't obey him.

Despite the sounds he heard from whatever lay beyond his eyelids, in his mind, he heard Captain McCormack's voice.

I got them where they were going, but there's one lady on land I don't try to screw around with, and her little bird said leave.

Raynt fidgeted, but he felt hands on him. He heard Nchoji speak soothingly to him, both in Wo'Huzziet and in common. Sleep tuned out most of what he said. When he awoke, he heard cheers and a celebration from somewhere, but he still couldn't open his eyes.

The healer's voice returned. "Rest, friend. Rest."

There was little Raynt could do to stave off the exhaustion, though he felt his fingers move again.

The healer laughed. "You are just as we thought: relentless. Rest. Most of the ray's poison has been drained, but your nervous system needs the sleep."

Without argument, Raynt drifted off to sleep. His mind startled when he saw a giant bird, circling through the sky far above; its vision trying to connect with his own. Wondering, prying at the edges of Raynt's consciousness. It returned whenever he sensed he was alone or heard cicadas or some other insect outside. He felt a gentle breeze on his skin. Somewhere nearby, a waterfall let forth a cascade of calming sounds. But there was another woman's presence, testing him. Wings soaring in the air. His body tensed, but he still couldn't move, even if it shouted at him to be aware of a predator. To flee. Or fight.

You, he heard a female voice say—but inside his mind. *You are special, aren't you? It has indeed begun. The Oppressor seeks his domination, but he is weak now. So weak. A Chosen has come to the boundary, but what do you seek in my domain? Your sister, if she even is? No, your friends. But why?*

Then Raynt saw her eyes, an image floating on the back of his eyelids. Silver and deep, cold and calculating. The skin around her eyes was tight, pale as Alain's.

Alain. He's dead, child.

No. Impossible.

Oh, I was there when it happened, the woman's voice said inside his head. *It's very rare for one of us to die, but it does happen. You should know. He came to me. Came to us. I know what he wanted, but did you honestly think I'd let you win? I wish I could see the look on his father's face when he finds out who sacrificed him to my glory and The Taurs that guide us.*

If Alain was dead, what of Shai? Bedel?

Reason? Her eyes widened, and she heard the bird caw, furious and surprised. *Reason!* Her voice had turned demanding. The amusement she had projected before had gone. Instead, she was terrified. Furious. *What does Reason have to do with all of this? You slew one of my servants. There are consequences, Chosen. Tell my old friends Reason will not stop me again.*

"Be gone, witch!" someone barked next to Raynt.

Raynt felt the bird's presence, felt the long beak against his cheek; felt its hot breath. Then, felt a different sort of heat. Feathers drifted on top of him, as flesh broiled. The bird's cry was painful. He heard wings flap, felt the wind on his face. Bowstrings twanged; arrows whistled in the air.

Reason will not stop me again! The woman shrieked, but her voice was one with the bird's. Her eyes were wide, full of fury, and dark fire swirled within her, dying those eyes black. *I will find them. I will chase them to the ends of my domain and beyond! And then I will burn down your precious world.*

That last point seemed to drift on the wind. Her eyes faded from his mind. Raynt felt his body heave for breath.

"Ancients preserve him!" Nchoji! Nchoji was in the room.

Raynt felt hands on him again, prodding. Was that hot liquid blood? Had he lost more blood?

As if echoing Raynt's thoughts, Nchoji said, "What's wrong? What did it do to him?"

"Please, Nchoji, let us work," a male voice said, clucking frustration. "Keyauri, see him out. And someone shut the window! Theantros help us. She found our paradise at last. Sleep, Raynt. Sleep."

"Come, Nchoji Rda," the familiar Wo'Huzziet female voice said. She sounded like peaceful waves, gently rolling onto the shore.

His body had no more resistance left to give. Raynt slid back into sleep, though he was uncertain whether it was fitful or replenishing.

CHAPTER 14

Light refreshed Raynt as if he stood baking in his family's fields. Except, the light streamed through the windows, bathing a wood-paneled room, filled with bookshelves. Sitting at a scribe table, was Raynt's adopted brother, writing intently in a journal. He recognized this room as the Commission's Library in their hometown of Gloriweedum. That was impossible. Raynt knew he was in a bed, recovering. But he heard the librarian, Stamford Farr, droning on out of view about legal procedures for presenting a proposal to the city council. Raynt hadn't seen Stamford since the mountain ordeal, when they had met the Immortal, Alain.

"Ian?" Raynt whispered.

Raynt's brother paused, quill shaking in the air. He started to turn from the table. Above Ian appeared a painting, as if it were part of the wall itself. Blue fire met streams of golden sunlight, while from the lower corner, dark shadows, lined with red flames, consumed both. Those images moved, flowed in a circle, like a stirred drink. Each fire flared brighter than the others, but they could not blend, even if they seemed to consume the others—dark fire, starlight, golden rays. At the moment each seemed flared, greater in power, as the others faded, and then all at once, they shined together.

Entranced, Raynt looked down from the painting, but Ian was gone. The room and the painting vanished.

Raynt woke, though even that took effort.

"Good morning," a voice he recognized said, though the speaker was out of view.

"Where am I?" He groaned, straining to move his arms.

"Inimorin, on the big island of Cronop."

Even that name was familiar. *Why?* Bright sunlight filtered from an open window above his head. Raynt felt a blanket and a pillow beneath him. "Is this real?"

"We feared you were hallucinating some. You received a high dose of a powerful poison. In addition, the pirate's blade punctured a lung. All things considered, you've recovered faster than we imagined."

Another groan escaped Raynt's lips. His fingers felt for the wound, but he touched smooth, pink flesh.

"Our healer, Keyauri, is quite skilled. That does not mean you should rush off and try to duel another essencer, friend."

"Who are you? I can't see you. The sun is so bright."

The voice clucked. "Of course. Do not fear."

Bare feet padded across the floor. Raynt raised a hand to cover his eyes and tried not to gasp as a short, green Goblin came into view. Raynt's mind flashed back to the battle, the sheer savagery of the Goblins who had come to their rescue against the Baktur.

Raynt's vision cleared, and he stared into the Goblin's yellow bulbous reptilian gaze as the long, thin, extended mouth smiled. Shock seemed to rip out the bed, floor, and ground below him. It wasn't just the Goblin. He had tattoos Raynt had seen before. Runes that encircled his eyes and mouth and ears, with lines drawn like rays from each. The only time Raynt had seen those were on the Speaker of Men, who resided in a small palatial estate within Cardor's capital. The Speaker who had overseen the complete reform of the religion he was supposed to lead, including supporting slavery, sex trafficking, and the sanctioning of murder against those who did not share the church's faith.

Since Raynt, Bedel, and Shai had climbed that mountain, it had all been so they could save a reported new Speaker and his daughter! Now Raynt remembered clearly; Captain Forbens of *The Red Hand* had talked about a Goblin shaman.

"Impossible," Raynt said. "The Goblins killed their Speaker."

"And I am looking at one of the Chosen. Strange how the cosmos has a way of sorting itself out, isn't it?"

Raynt shook his head in disbelief. "You saved us?"

The Gaul nodded. "We did, after my friend Captain Forbens sent word you may need help. I'm glad we sent most of our warriors. Easier to overwhelm Baktur with equal numbers."

No one overwhelms Baktur, Raynt thought absentmindedly.

"My name is Muriumek, Speaker of Gaul." The Goblin bowed. Raynt realized that this was the one who had greeted them in the street. Either the edge of death or the darkness of night had kept Raynt from noticing the tattoos. Muriumek continued, "We are not your average Goblins, my friend, and would prefer our race's original name."

Raynt shook his head, then nodded. He wanted it to make the casual sense with which Muriumek explained it, but instead, he felt confused, overwhelmed, and reality-challenged.

"Gaul, of course," Raynt said. "My apologies."

"No need. We're very familiar with our reputation. There is a reason we live on an island in the middle of the sea, after all."

All of a sudden, Raynt's stomach growled. Muriumek gave a big, toothy smile then hopped across the room to bring Raynt a covered bowl of soup. "Specially made to replenish your strength. One of Keyauri and my own recipes." He clucked, which Raynt supposed was the Goblin—Gaul—way of laughing. "Our friends, the Wo'Huzziet, and we share common needs. It is, if you pardon my saying, quite symbiotic."

Raynt finished the soup quickly and tried to stand. He could feel his limbs again. Muriumek nodded contently as a Wo'Huzziet woman entered. Her patterned orange, brown, green, and blue dress was a beautiful and stunning contrast to the cream-colored walls. Her curly hair was up in a hairstyle Raynt was unfamiliar with—it had volume, yet spread like the rim of a hat above a blue, purple, and orange bandana. A necklace of shells and pearls clung to her neck on a purple string. She was elegant and stunning.

"Healer Keyauri, our patient is awake," Muriumek said, smiling.

The middle-aged woman crossed the room. She offered a quick smile as she took Raynt's arm. He felt her aether join his in a healing bond. It was like she saw within him completely, totally. "Impossible," Keyauri whispered.

"What is?" Muriumek asked, although she ignored his question. That didn't seem to bother him in the slightest.

"How old are you?" she asked Raynt.

"What does that matter?" he answered. Truth was, he may only be twenty-five years old.

"It's a strange world. We Wo'Huzziet are some of the last free of our peoples, yet we live with Gaul, who are estranged from their people. One of our Rda brings you whom the Sorceress, an Immortal, pursues to our doorstep. Immortals are being hunted, you know."

Keyauri emphasized that last phrase, as if it was common knowledge. Just as Raynt was about to ask about Alain, Muriumek said, "He was dying. We couldn't have just abandoned him."

"Not at all!" Keyauri said, nodding vehemently. "It is not our way. Raynt, do you know who your parents are?"

Raynt's cordial smile vanished. The truth was, he only

remembered a Glymph woman who carried him as an infant through the Zeller desert. She died giving him the last of her water. He could still see her face, feel the prickly, peeling skin of her lips as she kissed him. He remembered trying to play with her, and she would not wake up. Then a healer and an essencer had rescued him, and later he was adopted.

"With respect, Lady Healer, it's none of your business."

"Perhaps you are right," Keyauri conceded, but her brown eyes were passionate as they gazed into his. "But it should matter, you know? Have other healers mentioned this to you?"

Raynt thought of the healer who saved him, Susanne, and Xathon's wife, an Elf, or his sister-in-law. Raynt shook his head.

Keyauri pursed her lips, as if trying to piece together a puzzle. Even though he knew he sounded rude, she would be able to feel his emotions through the bond. *Please*. He didn't know why, but he called the image of the Glymph woman to mind, allowed her to see the emotions.

I'm sorry, he thought he heard Healer Keyauri's voice through the bond. Before he could confirm, she gently put his hand down. The aether of the healer bond receded into her.

Keyauri smiled. "You are healthy and healing well, Raynt. Your body has completely purged the effect of the poison from your body, and your lung has continued the healing we started when you arrived. It's safe for you to walk. I know Rda Nchoji will be happy to see you." She smiled again, bowed slightly, and spread her arms to her sides. "Welcome to Inimorin-Droth-Zaet. May the peace of the valley sustain you."

Keyauri stopped at the door, glanced back at him. Raynt saw deep pensiveness in her eyes. She looked concerned, yet pleased. "Enjoy Inimorin-Droth-Zaet, Agent Raynt," she said, though Raynt could tell she had wanted to say something else.

When she was gone and Muriumek pulled out fresh clothes for him from a pack, Raynt stood. At first, his legs wobbled, as if the floor itself was unsteady. As he was about to topple back to the bed, Muriumek reached out, steadying him. His webbed hand felt odd on his elbow. He wore a full white gown, coming down to his knees. He wasn't used to being this undressed before others.

"Better?" Muriumek asked.

"Aye," Raynt said.

Muriumek nodded pleasantly and turned to give him some privacy. Raynt dressed quickly. His muscles stretched. It felt good to move.

"What did Healer Keyauri want to say?"

Muriumek smiled. "If I told you I knew someone who suspected, would you listen to me?"

"Where is this someone?"

"Far from here. He knew the Grand Essencer, though. Long ago. As a Speaker, we also have a bond, though unlike most others. I can hear the thoughts of my fellow Speakers." Muriumek was about to say more when a man entered.

At first, Raynt didn't recognize him in the navy-blue coat with a brown and silver hem, but he knew the jeweled hilt of the sword sheathed at his waist. It had belonged to McCormack. Above it was hung a baklana—the same one Nchoji had used to kill McCormack.

"Hey, my friend!" Nchoji exclaimed, arms wide. He crossed the room and hugged Raynt in a bone-crushing grip.

"Good to see you, too," Raynt coughed, patting him on the back. He wasn't used to the familiarity of it all, but it felt good, welcome. It made him dismiss the curiosity Muriumek was trying to explain, and the Goblin looked troubled by that.

"I am delighted to see you awake," Nchoji said. "There is much you missed."

"I've caught on to that. In my dreams, I remember hearing your voices and the voices of a woman."

"And a giant bird in your window?" Nchoji said, eyebrow raised.

Raynt nodded. "The Sorceress of Avoc? Was that her?"

Muriumek came over. "Aye. You saw her avatar, the Velheron. If she spoke to you, well, we are below the Keeper's boundary. Where the avatar flies, she can see and project her thoughts, as well. Like a communication jewel, but when she enters one's mind, it can be painful."

"Have you experienced her?"

"No, but I have felt the mind of a dragon before, and the power of dark fire essencers." Muriumek sighed. "There is much corrupt in our world. Above the Keeper's border, the northern nations are safe from her reach, for now. We'll return you there as soon as we can."

"What of my friends? Nchoji, I can't leave without some news. The Sorceress claimed she killed Immortal Alain. Is that possible? Is that what Keyauri was referring to?"

Muriumek sighed and leaned against the doorframe. "Come, see the council. We shall discuss it there."

"Aye," Nchoji said, eyes wide. He gripped Raynt's shoulder in his large hand. "I have a surprise to show you in the harbor. Captain Forbens waits for us there."

"After the council?"

"Good," the Rda warrior said, grinning.

They exited the room and made a left down the hall. Raynt blinked as he saw two doors of a dark wood, wide opened to let the breeze and bright sunlight through. Beyond was an arched walkway suspending a wood trellis above. Light green vines and beautiful flowers covered the ceiling, providing a bit of shade. When he stepped into the corridor, Raynt couldn't help but gasp. From this height, he could survey an entire courtyard around the L-shaped hospital. Crescent hills towered above a lush valley. Rocky cliffs gave way to steep inclines and dense tropical forest.

Raynt could barely make out the shimmer of a large lake that fed a beautiful waterfall, cascading down mossy rocks. This far away, sound wasn't deafening, only pleasant. The air was clean, with none of the smog or atrocious odors that were present in most cities. The waterfall sent up a mist as it poured into a clear blue pond. Wo'Huzziet gathered around the waters, chatting or drawing up buckets and jars, while young Gaul and Wo'Huzziet splashed in. Macaws took flight through the trees and across a small marketplace, where several dozen people gathered around vendors, especially those selling spices, fresh produce, and salted meats. Adobe homes surrounded the marketplace, with a central street that ran clear from moderate-sized river docks in the south to a columned outdoor amphitheater, where six stone chairs sat side by side. Near the amphitheater was a domed building and Raynt could see a group of elders chatting inside in colorful robes —Wo'Huzziet, Gaul, and the person moved so fast Raynt blinked. He couldn't have seen what he just thought he had. Clearly, the individual must have long white hair, and those pointed ears were Elven. Even if the person had looked like a white tiger.

Raynt noticed Muriumek and Nchoji watching him carefully.

In the courtyard of the hospital were a group of young Goblins, speaking with an elder. In front of them was a table covered in bloody meat and another in fresh vegetables. Each of the young Gaul, male and female, looked strong, fierce and ashamed. One reached for the meat, and the elder's hand flashed. A switch slapped the hand down. Even from here, he could hear the elder say: "Gaul do not eat people. Even if we fight with our teeth, we do not consume the flesh of a person! You four will now eat, for you shall begin your time of cleansing and meditation, refocusing your aether unto the value of life—even the lives of our enemies."

As the young warriors slowly, begrudgingly, sat around the

table with the vegetables, two other Gaul came and removed the table with meat.

"What is this?" Raynt asked.

"Our community," Muriumek replied. "As for our young soldiers, they have to purge themselves of the blood craze and re-center their minds and impulses on that which allows us to enjoy symbiosis with our neighbors and fellow people. It allows us to realize that Theantros set us free from the blood craze, and that we are not our ancestors. This makes us different from Goblins. We are not cannibals, but sometimes, after a battle, we need to remind ourselves."

Raynt looked at the waterfall again and noted that, when he stepped further south, he could see that there were two waterfalls, not one. The second began a creek that fed the river winding away to the south. There was a small bay there where two ships were anchored. One clearly was *The Red Hand*. The other was black, a warship that looked all too familiar.

"I must still be recovering, I thought I saw *Batoidea*."

Neither of his companions said anything.

"Nevermind."

"As you wish," Muriumek said. "Come, I want to show you one more thing."

They reentered the hospital from the southern door of the veranda. Down a flight of stairs, they entered another corridor. Doors opened to reveal a large room full of beds. Wo'Huzziet, a few Branairds, and even a couple of northerners lay in them. Each was in a different state of pain. Keyauri and a few attendants moved throughout. Raynt hesitated, looking in.

"These people are sick," he murmured. "With what?"

Muriumek looked grieved, then waved them down a different hallway, to a stairwell that descended deep below them. They followed Muriumek, who stopped at a door and whispered at it. Raynt blinked, realizing he saw the doors alter from one essence to another, from solid rock to water to air that formed a portal around them. Muriumek ushered them through. It was a long room. One rock wall was covered in blue, glowing mushrooms and a dark green ivy, while a single strip of white light swirled in a tube above them, illuminating the center of the room. Muriumek led them around the rich soil there, where flowering ferns grew.

Several Gaul and Wo'Huzziet moved between tables, crushing and blending mushrooms and ferns together with some sort of seed.

"Apothecaries?" Raynt asked.

One of the Gaul, a woman with long dark hair, glanced up. She clucked, long lips pulled back into a smile, and then returned to her work.

Muriumek also clucked. "One might think. No, we prefer to think of ourselves as chemists, a rare field of scholarship, even if we do create a cure."

"For what?" Raynt asked, glancing between the busy workers, the plants, and tables with glass, small oil burners, and mortar and pestles.

Muriumek nearly answered, then saw someone approaching. He gestured to them. "Healer Wavos, this is Raynt Lacrause of the Magical Affairs Commission."

Raynt turned, then froze.

A tall cat-like figure came from an adjacent cave. His hide was orange, his eyes had an even deeper orange depth where one might expect them to be white, while his pupils were pitch black. A long tail stretched from his white coat over dark trousers and a blue tunic. A second cat-like figure followed him, dressed in much the same way, although her tunic appeared to have patterns similar to Keyauri's dress. They each carried baskets full of harvested ferns, which they brought to the tables. Raynt expected them to have paws, but though their hands were large, they had fingers.

Wavos stepped close, his black nose moved, whiskers shaking. Wavos' voice was deep, like a smithy's bellow mixed with a growl. "He is different. Chosen?"

"He is, my friend," Muriumek said. "Latana believes there is more to him, though."

Wavos grunted. The cat-like woman purred. "She would know," she said, using her claws to trim leaves off the fern branches.

"My apologies, Healers," Raynt began. "I don't recognize your race."

"You aren't meant to," Wavos growled, although his lips peeled back over long, sharp teeth in a smile that rivaled Raynt's attempts to intimidate others. It was impressive. "Is he why the Velheron found us?"

"No," Muriumek said. "We believe the Sorceress was tracking the *Batoidea*. She likely employed Captain McCormack, based on a few of the surviving pirates' testimonies."

What had McCormack said? *A little bird told me.* The pirate had a strange definition of "little" if he meant the Velheron.

Nchoji frowned. "Had I known, I wouldn't have sailed her so close. I might have kept a few more of the bastards alive, too."

Wavos shrugged and settled on a stool. Neither of the cat-like folk or the Gaul wore boots. "They had justice coming."

Raynt didn't know what to ask or say next, so he turned to Nchoji. "We took the *Batoidea*?"

The Rda warrior grinned. "I mentioned the surprise in the harbor, yes?"

"Crows be damned!" He shook Nchoji's hand. "Well done! I want access to prisoners."

"It will be done," Nchoji answered. "It now belongs to the Inimorin collective. I am its captain."

Raynt grinned. Having Nchoji as captain of a powerful ship like *Batoidea* was fortunate. He was keen on allies.

"You have ancestors of the Glymphs?" Healer Wavos asked, using one clawed finger to point at Raynt.

"I do," Raynt said, acknowledging the cat-like man.

"I have ancestors who were Elves, human, and lions and tigers," Wavos responded. Raynt realized the woman was watching him, chuckling and purring contently. "Do you know why?"

"No."

"The Velheron came to you because you are Chosen in the new star cycle. Perhaps more than that, by your smell. I can't place it." He sniffed again in Raynt's direction. "The Sorceress made the Velheron, crafted it. She crafted a race of beings called minotaurs, and she sent Jacob Morbrook to the Goblins to convince them to be an experiment, one of a kind. One more terrible than we can imagine and have yet to see."

Morbrook? Raynt thought. Xathon's last name was Morbrook. He wasn't familiar with a Jacob could that be Bedel's brother he sometimes spoke of?

"How do you know this?" Raynt asked. "And is this Morbrook related to Xathon?" Muriumek and Wavos' nod answered that question. "Why do I not know your race?"

Wavos purred. "The Felin were her first creation after the breaking. We live on islands south of Mursia across the sea. She couldn't control us, and we retained our intelligence. There would have been war, and we would have won. So my people stay away from all the others, because not even Muriumek's god, Theantros, gives us a Speaker of our own, since we are not one of his, but hers."

"Felin," Raynt repeated to himself. "It is a pleasure to meet you."

"Perhaps," Wavos growled.

"My friend is modest," Muriumek clucked.

Nchoji leaned forward. "He looks like he could rip our arms off, not modest at all."

Both Felin laugh, a deep, roaring bellow that echoed off the cave walls. "We won't harm you, as long as you are friends of the Inimorin-Droth-Zaet commune. We are here to heal what our cousins, humans, wrought on each other."

"The disease," Raynt said. "How did it spread?"

"Slavers," Nchoji answered, crossing his arms. "Those who are sick are culled by the Coalition, so not to contaminate the north, but it is a virus born of dark fire itself, they say."

"They," Wavos growled. "Meaning *we*, are right. It is how she makes her monsters. She has a formula, one we don't even remember. But to use it, she manifests dark fire. So much evil can come from one thing—nothing but raw power. So the virus was made, given to the slavers. When they raped and pillaged, they brought it. You did not think that she destroyed an entire civilization of a million people in half a century by war alone, did you?"

"We are not told this," Raynt said.

"Why should the north teach this?" Nchoji scoffed. "It is our problem. It is why we came here, to Cronop, to find a cure. Then we met friends who taught us how to make it, but it is no cure. It just delays the end or prevents transmission of the Slaver Coalition's virus."

"But the slavers should have died by this, too, shouldn't they?"

Wavos' claws withdrew into his fingers, which he wagged at Raynt. "This! See! This is what I have said, is it not, Muri? Why do the Slavers not die, but only the people south of the Keeper's border?! I think I know, but your people have young minds. You do not know the Blood Sages."

"They are stories told to frighten children or those traveling."

The Felin woman growled. With one swift stroke of her claws, she trimmed an entire branch then dropped it in her growing pile.

"We were stories, once, too. But no one understands. No one hears. The power of erasing a civilization for the sake of the Sorceress' science and her magic. She isn't the only one who does not teach. Your Xathon Morbrook. The Elven House of Menai. They keep you all blind, and the Blood Sages satisfied. When you know, when you understand, then you will see."

Nchoji nodded, jaw tight.

Muriumek sighed. "They are correct, Raynt. When a culling is needed, of both slaver and slave, they are given in sacrifice to the nameless ones. Fear them, indeed."

"Where are they?" Raynt asked.

"If my people knew, we would destroy them," Wavos said.

"If the Sorceress killed Alain, would she have fed him to the Blood Sages?"

The Felin woman snickered. "Even she is afraid of something. They are not in Avoc, nor near any Immortal."

"Are they The Taurs?"

"No," everyone answered at once.

"If Alain is dead, where would his companions have gone?"

At first, no one answered, then Nchoji pulled a map from his jacket. "As Rda, I have been in charge of taking shipments of our cure to the dwelling places of the last of my people. These are their locations. Look at it, but I will burn the map before I let anyone take it."

"I understand, my friend. Thank you."

Muriumek cleared his throat. "My colleagues may have an answer, if you believe I hear the Speakers of Theantros."

Wavos growled in frustration.

"I echo that sentiment, my friend, but I am not my god."

"No, and for that I am thankful," Wavos said, then resumed shredding ferns. A Wo'Huzziet came over, smiled, and bundled a pile, then took it over to a machete and large wood table. He proceeded to cut the pieces even smaller.

Wavos set the empty basket underneath the full one, and they kept working.

"Okay," Raynt said. "Where?"

"Alain abandoned them where the Wo'Huzziet have appointed a new high chief."

"Until you find us Naminia," Nchoji added.

Raynt nodded firmly. "Where?"

Nchoji and Muriumek pointed at the same time, to a marked place south of the ruins of Ntokup.

Raynt's heart fell. "They're so far south, almost to the jungle regions."

"But they were alive just two weeks ago."

"What about now? If the Velheron followed the *Batoidea*, she would know" Then the pieces of the puzzle fell together. "That's why Alain left. So she wouldn't understand who he was traveling with."

Muriumek nodded.

Raynt inhaled sharply. Whatever Bedel and Shai had been keeping from him during their mountain climb, meant that Bedel had some tie to the Sorceress. "That's why she became angry when she heard my thoughts about Bedel. He did something to her."

Wavos and the Felin woman paused. A fern dropped from his hands.

"That name," she whispered.

"No," Wavos said. "We do not speak it. We will not. We sought freedom, he should keep his."

"What is special about him?" Raynt pressed. "What did he do to her? What reason does she have to hate him?"

Wavos blinked, growled, and then lowered his voice. It still made Raynt's chest rumble with the sound. "If you love your friends, you will stop asking those questions. If the Sorceress has read your mind once and spoken with you, then she may try again. If she does that and finds you know, your friends are doomed most certainly."

Muriumek folded his hands. "But surely we should teach them about the cycle."

Wavos gestured dismissively. "What you and your colleagues do is no concern of mine. But I warn our friend, Raynt, guard your friends' lives with your mind."

Raynt glanced again at the map. There would be no way they could get from that location to Wonbai in Zeller to retrieve the war plans at that distance. They'd have to travel days and without a ship, even longer. "We believe the Sorceress is helping plan a war. A mutual friend of Nchoji and mine set up a time to exchange information, but Bedel and Shai will never make it. I can't go to Zeller."

"Let me," Nchoji said.

"No, the Baktur know us, now. You can't."

"I can," Muriumek said. "I can even bring a mutual friend. We will go to Wonbai and retrieve this information for you."

"Baktur will kill you on sight."

Muriumek clucked. "My own people tried to do that when they attempted to feed me to a dragon. It did not work out as well as they hoped. I am hard to kill."

Wavos and the other Felin growled together. "You help the elders keep this community together. I know Keyauri will side with us."

"No doubt she will, as will the elders, and my mate and our children. But, I will not ask. I am a Speaker."

Wavos let out a bellow. "You damn fool! Going closer toward her? The Velheron saw you, Keyauri said."

Muriumek shrugged. "So it did, and so she did. That said, if I can help prevent a war, it benefits us all. Agreed? Now, how will I know to recognize your friends?"

"Not here," Wavos said, gestured sharply. "You two, alone.

Tell no one else. She cannot know. Perhaps that memory has faded."

"Doubtful," the Felin woman said.

Wavos shrugged his massive shoulders in agreement.

"Thank you," Raynt told them all.

"Thank us," Wavos said. "By stopping her before she breaks the world again. And we will do what we can to combat her villainy with our medicine."

The Felin woman growled, but it sounded like a laugh.

Raynt stayed a few minutes longer with them, before he, Muriumek, and Nchoji returned to the magically warded door. "I have one more request."

"What's that?" Nchoji asked.

"We have two ships here, correct?"

"Aye," Nchoji said.

Raynt smiled, surprised that his own lips peeled over his long canines. The Felin certainly helped him perfect his signature sneer.

"I need a ride home."

CHAPTER 15

Warm, salty Istantese Sea air blew through the open partitions of the palace wall, fluttering the page in Lady Ni'Dio's hands. It was a humid day, but she let her aether soak in the humidity around her, draining it into a bowl behind the dais. The din of the city below, the docks and marketplaces, the pens of the unenlightened, were but a murmur in the magic surrounding Clan Diotek castle. Now, she imagined a palace grander, taller, and even farther away from the bustle below. However, such a construction would rival the Matriarch Empress's——but they all knew her Glorious Enlightenment would be short-lived. Ni'Dio counted down the days until the next imperial moot, where some predicted she would overpower the Empress and take her title, even though the Empire of Istante already lived at the whim of Diotek. She and her father controlled the canal passage from east to west between the continents, and her father was one of the most revered diplomats and essencers in all the world. Not a day passed that Ni'Dio did not imagine surpassing him by sitting on the Golden Throne, yet she was not the only dancer in the world of fabric.

Lady Ni'Dio folded her white-painted hands, crushing her

father's missive between them. She glared at the kimono-clad slave laying prostrate on the floor.

Above him floated the teal coalescence of essences, Ni'Dio's crowning piece of art. The sphere rotated, pulling and releasing the strings of essence throughout the Istantese great room. The effect was a spectacular splash of color against the hanging cloth lamps, bamboo walls, and cream floor. The world fabric remained in constant movement, making paintings and armored manikins move with every pull. Her guests always recognized the coalescence as a work of art as they dined on rich food from her chefs. When her father was home, the whole room would be filled with essencers entertained with extravagant parties. Her favorite was when the slaves danced in the light of the essences. Or when she executed someone just below it. The colors that came from the beheaded corpse wove a majestic mural, even if it smelled.

In her single low chair—the only such furniture in the room— she knew that to the low-born prostrated before her, she seemed crowned in extended golden vines, roses, and sea dragons. Like the instruction of unruly slaves—called nayil—or the mastery of essences, everything was business or an art, even being the daughter-heir of the greatest essencer in the Empire. So as she studied the nayil prostrated before her, she considered her next creative endeavor fervently.

"Ambassador Ci'Dio was clear, Enlightened Majesty," the naye said. The slave dared rise to his knees, forehead still to the floor, hands clenched in front of him to prevent trembling. His companion, another naye, was wise enough to remain prostrated before his betters. "He wishes to offer you as wife and queen to King Aubert de Gerac of Franca."

So, her father wished to sell her. If anything, Franca had a sufficient slave trade and a flourishing navy and fishing industry. Sitting on the Francan throne as queen would have its advantages. But then, Aubert was a fat narcissist whose only redeeming quality was the siring of Princess Amelia. This news was disturbing. And all the nayil knew Ni'Dio did not like disturbing news.

She decided a splash of crimson black fury would look lovely on the tile. She may even let it dry there until her father returned. With a single stroke of aether, the coalescence illuminated like a captured rainbow. The essences of the Diotek Clan were hers when her father was away, and they sprang to attention like little servants wishing to keep their heads. Bright strings circulated, wrapping the servant in constricting lengths of water, air, and the forces within the world fabric.

The naye on his knees gasped. He choked, his body shuddered with an effort to breathe. Ni'Dio kept her red-painted lips taut and nodded to her attendant. The Elven woman, her translator, a slave and maid of Lodornatha, had a shaven head, exposing her exotic ears. Ni'Dio kept her nayil adorned in tight and translucent kimonos. Only the serpent dragon designs offered any sort of privacy and only the most loyal of those earned the most grandiose sigils of her clan. These slaves were hers, and she was their master. And forgetting to change into proper attire before addressing her was just as poor of a decision as delivering an undesirable missive.

"Lady Ni'Dio, Descendant of the Serpent-Dragon of the Sea, Kinshoukkun of the Lone Bridge and the Sea Gate, expresses her dissatisfaction at this proposed union," the bald Elven translator, Edelissi, intoned.

The man clawed at his throat, but there was nothing to pry away. Ni'Dio watched with satisfaction as the unenlightened naye flailed, slowed, and then went limp with a final sigh. When he suddenly bloated, Ni'Dio thought the colors were quite fascinating. For being a low-born and unenlightened naye, he certainly helped create beautiful art with the essences.

"Rise," Edelissi ordered the second naye.

The second scrawny slave shuddered and knelt. Next to him,

came the sound of a ripe tomato being torn apart. The surviving naye shook even more as the steaming hot blood pooled around his knees. Edelissi gasped and nearly clutched her stomach. Ni'Dio admired the flourishing colors of death. It had been a good choice under the coalescence.

Edelissi began to speak again, but Ni'Dio raised a hand. Even the nayil in the perimeter of the room, hiding in their places behind pillars, fell silent. She liked the color of fear around the other slaves, all recent acquisitions. Then she realized how beautiful her own hand looked in contrast to the shades of death on her floor. Her fingernails were immaculate and black, a stark contrast against her flesh; white-painted with a white and black tattooed serpent-dragon on each middle finger. The long, red-rimmed cuffs fell from her forearms, exposing elaborate tattoos incorporating a rose and dragon in an embrace that circled her wrist and forearm. Inked rune rings circled several fingers, a sign of her enlightened power. Ni'Dio let *Invisitus* essences raise the last messenger's chin so he could see her.

"You will return to my father at the World Summit in Peremaih," she said, her accent rich and flowing, smiling at the brightness of this masterpiece. "You will tell him I accept this marriage on a singular condition, that I am queen of Franca by this time next year, war or no. I require a male heir born, nestled in my arms, and raised in perfection. And I want Aubert's own crows to feast upon his body and his pigs on his head on a Francan platter, silver and beautiful. His heir, this Amelia, has made my businesses less lucrative in Cardor's Southern Province, and now his war has stolen profits for me. She will be made my slave, and within two years' time, her aether shall fill my gems as her head adorns the walls of my city. Can you remember this, naye?"

"Oh Enlightened Majesty, Descendant of—"

"Do you remember it?"

Shaking, he repeated her word for word.

"If my father cannot guarantee these terms, the marriage is void upon a Dance with us, and you shall sit naked and chained between us when we begin. Do you understand, naye?"

"Your wisdom is ever magnificent and your mercy as vast as the seas, oh Great Descendant."

"Leave me," she said, gesturing to a male Elf behind a pillar, just as scantily clothed as the Elven translator. He began to slowly wave a large fan of gryphon feathers up and down. She sighed, drawing in the power of the dead beasts to cool her body from the midday heat. Their bodies remained stuffed and on display elsewhere in the castle.

The naye bowed and crawled backward from her presence. The messenger, some highborn debtor she'd purchased from the Slaver Coalition's stock, left bloody imprints and streaks on the floor. No self-respecting highborn would ever have allowed themselves to be a debtor, but it did help his chances of surviving her court. Two other nayil women, Lodornathan Elves who had been standing behind a wood pillar, set to cleaning.

"Leave it," Ni'Dio said. "If only you could see the colors, you poor things. He sees it, don't you naye?"

The messenger hesitated. "Yes, Great Descendant."

She smiled as she dismissed him. The naye ran from the room. The women darted back into the shadows, bowing fervently as they went.

A partition at the back of the room slid open. Two Dwarven women, dressed like the Elves, entered bearing the afternoon respite as their menfolk carried in a table and chaise. They arranged the furniture by an open window. She saw their frantic glances at the bloated corpse at her feet, at the blood on the floor. Ni'Dio watched the short nayil work. She'd made them all shave. Hair on the unenlightened of any race was terribly unattractive, and when they were afraid, their skulls would light up with fascinating hues.

It made her muse on last week's shipment, from which these fools came. The last raid upon the Wo'Huzziet had certainly been productive with this new lucrative and exotic merchandise. She had nearly offered the essencer captains, a sister and brother mid-born from Cardor, positions within her own fleet. They had been most efficient. First, though, Ni'Dio had to tend her new portfolio. The potential new market would be lucrative, indeed, if she could break the Lodornathans, but they were stubborn folk and unworthy of her leniency. Still, some had fetched a considerable price with the Matriarch Empress, who preferred her servants in the nude.

"Such a nuisance," Ni'Dio said to Edelissi. It had been a remarkable but welcome surprise to find a Lodornathan fluent in the Istanton tongue. "My father plots, manipulates, and hides behind the battle glory of lesser beings, then wishes to marry me to a fat man with no wit or aspirations of greatness."

"He sired a powerful daughter," Edelissi said, staring ahead.

"That he did. Pity I must kill her to ensure my rule." Ni'Dio leaned forward. "Tell me, Edelissi: In Lodornatha, are there enlightened who could help establish my dominance among the lowly Francans?"

Edelissi hesitated. It was enough of a hesitation that Ni'Dio considered a thrashing, just to remind her to be forthright with her betters.

Edelissi stiffed as she felt Ni'Dio's wrath accumulate. "If it pleases your Wisdom, I once saw a woman who made a ring of fire from a candle and a chair from a stick."

Ni'Dio felt an eyebrow raise in curiosity. This sounded like magic of lore. "And what did your people say of her?"

"That she had the gift of gods like no one alive, save for you, your Wisdom."

"Indeed. Edelissi. Did you hear that Relchar and Eleanor

Rultritan are with boy child? They were previously unsuccessful in their union, do you recall?"

"Yes, your Wisdom."

"It seems chance the child is so healthy, does it not?"

Edelissi stiffened. "Yes, my ladyship."

Had this enlightened been called to Cardor? It would be an intelligent choice from the Cripple King.

"I wonder if this lost magic, the magic of Art, can create a child within a womb?" Ni'Dio cocked her head, observing her translator. The woman had been a ranger but daughter of a high house. They had requested a ransom. Ni'Dio had sent her ring finger back, wrapped in a letter of refusal and right of ownership. It would be hard to wear a noble ring without the finger. Edelissi had been loyal ever since.

"How do we find this woman, Edelissi?"

Ni'Dio's translator's jaw trembled, her eyes watered, her fingers curled briefly, but she held all of that within. Rare was the one with the courage to learn.

"With a map, I can show your Wisdom."

"It would pleasure me greatly," Ni'Dio said. She shook her cuffs and rose from the chair. "Excellent. Come. I hunger."

She stepped around her paint on the floor. When Edelissi followed suit, Ni'Dio paused and pointed. The Elf swallowed and dipped her slippers into the blood. They slurped with every step as they crossed the deep room to the chaise. The Dwarves served food and drink. Ni'Dio reclined, then used her *otemoshi* to pluck food from the platters.

Silent and lost in the thoughts of the last few minutes—and the possibility of becoming queen of a country and not empress—Ni'Dio stared out the open partition onto the city. Istantil was a land bridge between two continents. Over centuries, the artistic endeavors of essencers had created a stone castle and canal system stretching several miles. This was the Sea Gate, and it had belonged to Clan Diotek since Ni'Dio's ancestors built it.

She stared at the arched roads, knowing the large steel gears that operated lift mechanisms were hidden by gatehouses. Within, the lowborn manned the canals. The gears were inset with large jewels, so as the lowborn turned the levers, it drained their meager aether. The sight was a beautiful rainbow of color beaming from the windows of the gatehouses, lifting the middle of each bridge into the air with a spectacular arch. Granted, turnover was high depending on the number of ships passing through, but any position serving the enlightened allowed the lowborn a chance to better themselves and the pests they bred like rabbit litters. Soon, those bridges would be filled with Istante's historical enemy. She had not favored this treaty, but the new trade routes were tempting. Provided this experiment worked.

"Edelissi, it is upsetting to me that the Empress and my father have agreed to allow ten and ten legions from Zeller to use our thoroughfare."

The Elven translator nodded, standing just off to the side as her mistress ate.

"Do you think I should become queen of that fat man?"

"Queen is a noble role."

"He's been a widower for over a decade, and we have a decent financial arrangement. But him? I can't imagine myself—" Ni'Dio shuddered.

"Understandable, my lady."

Ni'Dio adjusted her position and continued her meal.

It was then that, just outside the main window, the sea erupted.

At first, Ni'Dio felt the tremor from the water, the large force pushing toward the surface. Ships lurched as a massive whale burst forth, displaying its great colored fins and diving to the depths a moment later. Its unique tail design lingered above the surface until it slapped down on the water with such force that a wave battered the small fishing vessels around it.

But it had been the figures on top of the whale that had drawn her attention. A leather harness had strapped them to the whale's back, while clear white shells streamed oxygen during the extended undersea travels. Fiery dark translucent reins stretched from the whale's mouth and blowhole to the foremost seat. As the whale dived, a pale translucent shield reformed, protecting the riders.

Ni'Dio's heart throbbed; she couldn't help smiling. She clapped, and nayil emerged from behind the pillars. They learned quickly, even standing long hours in a single position, waiting at her pleasure. The slaves gathered around the perimeter of the room. "Prepare for guests!" she snapped. "I want a feast and rooms prepared. Make my room smell of roses and incense."

"And the body, your Wisdom?" Edelissi dared ask.

Ni'Dio smiled. "Oh, I think our guest will like this master-piece." She paused and then clapped again. The nayil scattered to do her bidding. She reclined and waited. When it was time, she rose and went back to her throne. There was no knock, no announcement, only bodies of nayil flung through the double doors at the end of the hall like ragdolls. Oh, he had a way about him.

When the blood and bodies settled on the floor, Quin, son of Jocina strolled into Ni'Dio's great hall.

"My Lord Quin, Wizened One, a most pleasant surprise," Ni'Dio said, heart quickening. "I see our taste for art has not—"

She felt her jaw drop as he neared. His silver hair had become golden, and his once pale skin was now blue. His eyes appeared as ice, and obsidian-colored diamonds decorated his brow like a circlet.

Undeterred, she picked up her dress and approached. "What happened?"

Quin smiled at her. At least his red lips and fangs had not diminished. "A minor setback and a greater change upon the world, most Wise Ni, my love. May I present some new friends? We call them Vel."

He hooted, and a group of six cloaked figures followed him into the room. Beneath their coverings, the creatures were naked, but there was no anatomical reason for covering. Scales, black and in the shape of diamonds, covered them head to foot. Their noses had fallen away, slits remained. They were constantly moving, their reptilian pupils taking in everything. When they sniffed, a forked tongue touched the air, and when they opened their mouths, rows of jagged teeth could be seen. Their fingers were like the great beasts of the south, ending in black talons. The Vel's scales glittered like glass underneath her coalescence, shining and wondrous.

The monsters parted for another figure behind them. A woman. She, too, was cloaked, but Ni'Dio recognized the Voice of the South and the aura that enveloped her. Her leather and steel armor creaked or rustled with each step. Her largest weapons were visible hanging from some belt or another.

She was Kamalia, a half-Glymph woman. She never bothered with ceremonial attire, but at least she had learned some formality.

Kamalia bowed, letting her two sets of eyelids open and shut once as she extended a wooden box. Did her skin have a teal look to it? Normally, she was olive green. "My Mistress, Keeper of the South and Sorceress Empress of Avoc, offers you gifts upon your happy news, Wizened Lady of Diotek."

She spoke of Jocina. The Sorceress had eyes and ears everywhere.

"Quin, what is this?" Ni'Dio asked, hand hovering above the box, inches from Kamalia's face. A black diamond had formed on the center of her forehead, but nowhere else. It was true, her skin had changed color, a shade greener than his.

He circled the half-Glymph essencer ranger and opened the box for Ni'Dio. "This, my lover, is how we will govern the world."

Brilliant hues shone from ten rings, illuminating Ni'Dio's face. They were bright, beautiful, and now hers.

"Your mother, the high Keeper, has outdone herself."

"She's well-practiced at that."

"And what does she request in return?"

A leer crossed Quin's face, and she felt hot and ready to retire. "We merely want a criminal, my lady. A murderer, fugitive, and enemy of all that is Avocan. We believe she comes to Zeller. My mother has tasked Kamalia to return her. We also believe we have aligned interests."

Ni'Dio grinned, then let herself twirl in the midst of so many colors, so much life and death that the world fabric had gathered in this one room—her room. She laughed and strolled up to Quin. "Tell me more, in my chambers."

His cold silver gaze glittered lustfully. "As you wish." He glanced to the scaled men. "Behave, children."

The Vel hissed. Ni'Dio snapped her fingers, and a cautious naye took the box from Kamalia.

"Edelissi, refreshments for our guests. Wizened Kamalia, make yourself comfortable, dear. We will discuss everything you need in an hour."

"Two," Quin interrupted.

Ni'Dio grabbed a small fan from Edelissi, who was trying to keep some distance between herself and the hungry, roaming yellow eyes of the Vel. Ni'Dio fanned herself, letting her imagination run wild. "Two, then. But I am grateful to Jocina for the gifts and will wear them tonight for dinner."

She and Quin and she strolled in the direction of the corridor.

"I will need a ship," Kamalia pressed.

"Two hours," Ni'Dio repeated. Quin snickered. It was so easy to put even a lesser essencer in her place. Amused, Ni'Dio smiled at Edelissi, who was wise enough to retain a neutral expression. Yes, it was wonderfully easy.

The teal-skinned half-Glymph bowed. "As your Wise Majesty says. You are most generous."

"I know, dear."

Quin's voice was low as he pressed himself against her, whispering in her ear. "The Vel require fresh meat, Ni."

Admiring Jocina's latest experiments, Ni'Dio gestured aloofly. "Dwarf then. I can spare one of the six."

Quin laced his fingers in hers and led the way to her chambers.

CHAPTER 16

EDELISSI FINALLY ESCAPED THE GREAT ROOM, WHERE THE VEL had taken not one but two of the Dwarf naye that had been her neighbors, friends, and comrades in arms. She had seen dragons and drakes devour a person, but these—abominations—had ripped them apart gleefully and slathered themselves in the entrails. Kamalia had insisted upon another room, where she rested from her journey.

But for Edelissi, it was all she could do not to scream. Her hand clutched her mouth as her body was sacked by horrified shaking. She swallowed vomit twice and hurriedly cleaned. Her new "master" would never like the odor. Worse than rotting flesh, apparently.

Edelissi splashed cool water over her face and stared into the mirror above the washbowl. She barely recognized the Elf there. Bald, traumatized, molested. In the great room, she could still hear the Vel's hissing delight, the wild indulgence of being a monster. Down the hall, sounds of ecstasy echoed from Ni'Dio and Quin's dalliance.

The Elf slave gritted her teeth, dried her hands and face, and hurried to her chambers—the only benefit to being a handmaiden to the murderous vixen. With quill pen, ink, and parchment, she scrolled a quick note.

To the Roaster,

Ten and ten orders of imported Zelvatore nuts for our Avocan guests' dinner before they head north. Her ladyship prefers those sea-salted and will be grateful if we can prepare a large batch to take with us when we travel to Franca for the royal wedding. Also, two orders of noodles to celebrate a hunt. Make them artistic, light as the stars, and salted by the sea.

Edelissi quickly folded the noted, sealed it with wax—without a sigil—and slipped it into the fold of her robe. *I am,* she thought, *a ranger of the west, a daughter of a high house in Lodornatha, and I will find justice.*

She carefully watched the hall until she was sure it was empty. Light-footed and swift, she hurried to the kitchens. The taste of ginger and garlic was in the air. An onion brought forth tears. The cooks and kitchen maids acknowledged her with a curtsy. A good word from her may go a long way to keeping their lives. Where Ni'Dio saw "lowborn," Edelissi saw hardworking, desperate women trying to survive this tyranny. Someday, hopefully, she could help them and the other mistreated of Istante. They all had to survive first. She nodded back but continued. She had little time and must keep up appearances as the lady's handmaiden.

"Market boy!" she shouted.

The young Istantese boy appeared from underneath a plaster archway, where he had been repairing a straw basket. He wore a loose tunic, and oversized-trousers held up by a belt with an empty coin pouch. Unruly hair looked like a dog sat upon his head, but stars be blessed lowborn were allowed to at least grow their hair. Edelissi missed hers—and much more.

"To the nut merchant on Peling Street. Urgent." She handed him the note. "Please. Fly quickly."

The poor child attempted not to look through her robes but at her face.

"Best behavior," Edelissi chided, but they both knew it was not a rebuke.

"Yes, Naye of the Wizened," he said and ran out of the kitchens.

Edelissi sighed and leaned against a crate. The woman and her guests had murdered three of her friends today. After her company had fought with many others alongside the Wo'Huzziet against the Cardor slavers, she had lost so many. In truth, Edelissi was grateful her family hadn't come for her. They weren't essencers. Ni'Dio would have slaughtered them in her perpetual boredom.

She passed through the kitchens, sampled food for the evening meal, and then returned to her post. She closed her eyes, trying to block out the sounds throughout the castle.

"Uncomfortable, Elf?"

Edelissi opened her eyes, hardening her emotions. She bowed low, knowing the kimono still exposed parts of her she had once hoped to reserve for a husband.

"It's uncomfortable to watch an Elf groveling," Kamalia, half-Glymph, said. "Especially one from Lodornatha. Up now."

Edelissi rose even as Kamalia adjusted her leather belt and cuirass. She wore steel toe boots and thick gauntlets. A large curved sword hung from one side of her belt, a knife from the other, and a quiver and bow behind her. In the center of her chest-plate was engraved a six-winged heron, the sigil of Jocina.

"You've heard of me?" Kamalia asked as she took a seat across the hall on a chaise, crossing her legs below the cuirass.

"All Lodornathans know the dragon slayer from Avoc."

Kamalia grinned, showing off her long canines. She blinked again, two sets of eyelids—one vertical and one horizontal—closed in succession. "Gods, bloody stories and tales. Here."

Kamalia unclipped her cloak and tossed it at her. Edelissi grabbed it easily out of the air, so not a part of the fabric touched the ground.

Edelissi froze, realizing her mistake. Was this a trap?

"A ranger, so I thought. Cover yourself. You deserve it."

"If my lady—"

Those canines showed again as the warrior gestured down the hall. "Your lady is predisposed with my lord, if you haven't heard."

Edelissi bowed her head in thanks and quickly wrapped herself. She sighed, embracing modesty she thought was forever lost.

"Sit and tell me who I speak with."

"Edelissi Naye, Lady Kamalia."

"Edelissi. Captain Edelissi?" Kamalia leaned forward, leather creaking. "Gods. They should have slaughtered you on the field, not dragged you back to this living Kerdum."

She couldn't stop the curl of her lip.

"If ever I find this Claudya and Kestov, I will give them the same greeting your lady sent your father." Edelissi gasped, looking at her missing finger. "Tell me, Captain—or should I say, 'Princess'? I'm supposed to hunt the former heir to Jocina's high priest. They think she's star-blessed. Do you?"

"I do not know."

A dark eyebrow curved upward. "Three ravens fly in three different directions from the city. North, southwest, and north-west. I'm grateful she hasn't broken you."

Edelissi looked past Kamalia through a window. Sure enough, small black objects darted three different ways. Good lad.

"I'm not going to say anything," Kamalia replied. She grinned, canines showing, like a predator looking at prey. Then she gestured down the hall. "Besides, they're saying enough, wouldn't you agree?"

"Your ladyship," Edelissi responded. How easy it would be to slip up, to crack a joke, and her struggle would be over.

"Smart woman. Stay alive, Captain. There's some bloody awful things coming."

"Like the men in there?"

Kamalia chuckled. "Gods, they're just the start. You know I'm parting ways with them here. They head north. I'm going to Zeller."

"To hunt the fugitive."

"And bring back the artist your lady wants. This artist is the only essencer, other than the Sorceress, known to create life. I imagine you're wondering the same thing I did: how terrible an idea this is! Bringing someone like that, here, against their will." Kamalia sighed, leaning back. She had high cheekbones and curved eyes, the faint hint of pointed ears. "There are things we say to survive. My guess is an artist of this caliber may be very interested in that jewel I saw in the coalescence."

Edelissi remained still, calm. A bead of sweat ran down the back of her neck. She would not think, not let any emotion beyond her quintessence show.

"I wonder," Kamalia said. "Could an artist like that retrieve the jewel?" Their gaze was long. "Don't ever let *her*..." Kamalia gestured down the hall. "... understand who *you* are."

Edelissi exhaled.

Kamalia resumed her casual posture. "Besides, I much prefer a ship. I think I'll be scrubbing the smell of whale out of my armor for a year."

"Your ladyship, if I may inquire personally?"

"Do so."

"The black diamond on your forehead and Lord Huiquin's?"

Kamalia's expression saddened. "There are things you can't come back from, Captain Edelissi. If you notice any strange vines with thorns and purple buds growing anywhere, don't touch them.

At least with Elf blood, you'll keep a part of yourself. Those six Vel were once Men, Dwarves, and Goblins, if you believe it. There are more."

Kamalia's armor creaked again as she shifted. "Their hide is as thick as a drake's, and they're slippery little bastards. If we're wrong, and the rumors are true about these blue stars and why Priestess A'banna and her father fled their city, and if this Shai has the same magic as Jocina, we're condemning a whole world, Edelissi. What do you think about that?"

"I'd rather die, Kamalia Elf-and-Glymph Blood."

Kamalia gave her a weary smile. "That's the nicest thing any Elf has said to me." She stood but hesitated. "If I happen to encounter, say, messengers from House of Onoarel in Lodornatha, what should I say to them, Princess?"

Edelissi swallowed. "Everything you said to me. And I am strong."

"I can see that. Stay so."

"I thought you were the servant of Jocina?"

Kamalia nodded. "Voice of the South. Oh, yes. But my mother wasn't Jocina, and I can't figure out whether or not dear old half-brother is trying to supplant her or not. No matter. If he or she rules, there won't be a world for me to hunt in. They plan on remaking it, all of them, you understand." It was Edelissi's turn to raise what little eyebrows she had.

"I'll need my cloak back, Captain. Best not draw attention to yourself or that market boy."

Edelissi's hand froze as she started to remove the garment.

Kamalia frowned and placed a gauntlet on her hip, above her dagger. "I roam the wildlands, Princess. I don't live in Avoc, no matter what the tales say. I'm the Voice of the South because I tend to the land and its inhabitants. All of them. I said I will remain silent and by the honor of the land I will."

Edelissi slowly removed the cloak. "You don't have to pursue them. You are nothing like them." Her eyes flickered down the hall.

"Unfortunately, I do," Kamalia said, refastening the garment. "No matter how much I agree with you. I have that bloody reputation to uphold. And my word."

"Watch yourself, then, in Zeller."

"Baktur? Of course." The half-Glymph scoffed as she readjusted her sword and was ready. "They share our shadows."

"Thank you for your kindness, Kamalia, daughter of Hurmlen."

The half-Glymph smiled, gave a partial bow. "Thank you for the intelligent company, Princess Edelissi Onoarel, ranger captain. I am not often with an equal."

Kamalia clutched the hilt of her sword and headed down the hall, armor clattering and creaking as she went.

Edelissi stared, stunned, and let herself sit for a moment longer as the other sounds of the palace were briefly muted. She felt her missing ring finger—which itched—and then drifted down to the long scar on her wrist where the drake had pinned her against rock. Her face twisted a bit into a snarl, she quickly replaced her emotions with the nothingness a slave should have. She would survive this.

Edelissi glanced down the hall again as Kamalia turned the corner. Kamalia stared confidently at her before disappearing.

Then she realized, all too late, that if Kamalia was not an ally, then Edelissi of House Onoarel had just assisted in destroying the world.

Trembling, she went to the kitchen. She had mundane, nayil duties to attend to.

CHAPTER 17

BEDEL FELT SOMEONE WATCHING HIM FROM THE SHADOWS AS HE left Shai's hut—or the one they had shared for nearly a month here. He could still hear her snoring, though the dawn sun had risen. It wouldn't be long before they departed, but even A'banna agreed—they needed an hour or two of rest. The satchel with all of their key evidence was packed, as was a second one with copies, as well as the tattered remnants of Huahanna's book, and the imager beside it. Bedel crossed over to a water barrel and splashed his face. The shadows moved.

Bedel slid into a defensive stance, feet apart, hands raised.

"At ease, my friend," Martuza said, stepping out of the shadows of the building.

Bedel dropped his hands. "Similarities between the Rda and Baktur abound."

Martuza chuckled and ran a hand through his long gray hair. "It has been a long time since I replaced my vows with one of stewardship, but we never give up our ways. Walk with me."

Bedel fell into stride with the chief.

"I have no weapons or gifts I can give your people as you

leave," Martuza began. "Except knowledge. That, I think, is your greatest shield."

"You know where the Gate is," Bedel whispered.

"Not just I. The Sorceress sent one of her birds to watch the fall of Ntokup, so she knows that the rumors we spread with the help of the Elves are false. The tear is not in the north. It cannot be."

"Why? Is it in Ntokup?"

"Beneath it, in the catacombs of an old tower, was a place the Immortals once used. It was there that the breaking began, although it had greater power of destruction than others."

"Why not just close the tear between realms? Shut off The Taurs and The Caurs forever?"

Martuza's brow furled. "And wait for the gods to kill themselves? Then we would not have moments of blessing, like yesterday, where they showed us what you and A'banna are capable of, beyond our reasoning. No, our elders chose to keep it open not because it is an exit into our realm, but an entrance into theirs."

"Excuse me?"

Martuza fell silent as they rounded a few huts. People moved inside, quiet chatter. At a community oven, women were already baking bread as children helped cut vegetables. A man with an apron entered the smokehouse, where meat from the raptor dried.

The people waved at them. Martuza nodded, then led Bedel to a quiet part of the wall. In hushed tones, he said: "In all our years, The Taurs never appeared inside our city, always outside trying to enter in. No, but the tear itself is in the very web of the world fabric. However, our ancestors began to rebuild after the breaking. They started at Ntokup, but now it will end somewhere else. That is for you to find. I will send a guide, and he will show you where the entrance to the Gateway is. I warn you, it will take an essencer of great strength to even access it. The McCormack family was thorough in their genocide and erasure of our culture and history, more than they know. Even then, it cannot be opened without the seventh stone."

"What stone?" Bedel asked, trying to make sense of what Martuza shared.

"We call it the jewel of the High Clan. Only the heir or heiress of the high chief or chieftess may house it."

"House a jewel? You mean inside of her?"

Martuza's head bobbed side to side, his long-braided hair crossed his face. "We learned many things from the Elven Memory Larks, or perhaps they learned things from us. Lark jewels may be taken, you know, shaped into something else, a weaving that is so unlike it, the jewel is not even noticeable. The chieftess is unlike anything else you know."

Martuza grabbed Bedel's elbow, his grip hard. "Find Naminia Bloodskull, enter the domain of Transcendence, and petition the Weave Master for the Rite. It is the only way for you to be spared, my friend."

"Enter Transcendence? The Realm of The Taurs and The Caurs?"

"And petition the Weave Master for the Rite."

Listening to the fervor with which Martuza shared these things frightened Bedel. The chief was strong, but here, he seemed desperate.

"Why not close it from here?"

"How useless would one be to brick up only one gate of a city, when there are many? The front gate leads you to the Tower of the Weave Master, but others take you elsewhere. Seal them all, seal a few, or seal none. It is up to you. But the breaking was greater than you know."

"Martuza, if you know this, you know it will kill me! And now A'banna, too."

"Not if you petition the Weave Master himself. He should listen, I think."

"What happened to 'everyone dies'?"

"It is the path of the ancestors, Bedel," Martuza said. "But not every ancestor has the power of gods. Your ancestor sealed the Gateway. You must open it, but you will need my niece, Naminia, to do so. I do not know if we can meet again. We will leave here soon. The danger of retaliation from the south haunts my dreams, Starblessed. Bominga will show you the way inside. When you return to our lands—if you return—you must search the wisdom of your ancestor to do what must be done."

Bedel's mind wheeled from all of this. He didn't have to die? The original him knew? Original him? What did that mean? So he had a biological family? Who? How did he end up in a 'jar'? He'd have to enter Transcendence and speak with a god none of them believed in? Why not! What else could be crazier? To do any of that, though, he needed Naminia, the heiress stolen by the Slaver Coalition, who surfaced briefly to testify, only to be abducted again five years ago? Raynt and the King's Men were tracking her down, but they needed this portal to enter the Weave Master's home directly? Bedel could live?

"I don't know my ancestors, Chief Martuza."

The elder man broke into a grin and clapped him on both arms. "Which is why you must find a way to reconnect with them, someday. You have one chance at avoiding the death the allies of my people would have for you—and two women who will fight for you with love I see only from those with deep devotion. You will find out who you are, Bedel Starblessed, our Gatekeeper, or history will continue its cycle, round and round we go, until one day perhaps our people forget history and one day, our enemy wins."

Bedel blinked, sighed, and stepped back. "What did you say? About the cycle?"

"It continues."

"Circular," Bedel said. "In mathematics, a circle is pi, 3.1415."

"So it is."

"If we change the cycle, how many of us do you think would be required?"

"As many lives and deaths as it takes," Martuza said. "Even mine."

He held out his hand, and Bedel grasped it above the wrist. "You bring me hope."

"You bring us hope, Starblessed. Come. It is nearly time for you to leave."

MURMURS OF SURPRISE AND AWE CAME FROM THE CROWD AS THEY pressed in around the table. Old men placed little boys on their shoulders just to see the new, shimmering silver blades, shield, and bracers. Rangers stood on either side at full attention, making sure no one touched the items on display.

A'banna couldn't believe they'd made them together. Shai emerged from one of the huts, dark circles under her eyes and bandages around her wrists. She was exhausted, and her few injuries didn't help. A'banna had seen those before, when an essencer gave too much aether to the world fabric as payment—or bribes as Shai called them. Still, the few mistakes A'banna or one of the youth assistants had made in moving the weapons too quickly didn't fully make sense. Why had it hurt her?

The crowd cheered when Shai neared. She grinned, waved at the crowd as if she were at a performance. It was remarkable, regal even. The disrespectful and, at times, vulgar woman had turned into a fully gracious host, but Shai was also a beloved artist and performer. A'banna had to confess, she admired Shai for it.

Rangers gathered horses and supplies near the gate. The horses neighed and bucked, none too pleased about the guests on the other side of the boma wall. A cart loaded with furs, hides, and baskets of provisions was pulled forward.

"Ladies and gentlemen," Shai's voice boomed. "It is with great pleasure that I present gifts from the people of the stars to their Chosen instruments."

A'banna gawked. No ceremony was needed and was uncalled for.

Shai presented the baklana sword to Bedel first. A'banna could feel the awe he had for the weapon.

"Used by the great assassins and followers of the balance, the baklana is a weapon fit for any warrior with the skill to use it," Shai declared. One of the Wo'Huzziet women brought forth a leather baldric specifically fashioned for the weapon. They fastened it on Bedel, and he sheathed the sword. "And for any spy, a well-concealed weapon with a little extra protection is always welcome." She lowered her voice. "Give me your hands."

"Nice show," Bedel said, holding his hands out.

"Of course," she said, fastening the bracers to him. She slid jointed plates out from inside the bracers. They fit over his hands, forming gauntlets. He twisted his wrist, and a blade popped out.

"Incredible," Bedel said.

"The power of art in our little magical realm," Shai said with a sly smile.

She turned to A'banna. "For our Leviathan, I present two Wo'Huzziet knives and the gift of this shield."

A'banna was given a belt that could sheathe the knives to her thighs and a medium-sized shield—slightly smaller than she was used to—with four thick spikes squarely centered. Inside each spike was a different colored jewel—pink, blue, yellow, white— all in the shape of the tear drop from her father's imager. "I don't understand. What are these jewels?"

"My contingency plan," Shai whispered. "Store yours or Bedel's aether and quintessence in the jewels, and you have a chance to survive. I'll teach you how later. I happened to have acquired these from an immortal benefactor and have been saving them, as he said I would."

A'banna reacted with a gasp as Shai proclaimed something she didn't hear to the crowd, who applauded. A'banna held the shield, examining the curved runes weaving in and around the spikes, center, and jewels. Shai had taken the gift of the gods and made it something precious, hopeful. A'banna slid her arm into the two leather straps and grasped a small handle set into the back of the shield, guaranteeing a firm grip. The balance was more exact than any Avocan shield, lighter, but firmer. The shield itself was thick. She punched the surface, causing Shai to glance her way.

"This is a good shield."

"I know," she said, smiling.

Shai held up the steel arrow. "I sensed I needed to make this. Whether or not it has a purpose, it travels with us to the north. Perhaps one of the other Chosen can use it." She wrapped it in leather and picked up a curved, almost triangular blade. "And to the Wo'Huzziet, our gracious hosts, I give a spearhead. Attach it to the spear of your chief and use it bravely in the battles to come. I must caution, though, that I do not know if the magic of this metal will work without the bloodline of the ancients or the stars running through you. Be careful and be blessed."

The crowd cheered. Chief Martuza Cougareyes bowed and received the spearhead in awe. It lacked most of the runes, but it was still beautifully formed and a sharp weapon. Martuza held the spearhead aloft. "This weapon shall serve the honored Rda of any Wo'Huzziet tribe, so long as they are the greatest among our warriors. We thank you, Lady Shai."

"It is my honor to count the Wo'Huzziet as our friends." Shai offered a genuine smile. "Thank you, Chief Cougareyes, and all of you. All of these weapons, if history has taught us anything, will never lose their sharpness. But take care of them, for they are most rare. Thank you for your gracious patience as we sojourned with you."

Martuza stepped up onto the platform of his longhouse. "Friends, allies, Wo'Huzziet. These last four weeks, we have seen great things. The Immortals came, the Speaker for Men was renewed, and we have been blessed with Chosen and the presence of The Caurs. We must never forget that the edge of our future lies in understanding our past, so with the blessing of all our ancestors upon you, we send your company on your way. You shall not journey alone. Rda Bominga and two of his warriors shall run with you."

Idrin shuffled uncomfortably but said nothing.

Martuza presented the spearhead to the elder Rda, who held a wooden shaft. He fitted the spearhead to it. As the village watched, the steel seemed to merge with the spear. Tendrils of starlight steel melted down around the wood, reinforcing it. Bominga gasped and nearly dropped the spear, but the tendrils passed harmlessly under his hand, forming a seamless end of starlight steel from one end to the other. A'banna turned and saw Shai lower her hand. Silvery aether retreated back into her aura. She winked at A'banna.

"Every great gift needs one who can wield it," Shai proclaimed. "May the ancients bless and preserve you and The Caurs give you bounties beyond imagination."

The Rda's one eye blinked, staring at the weapon, before he dashed into complex drills, ending with the spear splitting a thick log set out for the fire. The weapon was nimble but lethal. He pulled the blade out with ease. Bominga brought the spear to rest on his shoulder and bowed.

Shai bowed and quickly left the table. Bedel said his farewells, so A'banna followed Shai.

"You don't believe in gods or goddesses," A'banna said to Shai.

"But they do, or at least in their ancestors. If I have to say a few words to get favor from a people, I will. You never know when you'll need a friend next."

They passed Idrin, who stood by the carriage. Idrin scratched behind his ferret's ears as the two watched the women near.

Her fake smile disappeared. "Let's get on the road."

"And the last blade?" Idrin said. Both he and the ferret's eyes seemed to move as one, tracking Shai.

"Idrin, I can't use its magic. Call it a smith's payment."

"May I see it?" A'banna asked.

Shai frowned and reached underneath her tunic to pull out a small, sickle-like dagger, round like a talon with a horizontal grip.

"A raptor's claw," A'banna whispered, examining the Belasna runes that ran up and down its curved length.

Shai shrugged as she took the weapon back and hid it again. "I was inspired, but a spy doesn't readily reveal her tools."

"Beware the cost of meddling too much in magic that is beyond you," Idrin said.

Shai patted him on the chest. "Oh, dear ranger. Who is the only one north of Avoc that can use the magic of Art?"

Before anyone could reply, Bedel approached. A'banna discovered she was staring, and that he liked it. He was dashing with that sword at his back, the silver bracers shining below the arms of his tunic. So unlike Quin had ever been.

His cheeks reddened. Shai looked away. A'banna wished she could run and hide.

"We depart," Bedel called.

The last of the Wo'Huzziet gathered around the gate, wishing the group fair travels and other blessings in a tongue A'banna still hadn't learned. It made Bedel happier, which made her more content. A'banna chose a horse that hadn't been saddled and leapt up without aid. Whatever Bedel—and the others—had done, her body had healed astonishingly well.

A'banna moved her horse beside Bedel's. He gave a swift nod but kept his thoughts focused on stone and blinding light. Sunlight glimmered off his new arsenal; his jaw was set. Bedel had made up his mind, but on what, precisely, he hadn't shared. For a short time, perhaps, the gods of the stars had given him—and Shai—to her. She'd embrace what little time they had with joy, no matter what others believed.

The elder Rda, Bominga, came to stand beside her horse. His new spear caught the sun. Behind him came two of the younger warriors. All three carried a spear, short sword, and a tall, tear-drop shaped shield covered in painted hide, so as to blend in with grass and trees. They wore shorts, vests, and sandals, secured by leather straps around their legs, and a belt with pouches of provisions.

When the gates opened, the great beasts that roamed the fields neared. The raptors lined up again in procession. A hushed whisper floated through the crowd of onlookers. Then, one by one, the raptors followed the golden-haired lion as it strode side-by-side with A'banna's horse. She looked down at the majestic cat, a perfect predator, and instead of fear, she felt pride. She was bringing a gift to a friend she hadn't met, yet. An ally. A companion.

The raptors followed at a trot behind, with the alpha female in the lead. Behind them, Idrin and the other rangers followed. A'banna shifted and could see Shai in the wagon, staring ahead with awe and even a twinge of fear. The Wo'Huzziet kept aston-ishing pace with the wagon, their footfalls silent on the road.

Riding tall and proud, A'banna turned to look back at the settlement. Martuza stood in the open gate of the village, fist raised above him. Their caravan crested the hill, and he stepped back through the gate; he was the last she saw of the Wo'Huzziet before entering the great wilderness beyond.

THE LONG ROAD HAD ONCE BEEN PAVED WITH WIDE, SMOOTH stone. It wound through rocky plains or barren savannah fields. The Great River was on their east, flowing south to north, a perpetual guidepost. The road was a treasure of some era, some bygone history that had died long before most of A'banna's companions' memories had a chance to be cradled in the womb. It felt wondrous that this artery still existed—and even more exciting that it connected the five great tribes to the outside world.

At first, only the animals ran from them. The orange and black spotted giraffes, striped zebras, hairless scaly yehts and their smaller hornless kin. She even saw long-necked behemoths, heard their large feet shake the earth with every step. The animals all fled from her company's approach, galloping or striding farther west and beyond view as fast as possible. Elephants herded their young, trumpeting at the raptors. Lion prides approached the road, bowed to the lion trotting beside her, then darted back into the grass or thickets. Every animal ignored or feared her touch of aether, the connection the animals of the south did not shy from. Strangely enough, the raptors did not pursue.

The lion did not hunt. It just accompanied them.

Her.

The rest of the beasts that she had so come to treasure ignored A'banna or were frightened of her. To them, she was a raptor astride a horse, a hunter they sensed was being hunted. That is all they would share amid their panic.

The three Wo'Huzziet took notice. She could hear their rhythmic breath as each of the three warriors kept pace with the others. None spoke. They only ran. The rangers seemed content to be quiet also, keeping their counsel to themselves. It was a different sort of travel than she was used to. Even nature used to be her companion. Now, there was only silence, and in that dreadful quiet, memories threatened to return. The entire turn of her life crept at the edge of her mind, so much so that she wished for the animals to think something. Anything.

You can't control the whole world, Bedel said. *Let the animals be as they prefer.*

A'banna craned her neck to watch a herd of wild auroch galloping away. *I try to control nothing,* she thought. *I am used to their counsel, and now they flee from us, even with the raptors as if in a spell.*

One you did not weave.

The stars did. They were a gift.

You can scarcely call the army building siege towers outside a nobleman's walls a gift. It is the same for them.

They locked eyes for a moment, deepening their connection.

They say we see ourselves as the hunters but are being hunted.

Bedel tensed, the leather of his saddle creaking. *Any idea by whom?*

A'banna surveyed the landscape. *Silver eyes and a Voice in the shadows with a pride of unknown. Some say men, others snakes, large lizards, or Goblins. But none understand. And the raptors—*

Bedel turned. "Idrin, tell our people to keep an eye out for any pursuers. They may take the form of a man but look like a reptile."

"Aye," the ranger replied, sending the command down the line.

"A'banna," Bedel said aloud. "We'll be at another village soon, but Martuza said they severed their ties with the Wo'Huzziet nation, so it's possible the Wenta tribe won't let us in. If they do, we'll rest there for the night behind a boma wall."

"She's coming for me," A'banna croaked, shamed at the fear in her voice. "And if she catches me, she'll catch you."

"What I've been trying to say all along," Shai called forward. "Sorry to eavesdrop."

"Hardly," Bedel said.

Shai made a dismissive grunt, and they fell quiet. The only sound was that of the wind upon the tall grass; whistling through rocky formations, rustling leaves, and rippling the surface of ponds and pools. Some contained water drakes, sunbathing on the shore, massive jaws wide, waiting.

A'banna felt the skills she had learned as a hunter returning. She saw and heard everything, filtering it as needed. It was the only way to contain the fear and retain hope.

Later that night, when they neared the first outpost of the Wenta Tribe, the walls were unlit, and the gate barred. Arrows creaked under the tension of taut bowstrings. Faint sounds of controlled breathing came from within and its wooden towers.

Only a single man stood outside the gate. A lion's skull rested upon the Wenta herbalist's head as bones covered his colorful hide garments. Barefoot, he stomped the ground and shook his staff, which was topped with the skull of a sabrecat. The sudden rattling of bones, the stomping of his feet, and the dark arrow-heads glistening in blue starlight needed no translation for Bedel, but A'banna could only understand from what Bedel thought.

The Wenta tribe condemned the raptors and lion as possessed by evil Taurs. They had no desire to let them sleep on their doorstep. Rda Bominga stepped forward to reason with the Wenta herbalist but was rebuffed. Wenta was no longer Wo'Huzziet and would not shelter those who created the division.

Bominga scoffed, turned, and shuffled four times in the dirt before moving on. He shook his head at Bedel in regret.

"We ride on," Bedel said. A'banna could feel his frustration.

As the company passed the walls, A'banna said, "What did he say?"

"That they dream of silver eyes and of you," Bominga said between breaths, running beside her horse. "The ruins of Ntokup are near. The Wenta Tribe suffered in its defense. Now they suffer stubborn minds!"

"We make for Ntokup," Bedel said. "Let us camp there, instead."

A'banna glanced back, but the outpost had already faded into the shadows.

* * *

Blue haze shimmered over the next hill, as if a thousand lights were there. Bedel thought he saw the brilliance glow even brighter, at one point, but as the road curved around an outcropping rock, it dimmed. Trees, dark in the night, seemed to make the light flicker as they rode past. A growl came from the left, as yellow feline eyes followed them, then darted away into the underbrush. The ground grew steeper, rockier. Above, the blue stars outshone the moon as the group crested a hill.

Bedel tightened his hands on the reins of his horse, leather creaking in his hands. Martuza's words echoed in his ears. He had mysteries to solve, and one night here would not answer them. Not, yet.

"Oh, bless the gods," A'banna whispered beside him. "I thought you said the city was ruined? It shines bright as the stars."

"It is an illusion," Bominga called.

The city rose shockingly tall inside an outer ring of walls. Many of its buildings were towers unto themselves, some connected by bridges. Many towers shined like mirrors. A smaller river streamed from the east to flow into the Great River, while a ring of mountains, just taller than the highest building, formed an outer circle around Ntokup. In the moon and starlight, Bedel could make out a forest to the south, no doubt only a sanctuary for wild animals now.

"We must hurry if we wish to camp," Bominga advised.

"Agreed," Idrin sounded off behind them.

As the company drew closer to the city walls, the light glistening off the buildings dimmed, allowing Bedel to see the city clearly in the unnatural blue light. The area of the walls still standing easily reached sixty feet high, but whole sections had crumbled. Some had been built back up with palisade replacements; others still held shadowy lumps of decaying corpses. Bedel's breath caught in his throat, his stomach heaved. The closer the paved road came to the city, the more pockmarked it became, often with boulders sitting in craters they guided the horses around, or open craters that had seemed to explode from the ground. Bedel's horse stepped in a shallow one. Water splashed under hoof.

The road curved toward the city. Ntokup's gates had shattered. Once there had been a great arch with matching towers above it. Neither towers nor arch remained. It didn't stop his imagination retelling this mega-metropolis' grandeur. What had it felt like to enter these gates? As Shai's horse drew near, she lifted a lantern, shining light onto the walls. Hundreds of symbols were carved there, including a staff of bones, a skull, and a cougar. All the tribes of the Wo'Huzziet gathered in one place. Bedel shifted in his saddle, meeting Shai's gaze. This had been complete genocide.

Once through the gate, off to the northwest, buildings lay in ruins. Weeds, vines, and other vegetation grew on free-standing walls or the odd short brick building dotting the ruined landscape. Many buildings still standing had no walls, no interior, just frames like skeletons stripped of flesh and muscle. Near one of the shattered sections of the wall, trees, buildings, and stone seemed sprayed inward, as if a wave had generated from that sole penetrating point, carrying everything across several city blocks inward. Parks and green spaces were overgrown. Crows took to the air as the street disappeared beneath an overgrown tree canopy. Suddenly, the vegetation ended, exposing the tall reflective towers which appeared to be made of glass, and though many of these glass walls remained intact, others had been completely shattered. Glass crunched beneath the horses' hooves or the wagon's wheels.

The city was eerily silent, even as they passed a street that had broken down market stands and open entries into shops. Then there were the odd, dark shapes in the road, more skeletal than anything the buildings could be.

"They were left in the streets," A'banna whispered.

"And the wall," Bedel said.

"Everywhere," Shai whispered, hoarsely. A'banna turned to look at her, into the lantern light. Shai shrugged, though her expression was far from dismissive. "Better if you didn't notice."

"The Sorceress massacred my people," A'banna spat. "I will notice."

"Yes," Bominga said at last. Bedel could see him studying A'banna in the starlight glittering through building frames. "They were left to rot for the vultures, crows, and animals. We buried or burned as many as we could. We left the invaders. Or those we couldn't dig out in time."

"I had no idea," Idrin said. "Rda, friend, I did not know."

"To the south beyond the walls was the dock," Bominga said, pointing. "The Lodoronathan battalions fell there, or were taken."

There were whispers between the rangers behind them.

"I see," Idrin whispered. "I should have come sooner."

"Yes," the Rda elder said. "You should have. Did you think

barrels of wine could help us mourn our dead and the fall of our nation?"

"Never" Idrin began. "Forgive me."

Rda Bominga grunted and led the company down a wide, long street. Many of the buildings appeared more ancient than the glass towers. Carved stone reliefs decorated lower levels of the towers, with broken marble steps leading up to empty doorways and windows, like giant skulls.

"This is more ancient than even our cities of Avoc," A'banna said. "How?"

"Our secrets are lost to the death and destruction of war," Bominga said.

The company rounded an empty stone fountain, covered in brown leaves and vines. A stone structure faced them, only its pillars remaining upright amid shattered rock. Parts of the stone were charred black, while so much of the building had caved in on itself. It was impossible to clearly see at night.

"Behold, the ruins of our Archives," Bominga said. "We shall camp here."

"Here, let us," Pol the Dwarven ranger, taking some of the reins. "Captain."

Idrin didn't speak as he dismounted.

Bedel noticed—because of A'banna—that the two young Wo'Huzziet warriors stayed quiet.

A'banna approached Bominga. "Were you here?" she asked.

"Most of us were, Starblessed," he said hoarsely. "Why we survive is still a mystery."

A'banna shivered as they stared out onto the crater of the Archives. A few steel or stone pillars protruded like ribs from the building, but below, it was hard to see anything but rocks, charred or not.

"I was there when my people rose up to fight the Sorceress. They followed my father, but they fought."

"It is for those of us who survive to find purpose. Come, there is natural covering this way."

Bominga led down into the crater, where the destruction had spared a few rooms. Four rangers stayed on the high ground, spreading out to keep watch. Another two took the horses inside the shell of a building half a block away. The space had been emptied of whatever had been there, but there was a pocked roof and a solid floor. Around a corner was another room, with a steel-reinforced door. From a pouch, Bominga produced a key. The door creaked open.

"Crows, it's beautiful," Shai murmured as the Rda lit torches. The room had been converted to a small armory. Ancient Wo'Huzziet armor, covered with dust, lined one wall. A'banna and Bedel approached helmets with long steel-coated antlers and layered leather cuirasses painted in green, brown, and blue hues.

"From the Yakoni Tribe in the northern plains. This is all that remains of them."

Bedel grasped the breastplate, holding it like a sacred relic. "It's light, still firm."

"If you require armor for your journey, you may help yourself to a set."

A'banna turned. "Rda Bominga, these are artifacts of your people. Are you sure?"

The old man with one eye smiled. "Yes, Starblessed, I am sure. Come, we have stored food here."

"In the morning, I would like to visit the docks," Idrin said as they sat around a fire with little smoke, its light blocked by three walls.

"We can take a little time," Shai said. "An hour or two."

"Thank you," he said, looking across the fire.

"We have all suffered these last few decades. At least your people came to help."

"Yes, and they fought like wild warriors." Bominga used a

stick to stoke the fire. Red sparks, picked up by the wind, illuminated his face. "They were overrun. I fought atop the walls, repelling the invaders until at last only I stood. But I saw from my post how Claudia and Kestov launched themselves into their ranks. Lodornathan warriors are fast, but these two used the world fabric against us. They carved through the ranks, beat or slaughtered the rest, and then when the survivors were rounded up, put onto the ships We had asked for your army, and you sent three battalions."

"My sister was here. Her name was Edelissi."

Bedel instinctively reached out, putting a hand on Idrin's shoulder. "I'm sorry—"

"I failed her. I should have abandoned the watch on the walls."

"Captain," Pol said, coming to join the circle. "The dragons tried to make a breach over the days the army was gone the days that Ntokup fell. Had we come, they would have gotten out."

"She was outnumbered," Idrin whispered.

"We're always outnumbered," Pol said.

Bominga cleared his throat. "This is Evaz." He rested one hand on the young Wo'Huzziet next to him. "He is my sister's son. He is all I have left. We, too, were outnumbered."

A'banna reached out to one of the young men, Evaz, who reached back. They gripped hands.

"The Sorceress is playing us all," A'banna said. "She hurt your people and mine, so she can get whatever it is that she truly wants. It's all a distraction until at last, she makes her move."

Shai let out an exasperated gasp. "Even if she sent her mutant bird to watch the proceedings, it doesn't mean she orchestrated the battle, or that she controls the Slaver Coalition. We have enemies everywhere. What should concern us is how many of them are coordinating together."

"And after that?" A'banna said.

Shai leaned back against a stone wall. "We take them apart. Piece by piece."

⚬────◖◉◗────⚬

NOT LONG LATER, THE GROUP SETTLED DOWN TO SLEEP. BOMINGA and Pol left to scout, then returned, rousing Bedel and Idrin.

What is it? A'banna thought to Bedel.

Tracks? What kind?

Bedel waved her forward. Shai seemed to sleep through it, recovering her strength. Evaz and a ranger took watch. The group followed the Rda and ranger up the crater and down the broken stone stairs. They crossed the street opposite the Archives. All grassy areas had grown over, just as this had. Except the grass had been beaten down into dried mud, surrounded by hoof prints.

"I'd say boar," Pol said. "But I haven't seen or heard any animals since we entered."

"No," A'banna whispered. "Only birds. Listen."

Even the crows had gone silent.

A'banna glanced up at the group. "These aren't boar tracks." Her voice caught in her throat with a flood of memories. "They're Marchers. Minotaurs. The Sorceress' hunters!"

"If those are minotaur tracks," Bedel said. "What's this?"

A'banna crouch-walked to him. There, in the dirt, were thin, long footprints. Three digits, ending in the imprint of a claw. Another set. And another.

Not far away, in the stables, the horses whinnied. Wings beat the air, somewhere close, not high.

Fear reached down through her, yanking deep to cause some nausea. A'banna held her hand to her throat, desperate not to scream.

Shai rolled over, groaning. Her back ached, and not just from sore muscles from the trip and a night of smithing. Reaching beneath her bedspread, Shai withdrew a pebble. "Fabulous."

All of a sudden, a dark face hovered inches in front of her. Instinctively, Shai reached for her knife, but in the glowing embers of their fire, she paused.

"Evaz! Careful."

"Quiet," the Rda-in-training whispered, then snuck along the broken wall, carefully pouring ash over the fire.

"What is it?"

Then Shai heard deep, nasal breathing, like an animal. It snorted. Rock ground stone as it heaved. Shai heard the crash before she saw the boulder tumble out of view. A gentle wind blew across the city, sending up dust and ash into the partially covered room. They were downwind of whatever was outside.

It moved, each movement seeming to shake the ground, jostling rock.

"She wants this moved tonight."

"Entrance is here," something shrill sang. It sounded like a bird and a woman.

"Shit," Shai said, crawling on all fours to the wall, just as the shadow of the big thing fell across the room, enshrined in blue starlight.

The shadow looked like a cow, or a boar, standing upright like a man.

Evaz pressed into her, short sword drawn but hidden behind his shield. The young man shook.

Shai placed a hand on his arm.

Wide-eyed, he turned to look at her. She shook her head, then gestured to the armory. *Where the Kerdum had everybody gone?*

Once inside, Shai started fitting the Yakoni tribal armor. Evaz followed her lead, which was good. The boy wasn't wearing much to stop a blow. *I hate helmets,* she grumbled to herself, then picked up one with the antlers. Though it was well balanced, she felt like she had extra weight on either side of her. The usual acrobatics wouldn't cut it in this. *Shitty to move in.* Evaz grinned at her from beneath one, and she tried to smile back. How green was Bominga's kid, anyway? Wasn't he supposed to be—

Her thoughts cut off as wings beat the air.

"Find it," the woman's voice said, though it had the cadence and tone of a bird. "Even if you spend the rest of your lives digging."

Shai crouch-walked back to the main room, pausing as the minotaur's shadow fell over a gap in the wall. If it got wind of them, saw them at all, all it had to do was reach down with hands capable of throwing a boulder and crush her skull inside this silly helmet. Fighting against the fear, Shai slowed her breathing. They had to get out of here. Find the others.

The bird cawed as someone screamed. Shai caught sight of a person falling from a great height, breaking like a melon on the ruins below.

Through the gap in the wall, Shai saw two minotaur shapes descend on the bloody corpse, pulling the ranger apart, piece by piece, eating the flesh of a leg. She grimaced, swallowing bile.

"Rangers!" the woman's voice came, but from a different direction. "Kill them all. Bring me Reason and the priestess."

Across the crater, three Velheron landed, beaks touching. The beasts were huge, six-winged each, but there was little detail Shai could see this far away in this light. But there were three birds. Not one. Not two. One, walking closer to the others, bent its knees and moved with a slight waddle, but otherwise appeared very human-like.

Bows twanged. Arrows whistled through the air. The Velheron screamed and took flight. Shai and Evaz unsheathed their swords.

The minotaur was still on the other side of the wall, grunting out commands. Shai lifted her fingers to count down.

Three. Two. One.

She and Evaz launched themselves through the opening, blades out and nearly ran face-to-face with the ugliest excuse for a creature Shai had ever seen. Yellow-black eyes stared down at her. White horns and tusks curled up, sharp and painted with silver and blue. It was at least seven feet tall, more muscular than the toughest human, and it leaned down, waving its axe and hammer to the sides. Spittle flew from its mouth as a scream escaped yellow-toothed, bloody jaws.

Shai cursed and dropped to her knees as it swung the hammer horizontally, smashing the broken wall they had just hidden behind. Evaz grunted, and she heard his body hit somewhere. Stone and dust showered her as she wheeled backward, her sword slipping from her fingers, tumbling blade-over-hilt into the crater. The monster roared again. Shai felt terror as the boar-man she had mocked as fiction raised the axe for a downward, execution-like arc. Shai fumbled at her belt for the raptor-hook. It had to be there. And then she gasped. Dozens of torches filled the street around the Archives to the northwest, illuminating dozens more of the monsters.

She had nothing left to say. The minotaur above her snorted.

Four arrows thudded into its open mouth and eyes.

"Run!" Pol the ranger shouted.

Shai stumbled to her feet and ran over to Evaz, who laid prone.

"Come on, kid, wake up," Shai said, grabbing the warrior and turning him over. His helm came off, too loose for his head. Blood covered his nose and mouth, and his chest had caved in, blue, broken. His eyes looked off to some distant sunset, some fabled ending of the pain of his people. A day when the Wo'Huzziet began winning.

"Oh, gods, no." Shai sniffled, falling backward, suddenly devoid of strength. "No. Come on, Evaz. No!"

The ground thundered beneath her. A minotaur approached.

"Shai!" Bedel shouted as he fought up the stone stairs. Two minotaurs ran at him and the group of rangers. Bedel used two hands on the starlight baklana, parrying away one of the monster's scimitars. A'banna rolled across the step and came up behind the creature, plunging her knife into its knee. The minotaur roared. Idrin's sword couldn't move fast enough. He and Pol dueled the other. Rda Bominga was right behind them; pivoting, he stabbed with his spear into the minotaur's eye, twisted, and yanked it out. It tumbled forward, but he left it for the rangers to kill. The Rda elder darted up the stairs and skidded the few feet into the crater to their level. A ranger had already beat him there and tried hoisting Shai up.

Wings pounded the air. Wind whistled. A black shape sailed across the crater, its beak like a spear. Shai felt the ranger's hands loosen as it was shoved away, impaled by the Velheron. The massive mutated crane shook its head, sending the corpse falling to the earth. It took to the air and dove toward her as a minotaur closed in. Shai stayed where she was, in front of Evaz, dressed in that ridiculous armor, raptor claw held up threatening.

She could feel the wind from the Velheron's wings—and then heard a sickening thud, a woman screaming as the bird smacked into the rubble, a starlight steel spear protruding from its body.

It was the chance she needed. Shai grabbed Evaz's loose helm in both hands and wielded it like an axe. It blocked the minotaur's downward strike. The antlers groaned, cracked, snapped under the monster's strength. It roared at her and Shai roared right back. Just as the helm gave way, Shai stepped to the side, throwing the minotaur off balance. Rda Bominga ripped the spear from the dead Velheron's corpse and spun, throwing it like a javelin. The beast gurgled its protest as it tumbled beside its fallen comrade.

Shai turned, stumbling to Evaz's body. Bominga fell to his knees, weeping. "My son! My son!"

She wanted to hold the old man, tell him his sacrifices wouldn't be in vain, but those were just words. This was Ntokup, the city that had once boasted life seemed cursed to be death.

Minotaurs charged the stairs. Thick, three-fingered hands latched onto the Archive's ledge as the creatures heaved themselves up. Dozens roared and charged across the crater.

Bominga seemed lost in his grief.

Shai felt confused, dazed. She touched the back of her head. It stung. Her fingertips were dotted with warm, wet blood.

On the wide stone stairs, A'banna screamed as she fought two of the minotaurs, back-to-back with Bedel. He led a minotaur away from A'banna, dodged a swipe of an axe, then used his baklana to slice up and across, opening one of the monster's throats. Another grabbed Bedel by the throat, but he thrust out, starlight steel blade releasing from his bracer into the minotaur's cheek. He kicked twice as he used that blade to carve up its face, enough that it let go, so he could bring it down with the baklana. More surrounded him. Bedel wiped blood off his lips, sneered at them, and braced himself. A'banna bobbed and weaved around the minotaur after her, pivoted, stabbing it in the back of its neck before ducking beneath a thrust and cut of its scimitar. Idrin and the remaining rangers formed a line on the stairs, trying to prevent them from being pushed up and into the crater, and thus losing the high ground.

Overhead, two Velheron circled, cawing, waiting.

The other Rda trainee darted up the stairs, face grim, tears on his cheeks. He pivoted, stabbed a minotaur with his spear, then closed the distance.

Bominga shouted something in their Wo'Huzziet tongue as a Velheron dove.

"We have to run," Shai said, shaking him. "Bominga! I'm sorry!"

The Rda clutched his son, then the starlight steel spear. His tears were still drying on his cheek, and shadows danced off the gaping eye socket where his other eye had been. Clenching his teeth, tensing, Bominga crouched on his toes, as if ready to run.

"No," Shai whispered. "We can't stay here."

"I am Wo'Huzziet," Bominga said. "And this is Ntokup, the city I alone survived to save."

Bominga sprinted past her, wielding the spear so quickly it seemed to bleed blue starlight. He carved down minotaur after minotaur in his path. Two, three, they tried to surround him. There was no way Shai could get to close with those flourishes. He might accidentally spear her, but her magic came from art itself. She felt down deep into the broken stone of Ntokup, listened to the rock and dirt and burned rubble as it spoke to her, *Soliditus* essences answering her call as if she conducted a symphony.

I make something from nothing, Shai thought, *or from something else.*

"Crows take you," Shai said.

The stone ruins across the crater shifted, changed. As powerful as the monsters were, they weren't steady. Stone beneath the cloven feet of the minotaurs turned into sharp blades, spaces apart. The minotaurs fell upon them, impaling, slicing, gouging. She spoke to their blood, to the dark fire like oil oozing within it, and turned it back into their mouths and snouts, clogging their breath. The minotaurs clawed at their faces, desperate to breathe as they drowned in their own blood, shed by the blades they toppled over onto.

Behind her, the lion and raptors roared. Ranks of minotaurs turned from her companions to face the newcomers, but the giant birds and the lion plowed into their ranks, tearing, ripping, slicing, biting.

"Press the assault!" Bedel shouted.

"Rangers on the Starblessed!" Idrin ordered.

Bedel and A'banna pushed the minotaur ranks down the stairs, into the animals who flanked them.

Bominga left a trail of bodies in his wake, while those minotaurs who tried to get to him tumbled into her trap. A group tried to flank him, but Shai would have none of that. A collapsed wall turned from stone to thin steel blades and spikes. Like a trap, the wall sprang back into place, then down as a lantern still clinging on its opposite side became a stone, driving the trap down.

Cheers came from the stairs as the group slaughtered the last of the minotaurs. Overhead, the two Velheron shrieked madly, then peeled off, flying in opposite directions, their wings blocking stars as they glided past.

Shai turned away from the gore. She pulled off her antlered helm, then tumbled next to the Rda kid, Evaz. One more dead Wo'Huzziet. One more they failed. And Evaz had saved her life. She reached town, intertwining her fingers with his, and wept.

Moments later, Rda Bominga approached, spear held at his side, covered in his enemies' blood. He was met by the remaining Rda lad and A'banna, who sprinted up the steps two at a time.

"No," she moaned, falling to her knees beside his head.

Bominga groaned, set the spear aside, and laid down next to his son's body. The grief came, heaving the elder's body. He screamed, covered his face, rose, and buried his head in the cleft of his son's neck, pulling the boy close.

A RED SUN ROSE OVER THE NTOKUP VALLEY. THE RIVERS AND waterfalls reflected the golden-red light and the crawling clouds. Rda Evaz was buried in a field of green, not far from the Archives. What Shai had created the night before, how she had defeated the minotaurs, was impossibly horrific. Now, stone creaked. Dust slid off as rock smoothed over. Shai gestured as she stepped away from the headstone, shaped like a spear, in Evaz's honor. A'banna and Bedel stayed near Bominga for the ceremony, while Shai and the others stood across the grave. Bominga and the Rda lad sang a lament at the top of their lungs. A'banna recognized the tune and some of the methods of using the tongue to trill, so she joined in, until at last emotion overwhelmed her and she just trilled in the method of her people. She had grown to like the boy and some of the others in the village. The Wo'Huzziet were such like Avoc, except without fear of a malevolent goddess or her guides. But life had been cruel to the Wo'Huzziet, and Rda Evaz had suffered it.

Just as they turned to leave Bominga, Shai erupted into a beautiful, haunting melody. It carried music that made all the Lodornathans pause, trills that spoke to the Wo'Huzziet and

A'banna, and an odd beat, shifting changing, twirling as if the music itself danced. Tears streamed down Shai's cheeks until the music ended with her letting dirt drift through her hands over the grave.

At midday, the company left Ntokup. They left the minotaurs' bodies in the sun as carrion. Indeed, as they crested the road, leaving behind the gorgeous forest and the waterfalls and the once-magnificent city, a flock of crows flew overhead toward the city.

Not long after, Bominga and the remaining Rda held back.

"This is as far as we take you, my friends."

Bedel turned his horse and quickly dismounted. He saluted the Rda with a closed fist over his heart, then in the air, as Martuza had done. They reciprocated. A'banna and Shai joined them. At last A'banna embraced the Wo'Huzziet, kissing them both on the cheeks. "Until we meet again," she said. "I will keep Evaz in my memories often."

"You honor us all, Starblessed," Bominga said, bowing.

"We'll do everything we can to make Evaz's death not in vain," Shai said, gripping his hands in her own.

"Why? Two rangers were killed, also, no? But we made the Sorceress bleed as she invaded our city, and left her troops to rot along with one of her pet birds. We are Wo'Huzziet. She shall remember, now. Evaz and your men made it reality."

"Rda Bominga," Idrin said, bowing. The two warrior groups saluted each other.

"We will stay here for one day," Bominga said. "To watch the road. Then we must return and warn our people of possible retaliation. But we won the right to our lands. We will again."

"Yes, you will," Bedel said, shaking the man's hand once more. With another embrace, A'banna turned for her horse and mounted. The company set out, leaving the two Rda in the center of the great road.

A'banna wiped away her tears and leaned forward.

"Death and victory," Bedel said. "They often are the same."

"Death and victory," A'banna repeated. As their horses plodded along, she reached out. He took her hand, and for a moment, they rode together like that, watched from behind.

At a crossroads north of Ntokup, Idrin sent three rangers west to Lodornatha, carrying the imager, Huahanna's book, and a few other missives. A'banna strangely felt little attachment to the things of her past life. She had brought them to those who needed them most, that was all. In some ways, she felt more Wo'Huzziet now than Avoc.

There was no sign of the Sorceress or her minions following them, but neither had they seen the tracks at Ntokup right away, either. Whatever digging she had forced the marchers to do, they had disrupted it for now. Why didn't it bring A'banna more pleasure? Evaz and his people. Huahanna and their people. How many lives would the Sorceress claim? One disruption of a single operation would never be enough.

When the sun, at last, touched the horizon in the west, they sought a place to camp.

Large, craggy stone formations provided shielding north of their camp. Idrin ordered fires and doubled the watch. Bedrolls had only just been laid, the meal dispersed, and the moon had barely reached its zenith when the horses whinnied. A'banna and others ran to see what had happened, only to find the raptors and lion gone.

Something touched her mind. The alpha female. *The hunt.*

"They're hunting," she called to everyone. "They'll return after they finish."

"Like keeping dragons," Pol grumbled. "Sooner or later, instinct kicks in. Be glad we aren't on the menu."

A'banna wanted to say something profound, but instead, she found herself glancing at the skies, at the cracks in the rocks, at the tall grass the horses grazed near. She shivered, but there was no chill. Even Bedel was on edge, sharpening his new blades. Perhaps they still felt the battle. It weighed in the tension of her muscles, her shoulders, her back.

Shai sat cross-legged beside A'banna near a fire as they watched him trace the whetstone against the baklana.

"One of the fascinating things about starlight steel is the legend that they never need sharpening."

"Then, why does he do it?"

"Same reason I sit beside you. Only fools go unprepared." Shai slapped her shoulder—only partially playful.

"Shai," A'banna said, getting the woman to pause.

"Evaz's death was not your fault."

Shai bit her lip but otherwise returned a stony expression. "He was young, and I led him into battle unprepared. Of course, it was my damn fault, as much as it was Bominga's, or the Sorceress and the Slaver Coalition for erasing every fighting man of his people." Shai spat. "It was my fault, A'banna. But thanks for trying to make it hurt less."

"The song, was that from your people?"

"Yes," Shai said, pushing dark curls over her ears. "A Branaird tale of a brave young soldier who died unjustly at the hand of an opposing tribe. I altered it a little."

"It was beautiful."

"It was for the kid."

A'banna set her chin on her knees as she wrapped her arms around her legs. "No, not wholly."

A smile escaped on Shai's face, even as starlight made her tear glisten like a sapphire jewel. "Get some sleep, A'banna." With that, she headed to her own bedroll. A'banna thought she heard her say: "Please, don't make me like you."

A'banna hugged herself tighter. How could she heal a rift between two people that she had helped to make? Bedel continued tending the baklana, while Shai seemed to fall asleep quickly. Through the bond, A'banna felt Bedel's desire to have kinship with the sword go unfulfilled. He ached.

Say something, he thought.

What would you have me say? A'banna thought back.

Bedel blinked, then glanced up at her, holding the baklana out before him. *No, A'banna. Not you. Me. This sword. I had a memory—no, a sensation—that this sword should be… alive. Like it should speak, but it's just a piece of steel.*

Bedel turned his head slightly. Shai watched him where she lay. She rolled over, back to him.

What are you two hiding? A'banna pressed.

Nothing. Bedel sheathed the baklana harshly. *Just childhood fancy. Sleep well.*

His smile barely hid the colors of sadness in his aura.

A'banna settled into her bedroll, pulling the fur to her cheek. Only with her back turned did she feel him watching her, admiring her, fearing for her. For himself. For them all. In the midst of all of that, she sensed his shock at how beautiful she was.

I'm sorry, he began.

No, no. After last night and all the nights before it, it's nice to have something good to fall asleep to. I'm sorry about your childhood wish.

She heard him exhale sharply. *Thanks. This is my watch. Rest.*

Even in her dreams, A'banna felt Bedel, back to the fires, blade out, gazing into the darkness.

But there were two other silver eyes that scanned the whole south, widening when their aether brushed together. Malevolence coursed across A'banna's aura, like shocks on a rough cloth.

Yet another of my creations you stole, A'banna. Now, I've lost a precious Velheron, also. I will have you.

Get out of her dreams! And Bedel was there, standing before the Sorceress's face, sword drawn. She hissed, and her form sprouted six wings, morphing into a Velheron. Terror clawed at A'banna's dreams as she saw silver eyes, heard the cold sibilation of the woman's breath. The Sorceress was using a rare magic, *Long Sight*.

Six giant wings beat the air. Wind gushed across the campground, spilling a bowl and sending loose objects tumbling. A'banna felt the wind rush her, the caw of an unnatural predator who found its mark. The Sorceress's eyes narrowed.

A'banna, she hissed. *And you found quite the prize. Did you think I would leave you alone after Ntokup? After Raynt told me you found Reason? Or Did Reason find you?*

Fear stole A'banna's scream as her entire body tightened with the Sorceress's presence. A'banna felt her sleeping bag pull away from her, heard a rip, but she sensed Bedel even more. As the Sorceress saw through the heron, A'banna saw through Bedel. He leapt, slicing at the bird. It flapped its wings, shifting its large feet. Talons lashed out at Bedel, but he slashed at them, sword clanging against the creature's weapons. Several rangers loosed arrows, but the Velheron rose up swiftly on its six wings. One of the rangers, Pol, cursed.

"Nothing moves that fast!" A'banna heard Pol say.

"One of those things took out Nichell and Klaggen!" Someone shouted. Idrin. "Watch its beak!"

She tried to shake herself from the dream, but it felt like struggling against rope that tightened around her, squeezing the breath out of her. The Sorceress' embrace was like one of her precious snakes, constricting her.

You are mine, the Sorceress hissed again.

I'm losing consciousness, A'banna thought. *It is a snake.*

Be grateful I only brought the one, darling. Its brothers and sisters await your carcass back here.

A'banna cried out, but it came out as a hoarse escape of air. The snake constricted tighter, so A'banna tried to breathe in more air, as much as possible, to move her arms. The pressure just increased. With each hot breath from the snake, A'banna felt weaker. *Poison? What species?*

The Velheron dove. Its upper and lower sets of wings allowed its back to curve. Long, sinewy legs reached out with massive talons. Its toothy, long beak thrust out to stab or bite. The Velheron dove for Bedel. Claws and sword collided. Its long beak snapped as the baklana cut it.

"Crows, A'banna!" Shai muttered, very near to her. She heard something growl, snap, hiss. Her body tightened. A'banna felt sleep call her away, to a distant darkness and rest. She could barely breathe.

She heard Shai again, but she seemed so distant. A mass thudded against a shield. It jolted A'banna, so her eyes opened, focusing on the jeweled shield Shai had made. One of the spikes had a red smear. A large shadow rose, and a toothy, scaly maw snapped at Shai, who deflected the bite with the shield and brought a sword down on the head.

She killed the snake, A'banna thought, almost as if it were a musical piece. One of those tavern songs Bedel knew.

The Velheron shrieked, stabbing again at Bedel, but he rolled out of the way. The beak pierced dirt, trapping the bird for the briefest second. It was all he needed. He stabbed with his baklana, the blade cutting deep into one of the wings.

A sound mixed between a hiss and a shriek came from the Velheron. It pulled its beak free, thrust its head around like a spear, then beat its wings and took off.

Silver eyes glared into A'banna's soul. The woman drifted in her dreams, a banshee ready to draw her back to death, ready to spread vengeance.

Wings beat the air, rising higher. Wind lessened. The Sorceress growled, then spun away, fading into darkness.

A'banna felt the Velheron leave, flying south. It screeched one last time until it disappeared into the night.

"Bedel," A'banna whispered. She stirred, the foggy sensation of being drugged dissipating. She felt wrapped up in a scaly blanket.

"Quick, quick!" someone said.

"Sleep," he said, urgency in his voice.

A'banna started to stir, but felt two hands at her temple, massaging them. "Sleep," Shai whispered.

People heaved.

The scaly blanket pulled away.

A'banna sensed Bedel move closer, his breath on her cheek. She could smell him, a rough masculine scent, and felt his arms as he cradled her, as someone else gently prodded her arms and legs, releasing tension.

It happened, A'banna said. *This isn't a dream. You kept me asleep. How?*

I have you, Bedel whispered. *You're seeing through my eyes.* "Sleep."

She sighed, resting in the elusive safety. A'banna felt for a cloth blanket and pulled it up, despite the heat. Other eyes were watching now—rage, malice, hunger. Or was it her own terror? A'banna shut the projection of rage out as she had the decades of sleeping with venomous snakes living all around them. She dreamed no more that night.

⸻ ⬤ ⸻

"WAKE," A VOICE SAID, AND A'BANNA'S BODY SHOOK. "COME on, get up."

A marcher's hand closed around her father's throat, yanking him out of their makeshift tent, leaving Evaz's body in his place. She growled, her eyes flew open as she snatched a dagger and lunged upward. A'banna gasped as she met Shai's gaze; Shai's palm held the blade away from her throat.

Shai regarded her coldly. "This fury. When our next fight comes, I want to see it again. And again. Every time you fight alongside us. Understand?"

"Shai, I'm so sorry! I had a dream, a memory. I thought—"

Shai flinched as she slowly removed her hand, blood seeping down. A red dawn had come, its red and orange streaks filling the clear blue sky.

"Save it. There was too much magic last night. Do you feel it? The essences were hurt—and not by that bird tracking us. Crows, did it come from Ntokup? Was it one of the two that got away?"

A'banna paled at the mention of the Velheron. Her dream hadn't been a dream. The Sorceress had targeted her out of them all using *Long Sight*, but like the leading skills, the essences didn't feel pained. Any essencer could sense that. A'banna shut down some of the emotions tumbling within.

"You're right, Shai. The essences hurt, but not by the Sorceress' *Long Sight*."

"Glad we agree."

A'banna reached out with her aether, touching the world fabric. She saw the colors quake, like strings that had been loosened. The colorful tremor led beyond the rock formation, north, but near. The essences *felt* weak, as if something had cut them and tried to graft new essences onto them, like a farmer with a vine. This was a rare feeling, but it was close. The essences stilled, reluctant to share more of their pain with her.

Shai watched A'banna's probing. She could obviously see the aether at work. "That's what Bedel and I thought, also," Shai said. "Not many manipulations can hurt the essences. We're not alone. Get some food."

"Thank you for saving me from the snake."

"We're a team," Shai murmured. "And I liked what you did

for the Rda boy." Shai's expression steeled, hiding grief and guilt. Still holding her bleeding hand, Shai stood to leave, then looked down and over her shoulder at A'banna. "Oh, your pets are back."

Shai walked off, calling to a ranger for aid.

A'banna flicked off the blood from the knife. "I'm sorry," she called again, but Shai didn't answer.

The Sorceress had found them. Whether it was because she tracked them, or had gotten a hint from Raynt like Shai seemed to believe, but whatever it had been, they were being followed. A wave of fear coursed through A'banna, and then a quiet courage warmed the cold.

Bedel thought to her, *Whatever or whoever is near, we'll make it through together.*

I just hurt Shai.

Give her time, he answered.

I don't want to lose her, she thought.

Bedel turned from near the fire pit and smiled at A'banna. *Neither do I.*

Still ashamed, A'banna groaned and rolled out from the covers, jostling her boots for unwelcome guests. She thought of her father and their numerous trips into the wild. Every morning they had practiced this. She quickly rolled up the bedding, fastened it, and brought it to the cart. Pol nodded at her as he helped stow her gear. She offered him a smile.

"Did you sense anything last night? Any animals other than our companions?" he asked, his voice deep.

"Only the Velheron and the snake."

"The Velheron." Pol frowned, took another bedroll from a passing ranger and placed it in the cart. "Makes sense to call them that. No, your Grace, I wasn't referring to the Sorceress's sigil paying us a visit. There was scraping, like a drake in the mountains. We found nothing."

Her heart quickened, and she reached out, but there were no

other animals around, even if the horses stomped and jostled against the makeshift hitching posts. A'banna scanned with her aether. Nothing. A ranger roasted some sort of meat over a smokeless fire.

"Perhaps it was only the Velheron?"

Idrin approached, his ferret running every few feet, perching upwards, studying the rocks, then following once again. "Bedel drove the giant heron away," Idrin said.

"Wish we could have killed a second one," Pol said, shrugging. "But things are what they are."

"Indeed, my friend. A'banna Starblessed, we've heard the same sounds before in the mountains of the Dragon Wall, like Pol said. Sounds like a drake slinking through the rock, yet softer. And the essences are reluctant to respond to even us."

"But neither the Velheron nor the snake caused them?"

Idrin shook his head. "There is something off. Do you see anything?"

She blinked, letting the colors of nature fill her vision again. This time, she didn't focus on threads alone, but what moved on and around the world fabric. Every person and animal, every organic thing, carried a sort of aura, though they differed. She flinched at the thread of black and fiery red in Shai's aura but continued to turn. She reached out to the *cuelatchanli* and the lion. They were alert, studying the surroundings, but no more than usual. Always they felt like guards, living weapons ready to protect their entire pride. The predators had been satisfied by the meal the night before and the battle with the marchers. A'banna gagged at the thought, then kept reading through the connection. True, they slept closer to the horses. She stepped forward, speaking softly to them. They were agitated, as if something with nature itself felt wrong.

"The animals see nothing. There is something wrong. I wish we knew."

Pol grunted affirmatively.

"I think it came from the north," A'banna said.

"The Velheron came from the south," Pol muttered. His brown eyes locked onto Idrin's. It was as if their knowing gaze acted like A'banna and Bedel's *Zitaya*.

Idrin broke the tension by bowing.

"Thank you, your Grace," Idrin said.

"Grub's by the fire," Pol said.

A'banna smiled curiously. "Grub?"

"Breakfast," Idrin clarified.

Pol laughed. "We're less restrictive on our food options."

"I had good food with the Wo'Huzziet!" she said.

"Yeah, you're right. We did."

A'banna headed to the spit with the thick meat in a pot hanging over the fire. A few of the rangers had gathered there with Bedel, eating from wooden bowls.

Bedel approached her with a bowl of stew and chunk of bread. "Everything all right?"

Obviously not, she thought. He nodded.

A'banna looked again at the horses, the seemingly docile predators, and the rocky formation. "I can't tell. The essences hurt, but everything seems so normal. Maybe the animals are still unsettled by her. By the Velheron." She paused, pensive. In that brief hesitation, their hands touched against the hot bowl of stew. The flash of thoughts between them was dizzying but abruptly ended.

"Thank you for stopping her last night," A'banna said at last.

"Perhaps you should tell that to Shai, also," he chuckled.

"I did."

"I'm relieved. How's the stew?"

She glanced down at the large chunks of white meat floating in it and again at the spit. The meat was round, doubled up to save space. Long.

"No," she whispered.

"The Velheron dropped it on you. I'm sorry for *Leading* you into believing it was a dream, but either the bird or that snake was determined to kill you. A few moments more, it might have."

"You *Led* me to believe it was a dream?"

"Did I step over a line?"

"Yes," she said. "A small one, but let me fight back if I can."

"My apologies. I will."

This explained the hints of animosity A'banna sensed around camp. After Ntokup, if this was the start of the Sorceress' retaliation attempts, what was next?

"Besides, don't thank me yet," Bedel said. *Until we can figure out why the world fabric is in pain, we need to be careful. The magic feels ancient.*

The mountain.

Aye.

Then why do you want to go behind the rocks?

He blushed and then so did she.

It's getting harder to distance us, he said, even as he watched her start to eat. *You almost died again. I couldn't stop your father or Alain from leaving, and I'm afraid we'll lose you too.*

You Person Led *me into believing I was in a dream while a snake was crushing me?*

"In my defense, it tightened whenever you moved."

"I have training for this sort of horror, Bedel."

"So do I." He stepped closer, cheeks red. "I know you can handle yourself. I know that. Shai and I have worked together for a long time. We know how to help each other in a fight. When that thing came out of the night, I just relied on my training."

"Like the time you were pushed by a mountain?" she asked, shocked she had sensed that story.

His jaw dropped, and he hesitated. "Yes. A bit like that."

"Your friend, Raynt—I think he was in my father's dream."

"Aye, that's what I thought, too."

He smiled as she lifted a piece of hard bread. One bite sent pain shooting through her jaw.

Smiling, he rocked on his heels. "It's tastier if you soak it in the stew."

"I don't believe you," she said, almost laughing herself. "How did you hide that idea?"

His smile faded. "I'm a spy, A'banna. I don't always remember it, but when I get close to someone, I have to test whether or not I can also hide from them."

She thought of her father, how he hid the Speaker tattoos beneath warpaint. "That's absurd. It's how secrets and betrayals start."

Yellow, purple, and brown flashed across his aura. Regret. It showed most in his eyes. "We're nearing the part of the world where your ability to hide from others is going to mean life or death. For the both of us. Learning to hide from each other, even with this—" He laid a hand on the ethereal thread connecting them. "Is how we will outwit them."

"I do not want to lie to you, Bedel Riess."

He swallowed and looked away, but red crept up his neck—again. "This isn't getting easier."

Mouth full of stew and partially softened bread, she said, "I'm not trying."

"Neither am I," he said, smiling slightly. "About last night—"

A passing ranger shot them a look. Bedel held up his hands. "Not that kind of night, fool! Mind your own business!"

The ranger chuckled as he passed.

A'banna felt overtly warm. It certainly wasn't because of the stew.

Bedel's smile grew as he looked back at her. At first, they said nothing, stumbling over their words. Finally, Bedel helped her set down the empty bowl, and they walked around the rock crevice, putting space between them and any potential wandering ears. "About last night, the Velheron projected Jocina, didn't it?"

A'banna's warmth dissipated. She felt a chill. "She's found me. We call it *Long Sight*."

"Where I'm from, it's magic that only Keepers and dark fire essencers can do. We call it scrying."

"No, anyone who can *Lead* can do that, eventually. You and I have run with the raptors as if we saw through their eyes. I think Idrin does something similar with his ferret. I can't see any essence ties between a person and their avatar unless it's my own, so it's only a feeling."

The Sorceress had spoken to her through the *Long Sight* last night. At first, she had thought she had incorrectly heard Jocina's voice in Ntokup. There was no mistake now.

"Jocina's seen you with me!" A'banna gasped in horror.

"Bloody fields." Bedel hesitated. "She knows. I wanted to convince myself otherwise."

"I'm—"

Bedel held up his hand and nearly touched her face. His fingers were so close. Her breathing quickened. So did his. They shared thoughts, feelings. Trepidation. The need to find some way to prepare to fight against her. Attraction. Frustration. Need.

"Crows. How do we do this, A'banna?"

She blinked. His thoughts were a jumble—plans and ideas of the future, a castle in Zeller where a red dragon dwelt, beautiful images of him and her together, lovers alone in the wild, the Sorceress's eyes. Shai. "Precisely what are you asking?"

"Not you, too?"

She shook her head. "The longer you and I are joined I don't know if we should fight this. Until I met you and Idrin, all the men I knew other than my father lacked integrity."

"A'banna, stop."

"You saved me."

Their hands touched again. Hot shock raced through her fingers. She wanted more, but should she?

"I just met you," he said, eyes gleaming. "How is this possible?"

She cupped his rugged head in her hands. "I've been asking myself that since you pulled me out of the water."

Suddenly, she felt Bedel's will crumble under the pressure of the connection. Yet, deep beneath the tumult of feelings and thoughts, Shai's image was very vivid. They both knew. Bedel kissed her. Shai and A'banna were interchangeable in his mind, as A'banna could see it. He was afraid and gave himself over to her, the things he wanted to do, a host of them, and she felt immersed in passion. A'banna wanted it. He was safe. He cared. They knew each other. Those were beautiful things A'banna longed for. But Shai's image grew, an unresolved emotion burning through them.

The kiss ended abruptly, but they still held one another.

"My fault."

"I could have easily have thought of Quin, Bedel."

You did. You were thankful I didn't bite you.

She nodded. *You're nothing like him, Bedel. I've never known a kiss without pain.*

Concern, sorrow, and anger flashed through him. *I will not let Quin harm you again.*

She desperately wanted to believe. *I know Shai resents me, but she's my friend. I know you love her. We can't. But I want to.*

She could feel the torment inside him. He wanted to say yes and plunge himself into his connection with A'banna. But he wanted to sever the *Zitaya* and love Shai as he always had. *That future is gone for Shai and me as long as we are connected,* Bedel finally thought, shoving his emotions away. A'banna saw images of his training as an agent. Of a white-haired man dressed in red, who constantly told Bedel: "Push down your emotions. Don't even let them show in aura. Son—"

Bedel closed off that memory. He swallowed, then said, "A'banna, we're headed to Zeller. They have people who hunt essencers as part of their belief. On top of everything we're facing —what if we're moving too quickly."

She flashed some of the more sensual images back at him. "Your thoughts, not mine."

He desired to hold her, stroke her cheek, her hair. He tried to shut her out of those emotions, but he didn't want to. "All of these emotions! Hearing each other's thoughts! Shai is right. I can't ask her to do this. It isn't fair to her."

A'banna backed away, folding her hands. "You're right. This isn't fair to her. We could find a way to block our thoughts, you know."

"A few, but there will come a time when we can't. The *Zitaya* will only grow stronger. That much I know." His voice quaked, and he switched from verbal to internal communication. *For decades, it's only been Shai and me. You understand? I don't know how to do this. Us. I don't know how not to hurt her worse than I already have. But we can't do the three of us. It's not how we live there. She can't, for as much as she might say or act otherwise. She'd hate the idea.* "We need to make sure she is going to be okay."

"She needs us," A'banna agreed. She felt his gratitude surge through him. He wanted to kiss her again but restrained himself. Guilt ran through him. Their emotions were blinding them; they both knew that. Danger was still near, even if they didn't know of what kind. The essences outside of their aether still hurt. The graft was a sore wound.

Bedel crossed his arms, trying to keep himself from her. "When we're north of Zeller. In Cardor maybe."

"During a war?"

"I don't know. I can't hide from you."

"Nor I from you."

Blue colors flashed across his aura, unveiling all the passion and desire he struggled to keep guarded. He had finally gained a measure of control, like a wall with a gaping window she could reach through, even step through, but the wall stood as a request.

"We must start trying," Bedel said. "Harder. For both our sakes—and for Shai's. If a Sword of Baktur sees this cord, it won't matter if he or she believes one of us is not an essencer. They'll assassinate one to kill the other they can't see. I'm going to be on a mission. Idrin's agreed to accompany you, but that doesn't mean you're safe. He's not an essencer, at least, no more than the bond between him and his ferret. Besides, everyone in Zeller carries a weapon and is half-ready to use it all the time. It's not safe for you."

Every ounce of her being wanted to embrace him, but she hesitated. "Then we do what we can. We prepare."

He exhaled sharply. "Thank you."

His hand brushed hers, and then he walked around the rock back to camp. A'banna wrapped her arms around herself, closed her emotions inside, and suddenly felt nothing. It was horrible.

Knuckles wrapped against rock.

"May I come in?"

A'banna blanched as Shai circled. Her hand was bandaged, her black hair pulled up behind her ears. "I have a couple of ideas, but we need to talk."

A'banna couldn't find her voice. She felt like she had betrayed her only friend. When Shai nodded, looking into the wilderness, it only made the sense of guilt deepen. When A'banna finally spoke, her voice cracked. "What kind of ideas?"

Shai suddenly withdrew the dagger in the shape of a curved raptor claw. "Contingency plans. To keep the man we both love alive." Shai extended the dagger, handle first, to A'banna. "I did hate you at first, but I've gotten to know you since then. I don't want to hurt you. You're a good person, I see that now. There is so much more to you than the *Zitaya* bond."

"I felt we bonded while we were with the Wo'Huzziet, you and I. Was I wrong?"

Shai looked at A'banna and smiled, but her eyes and aura told a different story. "Bedel and I, we were convenience. No one outside of Lodornatha is even allowed to know what we do—and have shared. The House of Menai and the Magical Affair Commission sees to that. We spent a lifetime looking over our shoulders, being drawn closer together. We were the only ones who knew how the world would end and what they planned to do to Bedel. It was easy for us to become lovers."

"No matter what you've experienced, I don't believe you think your relationship was convenience," A'banna said. Shai scoffed, but the colors in her aura were clear as the strand of dark fire that swirled among them. "Shai, we are trying to undo the bond and stop the Sorceress, the war, all of it. We're trying to learn how to control it. I'm not even sure how the *Zitaya* formed, not really. I know he doesn't want to lose you. Please don't push him away."

Shai's jaw tightened, she blinked back tears but held the weapon steady.

"We want to fix this, Shai."

Shai let out an exasperated sigh. "It formed because both of you used the same magic discipline at the same time. Any good healer knows that a patient should not be using any leading skill while being healed. It's why I pushed so hard for the Wo'Huzziet medicine. It would have healed you in time, maybe, but they were so low on supplies I stole some. But then I saw the apothecary had already come. Bedel's healing worked, so they gave you their secretive medicine. I've never felt so damn stupid for stealing before. I made excuses, stood there, waiting, like a fool. Except, he kept *helping*. If he had listened to me, you wouldn't be here.

You were delirious, on the verge of death. I know you couldn't have stopped *Leading* the animals if you tried, and he's so damn yeht-headed. I love that about him."

Shai's glanced away, only for a second. The dark and red thread in her aura flared as it swam around the colors of grief and loss.

A'banna didn't touch the starlight steel dagger. "What is that?"

"It is a weapon that doesn't work for me, but it will for you. No one has ever tried to sever a *Zitaya* using a starlight blade, but it stands to reason, if we do this smartly, at least one of you could survive."

"And if we don't?"

"I'll kill myself after I've held you both bleeding out in my arms."

A'banna grabbed the dagger. Better in her hands than Shai's. "You were going to kill me."

Shai smiled. "I've thought of a dozen ways." The smile faded. "And I have none that lets you live. This is the only way he survives. If it comes to it—"

"I do it myself?"

"Yes, A'banna. You cut the *Zitaya* yourself."

CHAPTER 19

A'BANNA SLID THE BLADE INTO HER BELT. NINE RANGERS SEEMED to materialize from rock, grass, and shadow. Only when they moved did their cloaks give them away. One moment, A'banna hadn't considered them more than the wind, or a heat mirage. Their cloaks hid them when in plain sight. Arrows nocked and bows drawn, every blade was trained at Shai. They formed a semicircle around the two, a tight net without escape.

"Well, Idrin, I congratulate you," Shai said, raising her hands. "I should have seen through your little deception."

"My deception?" One of the rangers said, but they were all veiled. It was impossible to say who spoke. "You would use your grief to murder the world's salvation?"

Bedel rounded the rock. He hated the burden explicit in Idrin's words, but didn't want them to know. Or for A'banna to know. He held a ranger blade, not one of those Shai had crafted.

"I knew this was like Kerdum for you," Bedel said. "We could see it. But you'd have her commit suicide to get us back? When will you learn?"

"No one's committing suicide. Every viable concept I considered is built into the weapons. I don't control those. I can't."

"Stop lying," Bedel said. A'banna tried to reach out to him, but he had closed up most of that wall, shoving up a protective thought in that gaping hole he had left for her before. He was unreadable.

"It's what we do to live, or did you forget that, too? Did you forget what it was like to look over your shoulder your whole life? To wonder if that twitch in your father's eye or that new gesture meant he had discovered your lie? That we knew he was lying. Go on, tell me Martuza confirmed what we feared. What the historical texts hint at. Xathon, Mnai, every person who has ever sacrificed a Gatekeeper has done so in vain." Shai lifted her hands in frustration. "Come on, you dense people! What the Kerdum do you think the Sorceress's minions were doing in Ntokup? I can't lie for them anymore. I can't watch them slaughter you."

"So, you'll ask A'banna to die to try and save me?"

"It's not! I am not like them!"

"Yes, Shai, this is exactly what they would do," Bedel said. "Now, the whole truth. Or so help me—"

Shai's face twisted in anger. "It's Belasna engraved ferugial—starlight steel! Once I finished creating the weapons, the essences ignored me—but they work for A'banna, for you, Bominga, Martuza. Old Blood. Your ancestors' ancestors were Immortal, not just survivors of the breaking. I do not have the ancient blood-line—or the new one, apparently. It's a perfect flaw in the system. Once crafted, the smith cannot use their own handmade weapon. Strategic for The Caurs, agreed? But Old Blood can. As much as Idrin and I might wish, these blades were never made for Elves."

"Elves do not deserve the weapons. It was our people who broke the world." Idrin was still hidden among the rangers, a voice coming from multiple directions. His own voice echoed off the rock. Shai turned her head, slightly, so one ear was toward the rock. "Strategic? It's a safeguard from the bloodline that *would* use them. Elven Immortals. The Nameless Ones."

"Yes," Shai said. "Wouldn't want nameless Hurmlen or Jocina to get ahold of starlight steel, would we? They'd start slaughtering The Caurs faster than we could find a Taur." Her black locks shook with her fervent frustration. "Bedel, you know something must be done about the *Zitaya* before Zeller. One observant Baktur is all it takes to kill you both. Don't tell me that doesn't terrify you as much as the Sorceress's monsters following us. So, by all means, waltz into Baktur territory. I'm sure Jocina will help them find you. You heard her? And the Velheron?"

A'banna shivered.

A few of the rangers shuffled. Even with their fear, those arrows held steady.

"It's true I'm frightened, but now we know we have to do something. We have to fight. We can't sit back. She'll never let us," Bedel said.

Shai scoffed.

Bedel continued. "Regardless, you were going to commit murder."

"Originally, that was my intent, but after the last couple days, I stopped to consider an alternative." Shai's voice was exasperated. "You want to shoot me, fine. But Elven Intelligence in Lupacuo refused to send anyone else to get those war plans. Mnai and Nadael didn't even believe in that mission. They wanted the Immortal to stay north of the boundary, but someone else got their way. Not easy to do with House Menai. You still need me."

"I can get the plans," Bedel said. "You can leave."

"You are going to climb into the Veccil'ni's castle, maybe share his bed and steal them while the Red Dragon sleeps? Yeht shit and you know it."

"But you will?"

Shai smiled. "No. But I guessed war was coming, long before our fathers called us to that murdering mountain!"

A'banna felt a jolt through Bedel's emotions, like a lightning bolt. *She lied to me?*

At the same time, she felt a memory like a knife in the heart. Bedel on a mountain, falling, but Shai caught him. A woman in the rock had told him, *3.1415. Millions will die. Your presence permits a breaking.* He had refused to die.

A'banna teared up, confused, afraid.

"I spent the last six months arranging our next operation, and I've memorized every detail," Shai continued. "Baktur don't even look twice when I pass by. We're behind by a day now. If I'm not in Zeller within three days, everyone involved will abort. No defectors. No witnesses. No plans. No preparation for Cardor. Just guesswork. It's over. Go ahead and shoot me."

"And Raynt? How did he help?"

"Raynt was a small part of my plan. I just needed to keep our communication line broken."

"You hired the *Batoidea*? You knew they'd leave."

"It was a stupid damned risk, but yes! I didn't know the Sorceress used the Velheron, but when I saw it tell him to leave us what? I was right, wasn't I?" Shai slapped her chest. "Shoot me!"

Bedel didn't take the bait. A'banna stood against the rock, stunned, listening.

"Why the jewels in the shield? Flesh, mind, spirit, any essence?"

Shai sighed. "You used to be a lot faster, Agent Bedel. The goal is to transfer you inside the shield, as much of your quintessence, your identity, as possible. I based the concept off a formula I found in the Menai library, by a Glymph scholar, no less. She believed core consciousness could be transferred; pushing the boundary beyond what the Larks are capable of or what dark fire essencers do. Then, when we're satisfied we have you safeguarded, A'banna cuts the *Zitaya*. She dies, but I bring you back by draining the jewels and restoring all those essences into you again. It'll be messy. There's a high risk of short term memory loss or worse, but this the only way."

"No," A'banna said. "I refuse to believe it."

Shai cringed. "Damn it, Avocan."

"From here to Zeller, you can train both of us to hide our emotions. We limit the bond's use until we're free from these Baktur lands. We will find a way."

"Even when you're free you're still within range," Shai said. "They're masters of disguise. Better than Lodornathan rangers."

Someone grunted. It didn't echo. Shai shrugged. "See. At least I know that one isn't Idrin. If there's a fight, he lives." She pointed at the ranger who had made the error. "A Baktur would never make such a mistake."

Not a bow lowered. Bedel tensed. A'banna's hand went to a knife at her belt.

Don't. They're watching you, too, since you took the dagger.

Bedel wasn't looking at her, but Shai, yet he had seen her slight movement. Indeed, two bows had shifted from behind Shai. A'banna stared down the arrowheads.

I'm not going to hurt you, A'banna thought. *I don't want to.*

They don't know that, Bedel replied from beyond his mental wall.

Shai had heard the slight movement. "Avocan, learn quick. Lodornathans will always choose the Gatekeeper over a Chosen, just like the Speaker and Keeper chose you over themselves. If you still want to be naïve, consider this: Why haven't they said anything? Idrin's actually considering ordering them to fire upon you."

"And your ladyship once the Zeller mission is complete," another ranger said.

Shai snickered and kicked a light stone with her boot.

"Another not-Idrin. Reminds me of a game I used to play as a child: Turn the card over to find the fool."

A'banna took it all in, as if she were examining the forest for danger. Ten rangers and Bedel stood surrounding them. Like predators darting through trees. The cloaks were their cover, the veils their mask.

A'banna's breathing went harsh. "You want one of us to die."

Shai shrugged. "Was always in the stars, A'banna."

"That's not true, anymore," Bedel said. "We can find a way. If you trust me."

"Against the Sorceress? The Elves? They won't change because there are no more Rda with us?"

"There are ten rangers," A'banna interrupted.

Bedel and a ranger—must have been Idrin—exchanged a look and then both scanned the group.

"Three were sent to Lupacuo," she continued. "Two were killed in Ntokup. That should be nine, and there were fourteen to begin with, now there are—"

One of the rangers pivoted, bow moving from Shai to A'banna.

Clever, A'banna thought.

It was all in the design of the bow, the curves, the leather grip, the feathered arrows. A'banna locked eyes with the infiltrator, a ranger who blinked—two eyelids; one vertical, one horizontal, opened and closed simultaneously. A half-Glymph.

She knew this archer. Her eyes.

My house-sister!

What? Bedel said, swiveling to look.

"Kamalia?" A'banna gasped, her heart leaping with joy. "Sister! What are you doing?"

A black diamond beneath the false ranger's hooded face reflected light off an arrowhead.

That's new.

The archer pulled back and loosed.

A'banna felt the heat as the shaft drove through her abdomen, the heat of blood.

A'banna staggered backward, gasping, trying to hold the arrow steady. Hot, red life soaked her hands, clothes. Her vision blurred.

"Bloody weaving fields!" Shai screamed, rushing to A'banna as Bedel lurched over from the shared pain. "You killed him." She caught A'banna's head, helping her move. "Stay with me. I'm so sorry. Stay with me!"

"Not at all," the false ranger said, her voice deep and feminine. This half-Glymph woman—and there had been none in their company—had already nocked a new arrow and loosed it into the back of a ranger's knee. Another one of Idrin's men, an Elf, had drawn a knife and attacked her to the left, but with two blows from a heavy gauntlet, the Elf fell, dazed.

Shaking, A'banna struggled to remain conscious. To catch a glimpse of the half-Glymph's face.

It all made sense.

Only a few people she knew could make the essences hurt as if they had just had a graft of new threads. It had never felt natural, but the illegitimate daughter of Dark Judicator Hurmlen had abilities beyond compare, and she had shown A'banna when her parents took her in for several years. They had been a family, sisters, and they had been happy. Until she had come of age and Hurmlen decided to train his daughter as his pawn. A'banna had lost her foster-sister and her mother in quick succession. A'banna's mother had resisted the dramatic changes and was sacrificed for it. But A'banna had listened for stories about her foster sister, who had gone on to make a name for herself in the wilds of the south.

"Kamalia," A'banna groaned.

"I'm sorry, sister. Arrows can be survived," Kamalia said. How her voice had changed since they were children. "However, the monsters following me, aren't so easily survived. The Vel come. Fight!"

CHAPTER 20

SHAI TORE A SLEEVE FREE AND QUICKLY WRAPPED AROUND THE
base of the arrow shaft in A'banna's abdomen. She pushed down
hard, feeling hot liquid underneath her palms. Cursing, Shai
looked up at Bedel, who struggled to stay on his feet, gripping his
abdomen.

No, no, no!

All around her, rangers moved their bows between the
assassin and the rocks. Wind carried a cacophony of hisses and
slithering and clacking. Shai blinked in disbelief. *Scales? Claws?
Velheron and more snakes! Minotaurs?*

Her mind spun, trying to grasp everything that had happened.
She had to stop the bleeding and, if she had a few moments,
maybe she could start some sort of healing within A'banna. Turn
blood into skin, maybe? She refused to lose *them*. That had
ceased to be the plan in Ntokup.

Sunlight glimmered off scales as more monstrosities crawled
from gaps in the rocks. At first, they seemed so small, tiny lizards,
but then *inflated* as they emerged from the holes and gaps.
Rangers stumbled backward, stunned, before raising their bows

and taking aim. Shai gasped in horror, fumbling for her weapon which she had given to A'banna. Where had she thrown it? Shai thought she saw it shimmer in the grass, but didn't dare remove pressure off A'banna's wound.

"Move A'banna!" Pol said, patting Shai on the shoulder before rushing to his companions. Pol redirected his bow at a small scaly lizard emerging from a dark gap between two boulders. The Vel's joints popped as it stood upright. It had two arms *and* legs, much like a man. *The minotaur roared; saliva and hot, rancid breath in her face.* Only two terrors had ever frozen Shai: the memory of the minotaur, and now the sight of the Vel growing and tripling in bulk in mere moments.

Pol drove an arrow down the Vel's maw.

"Shai!" Pol snapped. "Move!"

The Dwarf's eyes locked with hers. There was no hostility, only concern, maybe something more. Had she been so blind? Pol *respected* her.

"I didn't know" Shai murmured, almost incoherently.

"Later!" Pol said, turning his back to loose an arrow. "Get to the captain!"

"Thank you, Pol," Shai murmured. Shai grabbed A'banna by the shoulders, pulling her away from the rocks. A glimmer within a dark crevice drew her gaze.

Yellow reptilian eyes focused on them from deep within the black fissure. The eyes slowly grew as the Vel pushed itself into wider space. Two long slits in its face constituted a nose, and its jaw extended in a V-shape. Talons on human-like hands reached out, gripping each side of the gap and pulling. The Vel contorted, slithered, and dropped from the gap with a hiss. It rolled, then sprang upward.

Pol launched himself between them, sword out. He drove the blade into the Vel's mouth and up, then yanked it out before its talons caught him in its death throes.

"Crows!" He said. "The Sorceress couldn't settle for more damned minotaurs?"

If Shai hadn't been retreating under cover, she would have laughed. This was insane. Shai quickened, yanking much harder than she intended.

"I owe you, Pol!" Shai called.

Pol dropped to a knee and loosed an arrow nearly as quick as Idrin. He didn't turn, but shouted back: "I like strong ale!"

Another ranger stepped near him, and they tried to pick off the growing Vel. Two arrows, two Vel, and the monsters dodged. The arrows hit rock and went spinning off into the air.

"Bloody fires," a ranger muttered.

"Vel kill with a bite!" Kamalia shouted, loping the head off one as it grew. "The larger they become, the stronger their scales. They swarm like drakes and Goblins!"

"Anything else we need to know?" Pol said. He and a few rangers drew their swords, closing the distance. Several Vel swarmed one of the men, tearing him apart even as they grew on top of the fountain of gore.

Pol cursed, his sword swiped away claws. Shai lost sight of him as she continued to drag A'banna across the grass.

A'banna's head rolled, trying to see. She moaned an inaudible word.

"What is it, A'banna?"

A'banna suddenly gripped Shai's arm. "Kamalia. My house-sister."

Shai let out a stream of curses. She could only guess what a house-sister was, but it complicated things. A'banna's eyes rolled back into her head. She was breathing, but perhaps her body hadn't been as healed as they first thought. Shai knew she was in pain—Bedel was doubled over not far away. He shuffled toward the rangers, visibly fighting beyond the pain.

Still swearing, Shai pulled A'banna behind the rangers. "Call the raptors, damn it. Come on, A'banna, call the raptors." Shai laid A'banna behind Idrin.

Their hostility was irrelevant and maybe even stupid.

"Until another day?" Shai said, watching the Vel converge.

"Indeed," Idrin said, loosing an arrow.

The ferret bounded over to Bedel as he struggled to stand. He'd paled. The ferret stood between his feet, snarling.

Shai risked a look at the rangers. Pol ordered them to fall back, as for every Vel they struck down, a fully grown one crawled or leapt at the front line. A ranger struck down a Vel, only for another, still growing, to leap forward and rip out his wrist with its teeth. Staying at the front was going to get more rangers killed.

"Fall back!" Idrin ordered. "Away from the rocks!"

Pol and another ranger formed a line in front of Bedel, Shai, and A'banna. In between volleys, Pol or Idrin helped Bedel move a little farther away. This couldn't go on for much longer. Two Vel reached their flank, leaping from boulders north of them.

Shai groaned, trying to keep pace. *The Avocan was so weaving heavy!*

"Loose and fall back!" Idrin shouted. He appeared at her side, making brief eye contact.

Shai grimaced but moved her hand. Idrin pulled A'banna back a few feet, giving Shai a moment to recover.

Arrows clanged against thick Vel scales, then tumbled harm-lessly to the ground. It was true; they were damn hard to kill once they were full-sized. An injured Vel curled long, clawed fingers around the shaft and yanked it loose. A long, unnatural jaw curved as a forked tongue licked the blood off the arrowhead. Wide-eyed, the ranger that shot it gasped and stumbled. Some shouldered their bows and drew swords again, but the beasts were driving a wedge between them, separating the group as predators isolating prey from the herd. With more coming out of the rocks, they couldn't use those as a natural defense. And they were surrounded by rocks.

"Perhaps we will have no need of conflict between us," Idrin said to Shai.

"Deal!" Shai shouted. She glanced left. How had Bedel fallen behind? His face was twisted in a grimace as he clutched his side. The *Zitaya* bond pulsated. A'banna's expression relaxed, as though her pain was relieved.

Bedel glanced at her, then sent more of his aether through the bond. Though the ferret danced and snapped at the approaching Vel from behind, Bedel seemed oblivious.

"No, no, no! Going for Bedel!"

Idrin loosed another arrow. "We've got A'banna. Go!"

Arrows did nothing, now. Vel crawled forward with lightning speed, undeterred. "Back, fall back!" Idrin said, drawing a long, curved Elven blade.

A Vel tumbled to the ground, headless. Its blood dripped from Kamalia's sword. Shai saw her staring at Idrin, mouth open, pale under her hood.

"Well damn the sting of mosquitos and bad fate," Kamalia muttered. A ranger saw her approaching the group and leapt to block her, using his bow like a staff. She casually deflected it, then shoved him down. He tried to stand; she kicked him with her steel-toed boot, spraying blood from the Elf's broken nose. "Stay down, fool."

Wide-eyed and furious, Shai shot Kamalia a look before darting to Bedel. The ferret hopped as she approached, but stood its ground between Bedel and the creatures. The monsters avoided the little furry brat. For that, Shai was grateful.

"The starlight weapons," Bedel muttered as Shai touched his shoulder.

"You have to stop feeding A'banna your aura. It won't help us."

Moaning, he turned a pained look at her.

"You beautiful fool!' she said, touching his face. "If you can reach Idrin."

"Yes. Get the weapons, Shai. They may work." He shuffled back to the dwindling group. Shai dabbed her wet cheeks with her sleeve. A Vel leapt at her. She swiveled, dodging its claws, then took off running back to camp.

To her left, a Vel with a misshapen neck shifted it back into place with a pop. It sneered at her, but arrows struck it from the side.

"Go!" Drelloss, a ranger, shouted. He and another ranger loosed arrows to cover the retreat of two injured and Shai's escape. "Hurry—"

Nimble and quick, the Vel dodged the arrows. A second darted from the side. They weaved and slithered like serpents, hunting like water or kimodrakes. The first Vel rose from its belly onto all fours and charged. Drelloss shouted in surprise as the Vel's foot clenched down on his hand, preventing him from drawing his sword. The Vel circled the ranger, claws raking whole chunks of leather armor and flesh. Drelloss struck with his other hand, trying to pry himself free. Claws dug into Drelloss' neck as it bit down, tearing away a chunk of face and neck in its toothy jaws. It shrieked, the sound was a horrible joyous noise. Drelloss' face was stuck in a half-scream, but without a throat or part of a jaw, it ended in a gurgle as the ranger dropped to his knees, eyes devoid of life.

The ranger with the arrow in his knee pivoted to shoot, but the two Vel rushed him, ripping into him with unchecked malice. Within seconds, as the ranger's body went through its death throes, the two Vel had split up, assaulting the ranger who remained shaking as he clutched his wounded sword hand and the ranger laying down cover. Four of the nine rangers had died within seconds. The ranger Kamalia had wounded struggled to his feet. A scaled rattle followed the green-black blur as it darted across the ground and dug its jaws into his neck. He had no time to scream. For the moment, the scaled-men were focused on the rangers.

Bedel groaned. "Shai"

She sprinted around the rock, scanning for any of those damned monstrosities. Shai skidded to a halt. The camp was a disaster. Several horses lay dead, and the raptors still ripped into a couple of Vel. The lion growled as it shook one of the Vel's heads free from its shoulders.

The raptors, maws bloody, glanced at her. She hesitated, remembering the hut all too well. The one missing an eye tracked her. She knew what that meant.

"We're on the same side here, now. Come on."

The raptor glanced at the rocks.

Shai ran to the cart and scooped up Bedel's weapons. She twirled, cargo in hand, and nearly ran into a Vel growing in front of her. It snarled, *grinned*. Long clawed hands lashed out.

The one-eyed raptor's jaws snapped shut over the monster's closest arm. With one muscular, rough whipping of its head, the raptor tore the Vel's limb from its body as the alpha female kicked high behind it. Its head rolled off the shoulders. The two raptors backed away from Shai.

"Thanks," she muttered. She pointed behind the rocks. "Um"

The raptors followed her hand and took off. Their claws clamored up the rocks; feathers flashed as they snarled and hooted.

"That works. Some damn good cavalry." Shaking, Shai ran for her life, desperate to get back to the others.

She didn't slow. Bedel hobbled, struggling to stay with the group. Idrin covered him as Pol and the others somehow held the fragile line. A'banna tried to sit, but fell back, panting, hand on the arrow.

A Vel charged Bedel. He turned, too late. Except the ferret guarded him. It bit the Vel's heels, allowing Bedel to escape.

Not about to abandon that cute, loyal, fuzzy-fuzzy critter! Shai grimaced, pulled out the baklana, and charged to join the ferret defending Bedel. "Go to Kerdum, you—" she swung, blade hacking into the Vel's neck, but only chipping away at the scales, drawing a little blood.

"Seriously?" she said as the monster hissed at her.

The ferret seized the opportunity. A master snake hunter, it used its claws to rapidly scale the creature before sinking its overtly large teeth into the neck. It ripped, pulled, and held on, dodging the desperate claw lashes. The ferret had brought the reptile down! Hissing, it ran a circle around Bedel's feet, triumphant.

Shai, still holding the starlight weapons, looked up at the sky. Had the stars moved since last night? "A little help?" she tightened her grip on the sword.

"Talking to the stars must be contagious," Bedel grumbled as she handed him his baklana in midstride, their fingers brushing for a brief, reassuring moment.

Another monster flanked Idrin's group. Without a word, Bedel and Shai charged. She slipped her hand into a bracer and flicked the blade free.

The Vel reared back, ready to pounce on A'banna.

"Idrin!" Bedel shouted.

At once, Idrin spun, sword out. Bedel leapt forward, his sword glistening silver-blue in the sunlight. Their curved blades hit hard scales, pinning the beast. The men shouted and drove the swords up, between scales, but Shai couldn't let them have all the fun. She darted between them and drove the bracer-blade through a long nasal slit.

The monster went limp.

"About time! Starlight steel works!" A'banna turned, trying to find Pol to give him the other bracer. They didn't need Old Blood to stab something, after all. Instead, she screamed. "Pol!"

Kamalia marched on the group with sword drawn. Pol had lost his bow. He fought with hammer and sword, using blunt force to keep Vel down. Two lay broken at his feet. Grunting, Pol swung up, knocking a third into another. Kamalia stepped into the gap. One of the monsters attacked her, and she cut it down with her broadsword. Kamalia's head swiveled toward A'banna, but she marched toward Shai and Bedel.

Shai sprinted, holding out the bracer.

"Stay back!" Pol shouted, stepping in her path.

"Stand aside, ranger," Kamalia said, raising her sword. "I will not ask again."

Pol glanced back at her, his deep Dwarven eyes determined—and sorrowful. Shai felt a lump in her stomach. How blind she'd been.

"Turn aside!" Pol said, raising his weapons. "*I* will not ask again."

Kamalia's heavy scimitar-like blade clanged against Pol's blunt weapons, faster than even he could swing. She grunted but didn't lose a step. She stepped forward, reached out with a spare hand, grabbed the hammer shaft, and drove her sword through Pol's chest. "I told you all to fight them— not fight me!"

Pol shook, red bubbling from his mouth and down his beard before he went limp. Kamalia shook her head and shoved him off her blade.

"Gods damn you!" Shai screamed. "Pol!"

Shai leapt into the air, bracer blade extended, ready to drive into Kamalia's neck—and the tall huntress caught her and threw her on the ground next to Pol. "No," she whispered, willing him to live, though the brightness in his eyes dimmed.

Evaz. Pol. Alain. Huahanna.

Angry at herself for letting a moan escape her throat, she reached out, fingertips brushing his blood-stained beard.

"No," Bedel moaned. The baklana sagged in his grasp.

Idrin howled, his grief turned to fury as he used his blade to cut Vel after Vel down. The ferret jumped between the monsters, ripping off scales on their throats or cheeks. Bedel stabbed and sliced. Idrin stepped back, closer to Shai and Bedel, sword raised at Kamalia. As the last Vel fell, the ferret circled Idrin, snarling at the huntress.

Idrin trembled. The last of his rangers were cut off from them by six more Vel. His eyes darted down to Pol. Shai scrambled to her feet, blade out in what felt like futile self-defense. She put herself between A'banna and Kamalia. Bedel staggered to her side, seething at Kamalia.

Kamalia addressed Idrin. "Prince Onoarel," Kamalia said urgently. "Your sister lives. Give me Shai the Artist, and we will rescue them both."

Shai glared at her as Idrin gasped. Then more puzzle pieces fell together. Idrin was of the High House Onoarel, thus heir to one of the Lodornathan thrones that had lost their Memory Lark to the Sorceress's dragon siege centuries before. His sister had been taken by the Slaver Coalition.

Had their mother given their sister her Lark gift as cover from dragon fire?

Idrin's story became even more tragic.

Shai sneered at Kamalia. "You attacked us!"

Idrin spun, driving his blade into a Vel's exposed neck. "You are no Onoarel-friend!"

"When we agree, you know you're crow meat," Shai murmured, standing awkwardly.

Kamalia removed her hood, revealing her teal skin. Her

warning was low and accompanied by the raised bloody blade, even as the scaled-men gained ground. "Fight me at your peril."

Shai moved to strike again, but Idrin caught her hand and held it back. She swiveled instinctively, locked a foot behind his, and pushed. He went down, pulling her with him. Idrin planted a foot on her abdomen and flipped her over his head. She slammed into the ground, the impact driving air from her lungs.

A Vel leapt at Shai, but Kamalia lopped off its head with a single swing of her sword. Its body fell to the ground with a thud at her feet.

"I am not the enemy," she said again. She lowered her sword, and Shai could see the blood dripping around Belasna runes.

Impossible, Shai thought. Kamalia carried and successfully wielded a starlight steel blade. That meant Hurmlen was Old Blood, or his mate had been. A few nurial houses, like Xikkan were known to carry the Old Blood. One of the last great houses had an ancient blade, as old as the breaking. *But this isn't that sword. The shape is wrong; too thick.*

Shai's mind spun with meaning, but all she could think of was the one man in the world who made her genuinely afraid: Kamalia's father, Hurmlen.

A sickening smack drew Kamalia's attention.

Vel ripped apart the last standing ranger. Seven were dead; their corpses split open in a dozen ways, crimson and wet, but not even the circling vultures dared descend for a taste. Two wounded rangers sat with their backs against a rock. One had his veil torn away, his Dwarven beard bloodied from the bite to his shoulder. He waved a knife at the monsters around them. One Vel croaked. The others turned away, leaving the two wounded rangers for the main group.

"What do you call this?"

"Horrific necessity," Kamalia whispered. "If you look dead, if we can stage it beyond reason, *she* may think I completed my job."

Shai saw a blur to her right. Bedel flicked blood off his blade, charged. A Vel tackled him. They rolled, but Bedel threw it off. It scurried onto all fours, charged again. Bedel rose to his feet, steadied himself. It launched at him, talons wide. Bedel's baklana flashed, parrying a strike. Black claws caught the blade. The monster hissed, a forked tongue leaping from its mouth. Something hot and black dripped from its mouth to the ground, wilting the grass at Bedel's feet.

Bedel and the monster rolled away.

She'd never make it. Where were the raptors? The lion? Weren't they coming? Hadn't they listened?

Bedel grimaced, drew back, but the Vel launched forward, knocking him back to the ground. His sword fell as they grappled. Bedel grabbed its wrists. He had formed a buffer of thick air between him and it. But as the monster kept slamming against it, bludgeoning itself against the unseen force, the air began to waver. It wouldn't hold for long. Shai saw him grimace in pain and exhaustion, just enough to lose the manipulation. The air shield dissipated; wind rushed out around them. Bedel struggled to keep its snapping jaws and claws away. Jaws and a remarkably nimble neck lurched downward. Bedel grunted as he barely moved his head in time. The monster, unfazed, shifted its neck and tried to bite sideways.

Shai stumbled forward, pain shooting up her ankle, slowing her. All she could do was watch in horror. "Help him!" she shouted at Idrin, though he stood between unconscious A'banna and Kamalia. Shai willed aether into her ankle, using the bruise's essence to heal herself. Too damn slow!

Shai saw a burst of *Soliditus* flow in and around Bedel's arm, boosting his strength. Bedel yelled as he twisted its arm right into its mouth. Teeth clenched, and it ripped flesh off its own arm. At that moment, the ferret leapt onto the Vel's back and bit at its neck, pulling scale after scale free with its teeth in a ferocious attack. The monster screamed, its breath foul and rank. Bedel kicked, kneed, trying to get some distance from the thing. He used *Soliditus* to enhance each blow, but the Vel was determined to kill.

A large, scaled, shredded corpse flew over the rocky formation, followed by two more. The female alpha raptor crested the rocks and dropped a dead monster's arm, shoulder, and head at her feet. She stomped hard, large talon cleaving the chest scales. She hissed. The majestically large lion stood beside her, scales stuck in its golden mane. The alpha raptor hooted.

The attack came from three sides, flanking the remaining monsters in a flurry of blue, green, red; claws slammed into the Vel. As the assault launched, the lion and the alpha female raptor leapt off the rock. One of the monsters jumped to meet it, but with a single slash of its claws, the Vel tumbled to the ground, a gash in its throat. Another tried to assault the lion, but it wrapped its paws around the creature, claws digging in. Jaws clamped down, they rolled, and then the lion shook the monster so hard, they heard a snap. The lion spat the limp monster from its mouth. It tumbled further and did not rise. The lion roared and charged into the monsters' midst.

At the last moment, the ferret leapt free. The single-eyed raptor appeared from behind a rock. It kicked, a curled talon ripping flesh and scales from the Vel's throat, blood and blue liquid splashing outward. The raptor sliced at the torso, spilling the monster's steaming guts onto the grass.

The raptor shifted, faster than the claws, and snapped down on its neck, driving it to the ground. The raptor used its curved claw to cut into the spine and, with a twist of its jaws, the Vel's spine snapped. It dropped the limp horror, hissing at it victoriously.

Bedel heaved, staring at his feathery ally. Shai gasped at the carnage, then flicked her gaze back across Bedel, the ferret, and the raptor. Shai could see enough colors to know it was thinking of the pack.

Covered in blood and a strange fluid, the raptor glared at Bedel. The same predator that had tried to kill them in their bed several nights ago seemed pleased to defend him. Its glare turned away from Bedel.

It nuzzled him.

"I don't believe it," Shai whispered.

The group of animals—raptors, a ferret, and a lion—cried out in aggression as they ripped apart the monster's ranks. The ground crimsoned with blood. Bodies were strewn around the entire area, but no more monsters emerged. The ferret joined in the final fray, and the raptors and lion seemed to welcome it. A minute later, the last Vel lay thrashing on the ground, a raptor gazing at it and its numerous wounds curiously. Finally, the animals all turned to look at the final threat: Kamalia.

With a downward slash of her sword, Kamalia finished off the last Vel circling the group. Kamalia tensed as all seven animals fanned out, surrounding her. She gripped her sword, tensed her jaw, bent her knees.

Gaining her feet, Shai smiled. "How does it feel?"

Kamalia didn't answer.

Idrin dashed forward, leaping in front of Kamalia, waving at the animals. "No! Please, no!"

At first, only the ferret seemed affected. It danced among the fallen monsters, checking for any trying to fool them. The animals hesitated, then stopped. The lion licked its paws as the raptors began preening.

Kamalia lowered her sword.

The only two other surviving rangers were in critical condition. One had tied a tourniquet around the other's shredded leg, supporting his weight even as he bled profusely around the neck and shoulder. They had to help each other stand.

"Idrin?" Shai said. "Let the animals finish this!"

"This woman knows my sister," Idrin said. "My sister helped lead our warriors alongside the Wo'Huzziet in battle against slavers." He shook, his voice lowered in anger, a sheen in his eyes. "She was taken. We were notified."

Shai glanced back at Bedel.

"So, we just let her live? Seven of your men are dead because of her and her 'necessity!'"

"As if you wouldn't have done the same," Idrin murmured. Kamalia locked gaze with him. They didn't speak.

Shai grumbled, "You ambushed me."

Shai dropped to her knees to check on A'banna, who was unconscious and breathing harshly. Circles of red had stained her shirt. The arrow had clearly missed anything vital, but getting it out would be messy. Shai smoothed the woman's hair and gripped her hand. "I'm so sorry," she whispered.

Bedel walked up the short incline to stand on a boulder near the infiltrator. Kamalia was within striking distance of their swords.

Kamalia looked to Bedel. "You are the Gatekeeper."

For a moment, no one spoke.

"There's no use denying it, and you suffer no danger from me," Kamalia said, her gaze fixing from Bedel to Shai. "I was hidden among you for much of the preceding confrontation."

"I'm no bounty. Try to take me," Shai hissed.

"Try, Shai Menai?" the half-Glymph laughed. "I could kill the last six of you without those abominations. I have no interest in that."

"Because you're outnumbered?" Bedel said. "Or is it the raptor or lion?"

"I've hunted both kinds. No, Gatekeeper. I've kept my word. I've shot the fugitive, apprehended the bounty, and tested the Sorceress's Vel. It's been a very successful day."

"That black diamond of yours is the same colour as the scales on those Vel." Bedel gestured at the monsters.

The Sorceress' minotaurs were bad enough, but these Vel had just taken out a company of Lodornatha rangers within a few minutes. Shai crouched down next to Pol's body. She glowered at Kamalia.

"They weren't going to hurt me," Shai whispered. "We would have deescalated."

"That did not appear to be the case," Kamalia said.

"He was a good man."

"Good men die," Kamalia whispered.

"You're a monster."

Kamalia touched the black diamond on her forehead. "True enough. A perk or curse of old Elven blood. Your companions are dead. This shared animosity will not bring them back. Sorceress Jocina and her son Quin are raising an army of Vel at an undisclosed location. Now we know precisely how lethal a self-replicating army of Vel are."

She turned to glare at the two surviving rangers. Both were shaking. They wouldn't last if their wounds were untreated.

"They need help," Bedel said. "That's a shock."

"Gatekeeper, didn't A'banna teach you anything?"

The teal-skinned half-Glymph threw off her ranger cloak, fully exposing her plated armor and numerous weapons. Leather creaked, and armor clattered softly as she strolled over.

"Those are my men!" Idrin shouted at her, waving his sword.

The woman came within striking distance of both men, who cowered before her.

"No, my prince, they were your men. Show them your arms."

They glared at her defiantly, even as they took a step back. Very unlike rangers.

"Shall I show them for you?"

Shai eyed the creeping blackness spreading along one of the ranger's veins up his throat.

"Too fast," Kamalia said as if it surprised her. She spun; her sword caught the sun and glinted. Shai and Idrin shouted as the two Dwarven rangers were cut down. A sickening smack echoed against the rocks as the bodies fell without heads. She leaned forward, grabbed one, and pulled his sleeve away from the arm. It was scaled.

"How?" Idrin said in horror. "What witchcraft is this?"

"It's the same thing that would have happened to me if I didn't have Elven blood in my veins. It is what will happen to any army that opposes them. As I warned you: Vel kill with a single bite." The woman grabbed the severed head of a Vel and forced open its jaws, revealing two curved fangs. The jaw moved on its own, the violent response of dead nerves. The fangs seemed to rise and fall with the closing and opening of the mouth. "Essence of dark fire is what the Sorceress calls the secretion. Similar to snake venom but highly contagious to anything that lives."

"We just forgive you?" Shai murmured as she tended to A'banna, wrapping a cloth around the arrow. "Not even I *wanted* to harm them after the battle."

"Noted," Idrin said, eyes hollow as he surveyed the field.

"Want has nothing to do with it, Shai Menai," Kamalia said. Shai bristled at the use of the surname. "Two more minutes and we would have had more enemies to contend with. No bites? Tend to the fugitive. We can still save her."

"Why?" Shai stepped in front of Kamalia. "Because she's your sister or she's a person we care about? Or did any of that matter when you led the monsters here?"

"I had multiple tasks. Would you have preferred I release them on the Wo'Huzziet? Or in the middle of a city where the infection could not be contained? There was no other way. Please. Tend her."

Bedel stood by the one-eyed raptor. "He has a bluish liquid on its snout."

"Reptiles have strong immunities to odd things, including this. The animal will be fine. Still, dress the wounds as needed. Now, Gatekeeper, we must discuss my bounty."

"Why?" Bedel snapped. The raptor stood next to him and snarled at Kamalia. The pack moved in front of Shai and A'banna.

"My oath and my word are my bonds, and no manipulation of what I look like will change that."

"This is yeht shit, and you all know it," Shai snapped. "Idrin, Bedel, someone keep pressure on this!"

She darted to the camp, scrounging for water, a saw, tools, and salve. Finding everything she needed and more, she ran back, dropping to her knees beside Idrin, who tended A'banna.

"The arrow missed vital organs," Idrin announced.

"I know," Kamalia and Shai said at the same time. They glared at one another.

Kamalia said, "I did warn you all."

"Ever so helpful!" Shai arranged the makeshift medical kit.

"She's correct," Bedel said. "You killed our men, our allies. Friends."

Idrin's hand shook briefly. Silently, he continued tending A'banna.

Bedel stumbled as he knelt to help.

Shai gasped, reaching for him.

"I'm fine," he said, though he took her hand as he sat down.

"I think you should watch A'banna," Shai whispered. She'd protest him being "fine" later.

Bedel's eyes flickered over to Idrin. He nodded once. Shai stood, crossed her arms, and glared at Kamalia.

"It will be no help if you do not return with me," Kamalia said.

"Not interested."

"You may be. Ambassador Ci'Dio of Istante has pledged his daughter Ni'Dio to the king of Franca. They wish you to create the same miracle you performed for the Rultritans."

Shai steeled herself. "What?"

Kamalia frowned, unamused. "If Ni'Dio becomes queen of Franca, she'll displace their princess, who I am led to believe may be Chosen by The Caurs."

"This never ends," Bedel said, tossing aside a bloody bandage.

"Events proceed swiftly in the north. The Sorceress is planting method after method to weaken resistance. Whatever she and The Taurs have planned, it will begin in earnest soon. We need your help." Kamalia touched the diamond repeatedly. "While I can still aid you freely."

"Who is we?"

The teal-skinned half-Glymph gestured around her. "Everyone who wants to survive what is to come. I can't hunt in a world where I'm being hunted by abominations and monsters." She looked to A'banna on the ground. "The fugitive knew that."

A'banna shrieked as the arrow was cut and slid from her. A poker, red from the coals, was pressed inside. Flesh sizzled.

"She is no fugitive," Bedel said. "She's your foster sister."

"House-sister, it is called in Avoc," Kamalia said, a fond tone leaking into her voice. "Her parents raised me for a time as their own, before Hurmlen stole me back to corrupt me. He failed."

"You murdered a man guarding us," Shai said.

"We have no reason to trust you," Bedel said.

"Prince Idrin, your sister, Captain Edelissi, is an attendant in Ni'Dio's court. She wishes to tell her family in Lodornatha that she is strong, and that House Onoarel should be ready for everything to come." Kamalia approached Idrin. "She has nine fingers, Idrin."

Bedel attempted to stand but gripped his side and sat hard beside A'banna.

Kamalia crouched, intent on Idrin. "I saw your sword. That is why I recognized you."

"Ni'Dio sent the letter to my father," Idrin said, wrapping bandages around A'banna's torso. "It was too much for him. My sister is all the family I have left. If you are lying, you will know the wrath *I* am capable of—and justice will be served for my family and my men."

Kamalia nodded. "Good. She's alive, Idrin Onoarel. I spoke with her yesterday. That fire within you lives still in her. Shai, if you return with me, you can help stop this union. A male heir will ensure King Aubert can discard Amelia. A Chosen with power and authority—think what Amelia de Gerac can accomplish! What if she loses it all?"

Shai wiped her brow with a sleeve. "You can't ask this of me."

"Eventually, I will not ask."

Bedel grunted. "Seems you've finally met your match, Shai."

"We'll see," Shai said, glaring at the half-Glymph. "We have a mission to accomplish first, Kamalia. It's in Zeller."

"By good fortune, I've booked passage from Zeller's city of Wonbai," Kamalia said. "They still think I'm slumbering in the cabin."

"Then how did you get here?"

Everyone hesitated, watching her.

"Jocina has been searching for you. Last night, she found you and dispatched me and the Vel. We used magic I prefer not to discuss."

Bedel sat on his heels. "You can *Vanish Travel*."

"Indeed," Kamalia whispered. "Vel are difficult to slow when small."

"Crows, that's how they're going to open or widen the gap

between realms!" Shai said, snapping her fingers. "They're going to cut a hole through the fabric. That's why the essences were so slow to respond to us. Your travel wounded them."

Kamalia looked to Shai. "If you're referring to why we need a Gatekeeper, Shai Menai, I presume to think *Vanishing* will only be a fraction of The Taurs' objectives. Millions of Taurs entering through a tiny space in the world fabric? No. They'll need something larger. Something the Istantese society is built on. We need your help."

Idrin passed a soaked rag to Bedel. "Kamalia. I know that name."

"A good ranger would. Your sister recognized me immediately."

Bedel dipped a new rag in misty red water before handing it to Idrin.

"The Voice of the South," Idrin said, sitting back on his heels. "The Sorceress's Voice."

Kamalia snarled, her lips pulling up over her large canines. "I am not and never shall be the Voice of one who desecrates the lands for pleasure and for war. My father is Hurmlen, former Dark Judicator of the Truth. My mother was nameless, a Glymph whore whom he took and later discarded after she birthed me. I was raised partially in Avoc. I know what this alliance of Jocina, Hurmlen, and the Veccil'ni are capable of. I hate Jocina, her son, and my father for what they are."

"Good," Idrin said.

Kamalia blinked, a corner of her lips curved upward. "You are Prince Onoarel. This is no chance meeting of all of us."

Sudden kindness softened her countenance, and she removed a gauntlet. A black diamond covered the back of her hand. Before anyone could stop her, she brushed hair off A'banna's face.

"Kamalia," A'banna whispered, eyes flickering open. "You shot me."

"My apologies, dear sister. Rest. We will explain."

A'banna exhaled. "I hate resting." She paused. "Fine, Bedel."

She moaned again but laid quiet as they tended her.

The half-Glymph nodded. "In Avoc, I knew few people like you. Your family instilled love of the land in me. I have never lost it, even if Jocina and Hurmlen hated me for it. While ranging in the wild last month, Jocina laid a trap for me with the vine. I am forever half of who I was; which is half of all of you."

A'banna reached out, grasping Kamalia's hand.

"I understand that feeling," Shai whispered, kneeling.

"Then know I fulfill my word. I give you my word that the fugitive A'banna has died to Jocina and Quin."

A'banna stirred, trying to sit up.

"Whoa!" Shai muttered, holding her down.

A'banna's eyes widened with horror. "He lives?"

"My sister, you broke him so much, the only way he could live was for her to make him as me. She sent him north to spread the Vel."

"We're headed north," A'banna whispered, trembling. Shai paused. She knew this reaction. She'd felt it personally.

"Take heart," Kamalia said. She locked gazes with Bedel. "We will find a solution."

"We will, A'banna," Bedel said. "I won't let him hurt you again."

Shai swallowed her emotions, hiding it behind a professional veil of steel.

"As to the rest of my word, know that Edelissi Onoarel is alive and strong. That there are more Vel and soon hundreds of thousands. They will plant this vine to create more Vel. I give you my word we will try to protect the Chosen and the Gatekeeper, rescue Edelissi and you, Shai, and stop The Taurs and the others from destroying our world. Or we will die a valiant death trying. I can do nothing else."

Bedel looked around the devastated camp, the many bodies, and the animals now lounging by a water hole. "No, Kamalia, Defender of the South, there is something else you can help us with."

Idrin stared out at his lost men. "What is that?"

Bedel sheathed his weapon, knelt to check on A'banna, then addressed them all. "We bury our dead. Burn the rest. And tonight, two days early, we arrive in Zeller."

CHAPTER 21

Coincidently, Father sent word from Greneld that our house's war-ram battalion is traveling for joint military exercises, and I am to serve as su'trekbok. Though I am loath to leave Ambassador Quika's side before the Summit in your Cardorian homeland.

— Vari, intercepted missive to Bedel Morbrook. 4076 AE.

The raptors did not like to be ridden. After nearly having a leg bitten off, Bedel gave up after his first attempt. He'd ride one of their last horses. The Vel had slaughtered most of their mounts. They were lucky to have three remaining.

Shai emerged from behind the detached wagon. An elaborate headscarf covered her hair, and for a shirt, she wore a tight cloth she called a tunic. Her pants billowed in the breeze, and she steadied the fabric with a touch of her hands.

Bedel stood beside her. "What if the portal closes on the *Zitaya?*" he asked.

Shai sighed. "Well, that's another method no one has recorded trying."

He rolled his eyes.

Shai nudged a small pebble in the dirt with her foot. "How's your pain?"

Bedel touched his side, the exact place he had felt the arrow pierce A'banna. "Less. It helps that she's sleeping. She needed more rest, and we took her straight into a long trek and then a battle. We'll be fine once she's recovered."

Both looked at their feet, then up at the emerging blue stars. On the other side of the rock wall, flames licked the sky. A farewell to their companions. "Kamalia was clever," Shai said, watching the flames. "With A'banna recovering, the bond is weak. You have a chance of evading Baktur."

"And you?"

Shai suddenly reached up, grabbed the air, and flipped high into the sky, higher than the flames. She landed, arms out, crouched on both feet. "Feel anything?"

He shook his head.

"Neither do they. I'm safe from everyone but our new friend."

"Hurmlen's daughter," Bedel muttered. "This keeps getting stranger."

Shai nodded. "I *can* do this without you, you know."

Bedel laughed. Her brash confidence was, well, normal from her. The more he gained A'banna, the more he lost Shai. "That's what I'm afraid of. You having to go this alone."

Shai smiled at his laughter. "I think you're afraid of having to do this without me."

Crows, did she have to see him like that? Of course, he was terrified of losing her!

Instead, Bedel scoffed. "Me?"

"Yes, you. Kerdum, Bedel, I was so terrified of losing you I tried to kill A'banna. I can only imagine how you're feeling."

"You lied to me and jeopardized the whole mission from day one."

Shai ran a hand through her hair.

"You knew why we were sent to the mountain. This coming war wasn't just rumor to you. You had Intel you didn't share. Then hiring the *Batoidea*? Why did you lie to *me*?"

Shai glanced around, but no one was within earshot. "I wrote our mutual friend, Vari in Ambassador Quika's service. He's invited you to dinner. You're going to meet with me and I'll have the war plans."

"You wrote Vari without telling me?"

"You can't play friends with everyone. You can't save everyone. I know you want Vari's family to become a safe place for Raynt, but he has to be on his own. There are great houses in Zeller trying to take down the Tressoni's, and the inter-marriage with Vari's brother..."

Bedel grimaced. "They are our friends."

"Vari is an asset, Bedel, not a friend. The moment you start to remember that you are an agent and a target, you'll treat him as a handler. I extracted information. Here." She took out a folded slip of paper, placing it in his hands. "He's been called to lead a legion of ram riders. Why didn't you know about this?"

Bedel's hand shook as he read his friend's subtle words and warnings. "How can I trust you?"

Shai raised her hand to slap him but dropped it to her side. "I'm looking out for you."

"You're lying behind my back. You wanted to vanish before this became more than just words and rumors. You would have left the kingdom to die?"

"Oh, don't get soft! Not until we're free from this mess, Bedel."

"Shai, you didn't answer me."

"Crows damn it, Bedel! I saw Hurmlen! I saw him. And your

brother." Tears streamed down her face. His heart beat so quickly, he could barely breathe. "Should I have told you? What would you have done? Chase after them, that's what! You would've gotten yourself killed. Or worse."

"Hurmlen and Jacob?"

"He doesn't go by that name now. He's working for Duchess Sapphira and with Hurmlen, the Veccil'ni, and the Judicator of Greneld. If Raynt and Sir Rurik from the King's Men followed up the hints I left them, we might even be able to verify they're working with the Slaver Coalition inside Cardor to bring Cardor, Lupacuo, and Franca down. I had to do this my way. Bedel, I couldn't let you do something noble and stupid."

He started to protest, but she interrupted him.

"Jacob is not your friend anymore. I briefed Xathon and Nadael. For all I know, that's why the Keeper and Speakers sent Alain and chose that mountain. Why do you think they let Stamford Farr there? Because he's reformed? They needed an insider. And Alain?" she shrugged in frustration. "I did my job. Just as you would have done. I kept you safe. Because I love loved you."

He exhaled sharply. "I am sorry, Shai. I loved you, too. I still do, but I can't trust you."

Shai shook her head, long curly locks fell in front of her face, obstructing her expression. She tossed them back with a gentle sweep of her hand. "You have a good heart, Bedel. I like being a spy. It's my life. I am still going to put it away one day. Just walk away into my cabin. I wish you could be there, but even if we could go back in time, you'd save her again and I'd make the same decisions, no matter if Alain had come or not. That's who you are. You try to save people and if they don't want to be saved, you let them go. This is me." Bedel looked up at the stars. "Bedel, ten years ago, you saved my life. You read those books with me in my grandfather's study. He would have made me disappear for that, if it weren't for you. But you wanted to know, too, no matter the risk."

"Shai."

She blinked back tears. "I was wrong to fight you so hard. To fight A'banna. I didn't want to lose you."

"You haven't lost me. We still care for each other. We still know what the world doesn't. Even if you can't enjoy friendship, you have allies."

"If I had trusted you," she blurted out. The words struck him, weakening a part of his heart. While A'banna was sleeping, he felt hollow. Alone. "I would have told you all I knew about the *Zitaya*. That I had stolen Wo'Huzziet medicine in my pocket! We could have bonded, you would know everything I want but can't tell you. All of this might not have happened exactly the same way. But I didn't want to abandon my work so cavalierly. Selfishly."

"I should have left when you asked me."

Shai laughed, wiping away tears. "Damn right, you should have."

There was more they could say, but it felt useless. Changing the fabric of time was beyond the ability of essencers.

"Shai, once you get to Istante who will aid you against Clan Diotek? Ni'Dio is insane, and she's marrying a man who has been a driving force enslaving your people. Who are you going to trust?"

Shai shrugged. "I know she's insane. That makes her unpredictably predictable." Bedel chuckled. "Seriously, Bedel. I used to think only Hurmlen scared the Kerdum out of me. Two of his children—Kamalia and this Huiquin—showing up in the midst of all of this? But then we got to see how the Sorceress works. His lover, the Keeper of the South, about to make another play to slaughter, conquer, and rule the world? Crows, I think I can handle Ni'Dio and Aubert. Besides, Princess Edelissi's surviving somehow, so will I. I also happen to like Istantese fashion. I won't have to wear those slave robes, you know. Highborn and all."

I don't like this, he thought. *The sense of being cornered. Of being trapped.* Perhaps Shai had been right to point out his father's negligence in teaching Bedel enough but not everything he needed to know about magic before sending him into the field. He nearly proposed they all disappear, until Kamalia walked by, tossing gear in the wagon.

"Finished, yet?" Kamalia raised an eyebrow.

"No, not yet," Shai barked.

"Well, hurry up. I'm preparing the *Vanish* portal now. Not all of us get so much time to leave our lovers."

Kamalia stormed off. Bedel and Shai watched her go.

"Did she?" Bedel asked.

"Crows, I have to know!" Shai murmured.

"You'll have plenty of time to find out," Bedel said.

"Don't remind me." Shai's aura flared with bright colors of pleasure, hope, and desire. And then the colors cooled. "I have to do this. If I don't go, none of us get to disappear—you, Raynt, A'banna, me. My mother's caravan or my assets won't be safe. Slavers, Hurmlen, Jocina, my father or grandfather. And they'll enslave or kill them. Jocina and Hurmlen are playing the nations like pawns. The Vel are coming. Boar-men! The stars are here. Like Kamalia said, there won't be a world for us to disappear into. No, all of you were right." She stepped forward and placed a hand on his cheek. "The life we hoped for is over, Bedel. At best, we die saving the world."

"Gods, maybe I'll even meet someone. The cabin might get crowded. Especially if Raynt oh, we'll build more."

Part of him wanted to reach out to her, hold her one last time, but that would have released a dangerous storm of emotions within her Elven nature. They both knew that. He looked at the wilderness around him as the one-eyed raptor nuzzled him. "Then we hope for the future."

"It's prophecy and magic cycles," Kamalia called over as she cleared a patch of grass and dirt.

Shai groaned. "If she continues being right, this will be an annoying trip! We're bloody fighting to stop the damn future. Let's rehearse this mission. Who are you?"

Bedel slipped into his training easily. He'd deal with the emotions later.

"A merchant from Clan Osana, a small house in Micelin. My master's been pursuing a personal collection of exotic animals and hopes to breed them as hunting hounds. Your menagerie helped connect me with this hunter who had just acquired a pack from her bounty."

Shai gazed up at the evening sky. "And though the troupe is headed south—"

"I require passage through Wonbai to Istanton. I'm looking to hire a freighter. And you?"

She smiled and winked. "That's confidential."

"Then I'll see you there."

She gave a wry smile before she turned to go, but he wasn't done yet. There was something that no one but Idrin, the late Pol, and Bedel knew.

"You did the right thing, stealing the raven that came last night," Bedel said.

She halted but didn't turn to face him. "It tipped off the rangers. It was selfish. We needed the menagerie."

"It's not selfish to send your mother away from harm."

"They're safer in the desert," Shai said. "But that bird wasn't mine. It was from Edelissi to Idrin."

"Shai. Edelissi wrote Idrin?"

She vacillated for a moment, then produced another thin, rolled missive and passed it to Bedel. "Idrin and I aren't exactly on good terms. You can give this to him. It's actually from an Elven Intelligence asset, writing for Edelissi. Istante has an army marching by land to Cardor or Lupacuo. So, likely Cardor. And apparently, she had other things she wanted him to know."

Bedel's eyebrows rose.

"It was marked by Elven Intelligence, Bedel. I'm authorized to open a message." She cleared her throat. "And pass it on. Via another messenger."

Bedel shook his head and slipped the message into a belt pouch.

"It's not about me," Shai whispered. "Princess Amelia needs aid, and as much as I can't stand Idrin, he's started pining over his sister. They survived dragon fire together, under their mother's burning body. I can't imagine. Any further news from his sister would put him at risk."

"Either of them could inherit the Elven Throne of Lodornatha someday. By then, I'm sure you and Idrin will patch up any misunderstandings." She chuckled. Bedel continued, "Thank you."

"That's correct." This time, they both laughed. Then Shai extended her hand. "Good luck, Master Osanu."

Bedel swallowed his grief. "Lady Shai."

Rocks tumbled, signaling someone standing on the edge of the cluster. The fire and early blue starlight silhouetted Kamalia, making her seem alive with light. Her hand rested upon her sword hilt. "It is nearly nightfall. Jocina will *Long Sight* again soon. We must away."

Idrin shouldered a bag and walked around the rocks. He had gathered arrows, bows, a few swords, and began wrapping them in leather. "I look forward to reading the letter from my sister."

"Of course, you had to hear, too," Shai muttered, glaring at Bedel.

"Let me help," Bedel said. He took the bundle and dropped it in the back of the wagon as Idrin secured the barding to a mount. The horse stomped once in frustration but allowed the ranger to continue.

Idrin and Bedel hefted the last of the gear into the wagon. "We will make them—Ni'Dio, Ci'Dio, the slavers, Hurmlen, Jocina— we will make them bleed for what they've done to us and the world."

Bedel held his gaze. "We will, your Grace. And you both will take your place on the thrones of Lodornatha. They will need your counsel with everything to come."

Idrin stood taller, prouder, despite the weight of grief he bore. He spoke facing the rock formation and the black smoke billowing like incense to the stars. "Once A'banna is onboard the ship, I must go. I will not follow you to Cardor but will track my sister, even to Franca." Idrin turned, and the men clutched forearms.

"Bring her home. Thank you," Bedel said. "For everything."

"And you, Gatekeeper."

"Call me 'friend.' Remember, they'll need you on that throne before long."

"May the stars forbid," Idrin said, cracking a slight smile. "I prefer the wild to politics."

Bedel began to turn, but Idrin put a hand on his shoulder. "If you should find a way to close the gate without expending yourself, do it. Once your mission is finished in Zeller and the plans delivered, you are dead to whatever your father planned for you. Make a new life for yourself and A'banna, free of the burden."

Overcome, Bedel clutched his friend's hand, and the two raised a sleeping A'banna into the wagon. The ferret hopped in beside her, curling up beside her hand.

"My magic will keep her safe," Idrin said.

"I know. One day, perhaps you will explain your bond."

Idrin scratched the ferret behind the ears. The ranger almost smiled. "One day. Perhaps."

Red and orange lit the sky in the west.

"It is time," Kamalia said, her voice stern. "We leave, or we die here."

Shai waved toward the road. "By all means, hunter, after you."

Kamalia cracked a toothy smile. "Bounty."

Shai shrugged. "So, this is what it feels like to be assigned a name."

"Yes, Shai Menai."

Shai raised an eyebrow but otherwise displayed no emotion. "Kamalia."

The group gathered around as white light split the air vertically. Colorful strings of essences recoiled, as if a knife had sliced through a taut rope. Essences tremored in pain at the slice. The light widened, like the rift of an eye, or a hole in space. Light shimmered; through the rift was another land, one of sand and rock, red and quiet. Green dotted the landscape, and to the west was a large hill covered in vines and a large, square adobe building with chimneys. A vineyard.

"Watch your feet and your head," Kamalia advised, then stepped through.

One by one, the group followed. Bedel stayed behind, watching each disappear from this location and stand in the desert on the other side of the portal. Idrin guided the horse and wagon through. Shai stayed close to the back of the wagon. The lion and alpha female led the pack, but the single-eyed raptor stayed beside Bedel.

"Well," Bedel said to the raptor as the group continued their trek across thousands of miles in a minute. "Does this make us friends now?"

The raptor swung its head to look at him, but only briefly.

They only sustained a gaze if they meant to harm. It snorted through the yellow-tinged snout and flared its blue feathers. *Mate of the beta mother. Claw brethren.*

Bedel smiled, trying very hard not to look it in the eye. *Claw brethren.* He liked that.

The raptor's maw upturned, as if in a smile, and it entered the portal. Bedel scratched his head, amazed. There were always risks, but it was nice to know the predator had his back. Sort of.

For only a moment, he was alone. Bedel looked up at the stars, shook his head in astonishment, and stepped from the tribal plains into Zeller.

He felt the essences tremble, as if stunned and in agony. The world fabric itself was alive, after all. Then came a flash of light, and the portal disappeared behind him. His stomach lurched, threatening to expel breakfast. In one instant, as he stepped through, his body felt torn in two and snapped back together in a blink. With that step, he hovered above a continent. Then it was over. Kamalia's *Vanishing* magic had given them what two days of steady travel would have required. The air was dry, but night had already touched here and the stars glittered like gems above them. Bedel shivered at the sudden change of temperature. The desert was a strange place.

Kamalia gathered the group and pointed toward the vineyard and hazy glow of light beyond. "Wonbai is over that ridge. We will arrive in the middle of the night, when the guards are drunk but the city is alive. Watch your footing for pits and vipers. Come."

Vipers were the least of their worries. The Swords of Baktur were headquartered in the castle of Winnago, high above the cliffs of Wonbai. Their leader, a self-described demigod called the Veccil'ni, was often called the Red Dragon. His presence was formidable, cold. The hunt for essencers was essential to their beliefs, to their way of life. Bedel and his companions had just left one sizable calling card.

Without another word, Kamalia began to trudge through dirt and sand. The company trekked on behind her. With every step, the world of the Red Dragon grew larger, closer. There were strange shivers, as if something cold passed them in the darkness, curious and with a slight hiss. As they ascended the incline and found the road, Kamalia broke up the two groups.

Idrin drove the wagon along the outer road to the docks. Bedel watched A'banna, sleeping soundly in back. Her body had been pushed to its limit. She still hadn't fully recovered from the physical trauma on her journey from Avoc. Kamalia's arrow, though perfectly aimed and not life-threatening, had pushed her body into a deep sleep. She didn't dream, and she didn't feel.

Kamalia stood beside Bedel's horse. "It's safest this way. For all of us."

"What if we can't control the raptors?" That wasn't what he wanted to ask.

Kamalia raised an eyebrow. "You haven't been in control of them since I found you. No more questions. The darkness has ears and eyes."

A sudden cold chill brushed past them.

Bedel shivered. "The Taurs."

"Be grateful you cannot see, Master Osanu."

He nodded. Kamalia made a show of rounding up the raptors, and they trudged onward.

Soon, tall plaster and stone walls rose above the desert. Behind them, the city of Wonbai shimmered. A tall, lone mountain climbed from the hills around the city. There sat Winnago Castle, seat of the Veccil'ni and home of the Baktur religious sect. The castle glimmered red and white under the blue light, as if the stars could not change its being. Shorter walls and long roads marked estates to the east, farms and other vineyards outside the city. A southeastern wind carried the smell of the sea and the sounds of a city at night.

Shai swore. "At the base of the walls…" Her voice trailed off.

Rows upon rows of large tents. Massive rams, horns curved and sharp, pulled their moorings. Large four-armed figures moved around campfires. Deep, guttural singing filled the night. Even larger silhouettes, some nearly twice as tall as a Man, moved through the camp. Bedel gaped as he surveyed the sheer number of towering Flygn, giant slaves and warriors who served the shorter but no less intimidating Glymphs. Flygn had two arms and the ground shook under their steps. One Flygn giant lugged a hairless dead yeht with broken horns to a farm pen and tossed it in. Campfires cast massive shadows on the city wall, larger than a manor, as the war-bred komodrakes took to their nightly meal. Unlike the water drakes of Avoc or the mountain drakes that Lodornatha kept at bay, komodrakes could not become dragons. They were fierce nonetheless and larger than any other drake kin. The shadows and the sounds of their feasting sent chills through Bedel, recalling the events of the Vel ambush.

If this war happened, Cardor's strength would be crippled. How could they then resist the Vel? Bloody fields, this was it. The prophecy. The cycle. The beginning of the end camped outside Wonbai's walls.

"Do you need more confirmation?" Kamalia said, standing between Shai and Bedel's horses on the ridge.

"I wish I could say no," Shai said.

"We need to know when and where they'll strike," Bedel murmured. He could see his breath in the cold air. "Judging by the camp size, I'd estimate at least forty thousand soldiers."

"Glymph and Flygn aligned with Zeller *and* Istante, and the Sorceress arranging for the Vel." Shai's voice was barely a whisper.

Bedel's heart pounded. "Shai, this is the Harvest holiday in

Cardor. Summit or no, most of the Royal Army will be on leave. And after this war, the Vel?"

The two agents looked at the hunter.

Kamalia nodded. "Keep to the story and do not stray from the road."

The procession began the slow walk down the hill. The raptors and lion glared at the beasts they passed along the way. A massive orange and black spotted sabrecat snarled at them from the camp's border. Long ivory canines gave way to his massive maw. The lion growled.

A lumbering four-armed figure stood from a rickety stool near the sabrecat. Torchlight glimmered off a thick steel pike in its hands. Bedel knew from experience the pike was a very heavy weapon and capable of skewering a fully armored knight.

"Halt," the Glymph sentry growled.

Kamalia, who stood a head shorter than the Glymph, faced him, hand on her sword. "I am the Voice of the South, bringing a bounty through the city. Step aside, or I will kill you where you stand."

The guard stepped forward, hands tightening around the pike. He was clad in overlapping plated armor. His helm had horns crafted in it, the darkness hid his eyes but not the canines behind his smile. "I thought the Voice of the South would be taller."

Kamalia stretched her neck, which popped. Before the Glymph could react, she darted forward, blade unsheathed. She slammed the pommel into his face and battered his neck with her gauntlets. One arm reached for her, but Kamalia slammed a boot into the back of his knee, driving him to the ground. She hit him again and again, sending his helm flying, then finally whipped the flat of her sword across his face. The Glymph sprawled in the dust, grunting. Using two hands, he pushed himself up, as the second pair went for long knives at his belt. But Kamalia's sword touched his spine. She brought the point down, enough to draw blood. Her growl was as deep as the sabrecat's.

The animals neared each other. Other cats joined the first. The raptors and lion snarled and stomped the ground, ready to charge. Glymphs emerged from the camp; warriors bearing weapons, heavy pikes and swords, and robed priestesses armed with large bows nocked with two arrows. Bedel's heart pounded inside his chest. It would be over if they fought now.

"Stop!" a voice ordered.

Growls and snarls came from a multitude of throats as one Glymph shoved to the front. He quickly glanced at the scene, with Kamalia ready to drive her sword into the sentry's neck and the animals ready to fight to the death. He paused at the animals and, in the faint light, Bedel couldn't determine his reaction to seeing the raptors defend the lion.

"Kamalia Huntress, well met," a Glymph rumbled. He wore a leather cuirass bearing the sigil of a rearing ram. Streaks of black, red, and green paint crossed diagonally from right shoulder to left hip. Two swords hung from a baldric at his back, and daggers from his belt. Like the archer who lowered her bow with its two arrows, all full-blooded Glymphs employed the benefit of having four arms.

Kamalia spat into the dust near the sentry. "Belu Vari, I did not expect you in the camp."

Bedel silently swore to himself. If Shai hadn't told him or shown him the letter, Vari's presence would have shocked Bedel. An army here with Vari leading House Xikkan's famed ram-riders into battle? Conditions were extreme. Vari enjoyed being in Ambassador Quika's employ and only visited this area to spend time with family. Quika was one of the most prominent Glymphs urging for peace between the nation of Greneld and the kingdom of Cardor. As if the situation wasn't bad enough. Bedel's heart pounded in his chest as he saw how many Glymphs, Flygn, and sabrecats had gathered around them. Shadows flickered above the priestesses, and Bedel could have sworn he saw winged furry creatures swirling above the lightly armored Glymph women. None were to be taken lightly, as Kamalia had just shown.

Glymphs jeered the guard for being taken down by a half-Glymph woman, while the priestesses and their private guards saluted her as she passed. Temporary allies at best, but at least Kamalia had won their respect. Bedel remembered listening to veterans of the Traders' War, which had destroyed much of this city two decades before. They told how the Glymphs valued battle prowess with honor and songs of praise and gifts—only to duel to the death for a chance at helping pass on that honor amongst friend and enemy. Like the raptors, Bedel held no true illusions here. Even Vari and Kamalia were both friend and foe.

Vari quickly surveyed the caravan, lingering on Bedel for a moment.

Come on, friend, don't say it, Bedel thought. In one breath, Vari could destroy everything.

"My lady had no need of my services at the Summit, Huntress. I'll escort you through the gate."

Bedel was careful about exhaling. Dozens of warriors monitored the procession. Pikemen took up position along the road, watching the raptors with unblinking eyes. Emerging from between a row of tents, a Flygn stomped up, its heavy breathing a reminder of its hovering shadow.

The gates were opened and heavily guarded by Zelvatore spearmen. Their steel and chainmail armor was surrounded by turbans and covered by tabards marking their house allegiances.

Bedel, Shai, and Kamalia exchanged words with the captain at the gate. He waved them through. As Bedel rode past, the captain said, "Good travels, Lord Osanu."

Like a narcissistic Istantese noble, Bedel only nodded.

The city was alive with movement. Soldiers walked from one

inn or brothel to the next. People were loud and partying. Kegs were opened in the streets as the men drank.

"This is not the Wonbai I remember," Bedel said, riding up to Shai.

"That's because it's the eve of war, my friend." Bedel glanced beside him as Vari lumbered next to him, eye to eye.

"Tonight, the infantry celebrates," Vari said, lips pulling over his teeth in what amounted to a display of frustration. "Tomorrow, the Baktur. Then they sail to war. Haven't you heard?"

Well, since Shai and I never told you that we know each other, and she just gave me your letter a few hours ago, no. But I can't say that. Thanks, Shai.

"Lord Vari," Bedel said.

"You dumb yeht. Quika would bash your head for coming here. Maybe I should. I warned you! You need to leave."

Bedel glanced at his Glymph friend and fellow intelligence operative. "We can't."

"Fine," Vari rumbled. "You want to brave the Baktur out in force, your choice. Kamalia?"

"We have passage booked. Can they leave port?"

"Better be tonight or tomorrow, no later."

Kamalia grunted.

"Is everything in place?" Shai asked. Her horse whinnied and stepped to the side, putting distance between itself and Vari's massive green hands.

"Tomorrow, then," Vari said. He swung his head back to Bedel and gestured at Shai. "Were you going to tell me you knew each other?"

"Oh, please, Vari," Shai shrugged. Bedel merely opened his mouth to interject truth, and Shai raised an eyebrow. "Eventually, we were bound to meet." She smiled, tossed her hair behind her shoulder. "I have so many fans."

"She—" Bedel said.

"Besides," Shai interrupted. "Lord Osanu's invitation was too tempting to ignore."

Vari snickered and shook his head. The Glymph began to turn. "Where in Kerdum did you come up with the name Osanu?"

Bedel grinned. "Oh shut it. Good to see you, too."

Vari grumbled and gestured for their caravan to pass. The raptors' eyes constantly moved, missing nothing as they traversed the winding streets of the city toward the harbor. When Bedel looked back, the Glymph had already turned back to his camp.

When they turned off the main road, Shai handed the reins of her horse to Bedel.

Shai opened her mouth as if to speak, but there was nothing left to say. She hopped off the horse and darted into the shadows.

Bedel steeled his mind and offered Kamalia the reins.

She, too, looked down the dark alley. "Thank you, but I prefer to walk."

He nodded, tied the leather straps to his saddle, and followed her lead.

A thousand thoughts ran through his head. Perhaps this was too complicated. Perhaps they shouldn't trust as many people. Half a dozen working parts made the mission more complicated than those frustrating new wrist clocks.

The city quieted farther in, until they reached the harbor. Seagulls flew overhead, squawking. Wind carried the aroma of a salty sea and odor of fish. Bedel enjoyed a good harbor, but not this time. They crested a hill, giving them a clear view of the water. Hundreds of ships stretched into the gulf. Many had the dark, triangular sails of Zeller's fleet, a source of Vari's family's wealth. Bedel felt essences tremble around him—which shouldn't happen in Wonbai. Baktur would have hunted these essencers down in under an hour. Yet, somewhere, a great number of essencers spoke to *Invisitus*: the air, the heat, the cold, the wind. Clouds formed over the water, but they weren't spinning. Not yet.

Theantros, no.

Kamalia kept their group moving. Separated from A'banna, Idrin, and now Shai, Bedel felt even more alone. He wasn't sure what it would take to fully trust Kamalia, but she was an unknown, and that was too dangerous.

Men and women steered clear of the animals as they loaded ships, crates, and provisions. Officers shouted as cranes lifted platforms of cargo on board and sailors checked and rechecked rigs and ballistae. Fletchers had set up on the edge of the docks, constructing siege arrows by the dozens. Carpenters worked quickly to supply the thick shafts. The cacophony of saws and hammers and coarse language of workers filled Bedel's ears. Inns, shops, trading posts, shipwrights, and freight offices lined the cobblestone street, facing the dock. Soldiers barked at a civilian captain who had just pulled his ship to dock, but no one secured the lines. The soldiers gestured angrily for them to depart.

Kamalia steered them to a seedier side of the harbor, where sailors stumbled out of taverns, and a man was still laid out from a fight that must have happened minutes before. All manner of people and professions called to them or tried to approach, only to swivel at the first angry glance from Kamalia or the lingering gaze of a raptor. Not far from the dock was an inn, lit up and in use. Men and women entered, some still waving empty tankards or carrying tavern wenches on their shoulders to some presumably private place.

"Wait here," Kamalia said and entered the inn.

Bedel shifted, keeping an eye on the raptors. The predators watched the commotion and sometimes sneered at nearby sailors or folks looking for trouble, who promptly kept their distance. Otherwise, the animals hunkered down.

Inside the inn, there was a commotion. Glass shattered as some drunken fellow was tossed through the grand window. The welts on the side of his face were the size of Kamalia's steel-covered knuckles.

A moment after the last shard ceased rattling, mandolin and flute players struck up a lively tune, and a usual rowdy tone returned from the inn's common room, even as a woman, likely the proprietor came to study the damage.

The inn's door flew open, swinging on its hinges. Out stormed a red-haired woman in white blouse and trousers. A leather belt suspended a curved cutlass from her hips. She was by no means unattractive, but her scowl said enough. She glared at Bedel, then the raptors and the lion, which sat surprisingly docile.

"Four times the amount," the red-haired woman said as Kamalia sauntered up behind her. "They'll be on my ship. If they get unruly, I'll skin them all and sell the feathers and hide, understand?"

Kamalia dropped a pouch in the woman's palm. "Thank you, Commodore."

The red-haired pirate snorted. "If he's not coming with me, who is?"

"The passenger will be on board before sunrise," Bedel said.

"She'd better be. I'm not sticking around this city longer than I have to. Understood?"

"Perfectly," Kamalia said, showing an elongated canine. Closest thing to a full smile Bedel had yet to see from her.

The commodore nodded once and then gestured to the docks. Bedel wasn't in the habit of dealing with pirates, but Commodore Magdalena had a rich history and a shockingly trustworthy reputation of accomplishing even the most challenging contract. And she wasn't a slaver; a rare find in the pirating world.

Before any dock master could say a word, the lion and raptors were loaded aboard a large freighter, armed with a siege tower and machinery aft. They rested inside a chamber typically used to ship livestock.

The one-eyed raptor paused, and nuzzled Bedel's side. *Claw brethren?*

Bedel let out a laugh and smoothed down a few feathers. "It'll be okay," he said. *Beta-mother will be here soon.* The raptor pressed in again, snorted, blowing Bedel's hair, and then entered the chamber. It settled next to the alpha female, who watched Bedel curiously.

Bedel turned to Magdalena. "It should go without saying—"

"Look, Master Osanu, as I told Kamalia, if they don't misbehave, I don't have to kill them. Trust me. I don't want to deal with weaving raptors on open waters, understand?" She gestured for one of the sailors to bar the hold door.

Bedel felt a lump in his throat, put his hand to the door, and turned to leave.

"Who are you, really?" Magdalena asked.

Hand on the stairwell railing, Bedel hesitated. "I don't really know anymore."

He left her pondering below deck and caught up to Kamalia, who handed him a pouch of coins. "Your horse."

"I might have needed that overseas."

"You might need this more. Your room is there." Bedel started down the gangplank and realized he wasn't being followed. "Where are you going?"

"You have a keen mind and a good heart." Kamalia hesitated. "The stars chose well. I have to hunt tonight, Master Osanu."

He sighed, looking over the dock. "I wasn't chosen. I was made by someone I never met, using the same magic as Shai and" Bedel paused. "Our friend. My father found me in a jar on a shelf, in unnatural heat and stole me from the essencers. He woke me but didn't set me free. All my life has been planned and purposed or repurposed. Shai was my escape, Kamalia. Know that. She was the only thing unplanned, the only joy until I met our mutual friend. We're trusting you," he said. "All of us. We shouldn't, but we are. We need to live and fight together."

Kamalia nodded. "You already know my father."

"Mine's mortal enemy," Bedel chuckled.

"Ah." Kamalia smiled. "Then we can make them pay together."

"Let's survive this, first." He extended his hand and Kamalia gripped his arm.

"I have already pledged. My word is my bond. You are dead to those who came before. Soon, I will be also. Then we will be free to protect what we love."

He nodded. "I suppose I'll see you after the war."

"I will bring your friends home to you, Osanu."

"Then I will introduce you to a friend of mine. You are only the second half-Glymph I've ever met."

"One survived infancy?"

Bedel chuckled again, watching the bustling dock. "I never talk about my friends. The real ones. Unless I have to. When this is over, maybe I will."

A genuine smile crossed her face. "It would be an honor. You must go and sleep well. Tomorrow, the city will be at its most dangerous and I cannot protect you, then."

"Travel safe, Kamalia Huntress."

Again, her lips started to move, but instead, she bowed. Bedel left Kamalia on the deck of the ship and headed back to the inn. He didn't eat. Didn't drink. He was shown to his room and found Idrin waiting, bow drawn. The ranger smiled and lowered the weapon. On one of two beds, A'banna slept soundly.

Idrin took the watch without a word. Bedel climbed into the second bed and stared at the beautiful woman across from him. He fell asleep smiling.

Hours later, he awoke with a start. Sun streamed in through the window. Both A'banna and Idrin were gone. Bedel touched the bed where she'd lay, imagining her presence. His silver cord stretched for a short distance, then faded. She was still asleep. Still hidden. He had grown so accustomed to hearing her thoughts —or even the raptor pack—but they were gone now. Their window had a view of the dock below, and Magdalena's ship was indeed gone, carrying A'banna to safety ahead of the army.

He looked out the window, where he could see the dock. A new ship had taken the place of Magdalena's. He let himself feel for one last moment, then shoved it all away. Idrin had secured Bedel's pack, and he changed quickly. One last identity to assume that was not his. One last time delving into the world of spies and espionage. One last time walking among killers he may not be able to see. Just as his father Xathon had always groomed him to do, to be. After this, Bedel was done with the Magical Affairs Commission. He would remain Starblessed.

If he and A'banna survived.

CHAPTER 22

ZELLER WAS PERISHING IN A FAMINE, AND YET THE PEOPLE OF
Wonbai had food. Not just food, but drink. And where there was
food and drink, nobles feasted.

Shai stayed behind the red curtain, checking her shoes, her
pants, her exposed belly and arms for what had to be the ninth
time. There were no bruises, cuts, or wounds. No scars. Nothing
that would make her performance look unpleasant, have anyone
ask questions of where she had been. On her way to the palatial
and heavily fortified estate of House Talacciaro, she'd passed two
mass open graves, no more than a day old. The Swords of Baktur
were not just feasting, they were celebrating a massacre of anyone
suspected of being an essencer—and they only went on these
mass killing sprees to release a part of themselves, a violent interior that the Veccil'ni said resided within them. Shai knew
because she had listened on as one of their leaders shouted out an
oration about a massive strike, a mission from the god of war
himself.

Thus, when Shai thought about performing in front of a group
of high-born Baktur, she fretted. Her magic wasn't like the others;
she added to the world fabric, rather than taking away from it.

Outside the curtain, the host began riling up the crowd. Shai waited, shook out her limbs, and slipped her fingers into zills, small cymbals. She had no intent to give anyone a reason to kill her publicly tonight. Instead, she was going to make them get off their feet and dance.

Several musicians from the club her small network of spies operated out of came on stage behind her. The lead musician, with his stringed baligar, and she exchanged nods. Everyone's life was at risk.

"Behold," the host bellowed from the other side of the curtain. "Traveling from all across Aelathia, the great, the wonderful, the mysterious, enchanting and beautiful Shai of Bombard!"

Shai spread her feet just so, raised her hands, and the curtain opened. *Let the show begin.* The crowd cheered as the curtains parted, the minstrels struck up a rhythmic tune, and she began to dance. The essences were hers. Colors came alive, light followed her, illuminating everywhere her feet touched, her hands moved. But she changed nothing nor forced the essences to do something they would need 'convincing' of. The zealous Baktur had never seen the like, and she held them in awe, just as she preferred it.

After the hour-long performance, Shai had been shown to a private bath in a luxurious marble tub, then returned to the bustling party. After mingling for an hour, Shai excused herself from the party. Her brightly colored striped Branaird skirts rustled as she slipped into a cloakroom. Her eyes quickly traced the room. She glanced underneath hanging garments; opened a wardrobe and the in-house privy, then returned to trace the walls for eyeholes.

"Did you really think that I would agree for us to meet here, in this room, if I had not already checked to ensure we would not be spied on?" The voice was sultry, elegant, sophisticated.

Shai turned and curtsied.

"My apologies, Lady Talacciaro. Paranoia is excellent for survival."

The Zelvatore noble smiled. Her hair was braided and hung over her shoulder. Her dress was blue with gold embroidered horses, and the shawl draped over her shoulder was a deeper blue with a gold hem. Her jeweled dagger hung from a silver and gold beaded strap that looped over her opposite shoulder. Shai had no illusions.

Nor did Lady Elayana Talacciaro.

"When my son first asked me to do this, Lady Shai, I had no idea that he truly meant 'one of a kind.' You are different than all the essencers I have ever met. By design or by coincidence?" Talacciaro walked across the room to a small cabinet, where she pulled out a bottle of wine. It was labeled with House Tressoni's crest. The two houses were in a blood feud after the youngest Tressoni daughter's assassination. Talacciaro glanced up, watching Shai feign surprise. "I do not judge. They make excellent wine."

She poured a glass and sipped. "Care for a drink."

"I can't, my lady."

"Of course not. We should never take note that light bends around you or that the cymbals seem louder than they should, or that you never hurt an essence, but you make it bolder. Stronger. Tonight, I saw you fortify the world fabric. This left me impressed."

Talacciaro took a drink and smiled.

"I live to impress," Shai said, sitting cross-legged in an armchair as Talacciaro settled on a chaise.

"How invigorating. How different. Did you hear of my assault in Cronop? Agents from the Magical Affairs Commission. Just ghastly. I was glad my son passed through. He saved me from this essencer, a half-Glymph. I heard you were friends."

Shai's heart beat a little faster. This wasn't going at all like planned. Why was she stalling? Why did she speak of Raynt?

"But you seem to have recovered well," Shai said.

"Thank you. Meditation helps, but if we're going to cease the yeht shit, we can just say medicine and physicians here are better than anywhere in the world that the Healing Order of Essencers has abandoned. Your friends are alive. Goblins slaughtered thirty of my husband's best soldiers, prevented a deal to purchase slaves back from the Slaver Coalition upon our arrival, and brought scrutiny upon my house for the death of Sorceress Jocina's pet enforcer. I am…" She paused, searching for words, then took a sip. "At a quite awkward place, Shai. I have what you want, but I don't know if it's of benefit to me."

Shai sat forward, elbows on her knees. "If you help us, it could save lives."

"And what about ours, Shai?" Talacciaro's voice grew hoarse, her face twisted in pain. "What about my people that are dying from starvation and thirst? Will Xathon deliver Advancers to work on our crops and water? Can I trust him? Can I trust you?"

Advancers were essencers limited in their magical abilities and tended to keep to infrastructure works. Shai thought they were probably more palatable to the Zelvatore powers-that-be than the presence of full essencers.

Shai nodded. "A very good question. Can you trust me? They sent me. My people didn't attack you. That's not Raynt's style."

Talacciaro's mouth twisted into a smile, very pleased. "No, Shai, it was not."

She stood, dress and shawl whisking against each other with every movement. Out of her sleeve, she pulled a thin envelope. "This will confirm what you already know."

Shai took it, hiding it in her slip. "Thank you. I'll press them on infrastructure aid."

"As will our ambassadors. I fear, though, that the gods of this land want this Summit to fail," Talacciaro said. "The question is, what do the gods of your land want?"

"Not more war," Shai said. She withheld to herself she didn't believe in deities. No need to frustrate the key asset.

"I hope that is so," Talacciaro said before heading to the door. She turned, jewelry softly clattering. She gave Shai a weary smile. "Leave when you're ready. When you see my son, ask him to forgive me. What I did kept us all alive. Goodbye, Shai."

Shai curtsied again. When Talacciaro left, Shai exhaled and leaned onto the vanity to stare at herself in the mirror. Her mind raced, but she didn't have time to plan or feel. She fixed her hair, slipped out of the room a minute later, and resumed mixing and mingling, flirting when necessary, all until she made it safely outside, where the musicians waited for her in a carriage.

"Let's get the Kerdum out of here," she whispered.

The driver whipped the horses into action. Shai kept her gaze trained forward, even though in her peripheral she could see Lady Eleyana Talacciaro on a balcony, staring off to the west as the wagon wheeled by, as if the only interesting thing to note that evening was the beautiful sunset.

CHAPTER 23

BEDEL FELT THE SHOULDER LONG BEFORE HE SAW THE LABORER IT belonged to, hefting a cloth sack of goods on his back. The jostling continued as Bedel wove through the throbbing mass of pedestrians teeming within Wonbai's expansive market district. People surged about him; he felt their unintentional pressure through his knee-length tunic, he smelled their body odor. Bedel kept his fingers loose; ready to trigger the hidden knife blades under his bracers. One hand continually brushed a concealed dagger and coin pouch, a deliberate attempt not to cover his nose against the aromas. That was but one reason to draw attention to his blade. The bracers were clearly silver steel and would fetch a hefty price for the industrious thief.

In a crowd like this, there was no need to tempt fate, a pickpocket, or worse. Gold and silver earrings jingled on men and women alike, but Zelvatores knew war and blood feuds, and so they adjusted their adornments accordingly. At their sash or leather belts, nearly everyone carried a crested dagger. On another visit, Bedel had seen someone use a pair of earrings as weapons, short sharpened blades gripped between fingers. Perhaps he should have kept the baklana rather than sending it with A'banna, but the traditional sword may have drawn too many other questions he didn't need.

A foreigner who'd purchased and shipped a pack of well-tamed raptors in the night. He saw more than one set of curious eyes follow him. Entrepreneurs considered this Master Onasu as a potential investor—but he needed to avoid their offers. As far as they knew, he was just enjoying the city for a few hours.

Olive-skinned Zelvatores and the darker-skinned Branairds went about their daily business, buying, selling, or avoiding eager merchants vying for customers' attention. Women ambled calmly with bulky baskets perched on their heads, chock full of everything from fruits to textiles. The air was filled with the overpowering scent of sweat and musk; to their credit, Zelvatores and Branairds valued and enjoyed this scent more than perfume sold to countesses, baronesses, or other nobility of the north. No one made overtures or voiced suspicions that Bedel was really from Istante. After all, it had been his Istantese features that had gotten him this mission. Bedel didn't count many as friends, but one of his fellow agents had wanted this mission. But it was a spy's game to blend in.

This had been a strange adventure, Bedel reflected, but this wasn't the time for distracting thoughts. A quick glance showed the silvery *Zitaya* cord dimmed less than an arm's length from him. He wanted to reach out to A'banna, send her a thought, hear from her in return, but doing so would jeopardize both of them. This was the best they could accomplish.

A camel snorted as it ambled by, pushing through the crowd. Its turbaned owner bounced with each exaggerated movement, and the large baskets hanging from its sides almost scraped Bedel's head. He dodged and weaved back into the pedestrian traffic, which only put him in the path of larger objects. Hairy, reeking yehts pulled carts and carriages. The animals' bloodshot eyes glared at everyone and nothing. A wise yeht master let them continuously chew from the feed bags at their neck—and a wise pedestrian never looked one in the eye. Though people in Cardor viewed them as beasts of labor, here in Zeller, their three lethal horns wore rings of silver or gold or bronze. Their large, hardened crests were similarly bejeweled. Lethality was highly prized in Zeller society. Even the porters wore curved swords, cudgels, and other weapons. For those listening to the rumors, it made them step from Bedel's path. Someone who could tame raptors was dangerous indeed.

The lumbering, aggressive yehts moved on. Their massive tails wagged behind as handlers kept them from stampeding or overturning cargo. Keeping a proper distance, bare-chested servants bore a sedan chair through the foot traffic. Thin, silk curtains veiled the occupants from the rest of the world, but cinnamon incense wafted out as they passed.

The vast nation of Zeller had known war for over a millennium, mostly with its neighbor, Istante. Their differing views on the world fabric's place—to be manipulated as Istantese essencers did or balanced as the Swords of Baktur taught—had led to near-perpetual conflict. The power of essencers was great, but not every Istantese was an essencer. He glanced down again at the *Zitaya* cord.

Still dim. That's good.

Confident, he continued through the crowd. He hadn't uttered one word of Belasna since they passed through the portal last night. No need to draw the attention to himself. Zelvatores were genuinely hospitable when in their homes or businesses, but they wouldn't hesitate to cut Bedel's throat in his sleep if they knew who he really was or what he could do.

Ahead, on his left, two Swords of Baktur roamed the streets of Wonbai. These trained assassins were easily identifiable by their black chturi fabric wound tightly round their bodies and their large, black turbans. Thankfully, they were unveiled, meaning they weren't hunting for people like him. Yet. This was the eve of their Day of Balance—they weren't planning on slaughtering essencers by the hundreds or thousands to restore a perceived balance to the world fabric today. It sickened him that Vari had already witnessed that genocide. But Bedel had overhead a shop-keeper say some of their brothers had sailed overseas weeks ago. If the essencer hunters saw the cord or identified Bedel's abilities, the last thing he would see was a baklana before his head rolled in the dirt.

Head down, Bedel slipped behind a woman juggling a basket of laundry on her head. The movement attracted a merchant's attention as he stood at the edge of a U-shaped stall. He charged Bedel, hands overflowing with gold and silver jewelry.

"Best price! Three Darics. These are pure gold and silver. Perfect accessories!" he said in Zellu and pointed at Bedel's brac-ers. Over the merchant's shoulder, Bedel saw the two Baktur stop at an olive stand. The woman filled a small basket for them. Afternoon snack.

"No, no," Bedel replied, dissolving back into the crowd before the Baktur completed their transaction, and leaving the merchant to seek out a new hapless victim.

Clear for the moment, Bedel continued to his destination, mulling over the situation. He'd attempted to send a messenger bird to Xathon, since he couldn't risk a communication via a jewel with the Baktur so close. Even that attempt had to be aborted, as three of them had neared the stall just as he had begun writing the note. As long as they didn't see the cord or the essences ignored him, Bedel was just another outsider to the Baktur.

Bedel changed lanes, avoiding two unveiled Baktur strolling by on his left. He controlled his breathing. The fanatic assassins didn't stop or give any indication they'd seen him.

The ironic thing was, shipping lanes to Istante had opened, but he couldn't go there and jeopardize that mission. Everyone smelled war, but not between Zeller and Istante. The longtime foes had finally found a common enemy. In their eagerness for war, darker horrors were coming. They were all blind puppets to Hurmlen and Jocina.

Short, flat-roofed adobe buildings lined the side street. Many had bricked porches, covered by cloth canopies suspended by wooden poles. The taller structures were inns, but each building housed a business, often with a table out front for their wares. Innkeepers waved people inside their establishments. He scanned the signs hanging on the canopies and entered one.

As he stepped down inside, hookah smoke swirled around his feet. The various aromas were strong—and toxic, but who was he to judge? A stringed baligar and hand drums crafted a rhythmic tune, to which four dancers moved in time. All around men and women reclined on large pillows on the floor, eating and drinking and smoking at short, round tables. The place was packed and quite loud. Indoors, body odors mixed with the dancers' perfume, spices beyond count, and the scented smoke.

A bejeweled belly dancer swayed hypnotically up to him, a tray of drinks carefully balanced on one hand.

"I'm looking for a friend," Bedel said in Zellu over the din of the room. He loved the language, guttural and throaty, and was glad this assignment gave him reason to speak it.

"Everyone's looking for a friend," she said, her shoulders tilting seductively. Her olive skin was lovely and, unlike the crowds outside, she was perfumed with something heavy. Her body never stopped moving, flowing as if she were but a wave on the sea. Sensual, hypnotic, and beautiful.

Focus, he chided himself. All that did was bring up conflicting images of Shai and A'banna.

Bedel scanned the room. "One with four arms?"

The dancer's chin jutted out in disappointment. "Our regular, eh?" She nodded toward a dark corner of the room.

Bedel flashed a smile tinged with regret. It was hard to blend in—let alone flirt—when someone might knife you, even a gorgeous dancer carrying beverages. But did he want to blend in, anymore? Everything was so different, so open with Shai. Either of them would have enjoyed a fling during a mission and not have second-guessed themselves.

Stow it, he ordered himself. Thinking about Shai would only embolden the *Zitaya* and perhaps wake A'banna. Then, he'd be dead.

He quickly made his way around the patrons, eyes drifting to the scantily clad dancers on the stage. Their elegant, amazingly fluid movements were distracting, as they were meant to be. This was an excellent place to drown out the troubles of the day. Or celebrate on the eve of an invasion.

At the back of the hookah bar was a deep booth, offering patrons a bit of privacy. As he rounded the side, a billow of smoke rushed out, tasting of mint.

"That stuff will kill you, Vari," Bedel said as one giant green hand gestured for him to sit.

Another hand offered the hookah hose as a third lifted a silver goblet for a long draught. When the goblet pulled away from the dark green face, Vari's broad lips curled back from his long canines. His four eyelids—one pair vertical, one horizontal—blinked simultaneously as he let out two streams of smoke from his nostrils.

"Everything will kill you, given the chance," the Glymph noble grumbled. "It's how we die that matters, my friend."

Bedel offered him a smile as he took the hose. *Weaving cere-mony.* He inhaled, letting the mint flavor fill his lungs. He coughed and handed it back.

Vari laughed and leaned over the table, one large green hand on Bedel's shoulder, shaking him in a friendly gesture. Bedel felt like the Glymph might break his neck.

"Bread, my friend?" Vari lifted up the platter of flatbread and savory dip.

"Sure. I can reach it, you know."

"Your arms are so tiny," Vari muttered. "Can they reach around a healthy woman?"

Bedel rolled his eyes. Their definition of "healthy" varied greatly. His did not include one with four arms who preferred biting to kissing. Vari laughed again. The booth trembled with his amusement.

"So, about our private party?" Bedel asked.

"The room is reserved and the ladies await, but let us eat first. An intimate performance requires food and patience."

Crows, we're being watched. At least Vari had eyes on whoever surveilled them.

Bedel fingered the bracer underneath his dark blue tunic sleeve but didn't dare look. Calmly, he scooped dip onto bread. *Kerdum, if it's time to die, might as well do so with a nice meal.*

Vari's upper arms spread out on the edge of the booth, nearly spanning the entire space. He drew another lungful of smoke from the hookah before offering it to Bedel.

"My brother's wife has invited us to dine with them."

What happened to 'leave now'? "Thank you, but I'm really looking to get home," Bedel whispered between bites.

Vari popped a couple of tomatoes into his mouth. Juice sprayed and dribbled down his chin. "When everyone's headed north? I'd stay."

"Are you staying?"

"No," he muttered. The squishing tomatoes made his words almost inaudible.

Crows.

"Come eat with us," Vari said, playfully swatting Bedel's

shoulder. Bedel braced himself for the impact. Vari knew his own strength. He probably liked to see people half his size batted around.

"This evening, I must find a way home."

The music and dances suddenly ended. Scattered applause filled the room. Vari and Bedel went silent, eating and smiling. Then the baligar began a catchy tune, and the dancers repositioned themselves. When the drums started, so did the dancing.

Vari leaned in, his brow creased. "Listen, you stubborn yeht, the road's impassable with the army marching. You'll just have to wait a few days until they've passed through. Like I said, everyone's headed north. No need to get trampled."

Bloody fields and crows, Bedel thought.

"Who is staying? Maybe I can find a place to stay?"

"My brother, his wife, and her family, but you know them. Farther south, there's some of my old kin staying. Not everyone likes moving such a long distance, by caravan or sea."

"Anyone that could put me up?" Bedel coughed again from the smoke. What he meant was, *Anyone I could reason with?* A potential asset, political insider, or dissident could be useful.

"Not many. One or two, but the rest of the family doesn't like to open a bed to a two-armed slant-eyes."

"Between us, you can drop the bigotry." Bedel glared at him, then smirked. "Well, the Empress has always wanted a cultural exchange program."

Vari laughed, his dual eyelids blinking. "Really? A program?"

Bedel shrugged and pushed the plate away. He really wasn't hungry anymore. "I'm adaptable. So, about that party?"

Sighing mightily, Vari tossed a chicken bone down onto the plate. He waved at a waitress, who acknowledged him with a smile as she moved through the crowd. With an elegant flourish, she gestured to a back door.

"Now, my friend, you're in for a treat."

"She always is amazing."

Vari's lip pulled back over a canine in a knowing smile. He nodded fervently.

"Better than amazing," the dancer replied as she escorted them to the back door, recessed underneath an arch. She leaned against the frame, close to Bedel. "Don't forget us."

He glanced at her. There was a hint of worry in the Zelvatore's expression, but she masked it with another pleasant smile.

"Enjoy, gentlemen," she said and then closed the door.

Inside, a woman in billowy pants and scarcely anything else bowed low. Bedel's jaw dropped at seeing Shai. She'd never specified who her assets had been. He should have predicted it. He of all people knew Shai had skills. Bedel heard the smile in her voice. "Vari and friend, welcome."

Bedel swallowed. Shai was beautiful, as always. All three exchanged a knowing look. The game would be played in case of any unwelcome listeners.

"Shai," Vari said. "My friend, Bedel Riess."

"Shai? I didn't know you were into belly dancing. Vari, I'm amazed!"

The dark-haired beauty smiled, her long locks falling over her slightly pointed ears. "I'm not."

Shai quickly crossed behind them and latched the door. "My cover doesn't allow for pleasantries, friends. No one can hear us over the din outside. We've practiced."

"Baktur?" Bedel asked, watching her move around them again, sorting through a short dresser.

"Well, they tolerate Shai of Bombard," she said. "You, however, better keep your aura inactive. Here." They glanced down at the thin, ethereal cord that disappeared like wispy clouds. She handed Bedel two scrolls. "This is everything my team could gain from the officers. Troop numbers, movements, everything."

Bedel scanned the scrolls and then glanced up at Vari. "Your people are moving in awful strong."

The Glymph grumbled and looked at the door. "You have no idea. Flygn cavalry. You saw the komodrake pen in camp. At least thirty. Ambassador Quika's been trying to stop it, but the power is in the bloodlust."

"Crows. Thirty komodrakes will wipe out cities. We'll be completely defenseless if the Vel attack."

"That's the intent," Vari said and paused. "What or who are the Vel?"

"Dangerous. I'll fill you in later."

Vari grumbled in dissatisfaction. "We think the Baktur are striking commission stations, taking out Advancers. Shai?"

"I concur," the half-Elven spy replied. "At this range, we should have no trouble hailing the Cronop station. I can't even reach my people, but we can still get a message out or close the distance between us and the nearest station."

"We can do both. Send the bird. I'll get closer.

"It's a lot easier to hit a barrier of magic than call jewels or rely on an animal's good senses."

Shai had outdone Bedel on cultivating assets here. He considered the warning. The magical barrier that covered Lupacuo lands in the north allowed for a projected thought message to travel along it until it dropped through to its intended recipient. They hadn't offered to share the technology, so Bedel had to hope for the communication network that utilized enhanced jewels and the advancers who controlled them.

"Won't argue with that," he said. "So how do I get to Cardor?"

Shai leaned closer. She definitely smelled of perfume. Something floral and sweet. *Focus.* A single blink told him she regretted the movement. They were over, after all.

"Look." She pointed at a map in his hands. "You've got an

army of at least twenty thousand Zelvatore cavalry headed north, escorted by Istantese infantry, through Istante. We know they're not headed toward us."

"Bordimore," Bedel said, looking at an eastern city on the map of Cardor.

"Yes," she said. "Some of the officers kept mentioning a name. Meetings had almost come to blows about his involvement. Have you heard the name Hurmlen?"

Shai's voice cracked as she said it.

Shai's hand brushed Bedel's against the map. He felt the tremor in her hand. Slight, barely noticeable. He let a single finger brush hers. It was the most comfort they could give each other. Now, Shai and Bedel had to let Vari come to his own conclusions, and hopefully, that would reach Ambassador Quika or someone with power enough to stop this madness.

"Hurmlen," Vari grumbled, his frown growing. His eyelids formed a rectangle around his pupils—the Glymph manner of squinting. "He's been to Mount Hazril to advise the Judicator on more than one occasion."

"Dark fire essencer?" Bedel asked. It was rhetorical. He tried to shut down the memories on board that ship two hundred years ago.

"Not just a dark fire essencer, Bedel," Vari said. "Hurmlen mentored the Judicator Vilmiz before abdicating so Vilmiz could ascend. That's all I know."

"You look worried," Bedel said.

Vari cocked his head and folded all four arms. "No, I don't."

"Yes, you do." He glanced back to Shai. "What else have you learned?"

"It's all in the documents," Shai said, pushing aside a tapestry that hid a door. "You both should leave. Lizzie said the Baktur in the dining room were unveiled, so they may not have noticed you."

Vari growled. One hand gestured toward himself, another at Bedel. "The pair of us? Not a chance."

"My thoughts exactly." She rolled her eyes, even if she offered a smile. "After the attack on Lady Talacciaro by a half-Glymph and two humans in Cronop, no one will give a second thought. Private guests usually use the back exit. That doesn't give you much time if the Baktur in the audience got suspicious."

"Where were they? I didn't see them."

"That's a problem, Bedel," Shai said. "They're everywhere. Keep your eyes open and don't use magic."

"Except you."

Shai shrugged. "Tricks of the trade."

He sighed, relieved she was still somewhat safe.

"Be careful, Lady Shai," Bedel said. Their hands brushed beneath the documents.

"Always. You, too. Bedel, tell Xathon when you get home that there are good people here in Zeller. They need the slaver ships to stop raiding, and they don't want war. Above else, they need essencers to restart agriculture and reverse the famine. From what I've heard, if this Summit fails, and there's a lot of people and self-proclaimed deities that want it to, then there is no coming back off of war."

He nodded. "I'll tell him."

Shai's face softened, only for a brief moment. In that brief glimpse, Bedel pictured her on the shore of a lake, with a forest around them. The cabin—the life—they had lost.

"Thank you," Shai said. "Now get home safe. We can't stop the war, but maybe we can help our peoples prepare for it. And you, big lug, help your mistress undermine it."

Vari shrugged. "We're working on it. She's at the Summit. Not going well, so I hear."

"Well, that's unsettling." Shai gestured at the door and held out a palm. "Two Darics. I'm not your average entertainer. Come on, gents. I have to work up a sweat in case I have new customers."

Bedel didn't argue as he handed her the coins from his purse. "Are you still going?"

"I gave my word," Shai said. Bedel was stunned at the sincerity. "Sure you don't want to come east with us?"

He nodded.

"Stay safe." Shai closed the door behind her as Bedel and Vari exited into the dirt alley. The gap between the tall adobe buildings formed a thin walkway, with garbage and sewage piled up.

Vari looked at him and shrugged. They quickly moved through the alley and into the street.

"How long were you two sleeping together?"

"Vari! Really?"

Vari tapped the side of his long, pointed nose and grinned. "A Glymph has a nose for these things."

Bedel glanced back at the door. "Oh, shut it. It's over."

"Is the Huntress available?"

"Seriously? Shut it. And I don't know."

"Kamalia fights well. They are good matches for you and I, yes?" Bedel rolled his eyes as Vari continued. "You're coming to dinner. Then perhaps you can explain."

"Seems I don't have a choice," Bedel said, looking up at his friend.

"No, my friend, you do not. None of us do."

They strolled through the city, casually scanning for tails, specifically of the Baktur type. By the time they reached the low adobe walls of the Tressoni Vineyard, the sun had set in the east. The heat of the day departed with the sun, and Bedel welcomed the chill wind. He glanced back as the disappearing sun glimmered around the infamous Winnago castle. Red stone glowed like firelight, an ominous heralding of the castle's resident, leader of the Baktur and professed demigod, the Veccil'ni.

"Is he going?" Bedel said, glancing at his traveling partner.

"Going? A wise man once said that war declared by two men is stronger than war declared by one. Hurmlen chose the Veccil'ni to lead the invasion."

Bedel stopped, his feet crunching on the dirt road. "Vari, what else aren't you telling me? Komodrakes? The Veccil'ni? They'll obliterate the Southern Province."

"That's the point. We've learned all we can." Vari scanned the walls around the vineyard and the road. "And who is the one withholding information? *The Vel?* Bedel, we all know this has been brewing for years. When people are hungry, they do strange things and align themselves with those who win their ears and their stomachs. War was inevitable. Come."

Reluctantly, Bedel followed the Glymph to the iron gate of the Tressoni hacienda. An attendant in white livery ushered them inside. They rounded an empty stone fountain, symbolic of the drought that had hit the southern continent hard. Coastal Wonbai had been spared thanks to sporadic rains, the edges of recent tropical storms that never seemed to make landfall. What was provided made this city luxurious living compared to the rest of Zeller and Greneld.

The large adobe home had curved clay tiles on its slanted roof. A stone veranda with gilded pillars marked the entryway, surrounding a fountain. Bedel could imagine the curved road they'd walked filled with carriages and sedan chairs, guests of their hosts in better times. Unlit lanterns hung between palm trees and potted bushes. The house of Tressoni, unlike others, had its own source of fresh water from a large, underground aquifer, making it the lifeblood of Wonbai. How they had managed without it being commandeered by the Veccil'ni, Bedel didn't know. The Tressoni family were in opposition to the Veccil'ni. The youngest daughter had been assassinated while being married off to the Talacciaro heir. Tressoni's strength and connection with

Ambassador Quika alone might help bring peace. Bedel thought about his travels further south within Zeller. He'd seen the children starving, near death, like skeletons with skin on. If the Sorceress or her agents helped fan this war using Cardor's upcoming harvest as bait, no amount of posturing from either side would keep the armies at bay. These people had much to die for. Hurmlen, Jocina, Judicator Vilmiz of Greneld, and the Veccil'ni of Zeller had struck a powerful alliance.

"Zeller only needed the push," Vari said, as if commenting on Bedel's thoughts.

"Aye. I wish things had gone differently."

Vari glanced down at Bedel with sad gray eyes. "As do I, my friend."

The large black doors of the hacienda opened, and children darted out. Two-armed, green half-Glymphs ran toward them. "Uncle Vari!" they shrieked in joy.

"Ai, ai, ai, what do we have here?" Vari leaned down and plucked the girl and two younger boys up as if they weighed nothing.

The hacienda door opened wider. A beautiful Zelvatore woman with flowing black locks stood beside a Glymph man who wore a fine blue tunic with gold embroidery. The sight of the two, glowing with pride, arm-in-lower-arm, was refreshing. If they could achieve peace, this was what the world might look more like. Both beamed at the sight of their three children, each snuggled into one of Vari's arms.

The Glymph stepped forward. He spoke in fine, eloquent Zellu rather than the harsh-sounding Glymph tongue. "Brother, welcome!"

"Dada, it's Uncle Vari!" one of the children blurted out.

"My boy, you're right."

With his one free hand, Vari stopped stroking his niece's hair and gestured to the man and woman. "Bedel Riess, my brother,

Ambassador Nadari Tressoni Xikkan, and his wife, Lady Phoebe Tressoni."

"Lord Bedel, welcome," Lady Phoebe said, bowing her head slightly. She wore the traditional chturi clothing, wrapped as a long maroon dress and tossed over her shoulder, pinned in place by a gold olive brooch at the top of an embroidered gold vine. A white blossom was tucked behind her ear. Long gold earrings hung to her shoulders, shaped like olives on a tree branch.

Bedel smiled and returned the bow, then shook one of Nadari's green, large hands. They were much softer than Vari's gruff callouses, and he certainly didn't have the same sharp lines in his face or the near-constant grimace. In some ways, he reminded Bedel of a younger, happier Ambassador Quika, before she had joined Princess Amelia in defying their fathers by urging peace between the nations and kingdoms. If the puppet masters planned on supplanting Amelia using Ni'Dio, then what would they do to Quika? Discredit her? If Shai gave King Aubert of Franca and his future wife Ni'Dio a boy heir, he would undermine Amelia's claim. Would Greneld's Judicator Vilmiz cast his own daughter aside for his war effort? What would that do to House Tressoni-Xikkan? The intermarriage between one of the wealthiest Zelvatore and Glymph noble houses still came with stigma in certain circles. That hadn't lessened the economic or agricultural power they wielded, though.

And where were the spies supposedly watching House Tressoni? Bedel glanced into the fields, where several gatherers had paused to watch them pass.

Their hosts ushered them inside, while the children continued to play with Vari. One even poked him in the eye, to which he exclaimed. "Oy!" Setting them all down at once, Vari charged after that boy. The half-Glymph child went squealing gleefully as they darted around a corner. Bedel couldn't fight the smile listening to Vari go on about how warrior-like it was to provoke a

Glymph like him. Meanwhile, the children laughed. The boy rolled into view on the floor grinning, as Vari charged after him, crawling on all four arms and both legs. Suddenly, the other nephew and niece charged Vari, jumping on his back.

The wrestling continued. Nadari and Phoebe turned to Bedel.

"They haven't seen their uncle since yesterday," Phoebe said. Her dark eyes shone serenely before a flicker of sadness passed over them. "His work for Ambassador Quika keeps him abroad for months at a time. His visits are much too sparse these days. They soak up every moment with him like roots do water."

She gave Bedel a slight smile.

But the waitress at the bar had called him their 'regular.' Bedel sighed, watching his counterpart with the children. He and Shai had always dreamt of something like this. Would he want it with A'banna instead now? Was it love if their magic forced them into it? Did it matter? If they survived, Bedel wanted a real life. If it came in the size of a cabin filled with children, laughter, love, he wanted it. He was certain Shai didn't want children, but A'banna did. A family. How many agents thought like that?

When he turned, Phoebe gave him a gentle smile. He imagined A'banna smiling at him, with the sound of children playing. She would have loved it here. Not Shai. The *Zitaya* cord pulsed.

Sounds lovely, Bedel thought.

Weave it, I let my guard down! Sorry. Bedel shut off his emotions.

"Vari told us about your predicament," Nadari said. "Come into my study. We need to talk."

Bedel nodded, following his hosts while Vari and the children played.

"Water or wine?" Phoebe asked as they entered the wood-paneled room, lined floor to ceiling with books.

"Just water, thank you."

"Ice?"

"You have ice?"

"We're fortunate," Phoebe said, nodding.

"Indeed," Bedel agreed. She gave a partial bow, hands outstretched, palm up, and crossed the room, exiting through a side door.

Bedel made himself comfortable on a couch covered in circular pillows, while the large Glymph ambassador situated his bulk across from him. The furniture had been built to accommodate both Glymphs and humans. It was designed with the sharp angles preferred by Glymphs, but the decorations showed the family's cultural diversity. The stuffed head of a sabrecat and horns of a yeht towered on either side of Nadari's chair. A Glymph scimitar, thick and angled, hung above a small tapestry of the combined Tressoni and Xikkan families' sigils. Decorative pillows were placed throughout the room. A multi-colored tile mural covered one wall, while a tapestry depicting the vineyard hung on the wall. All spoke of Zelvatore culture.

"There was nothing I could do," Nadari said as Bedel moved a pillow behind his back. "Please notify your superiors of that, when you return."

"They'll know."

"The phanstan is just a boy, and he's controlled by the will of the Veccil'ni. There's dark power in that man, much like Lord Hurmlen."

Bedel sat up straight. "You've met Hurmlen?"

The silhouette in the darkness, a long coat flapping in the storm. Dark fire burned around his sword blade. The man Jacob had hidden him from. Then Xathon plucked him up, blocking him from the heat until they plunged into the tumultuous sea.

"I've sat in council with him in the phanstan's chamber," Nadari said. "He and the Veccil'ni control Zeller. The Baktur are defiant against Cardor. Some of us have resisted, but our counsel is ignored, and all of our food relief shipments are commandeered by the Baktur and Zelvatore's military."

Bedel grunted. "They've blocked relief to urge on the war effort."

"Yes," Phoebe said from the doorway. As she rounded the couch with a tray, her shoulders were squared. She looked far more tense than she had been before. "And more."

Nadari said, "We've lost good workers and friends trying to get food to the south. All relief shipments return to Wonbai or Castle Winnago, but not to us."

"If you are searching for an economical answer to solving this war, we cannot assist," she said. "It is all we can do to keep basic shipments flowing and try to prevent the Veccil'ni's persuading the phanstan to confiscate our lands."

Phoebe served them two glasses from the tray. She laughed, but he sensed sorrow within it. "Whether it's to feed the masses, the army, or because the Veccil'ni as the God of War demands it, we are in a bind. I will let the two of you discuss it further. My love."

Phoebe nodded to Nadari, then left.

Bedel eyed the water in the goblet before taking a drink. "Is the Veccil'ni an essencer?"

Nadari's regard grew darker; he took a long drink of wine. "Worse."

"What can be worse?"

Nadari looked away then set the goblet aside. "We have to get you back to your people before the first wave starts. There will be three in total. By the end of it, they'll control half of your realm. This is the best we can do to help you."

"I understand. But ambassador, what can be worse? A dark fire essencer?"

"No. Veccil'ni means 'the Red Dragon' in Zellu, are you aware?"

"Yes."

"The Veccil'ni is no dragon, but the power he wields will crush the people of Cardor. They have to be ready. The first wave of warships leaves tonight."

Bedel leaned forward. He shouldn't have been surprised but had hoped for at least one more day. "Tonight! So soon? What about the Xikkan battalion? Surely Vari or you can withhold it?"

"And do what with it, friend? Xikkan's wealth comes from its war-rams. This war has been sealed by all parties economically, religiously, politically. Vari and I explored options, but as long as our father is the Xikkan patriarch, our hands are tied. And Tressoni has no army."

Bedel refused to be deterred. "Can you convince your father?"

Nadari shook his head. "You have much to learn of the politics of a Glymph nurial."

The Glymph ambassador clapped twice and looked to the door Phoebe had exited. Bedel turned, keeping one eye on Nadari and one on the door. A white-clothed attendant opened it, and two figures entered.

The first to enter was a man Bedel knew by sight. The pirate was infamous and wanted for murder and treason in Franca. With every step, Captain Dans Forbens' jewelry, woven into long dreadlocks and a braided beard, jingled. Cold blue eyes evaluated Bedel and Nadari. Forbens rested his hands on a thick belt, near a small crossbow and cutlass. Behind Forbens was a much shorter individual, hooded and cloaked. A Dwarf's shoulders and head were wider than a Goblin's to those who preferred slang. This clearly was no Dwarf. Bedel smiled briefly to the hooded Goblin —but if it hadn't attacked them, then that means it had its impulses in check. This was no Goblin. It was a Gaul and a welcome surprise.

"Well, Ambassador," Bedel said to Nadari. "I didn't realize you liked pirates."

"As always, my reputation precedes me," Captain Forbens said, hooking one thumb in his belt.

"There are warrants out for your arrest in every province of Franca," Bedel said.

"An enemy of Franca is a likely ally of those of us loyal to Zeller and Greneld," Nadari said over the rim of his goblet, his eyebrows raised. "We need allies, Bedel."

"I worked hard for those warrants," Forbens said. He pointed at Bedel. "So, do you want to get home or would you rather stick around for those Baktur bastards to disembowel you as part of a ritualistic game?"

Bedel shrugged. "When you put it that way." He turned to Nadari. "You trust him?"

"Since Magdalena's fleet departed this morning, Forbens is the fastest—and last—captain willing to travel north," Nadari said, still sitting. He spread his upper arms wide while gathering the bottom two to rest on his knees. "Otherwise, it's a long wait. With how dark ideals and politics are running in the area currently, allowing you to stay here for any duration outside of a dinner invitation with my brother is deadly for everyone involved, including my family. I won't risk them, even for an agent of Cardor. I'm sorry."

"I appreciate the honesty," Bedel said. He grimaced as he looked at the pirate captain. "So who's your friend?"

The hooded Gaul came forward. Green hands removed a hood, exposing a long nose and reptilian eyes framed by four eyelids, similar to a Glymph's. His ears were pointed, lips thin, hiding a jagged row of teeth. His tunic had various trophies and small trinkets sown into it, in Gaul fashion, but it bulged with the small companion's lean muscles. And he had Speaker tattoos.

"Dear Theantros," Bedel whispered.

"Hello, Bedel *Ries*. My name is Muriumek. Thank you for

what you did for our mutual friend, and tried to do for the others. We feel their loss keenly."

Muriumek's pronunciation of his name was off, but that could be attributed to his chirp-like dialect. More troubling, though, was how this Gaul with those specific tattoos around his mouth and eyes knew his name. The gift of Speaker had been returned to both humans and the Gaul.

Bedel tried to will all the prophecies and predictions away. He'd lost Huahanna and thus the gift of Speaker of Men, but here was another impossibility. The Speaker of Gaul stood before him. Bedel rubbed his forehead as a sudden headache came on. The mission still existed. *Save a Speaker. Great.*

"My name isn't *Ries*. It's Bedel Riess."

The Gaul cocked his head, very birdlike. "Curious. They didn't teach you?"

"Teach me what?" Bedel knew. What else could be hidden? Who knew what his ancestors were fully responsible for!

"How do you know my name?"

"Your friend Raynt told me before he instructed me to come find you." Bedel's heart thudded in his chest.

"Where is he?"

"Returned to Cardor. I believe he wanted to go climb a mountain in search of a princess." Muriumek looked up at Forbens. "A mutual friend. Raynt. We have to take him."

"Bloody waving Kerdum, Muri! I invite you to travel with me one damn time, and you're practically commanding my ship."

"Forbens. The stars are here, I am here, the Gatekeeper is here. It's time." Muriumek gestured to Bedel.

"Whatever. Fine." Jewels and beads jingled as Forbens glanced back at Nadari and Bedel. "Fine. You're welcome on board. Payment?"

"No payment," Muriumek said. "He's a friend."

"No, what! Are you out of your living Gaul mind?" Forbens muttered.

Bedel rolled his eyes and looked back at Nadari. He needed to know more about this Muriumek, anyway. He gestured to them. "How long have they been together?" Bedel murmured.

"Ha!" Nadari laughed. "I see why Vari likes you so much." He heaved his bulk upward, rising to his two long legs. "Time for you to say farewell. I wish you the best and a safe journey. Remember us when this is over."

"Wait," Bedel said. "Ambassador, you need to know something. Vari!" The lumbering Glymph made his way into the hall and stared at the pirate and Speaker of Gaul silently.

"I have a sense my wife needs to hear this, also," Nadari said. The quiet attendant at the door went to call on her. She entered, fingers laced tightly.

Bedel looked up at Vari first. "They're called the Vel," Bedel began. He shared with them everything he could without jeopardizing Shai, Kamalia, and Idrin's efforts to save Edelissi, reveal A'banna's identity or expose the full truth about Ntokup. It was easily spun to sound as though the Sorceress had tracked them north.

"I can confirm the Velheron," Muriumek said. "It recently attacked our village. It also tracked us."

"Ancients, save us," Phoebe said, eyes wide, glancing to the room where her children played.

"The war is a cover for another attack," Vari said, swearing under his breath. "I can't pull Xikkan troops back, Bedel."

"I know, old friend."

"We'll make preparations here," Nadari said, nodding at his brother and his wife. Phoebe's gaze hardened, and she shifted her stance enough that Bedel could see the dagger hidden in the folds of her dress.

Bedel continued, "The Huntress said to watch for a plant with a purple flower and thorny vines. It might be how the Sorceress is transferring it."

Nadari nodded, looking woefully out the window, at his vineyard. "My children play among vines every day."

Bedel grimaced. "Then teach them. As the Gaul said, the cycle is here."

Nadari's four eyelids opened fully. He locked gaze with his wife. She nodded once, firmly.

"My friend?" Vari said.

Before Bedel could answer, Muriumek said, "The other Speakers know, now. They'll spread what word they can and keep your identity secret."

"Huahanna's dead," Bedel told him. "The gift to Men is gone."

"I know. We shall see. The waters of Theantros are strong, unpredictable powers."

Forbens coughed. "Well, I love all this doom and end of the world talk, but I'd really like to get my ship out of the harbor before they close it to civilians. Shall we?"

Bedel shook Nadari's offered hand. "Thank you."

"Just get to your home safely. Phoebe will plead with her ancestors to watch over your travels."

Bedel nodded once. "I'm grateful. Keep your family safe."

Nadari's expression flashed that Glymph warrior flare that had been absent when they met. "They will be."

Bedel hesitated. "Nadari, I do have one last request for you."

"What is it?"

"When this is over, I have a friend who grew up without other half-Glymphs around. I think he'd like to meet your family."

"When the war drums stop beating, and the Vel are gone, my home shall be as his," Nadari whispered. A brief look of sorrow crossed his face. "It's a sad affair for many people. He is not alone."

"Raynt will be glad to hear."

Bedel approached the pirate-Goblin duo. "So when do we depart, Captains?"

Forbens frowned. "Ha, funny. Morbrook better pay well when we deliver you."

"I'm sure he will."

Nadari led them down a hall. Immediately, gleeful children charged their uncle. Vari gave Bedel a saddened glance before letting it disappear in the joy of his niece and nephews. Bedel soaked in the children's laughter as they tussled on the floor. His niece climbed to the top of Vari's shoulders, her small arms wrapped over his eyes. One set of hands tickled a nephew relentlessly. One hand went to his niece, and the third wrapped around the other nephew's torso, so his limbs dangled off the floor.

"Dada, we almost beat Uncle Vari."

"Almost, little warrior! Almost."

He shed them off with a shake. Each child tumbled harmlessly to the floor, rolling and laughing. Vari pushed himself to his feet.

"Safe travels. Perhaps we will meet in Cismore."

"Do what you can to stop the invasion."

"We are," Vari promised.

Lady Phoebe reappeared with an unlit torch and handed it to her husband. "The catacombs will lead them to the sewers," she said.

Nadari nodded. "Follow me."

The group passed through the hacienda and down a flight of stairs, past a large wine cellar, and to a metal reinforced door.

"For generations, my family has been buried here," Phoebe explained. "I ask you to not disturb their remains."

"Wouldn't think of it," Forbens muttered, earning a glare from Muriumek.

"Keep right, follow the tunnels," Nadari said. "There is a steel gate on the west end. Shut it once you're through and follow the underground stream to the city sewers." Nadari passed Bedel the torch. "Every hour you wait, the city will become more dangerous. The Baktur will find all three of you a handsome prize. Go with haste."

Phoebe lit the torch with a candle, smiled, and stepped back into her husband's arms. "May your ancestors guide you to peace," she said.

Bedel bowed and entered the darkness.

CHAPTER 24

A'BANNA AWOKE TO FIND HERSELF STANDING, STARING INTO THE empty face of a skeleton. Arms crossed over its chest; webs draped like lace had formed over the bones. Disintegrating cloth covered it. She turned, following a passage with brick walls. Footfalls echoed in the barren silence, and everywhere she looked, visible only in the fraction of the torchlight, lay the dead.

"Bedel," she moaned, gazing at someone's ancestors.

Bones popped, dust flew into the air in a cloud. A skeleton's head turned, and a viper slid out through the void of its eyes. Behind the viper were silver pupils.

You're running, the Sorceress hissed. *He's mine.* And the vision was gone.

A'banna awoke screaming.

CHAPTER 25

BEDEL HAD NEVER BEEN FOND OF BURIAL CHAMBERS. THE STENCH of decay and death, the stale air filled with dust. He kept the torch out in front of him, its light barely illuminating the next three steps.

"Kerdum, this is no place for a man of the sea," Forbens muttered from somewhere behind. Bedel ignored the pirate and kept moving. When he found a wall sconce, he lit it, spreading more light, even if briefly.

"So these Vel can hide anywhere?"

"That's right, Captain." This was the last thing they needed to discuss now. "Even in these ossuaries. They shrank and contorted to hide in the rocks but moved faster than a ranger's aim."

"And you never noticed them?"

"Best keep a lookout."

Forbens fell silent and muttered something about superstitions.

Bedel kept right at the next turn, eyeing the rotting corpses of the Tressoni ancestors on either side.

A sudden, cold chill blew through the tunnels, tossing up dust and webs and bone and cloth.

"The Taurs," Muriumek, the new Speaker of Gaul, said.

This will be you, a feminine voice said. A bird *caw-cawed* in the distance.

"Did you hear that?" Bedel asked, quickly turning. The fire flickered and flared with the movement.

"No," Forbens said. "Move on it. We should be nearing the stream."

Where is she, Gatekeeper? I feel her. The voice sighed as if exhilarated. *But I can't see her. I see you.*

Be gone, witch, Bedel thought.

She is dying, isn't she? You sent her away? That's why she runs without running. She has crossed the barrier of my enemy. Clever man.

Bedel picked up his feet, pushing past the dead bodies, brushing past cobwebs.

You're still here, little boy. Such a little boy. We made you, child. Without us, there would be no you. There never would have been a shelf where he found you, pulled the cords away, and let you breathe free air for the first time. But did he show you those who came before you? Hundreds of generations of you dead just like these.

"Be silent, witch."

"Agent?" Muriumek asked.

Air rushed past Bedel. *Who is that? I hear him.*

You are blind, aren't you, Jocina?

The Truth is never blind, she hissed. *It is merely concealed. Sometimes you have to rip the flesh off lies to find it.*

"Don't speak. Keep moving."

They discard you, did you know? Over and over until a cycle begins. But there is always a Ries. A Reason. Light and Darkness. Fire is star-light. The stars are fire. It is one and the same.

He felt a cold grip on his shoulders, the trace of a pointed talon against his skin.

You will see, Reason. Then you can choose. If you don't, they'll discard you over and over. Your life is not your own. Bedel Riess is a lie. You've always been a lie. A host of something required to die at the command of an Oppressive Wretch for a god. We freed you.

"You didn't free me," Bedel snapped, practically jogging through the crypt. *Where was that door?*

A door? A Ries always looks for a way out, but there is none, little boy. I gave you life, she hissed. *You were dead. The others didn't have the intelligence, the power, to remake you. I did. You owe me to listen.*

"I will owe you a sword in your gut when we meet, witch."

She cackled. *But we have met, Reason. Just ask your companion why those with the ear of Theantros mispronounce your name but always know you when they meet you.*

His heart pounded as he saw the door. He was running.

Your Reason is to die so they can live. Every cycle you are sacrificed, and the new you has no memory of the previous life. Sometimes they just take you out of the jar and cut you open, spilling the light out of you into the Gate. They don't waste time on you. I gave you life. We gave you a purpose. You are our precious pi, 3.1415.

Bedel paused, terror gripped him, draining warmth from his head. Somehow, he kept his mind clear. His hand was on the door.

Ah, so you know, darling little boy. I could always help you.

After a moment, Bedel found his voice. "My father may have done many things—cruel things; manipulations, lies, concealing the truth, but he also gave me a purpose. We will destroy you."

Oh, Reason, she began. Bedel opened the door and closed his eyes, allowing the other two to dash through behind him. He slammed the door to the crypt, dust fluttering into the air.

You are wrong. The Sorceress's voice echoed in his mind,

blocked out by the rushing stream of water to their left. The cold of Jocina fled, and only the chill of the cavern remained.

Bedel paused, braced himself with one hand on his knee and gasped for breath.

"What happened?" Muriumek asked.

"The Sorceress. She found me."

"Rogue waves, we should hurry." Forbens started down the tunnel but turned. "What the Kerdum are you waiting for?"

Muriumek waited by his shoulder. The Gaul was no taller than an adolescent. Leaning over, Bedel could look straight into those bulbous yellow eyes. "Why did you call me Ries? Why did Huahanna and Alain?" Bedel lashed out, grabbing Muriumek's collar.

"Why did you all call me Reason?"

"The Elves keep dark secrets, Bedel. You are not the first of your kind, nor will you be the last. But Xathon Morbrook and his son, your brother Jacob, stole you from the Elves of Mursia. They put themselves at risk, even against his own father-in-law, to bring you across the Barren Sea. They saved your life."

"Why?" Bedel asked.

"Can't you ask these damn questions on my ship?" Forbens snapped.

"So you wouldn't have to die," Muriumek answered, ignoring the frantic pirate.

"But the cycle is still happening."

"I fear good intentions mean little," Muriumek said, a gentle sadness in his voice. "For all of Xathon Morbrook's mistakes, taking you from the Elven lab was not one of them. Speaker Trevein of the Elves was there. He knows. He defended you against the assembly."

Bedel was shaken. He breathed deeply and started walking away, bearing the torch with him. Forbens hesitated, even as Muriumek waited.

"Every life is important, Bedel. Even yours."

"Is that how your people have justified murder to win a battle, only delaying the war?" Muriumek exhaled, but Bedel didn't stop. This was confirmation. "I thought I was Reason. Or was that Ries?" Bedel turned again, feet splashing in the cold stream. He ducked to avoid a low arched ceiling.

He could hear Forbens and Muriumek behind him, but the Sorceress's words rang in his ear.

"Elf blood." Bedel suddenly stopped. "My god, don't you see! The Vel. Elf blood. It doesn't affect Elf blood the same as it would all of us."

"So?"

"She said she saved my life and that no one else could. She's older than the history the Elves allow taught in most of the world. She worships The Taurs and is insane enough to destroy the whole world—but not the Elves. The Elves still live through it, keeping the scars of what the Vel does to them. The Elves aren't immortal, not like her, but some could have lived through the breaking." *Like the House of Menai,* he thought. *Crows, Father, what do you know?* "This is revenge for something they must have done—or something she failed to do. A vendetta," Bedel said, grinding his teeth.

He thought of Shai, Idrin and his sister, and of his adopted mother, Ismerdalia. Not all Elves deserved such cold wrath. Not all deserved to watch the world die as they were immortalized in the same evil.

He would save them but not the way everyone wanted him to.

Bedel grinned. "I can exploit a vendetta." He pointed at the Speaker. "Ask your friends what the vendetta is for. Even if something happened to her, destroying the whole world is not the way to find justice. I'm going to make this witch pay."

Muriumek stepped into the torch's radius. "Vengeance sparks dark fire, star-blessed."

"Easy to say when an entire race isn't just waiting to gut you to fix their problem."

Bedel turned away, jogging down the cavern, ignoring Muriumek's answer something about Goblins and a dragon.

The darkness seemed to crowd them, but eventually rock and stone became brick and sewage, the foul odor of excrement filling their noses.

"Wait!" Forbens said. "Hear that? It's the dock. This way!"

They moved quietly along the sewer's edge. Forbens located a drain, and they pried it open with the torch. Old nails snapped, and the bars clattered. Everyone paused, waiting to see if it had drawn the attention of all those moving bodies down at the harbor.

Bedel extinguished the torch and raised himself from the sewer. He reached down to help the Gaul, but the Speaker hopped through, rolling to a stop. Forbens followed and reached back in, replacing the drain bars. Hopefully, they wouldn't be tracked back—

Shadows *fluttered*.

Bedel spun, pressing the release on both of his bracers. The starlight blades shot loose, just in time for him to catch the downward strike of a baklana. The black-veiled Baktur grunted in surprise, then kicked. The cloth shoe was enough to drive the air from Bedel's stomach. He staggered backward, and the assassin lunged again. He scarcely had time to see two more hop from a ledge above the drain. Bedel dodged a thrust, parried the blade away and lunged forward with a strike to the shoulder. The Baktur swiveled, and the shadows cloaked him. Bedel blinked, trying to see the assassin's auras but the shadows seemed to conceal even those. He was blind and stalked.

Forbens had engaged a second, and Muriumek danced around the third. From his peripheral vision, Bedel saw the Baktur throw something that whistled in the air. Bedel dropped to his knees and leaned back as three star-shaped blades spun by. They lodged in the side of a ship, sending wood splinters into the air in a consecutive *chunk-chunk-chunk*.

The first Baktur rematerialized from the darkness, baklana raised for a downward kill strike. Bedel rolled forward, just as the blade lodged into the wooden dock. On his feet, Bedel kicked at the Baktur, trying to drive him away from the sword. The nimble assassin bent backward. Bedel heard a chain clank against the ground and barely saw the stick flying towards him. A sharp *crack* followed as the weapon struck his skull. Blood gushed, and his vision swirled. Bedel stumbled, trying to keep his balance. The Baktur swung the weapon again—two thick poles or cudgels connected by a chain. Bedel snarled and lunged forward, arms extended. A pole grazed his back. Bedel heard ribs on his right-side snap. Pain seized his right side. Breath came short. Stumbling, Bedel brought up his left hand, enough to deflect a swing on his bracer.

Light flared, enough that Bedel glimpsed the Baktur's eyes widen beneath his veil.

The Baktur growled as he closed the distance, pulling a curved knife from his belt. Ears ringing, Bedel dove forward, ramming his fists into the assassin's chest. He flicked out the blades. The assassin dropped his weapons and grabbed Bedel. They tumbled backward and rolled, each fighting to stay on top. The Baktur's hands closed around Bedel's throat. Bedel screamed furiously and used his thighs to trap the man underneath him. Hands clenched harder, cutting off air, but Bedel ripped the blades out and stabbed down desperately until the Baktur's arms fell limp.

Bedel gasped for air and rolled on his back, only to find fresh, sharp pain from his ribs. His mind thought in staccato sentences, telling him what he should do. His hands were slick from the Baktur's blood. Or was that his? His head pounded, and he blinked stinging blood from his eye. Light seemed to hover above him, moving whenever Bedel turned his head.

No, he thought. *No!*

Bedel willed himself upright, first on his knees, then swaying on his feet. Outside the weak stream of light coming from Bedel's wounds, darkness swirled, heralding another Baktur's charge. Bedel raised a bracer, parried the baklana once—with his right hand. Shooting pain broke Bedel's concentration. The relentless Baktur grabbed that arm, kicked underneath it, then drove Bedel to the dock, smacking his head into the wood.

Bedel lurched out, slicing the Baktur's hand with his bracer blade. The Baktur released him, but Bedel could barely breathe. He used his one good arm to crawl, but the Baktur recovered. Bedel rolled to his back, parried a downward strike once; twice. The Baktur stepped on Bedel's left hand, pinning it beneath his cloth shoe. He could only watch as the Baktur raised his sword and aimed for the kill—when another baklana cut across the assassin's back, through tissue and spine. The Baktur collapsed next to Bedel, dead, revealing Muriumek, who tossed the bloodied sword away and reached for Bedel.

"Come on," the Goblin said. "On board."

Forbens shoved each body into the water. "Get him moving!" the pirate said.

Bedel's vision was blurred. "I'm having trouble seeing."

"It's the head wound, Gatekeeper," Muriumek said. His voice felt like a thousand needles in Bedel's skull. Bedel felt Muriumek wrap a cloth twice around the wound, dimming the light.

They hobbled down the dock. Sailors darted down a gangplank. They assisted Muriumek in lifting Bedel up onto a ship and inside a cabin. He could hear Forbens shouting orders, heard numerous Zellu voices from the dock and the twang of arrows. The ship rocked. His ears continued to ring, drowning out most sounds. The rest—boots on the deck, Forbens shouting orders—

made his head throb worse. Muriumek appeared in Bedel's narrowing line of vision.

"Stay awake, Bedel," Muriumek said. He pulled back the cloth bandage, gasping as he stared at the beam of light. "Theantros bless us," he whispered. "Hold on." He placed a wet rag on Bedel's head—it burned. "You want to live so badly and prove the universe wrong? Then this is where you start."

Bedel, A'banna said. He felt her presence, warm and caring.

"Oh, my," Muriumek whispered with excitement and shock. "Huahanna's daughter? This is complicated. Can you hear me? Talk with him, A'banna. Keep him focused on your voice."

I love you, A'banna said. *Bedel? I'm with you. I love you.*

I love you, he answered. Bedel realized he was grinning. So was Muriumek. A new plan formed.

CHAPTER 26

Bedel Riess's head felt like someone punched him unceasingly from inside. If anything could keep him awake, though, it was a rough sea. Muriumek and Forbens tended to his head wound, but they refused to let the ship's physician work on anything but his broken ribs. For every success, it seemed he'd taken a beating, or worse—lost someone. At least the mission was coming to completion. He was almost a free man.

Forbens' ship, *The Red Hand*, was surprisingly equipped with what Bedel's agency called a router jewel. A red gemstone three feet in diameter, it had a convex surface and five precise facets. It was priceless, and, as far as Forbens was concerned, illegal. Jewels like these were the very foundation of Cardor's Magical Affairs Commission's communication network. It was one of Bedel's father's crowning achievements, boosting ethereal communication between advancers and essencers across extreme distances. When Bedel had awoken and saw it stored away in a glass container, he nearly shouted. Bedel bartered away all charges against Forbens. Happy to have secured a pardon in Cardor, Forbens reached out with his own aether and ignited a crimson flame within. Bedel sat beside it. He reached out to every

Magical Affairs Commission station he could think of. No one answered.

His excitement slowly vanished. The Baktur's vanguard had been terribly effective.

Wind howled. Tall waves rocked the ship. Bedel heard sails and rigging strain. Several times the bow of the ship crashed down, sending fresh pain through Bedel. The storms summoned by the enemy to propel their fleet also kept *The Red Hand* ahead of four Zeller warships, Forbens explained. He left shortly afterward. The crew needed to prepare for battle.

Continued sharp rocking and the thunderous waves caused Bedel to vomit breakfast and lunch and a horrible biscuit the physician had given him for a snack.

When Bedel laid back down in the bunk, head on a pillow, he glared at Muriumek. "What's wrong with me?"

"Where do I start?" the Gaul answered. "Sleep. The captain says we should pass the Cronop Isles tomorrow."

"No one is out there to help us. You know that, Speaker."

Muriumek pointed to the thickening *Zitaya* cord. "I wouldn't be so sure, Bedel. Perhaps you should ask A'banna. Huahanna had always said she was a fighter. Try."

At dusk, the crow's nest reported a second flotilla of four ships several hours behind the others. The first four warships were gaining speed, but *The Red Hand* rode the waves and the wind like they belonged to her. When Forbens entered the cabin after nightfall, he grunted and looked at his navigation charts.

"We can't outrun them in the Isles, and there's a southerly wind that's not helping us any. They're going to create a tropical storm out here, you know that?"

"I feel it," Bedel said, touching his head.

"We should've kept Nchoji and the *Batoidea* around, Muri."

"They have their own path, even if we don't recognize it."

Forbens scoffed. "Have you heard from your girl and Magdalena?"

Bedel relayed to them the plan A'banna and Magdalena were forming.

"Then we gotta make you dead, son."

"Agreed," Muriumek replied.

"Let me try my father again," Bedel said. "I could ping the thread off the router jewel in Cronop even if no one is using it. Or, you could."

Forbens shook his head. "Morbrook owes me a damned fleet of ships and full crew compliments."

"I'll let you two barter over that after we land." Bedel smiled, though even that was painful.

Together, Muriumek and Forbens helped Bedel to a swivel chair before the router jewel. For a good long while, they sat there, trying to find a thread to Peremaih.

Then, finally, a woman in the Magical Affairs Commission office answered.

Bedel grinned, though it hurt. Xathon soon appeared on the other side of the jewel, his image twisted along each angled side. Bedel had a flash of emotion push through him: anger, frustration, sorrow, relief, gratitude. Xathon smoothed his white mustache as he stared into the jewel. To his side, Bedel could see the purple-robed academy headmaster behind him.

This was his last report. His desperate request for aid. One of his last communications as an agent.

And his father's first word to his son?

"Authenticate."

"Operations Forever and Blistering Wind," Bedel replied, his excitement at speaking with his father fading swiftly. "Channel secure with assets online. Grand Essencer, documents and Intel retrieved from our mission in the far south to Winnago has been met with extreme resistance, starting with the woman called the Sorceress."

Bedel relayed it all. The political dilemmas facing the people of Greneld and Zeller, then the anticipated troop movements, units, and sizes. He told his father that there were powerful individuals in the adverserial nations waiting to ally, but that those potential allies lacked the power to stop the war.

"We do know there are forces within Zeller and Greneld open to peace. Their most pressing need is Advancers to counteract the drought and famine."

Xathon shook his head. "What of a tropical storm I've heard reports of? They seem fine to create that."

"Something tells me, sir, that's not the people willing to help them."

"That's a fine line, agent."

"Father, I've been on the ground. Shai's been on the ground. Raynt's been on the ground. Who are you going to trust? These people need Advancers."

"I'll look into it."

"Thank you."

"The Emissary?"

"He chose to return, sir. He and Speaker Huahanna are dead, but thanks to them, we've safely extracted his daughter, who carried his Intel, and delivered the Intel to Lodornatha. Our transport abandoned us, so we lost communication access until now. I have reason to believe that Agent Raynt assisted friendly forces in Cronop to take down the *Batoidea*, which should be several days ahead of me."

"Yes, it was seen south of Cismore on the Delado River. Raynt also reported in. I'm glad you're alright, son."

"Sir, no one is alright. The condition in Wo'Huzziet lands is devastating. Dragons are pressing against the rangers' defenses. The Sorceress is expanding her territory while confirmed to be working with Hurmlen and the Veccil'ni and possibly Jacob, Father sir."

Xathon's face twisted for a moment, but that shock and grief dissipated just as quickly as he'd shown it.

"What is our extraction coordinates, sir? Where are we landing? We've got a lot of ships coming your way."

"You can't," Xathon murmured.

"Excuse me?" Bedel said. His muscles tightened between his shoulders, and he nearly spat. "We're being tracked by warships and probably the Sorceress. While A'banna is north of the Keeper Boundary, I'm not. No one is responding to hails. It seems the routers have gone dark and the Navy hasn't responded."

"All our stations *are* going dark," Xathon said, letting the sentence itself send shockwaves through Bedel. "The Magical Affairs Commission's most remote stations are failing to make contact, or answer us. The routers aren't in operation. Our fleet— what's left of it—is tied up in conflicts west of Cronop and east near Istante."

"Conflicts? With whom?"

"The Sorceress uses monsters, you said?"

"Most of them she created, mutated from whatever they were before, including one that infects victims to duplicate itself in them. It mutates them, whether through a vine or a bite."

"Sea creatures have been attacking our ships," Xathon said. "If you make it through, count that as a success."

"The Sorceress and the others are making a play, Father. You have to increase security at the Summit."

"And frighten away the delegates—not all who have arrived, anyway? The world is on the brink of war. As you reported, this is our chance at peace. These isolated incidents may be nothing but provocation attempts—"

"Don't underestimate them. The Sorceress. Hurmlen. The Veccil'ni."

Xathon grunted. "I won't. Bedel, you cannot land until the Summit has played out, for good or ill. Having the *Batoidea* on our waters, even if it's under friendly control and Captain McCormack is dead, puts too much at risk. There have also been riots in Havenport after a recent King's Men mission shut down a key Slaver Coalition trading post. Son, sail east or up the Delado River to Cismore, but don't land in Havenport."

He mentioned the mission to rescue Naminia. If they could rescue her, reach the Gateway, cross into Transcendence, much of this would end. "Did the King's Men retrieve the target?"

"What target?" Xathon said, as if to say: *Stop asking.*

"The queen of Ntokup, sir."

Xathon's look turned dark. "You knew," Bedel whispered.

"I'm disconnecting—"

"You sent me down here. You knew." Before he could interrupt, Bedel pressed on. "The cycle doesn't have to play out as you think it does. If you know of Chosen, gather them. Inform them. Tell them we're coming."

"I thought you were about to tender your resignation."

Bedel scoffed. "I believe the Sorceress has a vendetta against Elves. What is it, Father? What did Lord Mnai do that he has been so keen on keeping us from discovering?"

"Bedel." Muriumek's webbed hand touched his forearm. "Let me."

Bedel shifted the jewel. "Oh, how forgetful. Father, I found another Speaker."

"My name is Muriumek, Grand Essencer. And you have a duty to the living, Xathon. It's time to do what you spoke about so long ago with Speaker Trevein."

Xathon's expression hardened. "I look forward to welcoming you to life above the Keeper Boundary, Speaker of Gaul."

"Grand Essencer."

"Son, get home safely. Deliver the plans directly to High Lord

General Bromswyn in Cismore, Agent Stamford Farr in Glori-weedum, or myself. Xathon, out."

The jewel's light faded. His father's distorted image was gone. That life wasn't gone, but Bedel had come out more assertive.

"They won't hurt you with a Speaker around," Muriumek said. "Even if that didn't go as planned."

"Bedel," Muriumek pressed. "Do you understand the cycle enough to train the Chosen, if you find them all? For example, your friend Raynt is a Chosen, representing the Letter, I believe."

Really? Bedel heard A'banna's excited voice over the *Zitaya. That's wonderful! When we find him, we Oh. Quiet. In my defense, you practically shouted that in your head.*

Bedel sighed and desperately tried not to think of a response.

Now not trying to think is supposed to stop your emotions from causing you to think? Not well done.

Please!

The last thing he heard from her was the sound of her voice, laughing and explaining it to Commodore Magdalena—and her laughter! *See, now you're not thinking of your family. Deflective humor.*

Shai's influence.

I'll see you soon, A'banna thought, then tossed up the same mental wall he'd been working on the last few days.

Bedel gently rubbed tension in his temples. If they survived, this might be a good joke, but for now, he had to focus. There was no reason to lie to the Speaker. "All I know is that The Caurs gave A'banna and I starlight steel for a reason. They want us to find the Dragon and give him the lion. Then, together, we'll stop Hurmlen and Jocina's plans. You look troubled, Speaker."

"As you said, none of us are truly fine," Muriumek replied. "It should not fall upon you to train them."

Bedel frowned. "I agree, but it's safer this way. The enemy

plans to use me, but A'banna and I have already changed expectations and prophecy."

Muriumek was about to answer when an explosion rocked the ship, blasting parts of the hull in view of the cabin windows.

"Too soon!" Forbens shouted, charging out onto the deck.

Bedel and Muriumek followed him. Square-rigged sails billowed windward as *The Red Hand* crewmen struggled to keep the pirate ship upright and traveling faster than her pursuers. Bedel braced himself against the deck railing, staring at the four triangular black sails spreading out to flank them. Cold, silver eyes linked with him.

Little boy, you're running, too! My poor little Reason. Let me show you what I can do. This will be fun.

A squawk and caw-caw drew Bedel's attention to a shape below dark storm clouds. A Velheron soared above them, its call a sour song, mixed with horrid glee and venom.

"She's here!" Bedel shouted. "The Sorceress."

"Theantros, save us," Muriumek replied.

"Drive her hard, men! I want every ounce of speed!" Forbens shouted, moving swiftly across the ship's deck. Bedel could see the captain's aether reaching out and touching the wood, the air, the water, driving the ship onward. Bedel glanced westward and, sure enough, the mountains of Cronop's big island could be seen. Any safe harbor was on the east side of the island. A mist poured out of the mountains, a confused storm headed in the wrong direction.

Muriumek stood at the railing, gripping it hard as he stared at the island and the mist.

Oh, so that is who you had with you? That Speaker for the Oppressor burned my bird. It's only a matter of time until I return the gesture.

"Hokano, if you're real, it's time," Bedel said.

Yes, send Hokano to me! We haven't spoken in so long. One

Immortal to another. Do tell him your little bond-mate slaughtered his son, would you? Oh, little boy, you are outside of your realm of understanding. A shame, really. What do you think of ice and blood?

Another flaming ballista bolt cut through the storm's darkness, slamming into *The Red Hand*'s hull. Wood splintered and cracked, blasting the crew as a sudden fireball exploded in its place. A sailor caught fire, stumbling around deck, falling into flammable objects until a merciless crewmate planted one booted foot on his chest and pushed the ill-fated man overboard.

"Hold fast and fire back!" Captain Forbens shouted aft as he tugged hard on a rigging. "Keep her moving, you sea rats, or we're all dead! Put those bloody flames out!"

Bedel braced himself against a guard rail, coming face-to-face with a bare-chested pirate distributing crossbows from a crate. All around them, other men—Elves, Glymphs, humans—all rushed about, carrying buckets and urgently trying to put out the many fires. There was no reason to conceal his magic any longer. Every Baktur on that ship knew they were here and had chased them for days. Bedel reached out with his mind, offering the sea aether. It answered with a massive wave; inundating the burning deck and soaking the crew. Fire steamed. Flesh sizzled.

Bedel glanced up at the swirling clouds above. The essences touched his aura, calling to him, asking him if he wanted to become one with the storm. He could be with the turbulence, the rain, the waves, the hurricane; all through the gift from his aura. Calm was beyond him now; there was nothing but the full completion of the maelstrom.

What kind of essencer wove this manipulation? Summoning a hurricane! First the mountain, then a sorceress, now this? In his connection with the world fabric, Bedel felt small; weak. As if all of his centuries of training had been for naught.

The clouds felt the static on the edge of the closest ship and struck with the white fury of lightning. Light and thunder split the air. Wood splintered, and men screamed as a ballista went up in flames. Any satisfaction was lost as his legs gave out from underneath him. Bedel clung to the rail and watched the fire spread. His vision cleared from the flash, but the clouds had been given permission. Streaks cut across the sky ahead. The clouds rotated faster. From the west, mist rolled forward, unrelenting. It would cover them soon, proving to be either an escape or their doom.

A giant beast erupted from the water, a flash of scales, dermal plates, spikes, and a long tale. The beast plunged back under the surface. Dozens of fins sliced through waves, like crows drawn to bloody fields. At first, Bedel though it was a whale cutting toward them, but the fins were webbed claws attached to massive, scaled arms. The dermal plates had rigid spikes in long rows from snout to tail. A pair of fibrous wings were folded to its sides, and it used them to propel itself faster through the water.

The sea dragon's body was lean and muscular, shimmering beneath the light of stars and storm. What once had been a water drake that roamed rivers and swamps had shed its infancy, becoming a monstrous creature terrorizing the sea.

"Harpoons!" Forbens shouted. "Portside!" Sailors darted forward as others used ratchets to crank back massive crossbows. Cold seawater sprayed them all as the sea dragon surfaced, a legend of the deep, shrouded in the fragile light of the night. Its throat rippled as it opened its toothy maw.

Liquid ice sprayed forth. A wave caught in the path of its breath froze instantly, before shattering into infinitesimal shards or solid lumpen hammers that rained down on the crew. The dragon's breath sprayed beyond the water. Flesh, wood, and metal crackled and groaned as it froze. Wide-eyed, screaming sailors, including two with a harpoon set on the crossbows, became ice statues. The harpoon and ballista shimmered as it froze. Even the hull became white and sleek, brittle. And then the dragon lunged.

Massive jaws and wide, cone-shaped teeth ripped three men up from where they had been frozen in place. Ice snapped. Only their feet, marked by bloody stumps, remained.

Bedel rushed forward, nearly slipping on the deck. It didn't even seem like wood anymore. It was pure ice. He tried to reach one of the men, whose eyes still wandered, though he couldn't move anything else. His mouth was open in a scream that didn't come. Bedel hoped he could break the man loose, maybe find a way to save him from this fate. Water sprayed. The sea dragon's shadow shifted. Bedel, still too far from the remaining sailor, dove back onto the wood as claws, as long as he was tall, cut into the ice like fissures in a glacier. Someone let loose a blood-curdling scream. The dragon's webbed hands pulled the frozen hull from the ship. Ice and wood shattered. A swath of the upper deck disappeared into the white, churning sea, dragging the sailor and the ballista into the depths with it. Cold water sprayed in its wake.

Forbens screamed a string of curses as that area of his ship caved in like snow. Water sprayed again as the dragon's tail slapped the surface. Forbens reached for one of the loaded bows, breaking off a frozen sailor's hands. Warmth fled from Forbens into the weapon. Ice turned to water, dripping at his feet.

Bedel stared at the gap in the deck. He could see into the cargo hold, where the beast's claws had ripped apart men, ship, and crates like a sickle to wheat. They were taking on water.

The three other warships advanced, flanking them on the starboard side. Bedel followed the massive sea dragon's shimmering shadow as it glided just below the surface. Forbens fired, the harpoon glancing off hard scales.

"Yeht me."

The first mate grumbled at the result. "Aft or stern?"

"May as well be both. Bedel, where in the dark abyss is that girl of yours?"

Where is the Keeper of the North?

Before Bedel could answer, the crow's nest burst into flame and the watchman fell to the deck with a shrill, horrified scream. A flaming stone tumbled to the deck. Bedel heard cranks grinding on the lead warship. A starboard ballista launched a flaming siege arrow at the warship. Pirates yelled as an officer chanted orders like a marching battalion song. Sailors rushed to douse the stone with water and wet blankets, but it left a smoldering trail that could still ignite the ship.

A terrible sound drew Bedel's attention starboard. Water cascaded as the sea dragon rose from the waves. It reared back, ready to spew its icy death. Before it could, another shape soared upward from the depths.

Jaws half as long as the ship closed around the sea dragon's throat. The dragon yelped, swallowing whatever icy chemical was in its throat. The colossal Maor Leviathan continued to ram forward, throwing the dragon onto the ocean surface and driving it underneath its wide body.

Bedel let out a triumphant shout and stared on in awe at the clash of the two titanic beasts. He saw a thin membrane slide over the leviathan's eye with each snap of its jaws. It had no arms or claws, just thick fins and a broad, toothy maw. In some ways, the leviathan resembled a combined whale, shark, and a water drake. Maor were bulkier than their other serpentine leviathan kin. Thick, protective scales formed armor as strong as the dragon's. Whereas a sea dragon was lithe and swift, a leviathan's charge hit with a single mighty bite; jaws snapping with more pressure than even the sea dragon could muster.

The sea dragon scraped claws along the leviathan's scales, ripping some free. The dragon slithered out of the leviathan's toothy grip and bit.

The Maor Leviathan's jaws closed around the sea dragon's torso, again ramming the dragon. The dragon snarled and its long neck twisted, jaws snapping at the leviathan's fin. The leviathan tightened its massive, toothy jaws around the sea dragon's belly and forced it beneath the surface. Tails and bodies pounded the surface water. The sea churned and then froze, forcing a pursuing warship to slow as ice crackled against its hull.

A false quiet settled over the shocked fighters, but the Zelvatore sailors quickly went to work attempting to steer their ship out of the frozen waves.

The surface ice shattered as the creatures spiraled in a rolling duel of death.

Overhead, the Velheron continued to circle around the battle, shrieking and squawking as the Sorceress' avatar.

Welcome back, Old Man! Bedel heard her shriek. *I'm so glad you could come. How many more of your disciples do I have the pleasure of slaughtering now?*

Muriumek ran up beside Bedel. The Gaul wrapped his long, thin fingers around the rail; his knuckles instantly white.

"Hokano, don't engage her!" Muriumek shouted, even though the two likely shared a connection similar to Bedel and A'banna. "Stay back!"

The leviathan bellowed. The creature's fervor was all Bedel needed to know.

Bedel could hear the Sorceress shouting in frustration. *So, you wish to hide behind these boundaries? Alain had more courage than you. No wonder you sent him! Fine, Old Man, avatars it is to be!* Bedel felt a surge of aether mixed with the cold of dark fire, *Beast Speech* summoning other creatures to the battle.

A low, rumbling caw filled their ears as massive wings beat the air. From the clouds burst an eagle—but it was also like a lion. The riderless gryphon's claws and talons were bared. The Keeper of the North's gryphon slammed and cut into the Sorceress's Velheron, whose long, serrated beak pecked back, drawing blood that fell to the sea.

"That's not something you see every day," Forbens muttered. "Ballistae, aim for the nearest ship and keep up the volley! If they want us, let their hands come away scorched red with our fire!"

Sailors cheered and resumed their defense against their human pursuers. Bedel felt a hand on his arm. Muriumek was there, smiling. "Hokano, Keeper of the North, wants you to know: He sent only the best."

"Tell him thank you. And crush the witch."

"It is not his pleasure, even though she had his son killed. He remembers another age. But he is bound to drive her back."

Bedel shook his head, not in the mood for myths and mystical talk.

In the sea, the sea dragon and Maor Leviathan roared, snapping and tearing chunks of scaled armor and flesh from each other. The dragon tried to wrap its long, sinuous tail around the leviathan's body. The leviathan released its neck. Its next bite sent a shockwave through the air, a rendering snap so loud it was deafening. The leviathan jerked, ripping the dragon's tail clean off in a fountain of dark red. The sea dragon shrieked, spitting its icy breath onto the exposed leviathan.

The mist rolled over *The Red Hand*.

"Gods damnin' us all!" a sailor shouted.

Ships groaned as they sped across the sea's surface, against the wind and through the mist. Sharp twangs preceded the whistling sounds of ballista arrows and tar-filled jars launched by catapults. The flaming missiles cut through the smoky haze. The volley rained down on the pursuing warships. Fire erupted on the enemy's vessels from both direct hits and explosions on the water's surface. Forbens' crew erupted into cheers. Bedel grinned as Commodore Magdalena's fleet joined the cacophony of war. He could feel A'banna on the deck of Magdalena's flagship. A'banna's relief coursed across the *Zitaya* bond as she felt his nearness.

We made it, she thought.

The Sorceress is watching all of this through the animals, Bedel told her.

So am I, A'banna answered. *There's also someone else. Can't be. Oh, stars! It feels like Alain, reaching out to me. He forgives me.* What he would have given to hear *that* conversation. *Bedel, we'll save as many as we can.*

"Light up these bastards and send 'em to the depths!" Commodore Magdalena's voice boomed from the closest ship.

More arrows and fire split through the mist as her entire fleet —twelve ships strong—burst from the haze. Ballistae and small catapults continued launching flaming artillery at the four warships. It wouldn't be long before they retaliated.

"Crows, you lucky bastard, you actually did it." Forbens grinned as he grabbed Bedel's shoulders and gave him a hard shake. Forbens turned to his men. "That's Commodore Magdalena, sea rats! Think she's going to give a damn when we're in port that she saved our fins. Charge us gold, more like it. Give those ships Kerdum if we sink in our filthy blood!"

Magdalena leaned over the rail of the closest ship. "You're welcome, you lying, cheating bastard!"

"Beautiful wench, ever I saw one!" Forbens shouted back.

"I didn't know you could tell the difference!"

They chuckled as the night lit up with their volleys. The mist began to clear, unable to be sustained under such intensity. It was then that Bedel could see A'banna clearly. Idrin stood beside her, spear in one hand, sword in the other. The ranger wore his hood.

He couldn't leave me alone, even for his sister, A'banna said through the *Zitaya* cord.

"Good to see you!" Bedel shouted. Idrin raised his spear in salute.

Sounds of flesh tearing preceded the sea dragon's head flying through the air and into the ocean with a definitive splash. The Maor roared victoriously and dove.

"I see four more warships hard off a'port!" a sailor called on Magdalena's lead ship.

"They used the mist and the sea beast's battle against us," Forbens said, drawing a farseer glass from his belt. Bedel could see clearly enough; those intimidating triangular black sails swayed back as they pressed forward. "We sunk two and got four more. Helm! Bring us about between *Woman's Fury* and the lead vessel."

"Magdalena's ship is called *Woman's Fury*?" Bedel asked, raising an eyebrow as he grabbed rigging to keep himself steady.

Forbens locked a thumb in his belt. "She's the best gods-damn smuggler in the whole Cronop Sea—though I'm the fastest, mind you. And you didn't hear it from me. You haven't known fear until you've seen her mad."

He grinned at Bedel and popped a pipe in his mouth. "Let's end this, Mr. Bedel, eh?"

Bedel felt the ship coming about. Just then, a loud splash, hiss, and screams filled the air. At first, he thought it was the lightning crackling against the sky. No such luck.

Wood crunched and cracked. Bedel and Forbens spun to see two sea dragons rise out of the depths, spewing liquid ice over one of Magdalena's freighters. They rammed the ship to a thousand pieces as its crew fell into choppy waters.

Forbens swore. In under a minute, the two dragons had reduced the ship to debris and plucked survivors from the water in their maws. The Maor Leviathan returned from its victory. It erupted from the surface with a roar, but the sea dragons pivoted, their lithe shapes barely escaping its jaws, and dove in together to attack.

"Muriumek," Forbens began. "Tell your Keeper friend we need a bit of extra help."

The Gaul nodded, sharpening a blade. "He's not Jocina. He doesn't enslave the animals like she does."

"Well, tell him to ask them nicely, weave it!"

"He's otherwise occupied," Muriumek said. "I suggest we prepare for close-quarters combat."

Forbens shrugged. "God-like powers, what do you expect from a bloody immortal Keeper? Aft gunner! Can you hit one of those dragons?"

The sailor manning a ballista spun to face him. "Captain, we got nothing but sticks and stones against those hides, sir."

"Lay down cover for the *Fury* and let's force the warships to back off, then."

"Aye, captain!"

"Muriumek, we need another leviathan." Forbens pipe dropped as he frowned. "Please."

The Gaul didn't reply.

"Sir!" the first mate shouted, pointing.

"Well, call the wenches and break out the axes, gentlemen!"

Cutting through the waves, one of the warships slammed into the side of *The Red Hand*. Both ships shook. Rigging and sails locked on the mainmast. The Zelvatore soldiers on the ship didn't hesitate.

"To arms!" Forbens shouted.

Bedel! A'banna called, but he didn't answer. She was in no condition to fight. Neither was he, really. But there was no choice in the matter.

Muriumek's eyes snapped open, and he grabbed Bedel's hands. "The Taurs approach from the north."

Bedel searched that frantic gaze. "How do you know?" Bedel spun and saw the *Windstream* nearing them.

Only the strongest essencers could create a large enough *Windstream* to fly. The only essencers Bedel knew of who could manage that were Xathon and Raynt, and neither one would keep company with The Taurs or utilize dark fire. This was a flying dark fire essencer. In truth, battles with the Sorceress from long-distance were far easier than they'd ever be in person. She had less control over the essences around her. A powerful dark fire essencer here would make things altogether worse.

As if I already didn't feel impotent enough!

You're far from impotent, Bedel. He could feel A'banna's confidence. *You can face him.*

A familiar feel to the aether streaming off the coming essencer made Bedel shiver. *No,* he thought, turning back to the battle.

One of Magdalena's ships burned as it cut through the water, oars pushing it forward at full speed. As one, the crew shouted as they rammed a warship at full speed. The ships locked. The fire spread. Before long, weapons clanged.

Bedel glanced back at the damage to *The Red Hand*. Zelvatore soldiers dropped off the enemy warship locked into *The Red Hand's* hull.

A three-pronged hook lodged into the wood at Bedel's feet. The line went taught. With a twist of his wrist, Bedel's knife sprang loose on one of the bracers. He sliced through the rope, but half a dozen other hooks had been launched over, pulling the ships closer together in their deathly dance.

Lightning split the sky and rain burst down.

Intimidating triangular black sails swayed back and forth as the sea surged with the unnatural tropical storm. Bedel helped Forbens secure the main mast line. He glanced backward. Already the lead ship loaded another enormous bolt into the ballista. One Zelvatore spun a crank, lowering the weapon, targeting *The Red Hand* below the waterline.

Bedel gripped the rail as he stared, stunned. His forehead started to throb from where the Baktur had cracked it open as they tried to flee Wonbai.

If the Baktur had tracked him to *The Red Hand* in port, what had happened to Shai? Vari? Nadari and his family? There was no way to know, and these weren't questions to be contemplating now with enemy soldiers climbing over railings with blades in their mouths. Spray burst over the rail of Forbens' ship. The force felt like a punch to Bedel's aching head. He braced himself, uneasy.

Bedel glanced back at the ballista's progress. Any moment, the spring would launch that massive arrowhead and pierce *The Red Hand*'s hull.

"They're trying to sink us!" Bedel shouted.

Forbens glared at him. "So that's what they're doing? Thanks for clearing that up, gods damn it!" He spun back to the crew. "What did I say? Fire back!"

A small, dark shape darted between sailors. "Dans, we need to evacuate the ship."

"*The Red Hand* is my ship, Muriumek, and you got us into this bloody mess!"

"No, Dans, a dark fire essencer is coming. I saw a Taur."

"And I saw my daughters!" Forbens scoffed.

Bedel felt Forbens' aether drawing from steel and iron *Soliditus* to strengthen the wooden hull. Water splashed out of the ship, as if rocked by a wave. Forbens grunted as he used wind *Gaseous* to convince *Liquidus* to not sink them. It was hopeless. The sea was too much for him alone. He wove the three strands together in a ward. The invisible tool would last for a little longer.

"This is my damn ship!" Forbens growled.

As Forbens finished weaving the ward, Bedel turned his attention to the warship. The sailor had nearly finished aiming the siege weapon. Bedel reached out with his own aether. Screws loosened. An iron plate popped off. Wood strained. Piece by piece, the entire ballista crumpled, bolt and all, disassembling. At the same moment, an arrow cut through the air and pinned the enemy gunner to a crate. The man gasped, but it came out as a bubbly gargle. *Woman's Fury* kept pace with *The Red Hand*, and Idrin had found a perfect shot. He lined up another. Bedel let his aether stretch along the warship hull, seeking another siege weapon.

A bald, tattooed Zelvatore leapt out of the cabin. With a slap, his own aether launched out of his aura, smacking against Bedel's. *Finally,* he thought, *I've been waiting for one of their essencers to show themselves.*

Bedel and the bald essencer stared at the colorful weaves developing in front of each of them. As the Zelvatore essencer summoned fire, gathering heat from the air, Bedel loosened the mast above his opponent. It was a race to death. But Bedel had one advantage.

The Zelvatore essencer's head snapped back when Idrin's arrow pierced his eye. The essencer crumpled to the deck; his fire manipulation burst apart into sparks.

Bedel raised his fist in thanks. Idrin raised his bow before notching another arrow, scanning for other targets.

Forbens rallied his crew and began firing bows and crossbow bolts over the gap, dropping would-be boarders in the air or on deck.

The warship jolted as a ballista bolt from *Woman's Fury* broke through its hull. Another warship passed the one tangled with *The Red Hand*. It began to come about to flank both *The Hand* and *Woman's Fury*. Wood cracked and the aft section drifted. Fire sprung up despite the rain.

"Captain! We're taking on water!" a sailor shouted.

"Bloody waves," Forbens muttered. Rain pelted the captain, soaking his dreadlocks. He ran a hand to clear his hair from his face; even he couldn't believe it. He glared at Muriumek and Bedel. "Better make a plan." He pointed as a warship began to cut them off from *Woman's Fury*. In their lantern light, Zeller sailors twirled grappling hooks. "We're about to get boarded and we're hours from Cardor."

"We stay with the original plan," Bedel said. "Muriumek, time for you to go."

"Oh no," Muriumek protested. "My place is here, yet."

"Not if these end up in a sea dragon's belly!" Bedel patted a copy of the war plans in his pocket. They were about to be boxed in! "I still haven't gotten ahold of the agent in Gloriweedum," Bedel shouted as more hooks clinked into the rail.

Ropes went taught and a choral, "Heave!" rose up in Zellu.

The Red Hand was yanked portside. Bedel's muscles strained as he held onto a rope to keep himself steady.

"Well, good ol' Stamford will have to wait for you. Take my bloody schooner." Forbens squeezed the Gaul's shoulder and patted Bedel's. "See you on the other side, gentlemen. Think there's room for me in Ibiloron-Bearune?"

"Always," Muriumek said, but Forbens had darted away from them. He joined his crew as the warship pulled the ships closer. Bedel could feel his connection with the essences of the ship and the sea. A barrier of water slowed the swirling sea from dragging the ship down.

Zelvatore soldiers swung aboard, their guttural war cries piercing the tumult of the storm. Dozens of crossbows twanged and bolts whistled through the night. Some of the swinging attackers yelped as the large arrowheads sank into them. Many fell off their lines. One flipped upside down, cracking his head on a rail as his momentum drove the arrow deeper. He fell between the ships.

Not to be outdone, planks rammed aboard *The Red Hand* and dozens of frenzied, scimitar-wielding soldiers sprinted aboard. The ship lurched as water filled the hold. Forbens had lost his concentration for a brief moment, and the ocean would not be held back. Some of the soldiers fell off the plank—they disappeared swiftly, pulled under the surface with barely a shriek. Guttural war cries were lost in the sharp clacking of sword against sword, or the wet smack as an unlucky soul met their end. The scene was repeated on the portside: two armies boarded *The Red Hand*.

Only desperate men would make such a move. They were after him and possibly Muriumek. They wanted the plans and confirmed kills.

Bedel was a weaving agent for the Magical Affairs Commission. He didn't back down from a fight. All of his career, Raynt and he, the supposed top agents, always pushed themselves to do more. Now, these pirates—not exactly innocent in their own right—were getting slaughtered.

"They're dying for you," Muriumek whispered at his side. Those words seemed to echo everything that had happened since Bedel had pulled A'banna from the drake-infested river. Muriumek's thin, wet fingers gently squeezed Bedel's wrist. "They believe, Gatekeeper. We need to go."

The din of battle, the commotion of men and women fighting, dying, monsters bursting out of the sea, roaring, giant terrors-on-wings assaulting each other overhead, it all faded. There was just Muriumek, Bedel, and A'banna across their connection. In that moment, with two Keepers battling one another, with blood flowing across the deck, Bedel felt Jacob's flight bringing him closer.

The mountain wanted to kill him.

The Elves wanted to use him.

Shai wanted to run away with him.

The Sorceress said she made him?

His father lied to him.

The Speakers manipulated him.

Bedel, I love you! A'banna's thoughts cut through the emotions like a knife. *Listen—*

And Jacob's ethereal touch, tainted with dark fire, helped him feel it all.

"We'll turn the whole world on its head," Bedel said to Muriumek, ignoring A'banna's interjections. "Have you thought of that? What if our very existence enables these cycles? What if we stop being participants? Would both sides lose power? Could we cancel the cycle itself? Destroy prophecy by not willfully fulfilling it?"

The Speaker of Gaulmen didn't release the Gatekeeper, but stared into his eyes, speechless.

"We should just run away."

Muriumek nodded, loosening his grip. His bulbous yellow eyes seemed to droop a little. All he said was: "The Vel, Bedel."

Bedel grunted with frustration. There was always something. The good of the realm. Saving the world. A woman in the river.

Is that all I am to you? What is this? These are not your —Bedel, stop shutting—

A war to stop. A prophecy to fulfill. Monsters to fight. Bedel glanced across the deck.

Zelvatore soldiers cut through a line of pirates, shattering the calm moment, bursting the unnatural quiet.

Muriumek tugged Bedel's sleeve, a little more urgently.

Bedel wrenched his gaze away from the battle and grabbed Muriumek with his free hand. "If you're a fake, I'll kill you."

Muriumek spread out his hands in acceptance.

"I am no pretender, so there's no need to try." There was no fear in the Gaul's eyes. Only sincerity. *Crows!* "Ignore dark fire's persuasion, Bedel! You are stronger than your brother."

"But he's my brother," Bedel whispered, a part of his heart desperate to reunite with the first loving face he remembered.

"The Taurs know that."

Reluctantly, Bedel joined Muriumek. They darted around to the foremast. Captain Forbens' personal schooner swayed as it hung upside-down, its own rigging tied inside. "Help me with the clamps!" Bedel shouted.

Muriumek danced up to the rigging, cutting or untying ropes with only the speed a Gaul could muster. He twirled, leapt, crawled, and moved unlike any person Bedel had seen. Not unlike an insect. The schooner righted and dropped over the starboard hull with a splash.

Muriumek landed on the deck near Bedel with a soft smack on his bare, webbed feet.

Bedel raised an eyebrow. "Clearly, you needed me."

"I felt some urgency," Muriumek muttered, scanning the horizon. The landscape of the Southern Province of Cardor was only a dark silhouette. They were so close!

"Bedel," Muriumek said, pointing. *Woman's Fury* flanked the second warship, bombarding its hull with her arsenal. Shapes darted across the short distance, even as flames began spreading across the ship. Then the hooting and screaming started.

"Ever seen a raptor fight?" Bedel said, his lips curling into a slight smile at the sight of his feathered predator friends. His claw brethren.

The massive raptors darted from aft to stern, cutting into frightened Zelvatore sailors and soldiers like they were bloody harvesters. Bedel saw Idrin swing onto the deck. Foe after foe fell before him. Those who tried to flank Idrin were surprised by a small, brown, toothy blur of a mountain ferret gnawing at their knee or ankle tendons. In a desperate gesture, sailors began turning their own ballistae inward.

"Idrin! Get them back to *The Fury*!" The ranger either didn't hear or was too headstrong to respond. *Stubborn yeht!* "Muriumek, go! I'll meet the Chosen at Wimble, if they're willing. I'll tell them what you told me."

Fires burned all over the deck, casting shadows of the men fighting. Blood splattered the deck with the rain.

Another cold wave of emotion washed over Bedel. For a moment, he remembered being cradled in an old man's arms. *The man's red robes were wrapped around Bedel protectively. Once, the redwood staff hit Bedel in the head. The man barely uttered an apology. He was only a toddler, after all. Then the man set him down, surrounded by the bodies and the blood, the dark silhouetted flames scorching everything. But Jacob had hidden him, gently, wrapped in a blanket to keep warm from the rain.*

Loud footfalls sounded from behind the foremast, emotions and memories shattered by reality. Bedel spun, whipping out a thin dagger as the Zelvatore soldier rounded. The dagger sank into his throat, and he fell to his knees, staring with shock. Bedel stepped forward and ripped the dagger from the soldier's throat. The dead man tumbled forward.

Bedel didn't have time to brace himself for the next wave of emotion and memory. *Marko the staff-maker was tied to a mast, impaled by dozens of wooden shards. Blood gurgled out from his mouth as another, who commanded the shadows, reached for Bedel. Blond hair fell over Elven ears, but his eyes looked as black as night. Xathon dashed between them, wild and feral.*

Defending his son, A'banna interjected, though she was not in the memory.

Bedel could see paternal and protective colors flowing around Xathon. Then there was ice and flame.

Bedel's body shook as the memory washed over him with the spray of a wave. Each release from Jacob's *Person Leading* made Bedel's head hurt worse, not to mention that the ocean water was literally pouring salt into the healing wound. Bedel steadied himself.

I'm with you, A'banna said. *I'm with you, whatever he tries.*

Thanks, Bedel thought. He wiped the dagger on the writhing corpse's body.

Wind essences trembled. Some were in fear, others aligning

with the command of one who drew them from the north. He needed to improvise.

Muriumek bailed water out of the schooner. Bedel grabbed Muriumek, eliciting a surprised shout, and stuffed two scrolls—copies—into his vest coat.

"They need you more than they need me." Bedel turned.

"Gatekeeper! They will need you for the Bloom."

"Don't call me that!" Bedel's head wound continued to throb as he tossed a short sword into the ship and cut the rigging with his bracer-blades. Muriumek called out as the schooner dropped into the sea. Waves sent the small ship away from the battle, carrying it toward the distant Cardorian shore.

"Besides, they have you," he muttered. "Mission, completed."

Bedel patted the original scrolls in his gambeson. *It is better this way,* he thought again. *He'll make it. He will. He's a survivor.*

So are we, A'banna responded.

Yes. We are.

The *Zitaya* bond surged with ethereal energy, nearly crackling like lightning. Bedel felt a rush of strength, as if A'banna stood next to him, not on a nearby ship. Together, they marched into battle. Soldiers rushed below deck; most had encircled the last of the crew. The sailors had been herded; back to back and cornered.

Essences welcomed Bedel's ethereal investment, and he did not withhold himself from his training. Simultaneously, he could feel every fiber of the ships, the sharks feeding on carrion in the bloodied water below, the abused wind as it pressed forward at the will of essencers like horses whipped by a carriage driver.

From afar, the essences revealed a cloaked figure flying through the storm. Bedel noted that he kept his distance from the Velheron and gryphon's ongoing quarrel. Feathers and blood rained down.

Bedel's brow furled. What did Jacob have to hide from the Sorceress, if Jacob was Hurmlen's lieutenant?

Reaching out with silver tendrils of aether, Bedel called to the discarded steel, bronze, and iron all over the deck. They were uncontrolled by any of the essencers in the other ships. Just like he had done with the lightning and with dismantling siege weapons from afar, Bedel found unclaimed essences. *Rise,* he thought, willing them into the air. He followed the essence strings as they combined: *Soliditus, Gaseous, Invisitus, Liquidus.*

The Zelvatore soldiers pressed around the crew, ready for the killing stroke. "On my mark, men!" Forbens shouted over the din of battle.

Bedel didn't hesitate. He drove the makeshift, floating weapons forward into the unsuspecting backs of the attackers. Wet smacks and cracks of rendered armor filled the night. The Zelvatore soldiers fell around them.

Forbens stood with his crew, dumbfounded at the bodies around them. To the port side, those still on deck of the Zelvatore warship hurriedly chopped ropes and threw planks to a rigid splash in the sea. Idrin had pulled the raptors and his ferret back, leaving a deck covered in corpses and maimed warriors. *Woman's Fury* herself pulled away.

Bedel leveled eyes with Forbens. Fires from all over the deck reflected in the man's face. "Abandon ship."

"Excuse me?"

The dark fire essencer's *Windstream* circled the vessel. They both felt it. Forbens' glanced up.

"Mating yehts," the captain muttered.

"Run!" Bedel shouted to the crew.

Wind snapped the blue cloak of the dark fire essencer as he hovered above the deck. Lightning streaked behind him, sparkling on star-shaped brooches and off the dancing black flame along the blade of his dueling sword.

Rumors had circulated before Bedel left: Duchess Saphirra had taken a Privy Counselor, a baron from the Ferrell Highlands.

As Bedel and Jacob gazed at each other for the first time in over a century, Bedel knew the truth behind the rumors. Jacob had assumed the identity of Baron Dietrich Von Schling, and thus was influencing the rogue duchess. He had a hand in this war. Maybe even it all.

"How could you?" Bedel said.

"It would have been so much worse if I hadn't," Jacob answered, his voice almost lost in the wind. "Much worse."

The crew scattered and the tangled Zelvatore ship tried to push off as Von Schling hovered over them, blue cape dancing like a flag in the wind. He met Bedel's gaze and smiled.

Jacob said in a booming voice, "It's been a long time, brother, but I didn't think it'd come to this. I did try to scare you off."

"I'm not a scared child anymore, Jacob."

"Damn it, Bedel," Jacob said, looking up at the swirling storm. "I'm trying. Do you remember me at all?"

Jacob descended, stepping onto the deck. His flame flickered, as if almost extinguished.

"I remember my kindly brother, who I loved to play with, who tried to save me from a madman. That madman is working alongside a witch who would destroy the world." Bedel pointed at the Velheron and the sea dragons. "I remember who you used to be. Be my brother again! Let these people go. Fight them with me, brother! Together, as it should be."

"What in Kerdum?" Forbens muttered.

Bedel barely paid Forbens a glance. The pirate captain had opted to go down with the ship, he guessed.

Jacob's face had softened even more. He lowered his blade. "You do remember? I wasn't going to let them do that to you. You were a baby. They still will try. I can't let them."

"If you help me, there may be no need to fight them too. Jacob? How did you become this?"

"There is a price for kindness from Elves." He gestured at

himself. "The Truth was not always like this, Bedel. We were good. We set captives free and we restored hope. But the Elves aren't the only ones who make you pay." Jacob's presence seemed to shift with the light. Gone was the white hair and aged face. A younger man stood there, with the weary, battle-hardened gaze Bedel remembered from his dreams. Jacob's fingers touched a ring on his hand, turning it. The image of an angry Von Schling solidified again, though Bedel still saw through it. "Two hundred years and Xathon has used you like a pet, a puppet. Don't make me kill you, Bedel. I spared your life once before."

Bedel felt shards of wood, iron, steel, and weapons start to move. He heard them yanked from corpses. Aether streamed from Forbens. The objects pointed at Jacob. Ropes untangled from the masts. The air became static around Von Schling, ready for a strike from lightning.

"No!" Bedel said, speaking to the essences he had just controlled but had since laid dormant. The static discharged. The makeshift missiles clattered to the deck. Ropes went slack.

"Damn it, man!" Forbens said. All of the essences, including his own ship, no longer listened to him. Bedel controlled them. And the sea swarmed into the breaches of the hull. They had a minute, maybe two. "Why? How in the weaving abyss did you do that?"

Bedel didn't acknowledge him, his mind full of the essences, full of the power. If he and Jacob fought—a dance of the essences —they could destroy all the ships. He could feel the world fabric: the ocean, the animals, the fabric on the sails, the fibers of the rigging, the chaos of the flames, the slow, desperate exhaling of the dying, the hunger of the beasts of the sea, every stream of the air around him. Above, Jacob controlled an equal amount. Their auras had expanded, dark fire and aether.

Somewhere, the Sorceress and the Keeper of the North still dueled with their flying animal avatars. They felt the conflict. The hesitation. The moment the hope of the world could die. The gryphon turned to strike, but the Velheron refused to let it pass. Bedel saw the Sorceress's silver eyes. He felt the Keeper of the North looming with a fist. Two titans of pure being, in and around their avatars; two pairs of ethereal silver eyes glanced his way as his own aura shoved against theirs. He felt A'banna, negotiating with the fish, mammals, and reptiles of the sea. She tried to speak, but there was too much power, too many thoughts and instincts.

And then there were the dark shapes, reptilian yet furry, with sneering, toothy maws, beady eyes and flapping bat-like wings. The Taurs saw him as they hovered in and around Jacob. One slithered from Jacob's mouth, extended its smaller pair of wings and flew above his shoulder, sneering. Bedel's aether slammed against them, stunning the realm walkers. Their wings flapped as they tried to stay hovering between realms, but they were invisible to the rain, the light of fire and the stars; silent predators making their own play. Bedel felt it all.

Golden light flared throughout Bedel's aura, as if someone had suddenly unveiled a bright lantern, only to hide it again in the darkness. The Taurs shrieked and flew a little farther away from Jacob.

Bedel raised his chin higher. Even the storm settled; the wind slowed, the rain stopped battering the deck, and the ocean stopped churning. All of creation waited in a single breath, attentive to him. Part of Bedel's aura brushed the wind essences suspending Jacob in the air. A slight threat he hoped not to be forced to take.

"Gatekeeper," Jacob said, horrified. "You became it anyway, didn't you? I tried, Bedel. How I tried."

Their auras flared, slamming into each other like waves of sound or rushing air. Bedel held his ground. Jacob's *Windstream* wavered, his cloak slapping at his ankles.

"Jacob, we need to end this. End the war. We can stop this. Stop all of them."

Jacob shook his head. "You know, Bedel, I may have a solution that will avoid me doing something I don't entirely want to do."

"Don't you?" Bedel whispered. Bedel's aether began spinning around Jacob's *Windstream*. If he tightened, Jacob could fall. Was it enough of a deterrent?

"Kerdum, brother. I'm just the forebearer."

Jacob Morbrook smiled as dark shadows circled around him. No, it wasn't just Jacob. The Taurs were smiling. Jacob shed a single tear, but his smile never faltered.

Bedel realized his mistake. In his pride, Bedel hadn't touched *forces* themselves. Temperature, for example. Hot, cold. The temperature dropped suddenly. Despite the ship sinking, waves pelting onto the deck, the air felt dry. The ship felt hard, like kindling. Bedel reached out with aether, desperate to slow the essences, but dark fire tasted sweeter to them. It always had. And Jacob had been filling it with tasty morsels of dark fire since Bedel first blocked Forbens' manipulation.

"Holy yeht shit—" Forbens shouted, darting toward Bedel.

Cold, dry air rushed through the entire ship as all heat was summoned into the center of the vessel. It happened so quickly, Bedel could do nothing. He felt Forbens tackle him, the hit shoving all air from his lungs. But it wasn't enough. They tumbled over the deck into the swiftly rising sea. Jacob unleashed the compacted heat with enough force that the ensuing explosion vaporized *The Red Hand* and everyone on it.

⁓——————⊶⊷⊶⊷——⊶⁓

The fireball tore into the nearby Zelvatore warship, obliterating its remaining crew and igniting it in the same dark-shrouded fire that smoldered in the floating wreckage of *The Red Hand*. Gusts of wind further spread the flames, touching a third small ship from the commodore's fleet. That wind went northward, driving troop transports to their second destination. Jacob Von Schling knew that Bedel and his companions had tried to prevent the war, but there had been no need to wait. The first strike had overthrown a Cardorian city and spread their forces for battle.

Von Schling hovered above it all, as *The Red Hand* and the Zelvatore warship sank. Despite the strategy playing out below him, Jacob—Von Schling—had to reconcile something. He scanned the dark, churning waters.

He nearly uttered, *Please*. That, however, would have informed The Taurs. They were quite efficient in punishing deviance from their Truth. Jacob would never stop protecting his little brother. He couldn't. But he just had. What did that make him?

Wood groaned, cracked. A mast split, its triangular sails padding the water and shoving survivors into the depths. The eviscerated hull of the warship capsized in a boiling torrent. Water churned as hungry sharks greeted desperate survivors. The Guides sighed with pleasure at the carnage, and their claws and grip eased on Von Schling, ever so slightly.

He didn't dare display relief at the ease of pain. He didn't even want to look at them now.

"I need to see someone," he spoke aloud.

The Guides hissed. One clawed hand pulled on Von Schling's shoulder, trying to get him to turn. He could see their bat-like wings flapping.

"The Goblin wasn't here. Use our contingency plan to eliminate him. Tell D'alamuz the asset is now in play, ready or not." The Guides unfurled around him, flying off back to the fortress of Cismore. Seven twisted creatures with furry faces, long snouts, scaled snake-like bodies, and sinewy wings took to the air, leaving him. He felt the cold drift away as they returned to Cardor. This was a brief break he wanted to use.

Jacob searched the skies. The Velheron had retreated a little south, chased by the gryphon. Both were bloody messes. *She* wasn't watching him. Which meant Jacob could undermine her in this one way—to save his baby brother.

"Come on, Bedel, damn it," Jacob whispered. "Be alive. I did all of this for you. To stop them."

But Jacob knew that Bedel would never hear that truth now: Jacob fought to protect Bedel from their own family. Jacob clenched his fist. This is what Xathon had driven him to. Xathon had the gall to send Bedel into this mission. This battle. This cycle. The anger that drove him to break Elven law and save the child had become, over two centuries, a fury that the young man hadn't been able to fathom.

What shame did their father have? Who was next? Mother? She alone stood with innocence among the Elves. She had fought for Bedel, too, when she had learned of him. Hurricane-force winds whipped around Jacob, but he pushed out his awareness beyond them and stayed stationary in his own pocket of air. *Yes, yes*. He could feel him.

Jacob looked down at the water, at the pirate captain dragging a body through the chummed waves to a piece of wreckage.

Bedel!

Bedel.

Jacob swallowed his relief. Then he saw the bond. The silver *Zitaya* bond! Who? A woman on the deck of a ship approaching them. Jacob smiled. Maybe his brother was happy, even if Jacob would never be.

The Zelvatore warships had taken out another two vessels of the smuggler fleet, pushing them to the Delado River delta. The path would be cleared for the rest of the army. The vanguard was already pressing through.

He looked again for his brother, but Bedel seemed to have disappeared in the waves and wreckage.

Dark fire be with you, he thought bitterly. Jacob summoned a new *Windstream* and flew northwestward for a family chat. Time to hold his father's feet to his own fire.

BEDEL FELT THE WATER, COLD AND DARK. ITS WAVES ENVELOPED him, moving him like a puppet. There were sleek shapes, gliding through the gloom, feasting on survivors. Bedel frowned, letting himself sink.

Arms wrapped around him, hefting him upward. The surface of the water broke over him, and he heaved in air. It was shocking; brutal. All the essences he had just held were lost or scattered. Some had ceased to exist and been transformed into another essence—ashes or debris. The ship that had been Forbens' domain was gone.

"Hurry!" Forbens shouted before softening his voice. "Damn the waves, Bedel. Swim!"

Dark fins cut through the water, shimmering blue under the stars.

"Those aren't dolphins, boy!"

Wood groaned as a massive ship steered alongside. He recognized it.

The fins grew closer, tails splashing water as they charged. Bedel felt something large push him as it swam by. He sensed others. A tail battered him. He felt Forbens jolt as one hit him, too. He could feel the sharks underneath that they couldn't see. They were coming, too. Those wouldn't just push them aside.

A white-clad figure dove off the ship, splashing near them.

"You've lost your minds!" Forbens shouted.

A wave of calm burst through the water. The sharks were not

hungry. These were not the lives they were looking for. They wanted harder meat. *Dragon meat. Your prey is dragon meat.*

All at once, Bedel felt the sharks change course. Something pushed him up, above the water, only to keep on swimming by. More fins swam dangerously close to him and Forbens, passing them by on a full charge to assist the leviathan in an ocean banquet.

Gasping for breath, he and Forbens treaded water. And then a woman's head popped above the sea. She smiled.

"Bedel, it's my turn to pull you out of the water," A'banna said. She swam to them, embraced him, and kissed him.

"I love you," Bedel said, holding her close.

A'banna grinned. "Bedel, I love you."

They leaned in to kiss again. Forbens grunted and splashed in the water.

"You know, this is great. I'm swimming in monster-infested waters after a sea battle with other warships out there, watching you make love like two yehts in heat."

Bedel and A'banna stared at him, humored.

"All I'm saying is, can we get on the bloody ship!"

They chuckled. Within moments, the crew of *Woman's Fury* lowered rope ladders and began hoisting all three back on board.

As they ascended the ladder, an eagle called, though it also sounded like a roar. Bedel and A'banna looked up at the same time. The Keeper of the North's gryphon, bloodied from the battle soared above them, heading north. The Velheron, missing at least two wings, flew toward the Cronop Isles, desperately trying to stay aloft. They heard the Sorceress scream through her avatar before it disappeared in the clouds.

Relieved, Bedel reached the top of the ladder. A sailor pulled him on board and pointed him to where A'banna sat in the center of the deck, leaning against a barrel. Commodore Magdalena fawned over her, wrapping her in a blanket and calling her 'sea goddess.' Bedel collapsed next to A'banna, who smiled.

She won't stop, though I've asked. I think these people are superstitious.

Bedel chuckled. *Indeed. You're a Chosen. Better get used to it.*

A'banna rolled her eyes, playfully. *I think I understand all your hesitation to be called Gatekeeper, now.*

Just wait until this becomes more than sailor superstition, but religion. They will treat us differently.

I enjoyed being normal for a little while.

Bedel squeezed her hand. *Me, too.*

Someone lowered a waterskin into view. Before Bedel could accept it, a blur of fur leapt into his lap. The mountain ferret nuzzled his cheek before scurrying back to Idrin, who held a waterskin. Bedel chuckled, accepted it, and took a long swig. Wine, not water, but it made this meager victory taste so much better.

"Yes, everyone, please, fawn off the shark bait! I'm fine."

Bedel and A'banna slowly looked at Captain Forbens, who had accumulated a puddle beneath him.

"Oh, Dans," Commodore Magadalena droned. "Are you going to need a new ship? I have an opening, apparently."

The commodore laughed. "It's all who you know. Isn't that right, sea goddess?"

A'banna's laughed, awkwardly.

Of all the friends we make, Bedel thought to her, but indeed, he was considering all those they were separated from.

Your charm, A'banna thought. She was grateful to even be here. Grateful for life.

Bedel looked at the distant horizon, and couldn't help but wonder how soon they'd see land—and if it would be on fire.

CHAPTER 27

MUD SLURPED AROUND SHAI'S FEET, THEN SLID OUT FROM underneath her. Dazed, hot, hungry, and sticky from the humidity, the last thing she wanted was to slide down the muddy hillside. She lashed out, grabbing a tree root. Kamalia had disappeared, continuing on whatever star-forsaken journey she thought they were on. Instead, the jungle slope looked painful below Shai; rocks, roots, and all. *She actually listened when I said I didn't need help. Damn it! Of all the times she couldn't have ignored me.*

With a fragment of aether, Shai called out to *Liquidus* and *changed* it. Water bubbled up from the ground, hardening, becoming one with the mud and the soil. Dry ground cracked, forming stairs. Shai swung her feet over to stand on solid, firm ground.

Hands on her hips, Shai looked around. That slope was a good drop. This little trek was proving to be more arduous than even a killer mountain.

Shai hated the jungle.

Once she had topped the hill using the stairs, Shai waved once and the stairs dissolved as water, making the ground muddy again.

That was how to properly dismiss a weave. Satisfied, Shai turned, smacking into an overhanging leaf.

A string of curses left her mouth. She heard Kamalia chuckling up ahead.

"I told you not to leave a trail!" Kamalia called back.

"I told you I didn't want to go into the damn jungle! That's what rangers and hunters and raptors are for." Shai used a damp part of her cloak to dab sweat off her face.

With every step, she could feel something crunch underneath her boots. Leaves and low-hanging branches tugged at her cloak and long-sleeved blouse. Speaking of the cloak, it was so damn humid that she was slowly boiling under it. But the mosquitos were larger here than they had been in the Wo'Huzziet village. The cloak offered some protection. She'd rather wander the streets of Wonbai and worry about a dagger in the back than the buzzing around her head.

"Tell me again why we went south instead of north?" Shai called to the woman in front of her. "You know, rescue the Elven princess and all?"

Kamalia moved stealthily through the jungle, almost cat-like. Despite her stature and the amount of armor and weaponry she wore, not a twig broke or leaf bent. Shai took a very minuscule measure of comfort that this was Kamalia's territory, so the Huntress's skills would be slightly better than her own.

First A'banna, now Kamalia. I'm losing touch. Have to get back on top of the essencer pecking order, somehow.

"There's something you need to see."

Shai swatted away a fly the size of her palm. She felt the impact and winced. Desert spiders had been bad, but these bugs!

"I've seen it," she said, wiping her palm on her cloak.

"No," Kamalia chuckled. "You're experiencing the south, just as A'banna is experiencing the north for the first time."

"I was raised in a Branaird caravan in Zeller, as if you didn't already know."

Kamalia slowed between trees and flashed her a wickedly humored smile, canine teeth and all.

"Of course, you knew." Shai didn't like being outsmarted, let alone by someone possibly deadlier than she was. *Okay, definitely deadlier,* she begrudgingly thought.

Monkeys heckled from above and leapt threw trees. One had the nerve to drop dung. Shai barely dodged it. "Charming."

"I rather like lemurs," Kamalia said. "Though I'm not sure they like you."

"The feeling is mutual," Shai muttered, trudging along.

A hiss came from a low tree branch near her. Shai's instincts kicked in—unsheathing her knife and swiveling to strike at the snake except Kamalia grabbed her hand. A small green snake slithered by.

"What the Kerdum, Kamalia, it's a snake!"

Kamalia kept the force against Shai's hand, even as she tried to strike another blow. "It is not one of those snakes. When you walk in the woods, you begin to tell the subtle differences, Shai. That is a green tree constrictor, but it is not a pet of the Sorceress. I know the difference."

Shai's muscles tensed, she pulled down to strike one more time, but Kamalia kept the hold strong. "How can you be so sure? What if it is just biding its time."

"There are subtle differences."

"Care to point them out?"

"This animal told you it was present, to guard itself and you. If it was from the Sorceress, it would have left no opportunity for you to defend yourself, just as with the constrictor that you told me attacked A'banna."

Kamalia loosened her fingers, and Shai pulled free and sheathed the knife. "Subtle differences, like you and the Vel?"

"Yes," Kamalia said, expressionless. "Or like my father and I. Subtle differences between potential ally or foe."

"The Elves don't understand that subtlety."

Kamalia shrugged before turning back to the path. "That depends. Edelissi did. Do you?"

Shai continued to follow, albeit watching the trees for any potential interlopers.

Kamalia paused, glared at her, and pointed at the forest floor. Shai's maneuver had left a single broken twig and crumpled leaves.

"Be more careful."

"Right, because we'll leave a trail," Shai said. "Maybe you could have thought about that before *Vanishing* us here. I'm sure that massive scorch mark won't attract a minotaur's attention."

"It will, in time," Kamalia said. "That's why we've hiked for two days."

"Very comforting." When Kamalia turned her back, Shai mockingly mouthed her words. "What's the next lesson, master? How to drink from my canteen?"

Kamalia shook her head but didn't answer. They marched on.

Another hour later, Shai paused.

"Wait," Shai whispered.

To her surprise, Kamalia paused.

"Listen."

Chunk, chunk, chunk. Shai knew that sound. It was an axe head against a tree trunk. Who were they coming upon?

Shai raised an eyebrow, waiting for any clue, but Kamalia nodded and gestured for them to continue.

The ground was always uneven, but they had been steadily climbing up an incline for a few hours. The tree line broke, exposing a rocky ridge.

Kamalia stayed behind bushes but urged Shai forward. The

sound of chopping increased. Then the rhythm of hammers. The rasp of a saw. A woman sang. Children laughed.

"What are you planning on doing?" Shai murmured. She slid behind the bush and crouched, looking over the ridge.

A swath of jungle had been cleared, tree trunks pulled from the ground. In the center was a large, stone home with a fence around a garden patch, and a larger perimeter fence made out of bone. Shai blinked as she took in the gateway, constructed inside the jaw of a dragon skull, blanched white in the sun.

"What is this?" Shai murmured.

Ten homes had already been built, plus several crude watch-towers. Hundreds of men and women toiled under the jungle sun below. They wore leather and colored cloths. Most of the guards had spears or round shields. A hunting party returned, passing inside the dragon's jaws to enter the developing village. The lead hunter wore a necklace with—were those boar tusks? They looked similar but minotaurs! Children chased each other in a game of tag, laughing delightfully. There were mothers down there. One worked on weaving a basket beneath a hide tent, while a young woman tended her baby.

Shai tore her gaze away from the new village of Avocans to Kamalia. For the first time since they'd met, Kamalia looked transfixed, her mouth slightly open, eyes focused, cheeks flushed. Shai followed her gaze to a woman who seemed to be in the center of it all, dropping off wood here, taking vegetables there. Every person stopped to talk with her—and the lead hunter and weaver, but they didn't hold Kamalia's attention.

The woman had beautiful dark skin, a round face. She was obviously quite strong. An axe was strapped to her back. She wore a necklace and bracelet of small bones.

Kamalia exhaled her tension, relaxing. She leaned forward, elbows on her knees, crouching on her toes.

"This, Shai, is Avoc-Nezlticoulti, or what is left of it."

"The city A'banna and Huahanna were from? Are these refugees?"

"Yes. Making a new life here."

"That woman, moving through the center there. She's different than the others. Why?"

Kamalia's brow furled. "Really? She looks as busy as the rest."

"I'm sure any woman who wants to keep up with you would have to be."

Kamalia chuckled. "Oh, you are fishing."

"Not on this one. I know that look. It's universal."

Kamalia's smile faltered, but she didn't try to hide it. "You don't trust my sister."

"Ha! That's very funny, coming from you."

"If I wanted her dead, she'd be dead," Kamalia said. "She's alive, Shai. I did what I had to do to get her out of this realm. Up north, she has a chance to survive."

"Yes, with the Vel running loose. They could slither down a chimney or through a mouse hole. Come on, Kamalia. None of us have a good chance to survive."

"Neither did they."

"Excuse me?"

"All three hundred and forty-seven, plus the two expecting, were inside the city when it fell. None of them should be alive. But they are and far enough away from the Sorceress and her breeding pits they don't have to fear retaliation, yet. She's busy, and there have been no scouts out this far."

"How do you know this?"

"When I found the first group, led by that weaver with her baby and the hunter, Torresin, they told me they saw Priestess A'banna in the street, right before they were certain they needed to leave rather than fight. They gathered other bands of people together and survived days in the jungle without pursuit. Then I found them and brought them here."

"Incredible," Shai said, sincerely. Survival took a certain amount of strength and courage.

"A'banna *Led* them, urged them to gather. Wispy fragments of her aether still swirled in their auras; I know it well. Without A'banna, these refugees would have all been slaughtered. I think the Sorceress was so intent on hunting A'banna down that she ignored them.

"So, Shai, when I tell you that my sister is a good person, a genuinely good person, and I'm thankful for her survival, believe me. She doesn't even know she saved three hundred forty-nine lives." Kamalia turned her torso toward Shai. "Where we are going, it will take all of our cunning to survive Ni'Dio. We have to work together."

"I'm aware."

Kamalia reached into her bag and pulled out a satchel; woven leather with some painted Wo'Huzziet ornamentation. Kamalia slowly opened the satchel, exposing the golden triangular imager with its finely carved jewels and Huahanna's journal.

Those should be far from here! Shai felt heat crawl up her throat, her heart beating faster, anger flaring in her mind. Shai's hand closed on her dagger and nearly drew it. "Crow-spawn!" she hissed. "What did you do to the rangers?"

Kamalia held out her palm. "Peace. If they listened to my advice, they're limping back to Lodornatha with word of what has transpired, including that Idrin chose to go with A'banna and Bedel, rather than with us."

Shai cursed, flicking the leather latch open on her sheathe.

"Neither of us can read this book," Kamalia said. "The imager is cracked in two locations, and even one of the jewels is damaged. We need an Elven Memory Lark's magic to extract this information and repair the imager. A Lark could even translate old

Belasna. Then you will have all the secrets you need to defeat the Vel and, ancients willing, the Sorceress herself."

"That's why we sent the damn satchel to Lodornatha," Shai growled.

Shai quickly evaluated her own aura. She wasn't being *Led*, so why did she hesitate? This woman could not be trusted! Though killing her would mean that Shai would never get out of the jungle, never escape, never fulfill her final mission. The desire to murder Kamalia here and now burned within her.

Kamalia shook her head. "It's vulnerable there. Can't you feel it?"

"Feel what?" Shai demanded, flexing her grip on the dagger. Suddenly, she felt less sure of herself, but there was no magic here. It was just instinct. Shai knew she was changing. She felt the heat of hatred too much now. Though her thumb stayed on the hilt, Shai lowered her fingers for a brief second, a moment of self-doubt.

"Change. There is so much you do not know, Shai, or so much you think you know."

"Yes, well, I haven't shared any of it with you."

"No? Perhaps not. Listen to me. I can feel the war has begun in Cardor. We were all too late. The stars themselves started moving. Did you notice last night? The cycle's constellations are converging."

"You're saying there will be a Bloom?"

"You understand the cycle lore."

"Of course, I do! Does everyone think I'm heartless? I didn't want A'banna hurt or bound to Bedel, I want them far from whatever is going to happen. She's a Chosen."

"The Gatekeeper."

"This won't end well for them. Then that bloody lion. You know what the lore says about the lion."

"First, the lion appears, then a dragon."

"But no one talks about that," Shai said. "No one!" Her voice rose, the words falling from her as a deep confession. All the truths that she and Bedel had kept secret rolled off her tongue in frantic crescendo. "The Caurs gave them a *lion* as a companion for another Chosen. Great. Also, for the first time in history, there's a man leading the former atheist Swords of Baktur, the Veccil'ni, calling himself the Red Dragon and son of the God of War. The lion and the dragon, Kamalia. It's so real. I still don't believe The Caurs or The Taurs are gods. I don't believe there is one. What I know is the world fabric is beyond full comprehension. Based on A'banna's description of both her dream in the river and her father's vision, the blond man in the north fits what the lore teaches about the Chosen Lion. But thanks to my grandfather, no one understands that. They'll call *him* the Dragon." Shai took a deep breath, slowing down, trembling. "They are so wrong! They don't know"

"Then the Bloom will end with a death."

"More than one. I tried to set up the pieces for us to survive— or win. I failed."

Kamalia raised an eyebrow.

Shai wiped away a tear. *Damn. I can't believe I'm crying!*

"You know much."

"Now you see why I don't trust Elves. Not even Bedel read that text. I don't know why I kept it from him."

"You loved him, even then. There are forces that would kill to conceal those truths."

Shai nodded. Kamalia glanced back to the bushes, at the sound of civilization nearby. "Then know that I have slain a dragon. If I can, I will help your friends defeat the Veccil'ni."

Why the surprise? Kamalia promised much including that she would honor her word. When all Kerdum broke loose, would she?

"If we are to rescue Edelissi Onoarel and keep Princess Amelia de Gerac in power, we must trust each other, or we die,"

Kamalia said. "If we succeed, we gain a Memory Lark and a Chosen."

Shai felt gooseflesh along her arms. "Edelissi is a Lark! I knew it!"

"I said nothing of the sort." Kamalia grunted. She carefully repacked the satchel. "What I did say, and what I meant, is that by the time we reach Ni'Dio and find Edelissi, traveling to and from Lodornatha to consult with their remaining Larks will be impractical. We will need a Lark quickly. When we save her, we gain a Lark and also avoid your grandfather's 'assistance' in Lupacuo. He is certain to slaughter Bedel as Gatekeeper, thus killing my sister and condemning the world we love. Do you trust me, Shai?"

Shai glanced at the village. The tremors of her avowal had stilled, but she expected reciprocation. Truth. "Who is she? The woman with the bone jewelry."

Kamalia breathed deep. "My wife, Cisoleau. This is our home, Shai."

Shai blinked back tears. In all her life, she would never have left herself that vulnerable to a threat. Shai glanced at Cisoleau, clapping and singing along with the children.

Shai dropped her hand away from her knife. "Damn you. I really, really wanted to kill you, and instead, I find us sharing secrets together. I don't share secrets."

"Neither do I. Neither do I have a desire to kill you, despite appearances to the contrary."

For a few seconds, Shai pondered the whole predicament. "This doesn't make us friends."

"Of course not." Kamalia's lip curled into a genuine smile!

Shai shifted her gaze to the villagers. "Will they survive without you?"

"Cisoleau knows the land as well as I do. There are enough animals that would help, if she requests. As long as the Sorceress is focused on finding A'banna and Bedel and spreading Vel in the north, they are safe. At some point, though, they will have to leave. I have that much time to find somewhere safe for them to go or to make it safe."

"So, Edelissi is a Lark? How do you know this?" If it was true, Shai didn't blame Idrin from keeping that from her. After all, Lodornatha wasn't fond of Lupacuo's secrets, why give their agent a secret they could use?

"I don't know, at least not definitively. The evidence is strong that a Lark is present in Ni'Dio's court. Ni'Dio keeps woven essences in her throne room. I had a chance to look inside her piece of artwork and saw an enhanced jewel of unknown essences woven into the very center of it. I also know that Ni'Dio takes pleasure in degrading powerful essencers who cannot beat her in the combative dance. A Lark could never use essences to harm. However, they can use them to keep or share history. A Lark would be a great prize, one she would want on full display."

"Like a translator or confidant."

"Who shares the dais with her, serving her in every way."

"Damn," Shai whispered. "What else?"

"Idrin and Edelissi's mother, Lady Onoarel, was a Lark. She was killed by a dragon, protecting her children."

Shai nodded grimly. "I was afraid of that. If Edelissi is a Lark."

"Aye. You understand. Edelissi is also well-known not just as a brilliant warrior and tactician, but as a councilor rumored to speak with the authority of ancients." Kamalia's gaze lingered on Cisoleau. "Ni'Dio sent a ransom note enclosed with the finger used by Larks for their ring. Edelissi is missing that finger. During my recent travels, I heard rumor from three sources in Zeller and the tribal lands, as well as from the rangers I took this from."

Kamalia patted the bag with the satchel inside. *Crows, Kamalia was an impressive and efficient agent.*

"Every source claims that one of the seven Larks in Lodornatha hasn't been seen since the battle with the slavers. What further evidence do you need to at least be suspect?"

Taurs, Shai couldn't find a reason to disagree!

"Fate has brought us all together, Shai. You need Intel, and we can get that, if we trust each other. Then we help A'banna and the others, but the cycle is moving faster than we can."

Bloody blue stars, Kamalia has a point. Shai waved at the village down the slope. "Now you've shown me a sum total of three hundred and fifty souls who will be affected if I betray you."

Kamalia nodded. "We all have much to lose. The question is now: Will you betray me? And if you do, know there will be no place you can hide where I will not find you."

"You drive a hard bargain," Shai said with a curse as she moved her arms away from her weapons.

"I asked for your life and the lives of everyone else. I never ask for something I cannot return." Kamalia touched the diamond on her forehead. "The Sorceress's machinations changed me. Being reunited with my sister and having everyone down there alive is all that keeps me alive."

Shai groaned, slapped her thighs, and then stood up, careful to keep a tree between her and the villagers. She reached down. "For what it is worth, good job gathering the Intel on the missing Lark."

Kamalia blinked; her jaw opening a little. "Thank you?"

"Yeah. Well, you're welcome. We better move out, then."

"Indeed," Kamalia said. She took Shai's arm and stood swiftly. The movement nearly pulled Shai off the ground, but she steadied herself. "It will take us days to reach a safe enough location to *Vanish* back. By then, the stars will have"

Kamalia gasped. Down in the valley, the woman with the

bone jewelry stared up at the ridgeline. Cisoleau lifted her hand with the bracelet in greeting. Even from here, Shai could tell she was crying, a smile on her face. Kamalia mirrored the gesture. She bit her lip.

"Forget it. She's your wife, Kamalia. We can stop if you want."

"No. She needs plausible deniability to be safe. As long as the Sorceress's attention is on A'banna and us, these people are safe. I let us leave."

Kamalia turned back into the jungle, disappearing into its shadows. Shai glanced after her, then turned back; meeting Cisoleau's questioning gaze and giving her a swift nod. Cisoleau stepped forward, but children swarmed her. She dabbed her cheeks, flashed a quick look back at the ridgeline, then started playing with the children, chatting happily.

A bug buzzed by Shai's ear. She felt a sting. She swatted something away. Damn mosquitoes. Good thing she had never planned to build the cabin in this area! Shai stowed her frustrations for another time. Just because Shai liked Kamalia a little more didn't mean she would tolerate the Huntress getting in her way. Besides, if hindering Ni'Dio meant hurting the Sorceress, then Shai was all in.

"Hang on, Edelissi," Shai whispered to herself. "We're coming."

Shai pulled up the hood on her cloak and followed Kamalia into the jungle.

EPILOGUE

Wind whipped at Raynt's coat and trousers. He was thankful he'd worn goggles to keep the flurry of snow out of his eyes. Here in Cardor, it was nearly harvest season, which meant that the snow upon Well Mount and the lesser peaks would soon spread to the lands below. For now, he felt the chill cut through his coat and used the essences to warm himself. The interior of his coat and trousers trembled, spreading heat through him.

A crosswind threatened to confuse Raynt's *Windstream* essences, so he thickened the flowing, invisible tube with another strand of air, then adjusted his arms and legs to slow his descent. It was harder to keep himself warm, but that was the cost of not falling to death. At last, he formed a cushion of air and swirling snow at the entrance to the ancient tower he had visited just a month before with Bedel and Shai.

At twilight, no lights shone from the tower. The snow and stone had a bluish tint to it from the stars above. It was strangely beautiful, which made this place feel more eerie. He could neither hear nor see any sign of gryphons or other flying creatures. Still, he could feel the essencer-who-inhabited-the-mountain's sight upon him, just as he had a month before when she tried to murder Bedel.

What do I think I will accomplish by coming here? Raynt thought to himself, frustrated at his own reasoning. He'd only have a single day to recover before the King's Men launched their mission to rescue the Wo'Huzziet high chief's heiress. Nchoji had sailed *Ntokup's Ghost*, formerly the *Batoidea*, as far north up the Delado River as he dared. He didn't want to enter Cismore's port as it was still under Slaver Coalition control. That made Raynt's time short. Still, Raynt felt proud of Captain Nchoji and his mixed crew of Wo'Huzziet, Gaul, and Felin. After they ferried Raynt south to his next mission, *Ntokup's Ghost* would continue to deliver their life-saving medication throughout the world—and now with twice the firepower of *The Red Hand*. Raynt couldn't help but grin. The whole world wasn't grim.

You've returned, a voice from the rock said, like a whisper on the wind. Raynt glanced at the stone beside the open door to the tower. An eye had formed in it, unblinking, watching.

"We need to speak," he said.

Why? The stars have come. The cycle had begun.

"I assume you can enter the tower."

It is part of the mountain. I am the mountain.

That was a definitive yes. Raynt had every intention to meet the essencer here. Tonight.

Raynt gestured inside. Stone ground as the eye followed him.

Snowbanks had formed inside the lower level that had recently housed the gryphons. Raynt headed to the stairs and climbed to the upper chamber. Just a month ago, this was the place of their clandestine meeting. Raynt traced the Belasna runes engraved on the stone round table. He couldn't precisely read them all, but he understood basic phrases. He waited in the cold and dark, with no fire to warm him. He could have easily used his daggers but resisted. He didn't want to scare the essencer.

All at once, the ground rumbled. Raynt spun, glancing at the stairs. They moved, a wave rolling uphill. A light shone in the circling stairwell, brightening the gray stone.

Raynt stood, astonished and excited.

A woman seemed to ride a wave of stone, with diamonds and jewels shining around her, as if they were part of her stone dress, or set within the roots of a tree which formed her hair. Yet, she was a woman; her bare arms and face were clearly flesh, and her eyes shone like emeralds and rubies and sapphires, never staying a single color.

"You wanted to meet, Raynt Lacrause," the essencer in the mountain said. The wave of rock seemed to flow along the tower's floor and walls as she moved, her hair billowing and spreading out behind and around her, all the way to the walls and ceiling. As she passed through the hall, the tower behind returned to as it had looked, nothing altered.

"Your Grace," Raynt said, bowing.

"I am neither grace itself nor a trivial rank of nobility, Raynt."

"Do you have a name or title you wish to be called?"

"The Mountain."

"Thank you for meeting me, Mountain."

She glided into the room on her platform of rotating, flexing, moving stone. Her eyes, still glimmering a rainbow of colors, connected with his. "Speak. You have my attention."

"Bedel, Shai, they're in danger."

"Yes," she said. "I warned you all. Up is was and still will be death."

"But not from you?"

The mountain rumbled as she slowly shook her head. The roots rustled. "Not today. Further, why should I kill a Chosen, Raynt Lacrause? You are but a variable, a part of the equation, neither a cause nor an end."

"Everyone speaks of this cosmic cycle, the stars being 'chosen.' By whom? What for? What is it I am supposed to do?"

She spread her arms out, while her root-hair rattled. "You ask me? Were you not in the presence of a Speaker for nearly a week? Why did you not let him explain it?"

"I… my friends needed my help. And I need theirs."

"Yes, sending him into a den of Baktur to meet the Gatekeeper and a Chosen." She sighed and stopped gliding, though her platform and dress continued to shift. "Raynt Lacrause, you have become hasty in your judgments. There are only five Chosen. We cannot risk you to be foolish."

"Then you will explain it to me?"

"No," she said, her voice like a thunderclap. "I am an observer."

"You tried to kill Bedel."

"Ah. Do you seek retaliation?"

"No. I seek enlightenment, Mountain."

"Bring me that glass."

"Glass?" Raynt murmured. He turned, searching for a glass. The room was bare, except a glass tumbler on the stone bench Alain had used when Raynt first saw him. Raynt lifted the perfectly round, diamond-like glass, as wide as his hand. It hadn't been there earlier.

"Scoop snow into it."

He did as she instructed from one of the open windows, then she had him place it on the table. Her hair-roots moved, but she did not blink. The snow melted immediately, and then the glass began spinning. The water inside of it churned in a fast-moving whirlpool.

"Your friend is the Gatekeeper. He is a cause and an end—that is why the enemy fears him." She cocked her head, gazing at Raynt as the glass spun on the still table. "When viewed mathematically, Bedel is the very reason we have cycles at all, because his predecessors all failed to kill the woman they loved."

"Shai? You want him to kill Shai?"

"That is absurd. She is new. She is only a variable. No, have you not understood what is plain before you? For as long as there will be a Jocina, there will be a Bedel. You cannot break the world without the other, because life must start from death. Bedel opposed Jocina before and after the first breaking, and sacrificed himself to save the survivors. For that, he is reborn, because of all the Immortals Jocina fears to lose, it is him. Yet, it must be him. For every time she seeks new power, the stars appear. They are all connected, but why I barely remember."

"Why not?" Raynt moved closer to look at the extraordinary woman. Even though the only light in the room came from her, she still seemed pale. Was this because she lived inside a mountain, away from sunlight?

Realization hit Raynt like a thunderbolt. Her face! Did Bedel and Shai know? Is this what they had been hiding?

"Are you their daughter? The daughter of Jocina and the first Bedel Riess?"

The Mountain opened her mouth, her eyes flashing red, then yellow, then orange, then yellow again. Then those jeweled colors seemed to dissolve as if they had been mere lenses covering her eyes. Her revealed pupils were clear. Pale. Her teeth were elongated.

"You are Immortal," Raynt whispered.

"How did you know Jocina birthed me?"

"I didn't," Raynt said, staying on his feet. "You tried to kill your father."

"My father died four thousand years ago. He helped us cross the boundary guarded by the Keepers, but when she came to the place you call the Long Bridge in Istante, he tossed me into Hokano's arms." Her arms reached out, palms up, fingers curling.

Pain strained on her face. "My *da* stayed behind to redeem her—or kill her. I don't remember." The emotion drained from her expression, and she grew still, like a statue. "She murdered him, took his body, his genes, his quintessence, and remade him. One day the Elves stole him away, and so now my father always returns, the power of my father returns with him, but he knows me not."

Then Bedel didn't know he or his ancestor still had an Immortal daughter. One who lived in a mountain. One who had tried to kill him.

"Mountain…" Raynt tried to speak but didn't know what to say. "I'm sorry for your loss."

"My mother is a rose. Roses spread. If it is a bad rose, they sting. They kill. They never end, though they wilt for a time. Underestimate my mother, and she will kill you, even if you stare at her in the face, she will come from behind, for she is a rose."

That made little sense. Raynt wanted to clarify, but Mountain gestured at the glass. The water had formed a deep indentation. "Over and over, god-men play games, numbers churn like water in a glass. They see the numbers, fractals, they give shape and allow them to divine how to manipulate the lives of mortals. Meanwhile, she gains power. The Taurs gain power. The Caurs lose power. My father is reborn. God gives speech to humanity's deviations. Humanity kills its speech. Humanity kills my father. For four thousand years, this has been the case. Except if someone were to remove humanity's ability to remake my father, to utterly reduce every trace of him except his memory, then there can be no formula with the calculation of pi. Do you understand? She loses power. There is no cycle. There is no destruction. No rebirth from the ashes. No new deviations who are lonely and without speech. Now, the latest mutations will kill for her. I see no humanity in them."

"You tried to end the cycle before it began."

"If da remembered, he'd thank me. I remember seeing him sit with Theantros by our campfires, talking into the night about the best ways to save humanity. They would let me sit with them to listen." She smiled. "I had a purpose, Theantros would say. He knew I would find this mountain. But mother would try to join in, but then Theantros would look at her with his all-knowing gaze. She was the one that escaped justice. The traitor hiding among us! She burned the world! Four thousand years is but an accounting of mortal time. The sky was cold in most places. The Taurs came. She guided them to us. To the survivors. They spared me for her sake, but killed my friends. But she knew. They all knew. Only Hokano and my father tried to stop her and the radicals! I still remember holding Alain as a baby."

The mountain trembled. Snow drifts tumbled off ledges and icicles cracked and crashed. Then all went still.

"I can't imagine," Raynt whispered, horrified.

"No. You cannot."

It all made sense, even why Alain had seemed to be praying listening when they first met. She had helped raise the emissary.

Mountain's voice evened out again. "Da would want our survival, but da is gone. Not even starlight steel speaks to the man wearing my father's face, his ethereal, his power anymore. Not yet. But he can do more than end a cycle. For the cycle is more than just my parents."

That must be it. In there, somewhere, was the answer to the riddle. Sure, this Immortal just confirmed the existence of The Taurs and The Caurs—and she also claimed to have met god himself; that her father used to speak with him, as friends discussing how to design a barn.

"What can he do? What is this Bedel capable of? Our religions say Theantros created a magic called the Well, a light that out-rivals dark fire or even starlight. Is the Well real? Is that the power the Bedel reincarnations have?"

"Ask a Speaker, Raynt. I am an observer."

Mountain gestured at the glass. A long shard of glass, almost as wide as the tumbler, lowered from the ceiling. Raynt hopped back, surprised. The rectangular shard hung above the spinning cup as if clutched by the air, then Mountain let it drop. The spinning tumbler completed its final cycle as the shard crashed down, pinning it. Water sprayed out, spilling onto the table. The remainder flowed back and forth, calming until it could spin no more.

Raynt watched, trying to figure out what the Immortal Mountain wanted him to discern.

"Not all the water is retained by the glass, but what is, becomes calm. Is renewed. So it is. Now that the cycle has started, my father can end everything so it can begin anew. But for that to happen, you will need to remember."

Raynt stepped back, away from the table. He was surprised at how much anger he let slip into his voice. "Remember what?"

"This is why you should have spoken to the Goblin." She turned and hovered toward the stairs.

"Wait! It's too late for that now. Why don't you tell me?"

"As I have said, I am only an observer. This I promise you, if you or your friends or your family or all the deviations and all the mutations of humanity are at peace and require shelter, you may come to me, and I will hide you behind my walls."

Mountain looked up, pale Immortal eyes shimmering with a mixture of sorrow and resolve. "Goodbye, Raynt Lacrause. It was pleasant to have seen my cousins again, before Alain had to die. There are so few of us left now. My mother and her Weave Master fought and killed most of them. Fear them both? I do. For our brief family gathering, I thank you. Until we meet again."

With that, the Mountain glided down the stairwell. Stone and hair-roots flowed about her, as if they carried her. Raynt followed, keeping to only the stairs that had ceased flowing. He stepped into the lower layer of the tower just as the Mountain turned. She smiled. And the floor rose up and swallowed her, then leveled out, as if it hadn't moved at all.

Gasping, Raynt leaned against the wall, then slid down it. He didn't know what to think. Or why. "Remember what?" he whispered. His voice echoed in the abandoned tower. This time, Mountain did not answer.

FROM THE PUBLISHER

Thank you for reading *Immortals,* book one in The Essencers of Aelathia.

We hope you enjoyed it as much as we enjoyed bringing it to you. We just wanted to take a moment to encourage you to review the book on Amazon and Goodreads. Every review helps further the author's reach and, ultimately, helps them continue writing fantastic books for us all to enjoy.

If you liked this book, check out the rest of our catalogue at www.aethonbooks.com. To sign up to receive a FREE collection from some of our best authors as well updates regarding all new releases, visit www.aethonbooks.com/sign-up.

SPECIAL THANKS TO:

ADAWIA E. ASAD
JENNY AVERY
BARDE PRESS
CALUM BEAULIEU
BEN
BECKY BEWERSDORF
BHAM
TANNER BLOTTER
ALFRED JOSEPH BOHNE IV
CHAD BOWDEN
ERREL BRAUDE
DAMIEN BROUSSARD
CATHERINE BULLINER
JUSTIN BURGESS
MATT BURNS
BERNIE CINKOSKE
MARTIN COOK
ALISTAIR DILWORTH
JAN DRAKE
BRET DULEY
RAY DUNN
ROB EDWARDS
RICHARD EYRES
MARK FERNANDEZ
CHARLES T FINCHER
SYLVIA FOIL
GAZELLE OF CAERBANNOG
DAVID GEARY
MICHEAL GREEN
BRIAN GRIFFIN

EDDIE HALLAHAN
JOSH HAYES
PAT HAYES
BILL HENDERSON
JEFF HOFFMAN
GODFREY HUEN
JOAN QUERALTÓ IBÁÑEZ
JONATHAN JOHNSON
MARCEL DE JONG
KABRINA
PETRI KANERVA
ROBERT KARALASH
VIKTOR KASPERSSON
TESLAN KIERINHAWK
ALEXANDER KIMBALL
JIM KOSMICKI
FRANKLIN KUZENSKI
MEENAZ LODHI
DAVID MACFARLANE
JAMIE MCFARLANE
HENRY MARIN
CRAIG MARTELLE
THOMAS MARTIN
ALAN D. MCDONALD
JAMES MCGLINCHEY
MICHAEL MCMURRAY
CHRISTIAN MEYER
SEBASTIAN MÜLLER
MARK NEWMAN
JULIAN NORTH

KYLE OATHOUT
LILY OMIDI
TROY OSGOOD
GEOFF PARKER
NICHOLAS (BUZ) PENNEY
JASON PENNOCK
THOMAS PETSCHAUER
JENNIFER PRIESTER
RHEL
JODY ROBERTS
JOHN BEAR ROSS
DONNA SANDERS
FABIAN SARAVIA
TERRY SCHOTT
SCOTT
ALLEN SIMMONS
KEVIN MICHAEL STEPHENS
MICHAEL J. SULLIVAN
PAUL SUMMERHAYES
JOHN TREADWELL
CHRISTOPHER J. VALIN
PHILIP VAN ITALLIE
JAAP VAN POELGEEST
FRANCK VAQUIER
VORTEX
DAVID WALTERS JR
MIKE A. WEBER
PAMELA WICKERT
JON WOODALL
BRUCE YOUNG

www.ingramcontent.com/pod-product-compliance
Lightning Source LLC
Chambersburg PA
CBHW032155180726
48284CB00001B/48